Praise for *The Lost Flowers of Alice Hart*

'I loved this brave and beautiful book. Alice Hart
has the strength and magic of an Australian wildflower
in bloom.' – Favel Parrett

'Not everyone who visits the central Australian desert
understands the landscape of it. Holly Ringland does and
shares her heart instincts in this epic telling. Each page arrives
to us like the first flight of the butterfly from its cocoon . . .
A literary gift.' – Ali Cobby Eckermann

'An astonishingly assured debut, *The Lost Flowers of Alice Hart*
is a story of love, loss, betrayal and the redemptive power of
storytelling, set in the blazing heat and ancient mythic landscape
of Australia's Red Centre. Written with intelligence, grace and
sensitivity, Holly Ringland's novel is both heart-breaking and
life-affirming, following the journey of her heroine Alice as she
discovers the strength of spirit to break the patterns of violence
of her past.' – Kate Forsyth

'*The Lost Flowers of Alice Hart* is a book that glows – in the fire
and heart of it; in the wonder and hope of it. Holly Ringland is
a gifted, natural storyteller and her novel – about finding magic
in the dark; about the power of freedom and the freedom of
story – is truly a light-giving, tender thing. A vivid, compelling,
utterly moving debut.' – Brooke Davis

'A complex, literary debut that _____ ___ dangerously fine
line between care and control. ___ writing is rich, vibrant and al__ ___
violent song of human conne___ ___
out for.' – Je__

'The best fairy tales traverse the darkest corners __
heart, and this beautiful novel is no exception. Questing and
magic, struggle and triumph.' – Myf___ ___

The Lost Flowers of Alice Hart

Holly Ringland grew up wild and barefoot in her mother's tropical garden in Australia. When she was nine years old, her family lived in a camper van for two years in North America, travelling from one national park to another, an experience that sparked Holly's lifelong interest in cultures and stories. In her twenties, Holly worked for four years in a remote Indigenous community in the central Australian desert.

In 2009 she moved to England, where she obtained an MA in Creative Writing from the University of Manchester in 2011. Holly has taught creative writing at Lancaster University, and to women in prison. For five years Holly volunteered as leader of a Greater Manchester storytelling project called International 16, bringing together 16 students from 16 countries (including the UK) to promote global friendship through stories.

The Lost Flowers of Alice Hart is Holly's first novel. She lives in Manchester.

The Lost Flowers of Alice Hart

HOLLY
RINGLAND

PAN BOOKS

First published 2018 by Fourth Estate,
an imprint of HarperCollins*Publishers* Australia

First published in the UK in paperback 2018 by Pan Books
an imprint of Pan Macmillan
20 New Wharf Road, London N1 9RR
Associated companies throughout the world
www.panmacmillan.com

ISBN 978-1-5098-5984-9

1 3 5 7 9 8 6 4 2

A CIP catalogue record for this book is available from the British Library.

Printed and bound by CPI Group (UK) Ltd, Croydon, CR0 4YY

Visit **www.panmacmillan.com** to read more about
all our books and to buy them. You will also find features,
author interviews and news of any author events, and you
can sign up for e-newsletters so that you're always
first to hear about our new releases.

For women who doubt the worth and
power of their story.

For my mother, who gave everything to
bring me flowers.

And this book is for Sam,
without whom my lifelong dream would
remain unwritten.

Contents

There has fallen a splendid tear
   From the passion-flower at the gate.
She is coming, my dove, my dear;
   She is coming, my life, my fate;
The red rose cries, 'She is near, she is near;'
   And the white rose weeps, 'She is late;'
The larkspur listens, 'I hear, I hear;'
   And the lily whispers, 'I wait.'

Alfred, Lord Tennyson

1

Black fire orchid

Meaning: Desire to possess

Pyrorchis nigricans | Western Australia

*Needs fire to flower. Sprouts from bulbs that may
have lain dormant. Deep crimson streaks on pale flesh.
Turns black after flowering, as if charred.*

In the weatherboard house at the end of the lane, nine-year-old
Alice Hart sat at her desk by the window and dreamed of ways to
set her father on fire.

In front of her, on the eucalyptus desk her father built, a library
book lay open. It was filled with stories collected from around the
world about the myths of fire. Although a northeasterly blew in
from the Pacific, full of brine, Alice could smell smoke, earth and
burning feathers. She read, whispering aloud:

*The phoenix bird is immersed into fire, to be consumed by the flames,
to burn to ashes and rise renewed, remade, reformed – the same,
but altogether different.*

Alice hovered a fingertip over an illustration of the phoenix rising:
its silver-white feathers glowing, its wings outstretched, and its
head thrown back to crow. She snatched her hand away, as though
the licks of golden, red-orange flames might singe her skin. The
smell of seaweed came through her window in a fresh gust; the
chimes in her mother's garden warned of the strengthening wind.

Leaning over her desk, Alice closed the window to just a crack.
She pushed the book aside, eyeing the illustration as she reached

for the plate of toast she'd made hours ago. Biting into a buttered triangle, she chewed the cold toast slowly. What might it be like, if her father was consumed by fire? All his monsters burned to ash, leaving the best of him to rise, renewed by flames, remade into the man he sometimes was: the man who made her a desk so she could write stories.

Alice shut her eyes, imagining for a moment that the nearby sea she could hear crashing through her window was an ocean of roaring fire. Could she push her father into it, so he was consumed like the phoenix in her book? What if he emerged, shaking his head as if woken from a bad dream, and opened his arms to her? *G'day Bunny*, he might say. Or maybe he would just whistle, hands in his pockets and a smile in his eyes. Maybe Alice would never again see his blue eyes turn black with rage, or watch the colour drain from his face, spittle gathering in the corners of his mouth, a foam as white as his pallor. She could focus solely on reading what direction the wind was blowing, or choosing her library books, or writing at her desk. Remade by fire, Alice's father's touch on her mother's pregnant body would always be soft; his hands on Alice always gentle and nurturing. Most of all, he would cradle the baby when it came, and Alice wouldn't lie awake wondering how to protect her family.

She shut the book. Its heavy thud reverberated through the wooden desk, which ran the length of her bedroom wall. Her desk faced two large windows that swung open over the garden of maidenhair ferns, staghorns and butterfly-leaf plants her mother tended until nausea got the better of her. Just that morning she had been in the process of potting kangaroo paw seedlings when she doubled over, hacking into the ferns. Alice was at her desk, reading; at the sound of her mother's retching, she scrambled through the window, landing on the fern beds. Unsure of what else to do, she held her mother's hand tightly.

'I'm all right,' her mother coughed, squeezing Alice's hand before letting go. 'It's just morning sickness, Bun, don't worry.'

As she leant her head back to get some air, her pale hair fell away from her face and revealed a new bruise, purple like the sea at dawn, surrounding a split in the tender skin behind her ear. Alice couldn't look away quickly enough.

'Oh, Bun,' her mother fretted as she hauled herself to her feet. 'I wasn't watching what I was doing in the kitchen and took a tumble. The baby makes me so dizzy.' She placed one hand on her stomach and picked crumbs of dirt off her dress with the other. Alice stared at the young ferns that had been crushed under her mother's weight.

Her parents left soon afterwards. Alice stood at the front door until the plume of dust behind her father's truck vanished into the blue morning. They were making the trip to the city for another baby check-up; the truck only had two seats. *Be good, darling,* her mother implored as she brushed Alice's cheek with her lips. She smelled like jasmine, and fear.

Alice picked up another triangle of cold toast and held it between her teeth as she reached into her library bag. She'd promised her mother she would study for her Grade Four exam, but so far the dummy test the correspondence school had sent in the post sat unopened on her desk. As she pulled a book out of her library bag and read its title, her jaw slackened. Her exam was completely forgotten.

In the low light of the approaching storm the embossed cover of *A Beginner's Guide to Fire* was an illuminated, almost-living thing. Wildfire shimmered in metallic flames. Something dangerous and thrilling rippled through Alice's belly. The palms of her hands were clammy. She had just touched her fingers to the corner of the cover when, as if conjured by her jittery nerves, the tags of Toby's collar tinkled behind her. He nudged her leg, leaving a wet smudge on her skin. Relieved by the interruption, Alice smiled as Toby sat politely. She held her toast out to him and he gingerly took it between his teeth before stepping back to wolf it down. Dog drool dripped on her feet.

'Yuck, Tobes,' Alice said, ruffling his ears. She held up her thumb and wagged it from side to side. Toby's tail swept back and forth across the floor in response. He lifted a paw and rested it on her leg. Toby had been a gift from her father, and was her closest companion. When he was small he had nipped her father's feet under the table one too many times, and been thrown against side of the washing machine. Alice's father forbade a trip to the vet and Toby had been deaf ever since. When she realised he couldn't hear, Alice took it upon herself to create a secret language that she and Toby could share, using hand signals. She wagged her thumb at him again to tell him he was good. Toby slurped the side of Alice's face and she laughed in disgust, wiping her cheek. He circled a few times and settled at her feet with a thud. No longer small, he looked more like a grey-eyed wolf than a sheep-dog. Alice curled her bare toes into his long fluffy coat. Emboldened by his company, she opened *A Beginner's Guide to Fire* and was quickly absorbed by the first story inside.

In faraway places, like Germany and Denmark, people used fire to burn away the old and invite the new, to welcome the beginning of the next cycle: a season, a death, a life, or a love. Some people even built huge figures out of wicker and bramble, setting them alight to draw an end and mark a beginning: to tempt miracles.

Alice sat back in her chair. Her eyes were hot and gummy. She pressed her hands on the pages, over the photo of a burning man made of wicker. What miracle would her fire welcome? For a start, never again would there be the sound of things breaking in their house. The sour stench of fear would no longer fill the air. Alice would plant a veggie garden without being punished for accidentally using the wrong trowel. She might learn to ride a bike without feeling the roots of her hair tear from her scalp in her father's enraged grip because she couldn't balance. The only signs she would need to read would be in the sky, rather than the shadows and clouds that passed over her father's face, alerting her to whether he was the monster, or the man who turned a gum tree into a writing desk.

That happened after the day he shoved her into the sea and left her to swim to shore on her own. He'd vanished into his wooden shed that night and not emerged for two days. When he did, he laboured under the weight of a rectangular desk, longer lengthways than he was tall. It was made from the creamy planks of spotted gum he'd been saving to build Alice's mother a new fernery. Alice hovered in the corner of her room while her father bolted the desk to the wall under the windowsill. It filled her bedroom with the heady fragrances of fresh timber, oil and varnish. He showed Alice how the lid opened on brass hinges, revealing a shallow underbelly ready to be filled with paper, pencils and books. He'd even planed a eucalyptus branch into an arm to hold the lid up, so Alice could use both hands to fossick inside.

'I'll get you all the pencils and crayons you need next time I go to town, Bunny.'

Alice threw her arms around his neck. He smelled of Cussons soap, sweat and turpentine.

'My baby bunting.' His stubble grazed her cheek. A lacquer of words coated Alice's tongue: *I knew you were still in there. Stay. Please don't let the wind change.* But all she could say was, 'Thank you.'

Alice's eyes drifted back to her open book.

Fire is an element that requires friction, fuel and oxygen to combust and burn. An optimum fire needs these optimum conditions.

She looked up, out into the garden. The invisible force of the wind pushed and pulled the pots of maidenhair ferns on their hooks. It howled under the slim crack of the open window. She took deep breaths, filling her lungs and emptying them slowly. *Fire is*

an element that requires friction, fuel and oxygen to combust and burn.
Staring into the green heart of her mother's garden, Alice knew
what she must do.

As the windstorm came in from the east and drew across the sky in
dark curtains, Alice put her windcheater on at the back door. Toby
paced by her side and she entwined her fingers in his woolly coat.
He whimpered and nuzzled her belly. His ears lay flat. Outside,
the wind tore the petals off her mother's white roses and scattered
them across the yard like fallen stars. In the distance, at the bottom
of their property, sat the shadowy hulk of her father's locked shed.
Alice patted the pockets of her jacket, feeling the key inside. After
taking a moment, willing herself to be brave, she opened the back
door and ran out of the house, into the wind with Toby.

Although she was forbidden to enter it, nothing had stopped
Alice from imagining what might be in her father's wooden shed.
Most of the time he spent inside followed the awful things he did.
But when he came out, he was always better. Alice had decided his
shed held a transformational kind of magic, as if within its walls
was an enchanted mirror, or a spinning wheel. Once, when she
was younger, she was brave enough to ask him what was inside. He
didn't answer her but after he made her desk, Alice understood.
She'd read about alchemy in her library books; she knew the tale
of Rumpelstiltskin. Her father's shed was where he spun straw
into gold.

Her legs and lungs burned as she ran. Toby barked at the sky
until a spear of dry lightning overhead sent his tail between his
legs. At the shed door, Alice took the key out of her pocket and
slid it into the padlock. It wouldn't give. The wind stung her face
and threatened her balance; only Toby's warmth pressed against
her kept her steady. She tried again. The key hurt her palm as she

pushed against it, willing it to turn. It would not budge. Panic blurred her vision. She let go, wiped her eyes, and brushed her hair out of her face. Then tried again. This time the key turned so easily the lock could have been oiled. Alice wrenched the padlock off the door, twisted the handle, and stumbled inside with Toby at her heels. The wind sucked the door shut behind them with a loud slam.

The windowless interior of the shed was pitch black. Toby growled. Alice reached through the darkness to comfort him. She was deafened by the rush of blood beating in her ears and the howling ferocity of the windstorm. Seedpods from the poinciana tree beside the shed rained down in sharp succession, like a clatter of tin slippers dancing across the roof.

The air was pungent with kerosene. Alice groped around until her fingers touched a lamp on the workbench. She knew the shape of it; her mother kept a similar one inside the house. Next to it was a box of matches. An angry voice bellowed through her mind. *You shouldn't be in here. You shouldn't be in here.* Alice cringed, yet still slid the matchbox open. She felt for the tip, struck it against the rough flint and smelled sulphur as a quick glow of fire filled the air. She held the match to the wick of the kerosene lamp and screwed the glass top back onto the base. Light spilled across her father's workbench. In front of her, a small drawer was ajar. With a shaking finger, Alice slid it open. Inside was a photograph and something else Alice couldn't see properly. She took out the photo. Its edges were cracked and yellow but the image was clear: a rambling, resplendent old house covered in vines. Alice reached into the drawer again for the second object. Her fingertips brushed against something soft. She drew it out, into the light: a lock of black hair tied in faded ribbon.

An almighty gust rattled the shed door. Alice dropped the hair and photo as she swung around. There was no one there. It was just the wind. Her heart had just begun to slow when Toby lowered on his haunches and growled again. Shaking, Alice lifted the lamp to illuminate the rest of her father's shed. Her jaw went slack; there was a strange jellying in her knees.

Surrounding her were dozens of wooden sculptures, ranging from miniatures to life size, all of the same two figures. One was an older woman, caught in various poses: sniffing a gum leaf, inspecting pot plants, lying on her back with one arm bent over her eyes and the other pointing upwards; another held the bowl of her skirt, filled with flowers Alice didn't know. The other sculptures were of a girl: reading a book, writing at a desk, blowing the seeds off a dandelion. Seeing herself in her father's carvings made Alice's head ache.

Version after version of this woman and girl filled the shed, closing in around the bench. Alice took slow and deep breaths, listening to her heartbeat. *I'm–here*, it said. *I'm–here*. If fire could be a spell that turned one thing into another, so too could words. Alice had read enough to understand the charms that words could possess, especially when repeated. Say something enough times and it would be so. She focused on the spell beating in her heart.

I'm–here.

I'm–here.

I'm–here.

Alice turned in slow circles, taking in the wooden figures. She remembered reading once about an evil king who made so many enemies in his kingdom he created an army of clay and stone warriors to surround him – except clay is not flesh and stone is neither heart nor blood. In the end, the villagers the king was trying to protect himself from used the very army he created to crush him while he was sleeping. Prickles ran up and down Alice's back as she recalled the words she'd read earlier. *Fire requires friction, fuel and oxygen to combust and burn.*

'Come on, Tobes,' she said hurriedly, reaching for one wooden figure, then another. Mimicking one of the statues, she used her

T-shirt as a bowl to carry the smallest figurines she could find. Toby fretted at Alice's side. Her heart beat powerfully against her ribs. With so many statues in the shed, her father surely wouldn't notice some of the smallest missing. They would be perfect fuel to practise making fire.

Alice would always remember this day as the one that changed her life irrevocably, even though it would take her the next twenty years to understand: life is lived forward but only understood backward. You can't see the landscape you're in while you're in it.

Pulling into the driveway, Alice's father gripped the steering wheel in silence. Welts had risen on his wife's face, which she nursed with one hand. She used the other to hold her stomach as she pressed herself against the passenger door. He'd seen with his own eyes the way she'd touched the doctor's arm. He'd seen the look on the doctor's face. He'd *seen* it. A tic twitched under Alice's father's right eye. His wife had been dizzy when she sat up after the scan; he hadn't wanted to stop for breakfast and risk missing the appointment. She'd tried to steady herself. The doctor had helped her.

Alice's father flexed his hand. His knuckles were still aching. He glanced over at his wife, curled into herself, creating a canyon between them. He wanted to reach out to her, to explain she just needed to be more mindful of her behaviour so he wouldn't be provoked. If he spoke to her in flowers, maybe then she would understand. Forked sundew, *I die if neglected*. Harlequin fuchsia, *cure and relief*. Wedding bush, *constancy*. But he'd avoided giving her flowers for years, ever since they left Thornfield.

She hadn't helped him today. She should have made time to pack breakfast before they left, then she wouldn't have been dizzy and he wouldn't have witnessed her pawing the doctor. She knew how he struggled with their town visits, and the medical staff having their hands all over and inside his wife. They'd never been to a scan or check-up during this pregnancy, or with Alice, that was without incident. Was it really his fault that she failed to support him, every single time?

'We're home,' he said, pulling the handbrake and turning the engine off. His wife took her hand away from her face and reached for the door handle. She tugged on it once and waited. His temper flared. Would she say nothing? He unlocked the central locking, expecting her to turn and smile at him gratefully, or maybe even apologetically. But she flew out of the door like a chicken escaping its coop. He tore out of the truck yelling her name, abruptly silenced by the windstorm. Wincing in the stinging gale, he stalked after his wife, determined to make his point. As he approached the house, something caught his eye.

The shed door was open. The lock was undone, hanging from the latch. A flash of his daughter's red windcheater in the doorway filled his vision.

When her T-shirt couldn't hold any more carvings, Alice rushed out of the shed into the murky half-light. A clap of thunder shattered the sky. It was so loud that Alice dropped the carvings and hunched against the shed door. Toby cowered, the fur along the ridge of his spine raised. She reached to comfort him and got to her feet, only to be slammed by a gust of wind, making her stagger backwards. Forgetting the carvings, she signalled to Toby and made a run for the house. They'd almost reached the back door when a shard of lightning broke the dark clouds into silver pieces, a downwards arrow. Alice froze. In that white flash, she saw him. Her father stood in the doorway, his arms braced by his sides, hands clenched in fists. She didn't need better light or closer distance to know the darkness of his eyes.

Alice changed direction and sprinted down the side of the house. She wasn't sure if her father had seen her. As she ran through the green fronds of her mother's fern garden, a terrible thought hit her: the kerosene lamp in her father's shed. His timber shed. She'd forgotten to blow it out.

Alice flung herself through the window, onto her desk, hauling Toby up beside her. They perched together, panting to catch their breaths. Toby licked her face and Alice patted him distractedly. Could she smell smoke? Dread sluiced through her body. She jumped off the desk and gathered her library books, stuffing them into her bag, deep within her cupboard. She shrugged off her windcheater and threw it in too, then pulled her window closed. *Someone must have broken into your shed, Dad. I was inside waiting for you to come home.*

She didn't hear her father come into her bedroom. She wasn't quick enough to dodge him. The last thing Alice saw was Toby baring his teeth, his eyes wild with fear. There was the smell of smoke, earth, and burning feathers. A stinging heat spread down the side of her face, drawing Alice into darkness.

2

Flannel flower

Meaning: What is lost is found

Actinotus helianthi | New South Wales

The stem, branches and leaves of the plant are a pale grey,
covered in downy hair, and flannel-like in texture.
Pretty, daisy-shaped flower heads bloom in spring,
though flowering may be profuse after bushfires.

The first story Alice ever learned began on the edge of darkness, where her newborn screams restarted her mother's heart.

The night she was born, a subtropical storm had blown in from the east and caused king tides to flood the river banks, cutting off the lane between the Harts' property and town. Stranded in the laneway with her water broken and a band of fire seemingly cutting her in half, Agnes Hart pushed life and a daughter out of her body on the back seat of her husband's truck. Clem Hart, consumed by panic as the storm boomed over the cane fields, was at first too frantic swaddling his newborn to notice his wife's pallor. When he saw her face turn white as sand, her lips the shade of a pipi shell, Clem fell upon her in a frenzy, forgetting their baby. He shook Agnes, to no avail. It wasn't until her daughter cried that Agnes was jolted to consciousness. On either side of the laneway, rain-soaked bushes burst into a flurry of white flowers. Alice's first breaths were filled with lightning and the scent of storm lilies in bloom.

You were the true love I needed to wake me from a curse, Bun, her mother would say to finish the story. *You're my fairytale.*

When Alice was two years old, Agnes introduced her to books; as she read, she pointed to each word on the page. Down at the beach, she repeated: *one cuttlefish, two feathers, three pieces of driftwood, four shells and five shards of sea glass.* Around their house, Agnes's hand-lettered signs: *BOOK. CHAIR. WINDOW. DOOR. TABLE. CUP. BATH. BED.* By the time Alice started homeschooling when she was five, she was reading by herself. Though her love of books was swift and absolute, Alice always loved her mother's storytelling more. When they were alone, Agnes spun stories around the two of them. But never in earshot of Alice's father.

Their ritual was to walk to the sea and lie on the sand staring up at the sky. With her mother's gentle voice telling the way, they took winter train trips across Europe, through landscapes with mountains so tall you couldn't see their tops, and ridges so smothered in snow you couldn't see the line separating the white sky from white earth. They wore velvet coats in the cobblestoned city of a tattooed king, where the harbour buildings were as colourful as a box of paints, and a mermaid sat, cast in bronze, forever awaiting love. Alice often closed her eyes, imagining that every thread in her mother's stories might spin them into the centre of a chrysalis, from which they could emerge and fly away.

When Alice was six years old, her mother tucked her into her bed one evening, leant forward and whispered in her ear. *It's time, Bun.* She sat back smiling as she pulled up the covers. *You're old enough now to help me in my garden.* Alice squirmed with excitement; her mother usually left her with a book while she gardened alone. *We'll start tomorrow,* Agnes said before she turned out the light. Repeatedly through the night, Alice woke to peer through the dark windows. At last she saw the first thread of light in the sky and threw her sheets back.

Alice's mother was in the kitchen making Vegemite and cottage cheese on toast and a pot of honeyed tea, which she carried on a tray outside to her garden alongside the house. The air was cool, the early sun was warm. Her mother rested the tray on a mossy tree stump and poured sweet tea into two teacups. They sat chewing and drinking in silence. Alice's pulse beat loudly in her temples. After Agnes ate the last of her toast and finished her tea, she crouched between her ferns and flowers, murmuring as if she were rousing sleeping children. Alice wasn't sure what to do. Was this gardening? She mimicked her mother and sat with the plants, watching.

Slowly, the lines of worry in her mother's face vanished. Her furrowed brow relaxed. She didn't wring her hands, or fidget. Her eyes were full and clear. She became someone Alice didn't recognise. Her mother was peaceful. She was calm. The sight filled Alice with the kind of green hope she found at the bottom of rock pools at low tide but never managed to cup in her hands.

The more time she spent with her mother in the garden, the more deeply Alice understood – from the tilt of Agnes's wrist when she inspected a new bud, to the light that reached her eyes when she lifted her chin, and the thin rings of dirt that encircled her fingers as she coaxed new fern fronds from the soil – the truest parts of her mother bloomed among her plants. Especially when she talked to the flowers. Her eyes glazed over and she mumbled in a secret language, a word here, a phrase there as she snapped flowers off their stems and tucked them into her pockets.

Sorrowful remembrance, she'd say as she plucked a bindweed flower from its vine. *Love, returned*. The citrusy scent of lemon myrtle would fill the air as she tore it from a branch. *Pleasures of memory*. Her mother pocketed a scarlet palm of kangaroo paw.

Questions scratched at the back of Alice's throat. Why did her mother's words only flow when she was telling stories about other places and other worlds? What about their world, right in front of them? Where did she go when her eyes were far away? Why couldn't Alice go with her?

By her seventh birthday, Alice's body was heavy from the burden of unanswered questions. They filled her chest. Why did her mother talk to the native flowers in such cryptic ways? How could her father be two different people? What curse did Alice's first cries save her mother from? Although they weighed on her mind, Alice's questions remained stuck, lodged in her windpipe as painfully as if she'd swallowed a seedpod. Moments of opportunity came on good days in the garden, when the light fell just so, yet Alice said nothing. In silence, she followed her mother as her pockets filled with flowers.

If Agnes ever noticed Alice's silence, she never said anything to break it. It was understood time spent in the garden was quiet time. *Like a library*, her mother once mused as she glided through her maidenhair ferns. Though Alice hadn't ever been to a library – to see more books in one place than she could imagine, or hear the whispers of collective pages turning – she almost felt she had, through her mother's stories. From Agnes's description, Alice imagined a library must be a quiet garden of books, where stories grew like flowers.

Alice hadn't been anywhere else beyond their property either. Her life was confined to its boundaries: from her mother's garden to where the cane fields started, to the bay where the sea curled close by. She was forbidden to venture further than those lines, and especially the one that separated their driveway from the lane that led into town. *It's no place for a girl*, her father would say, slamming his fist on the dinner table, making the plates and cutlery jump, whenever Alice's mother suggested sending her to school. *She's safer here*, he'd growl, putting an end to the conversation. That's what her father was most able to do: put an end to everything.

Whether they spent their day in the garden or at the sea, the point always came when a storm bird would call, or a cloud would cross the sun, and Alice's mother would shake herself awake, as if she'd been sleepwalking through a dream. She became animated, turning on her heel to sprint towards the house, calling over her shoulder at Alice, *First one to the kitchen gets fresh cream on her scones.*

Afternoon tea was a bittersweet time; her father would be home soon. Ten minutes before he was due, her mother would position herself by the front door, her face pulled too tight in a smile, her voice pitched too high, her fingers in knots.

Some days Alice's mother disappeared from her body altogether. There were no stories or walks to the sea. There was no talking with flowers. Her mother would stay in bed with the curtains drawn against the blanching light, vanished, as if her soul had gone somewhere else entirely.

When that happened, Alice tried to distract herself from the way the air in the house pressed on her body, the awful silence as if no one were home, the sight of her mother crumpled in bed. Those were things that made it difficult to breathe. Alice picked up books she'd read a dozen times already and revisited school worksheets she'd already completed. She fled to the sea to caw with the gulls and chase waves along the shore. She ran alongside the walls of sugar cane, throwing her hair back and swaying like the green stalks in the hot wind. But no matter how she tried, nothing felt good. Alice wished on feathers and dandelions to be a bird and fly far away into the golden seam of the horizon, where the sea was sewn to the sky. Day after shadowy day passed without her mother. Alice paced the edges of her world. It was only a matter of time before she learned she could disappear too.

One morning, after the rumble of her father's truck faded into the distance, Alice stayed in bed waiting to hear the kettle whistle; the glorious sound would herald the beginning of a good day. When it didn't come, Alice kicked her sheet off with heavy legs. She tiptoed to her parents' bedroom door and peered at her mother's body curled in a ball as lifeless as the blankets around her. A wave of hot and shaky anger swept through Alice. She stomped into the kitchen, slapped together a Vegemite sandwich, filled a jam jar with water, packed them in her backpack, and ran from the house. She wouldn't take the laneway, there was too high a risk of being seen, but if she went hidden through the sugar cane she'd surely come out someplace on the other side, someplace better than her dark and silent home.

Although her heartbeat was so loud in her ears she almost couldn't hear the cockatoos screeching overhead, Alice willed herself to run, past her father's shed and her mother's rose garden, until she'd crossed the length of the yard. At the boundary where their property met the cane fields, she stopped. A dirt trail ran through the tall green stalks for as far as she could see.

In the end Alice was surprised by how easily she could do something she was always told she should not. She just had to take a step. First one. Then another.

Alice walked so far and for so long that she started to wonder if she might walk out of the cane fields to find herself in a different country. Maybe she'd emerge in Europe, and catch one of her mother's trains through a snowy world. But when she came to the end of the fields, the discovery she made was almost better: she was at a crossroad in the middle of town.

She shielded her eyes from the sun. So much colour and movement, noise and clatter. Cars and farming trucks coming and going through the intersection, horns beeping, farmers with their tanned elbows hanging out of windows, raising tired hands to each other as they drove past. Alice spotted a shop with a wide window full of fresh bread and iced cakes. It was a bakery, she realised, remembering one of her picture books. This one had a beaded curtain over its entrance. Outside, under a striped awning, was a higgledy-piggledy of chairs and tables, with a brightly coloured flower in a vase on top of each checked tablecloth. Alice's mouth watered. She wished her mother was beside her.

On either side of the bakery, shop windows promised farmers' wives a whiff of cosmopolitan life: new tea dresses with narrow waists, large floppy hats, tasselled handbags and kitten heels. Alice wriggled her toes in her sandals. She'd never seen her mother wear anything like the clothes on the mannequins in the windows. Her mother only had one outfit for trips to town: a long-sleeved burgundy polyester dress and tan leather flats. The rest of the time her mother wore loose cotton dresses she made herself, and, like Alice, went mostly barefoot.

Alice's gaze drifted to the intersection ahead of her, where a young woman and girl were waiting to cross at a set of lights. The woman held the girl's hand, carrying her pink backpack for her. The girl's shoes were black and shiny, with frilly white socks at her ankles. Her hair was in two neat pigtails with matching ribbons. Alice couldn't look away. When the light changed they crossed the road and pushed through the beaded curtain into the bakery. A little while later they came out with creamy milkshakes and thick wedges of cake. They sat at the table that Alice would have chosen, the one with the painfully happy yellow gerbera, and they drank from their glasses, smiling milk-moustache smiles at each other.

The sun beat down on Alice. Her eyes hurt in the glare. Just as she was about to give up and spin around to run all the way home, Alice noticed a word on the ornate stone front of a building across the road.

LIBRARY.

She gasped and ran for the traffic lights. Jabbed the button repeatedly as she'd seen the girl do, until the light turned green and the intersection was clear. She sprinted across the road and through the heavy doors of the library.

In the foyer, she doubled over, panting. The cool air settled her hot, sweaty skin. Her pulse slowed in her ears. She pushed the hair away from her sunburnt forehead, and with it the thought of the woman and girl and their happy yellow gerbera. As she went to straighten her dress, Alice realised she wasn't wearing one; she was still in her nightie. She hadn't remembered to change before she left home. Unsure of what to do or where to go, Alice stayed where she was, pinching her wrists until the skin turned raw; pain on the outside softened the sharp feelings inside she couldn't reach. It wasn't until moving beams of coloured light fell in her eyes that she stopped.

Alice tiptoed through the foyer and entered the main library room, which opened around and above her. Her eyes were drawn upwards by sunlight streaming through stained-glass windows: a girl in a red hood walked through a forest of trees; a girl in a carriage sped away from a lone glass slipper; a little mermaid stared longingly from the sea at a man on shore. Excitement shot through Alice.

'Can I help you?'

Alice looked down from the windows, in the direction of the question. A young woman with big hair and a wide smile sat at an octagonal desk. Alice tiptoed towards her.

'Oh, you don't have to tiptoe,' the woman said, chuckling. She snorted when she laughed. 'I wouldn't last a day here if I had to be *that* quiet. My name's Sally. I don't think I've seen you here before.' Sally's eyes reminded Alice of the sea on a sunny day. 'Have I?' she asked.

Alice shook her head.

'Oh, well now, how wonderful. A new friend!' Sally clasped her hands together. Her fingernails were painted seashell pink. There was a pause.

'And you are?' Sally asked. Alice peeked at her from under her eyelashes. 'Oh, don't be shy. Libraries are friendly places. Everyone's welcome here.'

'I'm Alice,' she mumbled.

'Alice?'

'Alice Hart.'

Something strange flickered over Sally's face. She cleared her throat.

'Well, Alice Hart,' she exclaimed. 'What a magical name! Welcome. It'll be my pleasure to show you around.' Her eyes darted to Alice's nightie then back to her face. 'Are you here with Mum or Dad today?'

Alice shook her head.

'I see. Tell me, how old are you, Alice?'

Alice's cheeks were hot. Eventually, she held up five splayed fingers on one hand and her thumb and index finger on the other.

'Fancy that, Alice. Seven just happens to be the right age for you to have your own library card.'

Alice snapped her head up.

'Ah, look at that. Sunbeams are coming out of your face.' Sally winked. Alice touched her fingertips to her hot cheeks. Sunbeams.

'Let me get you a form and we'll fill it out together.' Sally reached over and squeezed Alice's arm. 'Do you have any questions first?'

Alice thought about it then nodded.

'Yes. Can you please show me the garden where the books grow?' Alice smiled with relief; her voice had found its way around the seedpod.

Sally studied Alice's face for a moment before erupting in hushed giggles. 'Alice! You crack me up. We're going to get along like a house on fire, you and me.'

In her confusion, Alice just smiled.

For the next half-hour Sally took Alice on a tour of the library, explaining that books lived on shelves, not in a garden. Row upon row of stories called to Alice. So many books. After a while Sally left Alice to herself to sit in a big, cushiony chair by one of the shelves.

'Browse about and pick out some books you like. I'm just over there if you need anything.' Sally pointed in the direction of her desk. Alice, already with a book in her lap, nodded.

Sally's hands trembled as she picked up the phone. While she dialled the station, she leant forward to make sure Alice hadn't followed her, but she was still sitting on the chair, the worn soles of her sandals poking out from under the grimy hem of her nightie. Sally fiddled with Alice's library form, gasping when the paper sliced into her fingertip. Her eyes filled as she sucked the blood from her finger. Alice was Clem Hart's daughter. She pushed his name out of her mind and pressed the phone hard against her ear. *Pick up. Pick up. Pick up.* Finally, her husband answered.

'John? It's me. No, I'm not, not really. No, listen, Clem Hart's girl is here. Something's wrong. She's in her nightie, John.' Sally struggled to keep her composure. 'It's filthy.' She gulped. 'And John, her little arms are bruised to buggery.'

Sally nodded along with her husband's steadying voice and wiped the tears from her eyes.

'Yes, I think she's walked on her own all the way from their property so, what's that, about four kilometres?' She sniffled as she tugged her hanky from her sleeve. 'Okay. Yes. Yes, I'll keep her here.'

The phone receiver slipped in Sally's sweaty palm as she hung up.

Alice added another book to the semi-circular tower she had built around her.

'Alice?'

'I'd like to take all these home, please, Sally,' Alice said earnestly with a sweep of her arm.

Sally helped her to deconstruct her tower of books, return the dozens to their shelves, and explained twice how borrowing library books worked. Alice was dumbfounded by her limited choice. Sally checked her watch. The bright light falling through the story windows had softened to pastel shadows.

'Shall I help you pick?'

Alice nodded gratefully. She wanted to read books about fire but didn't feel brave enough to say so.

Sally crouched to Alice's eye level and asked her some questions – name one of her favourite places to go – the sea – and choose a favourite story window at the library – the mermaid – then with a knowing nod, she touched her index finger to a slim book with a hard cover and bronze lettering on the spine, and slid it off the shelf.

'I think you'll love this one. It's about selkies.'

'Selkies,' Alice repeated.

'You'll see,' Sally said. 'Women from the sea who can shed their skins to become someone and something else entirely.' Goosebumps covered Alice's body. She clutched the book to her chest.

'Reading makes me hungry,' Sally said abruptly. 'Are you hungry, Alice? I've got some scones with jam, and how about a cup of tea?'

At the mention of scones, Alice thought of her mother. She was consumed by an immediate desire to be home, but it seemed that Sally expected her to stay.

'Can I go to the toilet?'

'Of course,' Sally said. 'The ladies' is just down the hall there, on the right. Shall I come with you?'

'No, thank you.' Alice smiled sweetly.

'I'll be right here when you get back. We'll have scones, okay?'

Alice skipped down the hallway. She pushed open the door to the bathroom. Waited a moment, then stuck her head back out to peek at Sally's desk. It was empty. The clink of cutlery and china came from further down the hall. Alice scurried for the exit.

As she ran home through the cane fields, she felt the shape of her library card in her nightie pocket, like one of her mother's flowers. The selkie book jostled up and down in her backpack; sunbeams bounced around inside her belly. Alice was so busy imagining how much her mother would love her library book, she didn't realise that by the time she got home her father would be back from work.

3

Sticky everlasting

Meaning: My love will not leave you

Xerochrysum viscosum | New South Wales and Victoria

These paper-like flowers display hues of lemon,
gold, and splotchy orange to fiery bronze.
They can be easily cut, dried, and preserved
while retaining their stunning colours.

A month after Alice discovered the library, she was playing in her room when she heard her mother's voice calling. 'We need to do some weeding, Bun.'

It was a tranquil afternoon. The garden was thick with orange butterflies. Her mother smiled up at her from under the brim of her floppy hat. It was the same smile she used to greet her father when he came home: *Everything's okay, everything's all right, everything's fine.* Alice smiled back even though she noticed her mother wincing, clutching her ribs when she reached for a weed.

Things hadn't been right since the library. Alice couldn't sit for days after her father took to her with his belt. He snapped her library card in two and confiscated the book, but not before Alice read it in one sitting. She absorbed the stories of selkies and their magical skins into her blood like they were sugar on her tongue. Her bruises healed and her father only punished her once; Alice's mother continued to bear his rage. A few times Alice had been woken in the night by rough noises in her parents' bedroom. The ugly sounds paralysed her. On those nights, she stayed in bed with her hands over her ears, willing herself to escape into her dreams, mostly of running with her mother to the sea, where they'd shed their skins before diving in. Bobbing together in the ocean, they'd only look back once before turning to the deep. On shore their pelts would turn to pressed flowers, scattered among shells and seaweed.

'Here, Alice.' Her mother handed her another tuft of weeds, wincing again. Alice's skin burned from her want to rid the garden of every weed, forever, so her mother could just spend her days talking to her flowers in her secret language and filling her pockets with their blooms.

'What about this one, Mama? Is this a weed?' Her mother didn't answer. She was as flighty as the butterflies, her eyes darting constantly to the driveway, checking for the telltale dirt clouds.

Eventually, they appeared.

He swung out of the driver's seat in full swagger, holding his Akubra upside down behind his back. Alice's mother stood to greet him with dirt on her knees and a bunch of dandelions clenched in her fist. Their roots trembled as he leaned in to kiss her. Alice glanced away. Her father in a good mood had the same air about him as a rain shower falling from a sunny sky – you could never quite believe the sight. When Alice met his eye, he smiled.

'We've all had a tough time since you ran away, haven't we, Bunny,' her father said, crouching while keeping his upside-down hat out of her view. 'But I think you've learned your lesson about leaving the property.'

Alice's stomach lurched.

'I've been thinking about it,' he said softly, 'and I think we should get your library card back.' She looked at him uneasily. 'I'm willing to go to the library and pick your books out for you, if you're willing to promise to follow our rules. And to help you keep that promise, I thought you might like some extra company at home.' Alice's father wasn't looking at Alice while he spoke – his eyes were searching her mother's face instead. She stood still and unblinking, her face stretched in a smile. Alice's father turned to

Alice, offering her his hat. Alice took it from him and lowered it into her lap.

Curled inside was a ball of black-and-white fluff. She gasped. Although the pup's eyes were barely open, they were the same slate blue as the winter sea. He sat up and gave a sharp yap, nipping Alice's nose. She squealed in delight; he was her first friend. The puppy licked her face.

'What will you call him, Bun?' her father asked, rocking back on his heels to stand. Alice couldn't read his face.

'Tobias,' she decided. 'But I'll call him Toby.'

Her father laughed easily. 'Toby it is,' he said.

'Wanna hold him, Mama?' Alice asked. Her mother nodded and reached for Toby.

'Oh, he's so young,' she exclaimed, unable to hide the surprise in her voice. 'Where did you get him, Clem? Are you sure he's old enough to be weaned?'

Her father's eyes flashed. His face darkened. 'Of course he's old enough,' he said through clenched teeth, grabbing Toby by the scruff of the neck. He tossed the whimpering pup to Alice.

Later, she cowered outside among her mother's ferns, snuggling the puppy against her heart, trying not to listen to the sounds coming from inside the house. Toby lapped at her chin where her tears gathered, while the wind blew through the sweet-scented sugar cane and out to sea.

The tides of her father's moods turned, as did the seasons. After her father burst Toby's ear drums, Alice busied herself teaching him sign language. She turned eight, advanced to Grade Three in home schooling, and read her pile of library books two weeks before they were due back. Her mother spent more and more time in the garden, mumbling to herself among her flowers.

One late winter's day a set of squalls blew in from the sea, so ferocious Alice wondered if they'd blow the house down like something from a fable. She and Toby watched from the front step as Clem dragged his windsurfer out of the garage and into the yard.

'It's a forty-knot northwesterly, Bunny,' he said, hurrying to load his gear into the back of his truck. 'This is rare.' He brushed the cobwebs off the windsurfer sail. Alice nodded, rubbing Toby's ears. She knew it was; she'd only seen her father ready himself to ride the wind across the sea a handful of times. She'd never been allowed to go with him. He started the engine.

'C'mon then, Bunny. Reckon I need a good luck charm on today's voyage. Hurry up,' he called, leaning out of the driver's window. Although the wild look in his eye made her uneasy, the disbelieving joy of being invited threw Alice into action. She ran into her bedroom to change into her togs and bolted past her mother, calling goodbye, Toby close behind. With a roaring rev of the engine, her father spun out of the driveway towards the bay.

Down at the beach, Alice's father strapped himself into his harness and dragged the board to the water's edge. Alice stood by. When her father called her she followed the deep groove the fin of his board had cut in the sand, all the way to the sea. He pushed his board into the waves, steadying the sail against the wind. The veins in his forearms popped from the effort. Alice stood thigh-high in the salt water, uncertain of what to expect. Her father readied himself to leap on the board then turned to her, his brows raised and his smile reckless. Alice's heartbeat knocked in her ears. He nodded his head towards the board. Toby paced on the shore, barking incessantly. She raised her arm and held her flat palm up to speak to him: *Be calm.* Her father had never asked her along before. She didn't dare refuse the invitation.

As she sprang through the sea towards her father, her mother's voice reached her. Alice turned to see her standing on top of the dunes, calling her name and waving her arms frantically, gripping Alice's fluorescent-orange life vest in one hand. Her calls rose from measured to alarmed. Toby raced away from the shore to meet her. In the water, Alice's father swatted her mother's worry away like it was an insect buzzing around his face.

'You don't need a life vest. Not when you're eight. I was king of my kingdom when I was eight.' He nodded at her. 'Hop on, Bunting.'

Alice beamed. His attention was hypnotic.

He lifted her onto his board, his hands firm and strong under her armpits, and positioned her at the front, where she leant into the wind. He lay belly down and paddled the two of them through the water. Silver fish darted through the shallows. The wind was strong and sea salt stung Alice's eyes. She turned back once to see her mother on shore, dwarfed by the expanse of sea between them.

Out in the turquoise depths her father leapt from his belly to his feet, and slid his toes into the straps. Alice clutched the edges, her palms scraping on the board grip. Her father heaved the sail upright, using his legs to keep his balance. Sinew and muscle rippled beneath the skin of his calves.

'Sit between my feet,' he instructed. She inched along the board towards him. 'Hold on,' he said. She wrapped her arms around his legs.

For a moment, there was a lull; the world was still and aquamarine. Then, *whoosh*, the wind filled the sail and salt water sprayed Alice's face. The sea sparkled. They sailed through the waves, zigzagging across the bay. Alice leant her head back and closed her eyes; the sun warm on her skin, the sea spray tickling her face, the wind running its fingers through her long hair.

'Alice, look,' her father called. A pod of dolphins arced alongside them. Alice cried out in delight, remembering her selkie book.

'Stand up so you can see them better,' he said. Holding on to his legs, Alice wobbled as she stood, mesmerised by the beauty of the dolphins. They glided through the water, peaceful and free. She tentatively let go of her father and used her own weight to balance. Holding her arms out wide, she moved her waist in circles and rolled her wrists, mimicking the dolphins. Her father howled joyously into the wind. Seeing true happiness in his face made Alice light-headed.

Out beyond the bay they flew, into the channel where a tourist boat was circling back towards the town harbour. A camera flash bulb popped in their direction. Her father waved.

'Do the hula again for them,' Alice's father encouraged her. 'They're watching us, Alice. Do it. Now.'

Alice didn't understand what *hula* meant; was it her dolphin dance? The urgency in his voice also confused her. She glanced at the front of the board and back up at him. This moment of hesitation was her mistake; she caught the shadow as it crossed his face. Scrambling to the board's tip she tried to make up the time she'd lost and stood on shaky legs, looping her waist and rolling her wrists. It was too late. The boat turned away from them; the camera flashes glinted off the water in the opposite direction. Alice smiled hopefully. Her knees trembled. She snuck a look at her father. His jaw was set.

When he flipped the sail around and they changed direction, Alice almost lost her balance. The sun was garish and sharp, biting at her skin. She crouched on the board and clung to its sides. Her mother's voice carried on the wind, calling them relentlessly as they crossed the channel back towards the bay. The waves rolled deep and dark green. Her father said nothing. She sidled towards him. As she nestled herself between his feet again and clung to his calves, she felt a muscle twitch under his skin. She looked up but his face was blank. Alice bit back on tears. She'd ruined it. She tightened her grip on his legs.

'Sorry, Papa,' she said in a small voice.

The pressure on her back was firm and quick. She pitched forward into the cold sea, crying out as she was engulfed by waves. Spluttering to the surface, she shrieked and coughed, trying to hack up the burning sensation of salt water in her lungs. Kicking hard, she held her arms up the way her mother taught her to do if she ever got caught in a rip. Not too far away, her father coasted on the board, staring at her, his face as white as the caps on the waves. Alice kicked to tread water. With a quick flick her father spun the sail again. *He's coming back.* Alice whimpered, relieved. But as his sail caught the wind and he sailed away from her, she stopped kicking in disbelief. She started to sink. When the water covered her nose, Alice flailed her arms and kicked hard, fighting her way upwards through the waves.

Tossed up and down at the whim of the current, Alice glimpsed her mother over the waves. She'd flung herself into the ocean and was swimming hard. The sight of Agnes gave Alice a surge of strength. She kicked and paddled until she felt the slightest shift in the temperature of the water and knew she was approaching the shallows. Her mother reached her in a flurry of splashing and clung to her like Alice herself was a life vest. When they could both touch sand, sure and solid beneath their feet, Alice stood and vomited bile, her retching a croaking, empty sound. Her arms and legs gave out. She gasped for breath. Her mother's eyes were as dull as a piece of sea glass. She carried Alice to shore and wrapped her in the dress she'd discarded before leaping into the waves. She rocked them both back and forth until Alice stopped crying. Hoarse from barking, Toby whined while he licked Alice's face. She patted him weakly. When she started to shiver Alice's mother picked her up and carried her home. She didn't say a thing.

As they left the beach Alice looked back at the frenzy of her mother's footprints on the shore. Far out on the sea her father's sail cut brightly through the waves.

No one talked about what happened that day. Afterwards, whenever he was home from the cane fields, Clem avoided the house. Instead he did what he would always do to relieve his guilt: retreated to his shed. At meals, he was distant and chillingly polite. Being around him was like being outside without shelter during stormy weather, always watching the sky. Alice spent a few sweaty-palmed weeks hoping she, Toby and her mother might run away to the places in her mother's stories, where snow covered the earth like white sugar and ancient, sparkling cities were built on water. But as weeks turned into months and summer started to soften its edges into autumn, there were no more outbursts. Her father's tides were peaceful. He made her a writing desk. Alice began to wonder if maybe he'd left the stormy parts of himself out in the deep that day when she'd seen the ocean turn dark green.

One clear morning at breakfast, Alice's father announced that he had to travel south to the city to buy a new tractor on the coming weekend. He would miss Alice's ninth birthday. It was unavoidable. Alice's mother nodded and stood to clear the table. Alice swung her legs back and forth under her seat, hiding her face behind her hair as she digested the news. She, her mother, and Toby would have a whole weekend together. Alone. In peace. It was the best birthday gift she could have hoped for.

The morning he left, they waved him off together. Even Toby sat still until the dust clouds that trailed after him billowed and vanished. Alice's mother gazed at the empty driveway.

'Well,' she said, reaching for Alice's hand. 'This weekend is all yours, Bun. What would you like to do?'

'Everything!' Alice grinned.

They started with music. Her mother tugged down old records and Alice closed her eyes and swayed as she listened.

'If you could have anything at all, what would you have for lunch?' her mother asked.

Alice dragged a kitchen chair to the counter to stand at the same height as her mother and helped to make Anzac biscuits, crunchy on the outside and chewy in the middle from too much golden syrup, the way she liked them best. Alice ate more than half the batter raw, sharing wooden spoonfuls with Toby.

As their biscuits were baking, Alice sat at her mother's feet while Agnes brushed her hair. The slow rhythm of the brush on Alice's scalp sounded like wings in flight. After her mother counted one hundred strokes, she leant forward and whispered a question into Alice's ear. Alice nodded excitedly in response. Her mother left the room and came back a few moments later. Told Alice to close her eyes. Alice grinned, relishing the feeling of her mother's fingers weaving through her hair. When she was done, her mother led Alice through the house.

'Okay, Bun. Open,' she said with a smile in her voice.

Alice waited until she couldn't bear the anticipation for a second longer. When she opened her eyes, she gasped at her reflection in the mirror. A crown of flame-orange beach hibiscus was entwined around her head. She didn't recognise herself.

'Happy birthday, Bunny.' Her mother's voice wavered. Alice took her hand. As they stood together in front of the mirror, fat drops of rain started to fall hard and fast on the roof. Her mother got up and went to the window.

'What is it, Mama?'

Agnes sniffled, and wiped her eyes. 'Come with me, Bun,' she said. 'I've got something to show you.'

They waited at the back door until the storm clouds passed. The sky was violet and the light was silver. Alice followed her mother into the garden that was glossy with rain. They came to a bush her mother had planted recently. When Alice last took notice, it was just a tumble of bright green leaves. Now, after the rain, the bush was thick with fragrant white flowers. She studied them in bewilderment.

'Thought you might like these,' her mother said.

'Is it magic?' Alice reached out to touch one of the petals.

'The best kind.' Her mother nodded. 'Flower magic.'

Alice bent down to get as close as she could. 'What are they, Mama?'

'Storm lilies. Just like the night you were born. They only flower after a good downpour.' Alice leant down and studied them closely. Their petals were flung open, leaving their centres fully exposed.

'They can't exist without rain?' Alice asked, straightening up. Her mother considered her for a moment before nodding.

'When I was in your father's truck the night you were born, they were growing wild by the road. I remember seeing them bloom in the storm.' She looked away but Alice saw her mother's eyes fill.

'Alice,' her mother began. 'I planted the storm lilies here for a reason.'

Alice nodded.

'Storm lilies are a sign of expectation. Of the goodness that can come from hardship.' Her mother rested her hand on her stomach.

Alice nodded, still unaware.

'Bun, I'm going to have another baby. You're going to have a brother or a sister to play with and look after.' Her mother snapped a storm lily from its stem and tucked it into the tail of Alice's braid. Alice looked down at its quivering heart, open and vulnerable.

'Isn't that good news?' her mother asked. Alice could see the storm lilies reflected in her mother's eyes. 'Alice?'

She hid her face in her mother's neck and squeezed her eyes shut, inhaling the scent of her mother's skin, trying not to cry.

Knowing there was a kind of magic that could make flowers and babies bloom after storms filled Alice with dread: more precious things in her world her father could harm.

Overnight the weather swung about and blew in another storm. Alice and Toby woke the next morning to torrential rain sobbing at the windows and battering the front door. Alice yawned, wandering through the house, dreaming of pancakes. She tried not to count the hours left before her father would be home later in the day. But the kitchen was dark. Alice fumbled for the light switch, confused. She flicked it on. The kitchen was empty and cold. She ran to her parents' room and waited for her eyes to readjust to the darkness. When she understood her mother was gone, Alice ran outside, calling for her. She was soaked in seconds. Toby barked. Through the downpour, Alice caught a glimpse of her mother's cotton dress, disappearing through the saltbushes in the front yard, headed towards the sea.

By the time Alice reached the ocean her mother had already shed her clothes on the sand. Although the rain hadn't let up and visibility was poor, Alice managed to spot her mother in the water. She'd swum so far out she was no more than a pale dot on the waves, dipping, arcing, thrashing her way through the water as if she had a fight to win. After a long time, she bodysurfed into the shallows and screamed violently at the sea as it spat her onto the shore.

Alice wrapped her mother's clothes like a pelt around her shoulders, calling her mother's name until her voice was weak. Agnes didn't seem to hear her. She rose from the sand, naked, haggard and out of breath. The sight of her nakedness silenced Alice. The rain beat down on them. Toby cried, pacing back and forth. Alice couldn't take her eyes off her mother's body. Her pregnant belly was bigger than Alice realised. Framing it were bruises, blooming along her mother's collarbone, down her arms, over her ribs, around her hips, and inside her thighs, like sea lichen smothering rock. All this time that Alice thought there'd been no storms, she had been gravely mistaken.

'Mama.' Alice started to cry. She tried wiping the tears and rain from her face. It was no use. Her teeth chattered from fear and emotion. 'I was worried you weren't coming back.'

Alice's mother seemed to look right through her. Her eyes were big and dark, clumps of her eyelashes stuck together. She stayed that way, staring, for a long time. Finally, she blinked, and spoke.

'I know you were worried. I'm sorry.' She gently unwrapped her clothes from Alice's shoulders and pulled them onto her wet skin. 'C'mon, Bun,' she said. 'Let's go home.' Agnes took Alice's hand and together they walked back up the sand in the rain. No matter how hard she shook, Alice made sure not to let go.

A few weeks later, just before the afternoon when she read about the phoenix bird, Alice and her mother were out in the garden among green pea and pumpkin seedlings. Curls of black smoke rose on the horizon.

'Don't worry, Bun,' her mother said, raking new dirt for the veggie patch. 'It's a controlled burn at one of the farms.'

'Controlled burn?'

'People all over the world use fire to garden,' her mother explained. Alice sat on her heels where she'd been tugging weeds from the freshly turned dirt and considered what her mother had said, incredulous. 'Truly.' Her mother nodded, leaning on her rake. 'They burn back plants and trees to make way for things to grow. Controlled fires reduce the risk of wildfire too.'

Alice wrapped her arms around her knees. 'So a little fire can stop a bigger one?' she asked, thinking of the library book on her desk about spells that turned frogs into princes, girls into birds, and lions into lambs. 'Like a spell?'

Her mother nestled seedlings into the rows of fresh earth. 'Yes, I suppose it's just like that, a spell of sorts to transform one thing into another. Some flowers and seeds even need fire to split open and grow: orchids and desert oaks, those kinds of things.' She dusted her hands and pushed her hair off her forehead. 'You clever girl,' she said. For once her smile reached her eyes. After a moment Alice's mother returned to her seedlings.

Alice went back to her work too, but all the while, out of the corner of her eye, watched her mother, backlit by afternoon sun, willing new things to grow from nothing. When her mother looked around the property and her face fell at the sight of the shed, Alice understood with swift clarity: she had to find the right spell, the right fire in the right season, to transform her father from one thing into another.

4

Blue pincushion

Meaning: I mourn your absence

Brunonia australis | All states and territories

*A perennial found in woodlands, open forest and sand plains.
Medium to deep blue flowers usually in spring, in hemispherical
clusters on a tall stem. Can be difficult to establish. May die
after a few years.*

Alice, can you hear me? I'm here.

The voice. Softly.

She drifted in and out of consciousness, only catching moments long enough to sense her surroundings. The sharp smells of antiseptic and disinfectant. The glare of a white-walled room. The sweetness of roses. Scratchy, starched bed sheets. A rhythmic beeping at her side. Squeaky shoes on a squeaky floor. The voice. Softly.

You're not alone, Alice, I'm here. I'm going to tell you a story.

Her tongue thickened with longing. She strained to answer the voice, to stay close to the smell of roses, but too quickly she sank back into the murky depths, her limbs heavy with the silt of memory.

Thin amber light shot through the nothingness that pressed in on Alice from all directions. She edged towards it. There was a hardening sensation under her feet, as if she'd reached the sandy bottom of the shallows after swimming in the deep. She realised she was on her beach, but something was very wrong. The dunes of silver-green seagrass were burnt and smoking. The sand was soot-black, and the ocean was gone, a tide lower than Alice had ever seen. She kicked her feet through the blackened shells of dead soldier crabs and cracked pipi shells, their pastel colours charred. Cinders drifted like flaky stars, and clumps of salty ash gathered in her eyelashes. Far off in the distance the low tide shimmered, orange embers under a dark sky. The air was hot and smelled foul.

I'm right here, Alice.

Tears burned her cheeks.

Alice, I'm going to tell you a story.

She searched the blackened shoreline. There was an acrid taste in her mouth. She sensed the heat on her skin before she turned towards the sea.

The embers shimmering on the distant horizon exploded into flames. Fiery waves rose, crashed and rose again, a stampede of glowering beasts. It hurt to breathe. An ocean of fire thundered towards her on the black sand.

Heat from the towering waves scorched her face. All she could smell was roses.

Wave after wave curled and crested, gathering strength as it raced towards her. She tried to crawl away, scrambling to get further up the beach, but she couldn't get traction in the soft sand. Trapped, she turned, helpless as the ocean of fire wheeled over her, a swirling wall of flames. Pressure surged from her gut, but when she took a deep breath, all that tumbled from her lungs was a silent scream of tiny white flowers.

She floated on coral and flaxen flames. What she thought was a sea of fire was not seawater at all; it was an ocean of fiery light. Around her it rippled, constantly changing, a flare of aqua, a splash

of violet, a burst of tangerine. She combed her fingers through the
colours as her body was immersed.

The room was dark. The scratchy sheets were too tight. The air
smelled so sharp it made her nose and eyes fizz. She tried to roll over
but was not strong enough; the bands of light transformed into
thick and flaming snakes, coiling around her body, burning as they
tightened. She coughed violently, crying for breath as her lungs
constricted. Fear snuffed out her voice.

Alice, can you hear me? I'm here.

She was outside of herself, watching the fire snakes consume
her body.

Just stay with my voice.

Sally finished reading the last page aloud and closed the book in
her lap. She sat back in the chair by Alice's hospital bed, almost
unable to bear the sight of her pale skin and bruises. How different
she looked, two years older than the young girl Sally first met on
that melting-hot summer day when Alice showed up at the library
in her nightie, dirty, neglected and vivid as a dream. Now she lay
lifeless, with her long hair spilling across her pillow and down the
sides of the bed, as if she were a character from the book in Sally's
hands.

'Can you hear me, Alice?' she asked again. 'Alice, I'm here.
Just stay with my voice.' She searched Alice's face, studying her
arms resting on top of the hospital sheets, looking for the smallest
movement. There was none, other than the rise and fall of her
chest, assisted by the machines beeping and whirring alongside
her. Alice's jaw was slack and there was bruising down the

right-hand side of her face. The oxygen tube pushed her mouth into a collapsed O.

Sally wiped a tear away as a thought circled through her mind like a snake eating its tail: she should never have let Alice out of her sight that day she walked into the library alone. Or, the quieter, deeper, harder truth: she should have tucked Alice into her car and driven her home to her house where she could have cooked her a hot meal, run her a bath and kept her safe from Clem Hart.

Twitching with regret, Sally sprang from her chair, pacing at the end of Alice's bed.

She shouldn't have listened to John when he said Sally had no legal rights. She shouldn't have accepted the story John relayed to her: after Sally called the station from the library, a patrol car went to the Hart property. Agnes welcomed the two officers in. Offered tea and scones. Apparently, Clem came home while they were there. *Alice is just a mischievous kid*, he'd said. *No harm done.* For John's sake Sally did her best to let it rest. But meeting Alice had an effect on her she couldn't control; she became all Sally could think about. A month or so after Alice visited the library, Clem walked brazenly through the door with the selkie book and Alice's taped-together library card, as if he had every right. Sally hid behind a stack of books and let someone else serve him. After he left, she shook so hard she went home sick. Ran a bath. Drank half a bottle of scotch. Still, she shook. He'd always had that effect on her. He was her darkest secret.

Now, years later, Clem Hart was all anyone in town was talking about: the charming farmer who had kept his beautiful wife and curious daughter locked away, like a dark fairytale. *So tragic*, some exclaimed. *So young*, others said, averting their eyes.

The heartrate monitor beeped steadily. Sally stopped pacing. The veins in Alice's closed eyelids ran like tiny violet rivers under her translucent skin. Sally wrapped her arms around herself. She'd met dozens of children in the library since Gillian died;

none had unsettled her like Alice Hart. It wasn't a coincidence, of course. It was because she was Clem Hart's daughter. From the night John came through the front door and told Sally about the fire, she'd gone to the hospital every day, reading to Alice while the police and welfare authorities huddled together outside, deciding her fate. Sally made sure her voice was soft, clear and strong, in the hope that wherever Alice was inside herself, she would hear her.

The door slid open.

'Hi, Sal. How's our little fighter doing today?'

'Good, Brookie. Really good.'

Brooke fussed over Alice's charts and checked her drip, smiling as she took Alice's temperature. 'You've made her room smell like roses. I think you're the only person I know who's worn the same perfume all their life.'

Sally smiled, comforted by the warmth and familiarity of their old friendship. But the sounds of the machines filled her head. Unable to bear listening to them, Sally started talking.

'She's doing really well today. Really well. She loves fairytales.' Sally held up the book she'd been reading. Her hand shook. 'But who doesn't?'

'Right. Who doesn't love happy endings?' Brooke smiled.

Sally's smile faltered. She knew as well as than anyone that happy endings weren't always what they seemed.

Brooke watched her closely. 'I know, Sal,' she said gently. 'I know how hard this is for you.'

Sally wiped her nose on her sleeve.

'I haven't learned a thing, not in all these years,' she said. 'I could have saved her. I could have done something. Now look at her.' Sally's chin wobbled uncontrollably. 'I'm a stupid woman.'

'Nope.' Brooke shook her head. 'Not on my watch. I won't have that kind of talk, you hear me? If I were Agnes Hart, God rest her poor soul, I'd be so bloody grateful to you, coming here every day out of the love in your big heart to keep Alice company, reading her stories.'

At the mention of Agnes, Sally's guts churned. She'd seen her a few times over the years. Twice driving through town, sitting in the passenger seat of Clem's truck. Once in line at the post office. She was a wisp of a woman. Fading somehow, as if she might vanish right in front of your eyes. Standing behind her in line, Sally could hardly bear the fragility of her shoulders. Her reasons for being in the hospital aside, sitting with Alice was the least Sally could do for Agnes.

'She can't even hear me.' Sally sagged in her seat. There was an ache behind her eyes.

'Rubbish,' Brooke snorted. 'I know you don't believe that, but sure, I'll let you wallow.' She nudged Sally affectionately. 'Every day you've been here has helped her recovery. You know that. Her temperature's coming down and her lungs are clearing. We're keeping an eye on her brain swelling, but things are good. If she continues like this, she'll be out of here by the end of the week.'

Sally frowned. Brooke, misunderstanding the tears in her eyes, leant forward to wrap Sally in a hug.

'I know, isn't it such good news about her grandmother?' Brooke gave her a squeeze and straightened up.

'Grandmother?' Sally asked, her legs deadening.

'You know, social services finding Alice's grandmother.'

'What?' she barely managed to whisper.

'Out on a farm out in Woop-Woop, somewhere inland, I think. Grows flowers. Farming's in the blood, I guess.'

Sally couldn't stop nodding.

'I thought John was the one who called her to organise it all – he didn't tell you any of this?'

Sally sprang out of her seat, hastily grabbing her things. Brooke took a cautious step towards her, offering a steadying hand. Sally backed away, towards the door, shaking her head.

'Oh, Sal.' Realisation filled Brooke's face.

Sally slid the door open and rushed down the corridor and out of the hospital that had now taken the two children she loved most from her life.

Alice hovered, cradled by a calm nothingness. No ocean, no fire, no snakes, no voice. Her skin tingled in anticipation. Nearby, a deep gush of air and the sound of wings. Flap, flap, swoop; up, up, away.

A single fiery feather beckoned, leaving a trail of shimmering light behind it.

Unafraid, she followed.

5

Painted feather flower

Meaning: Tears

Verticordia picta | Southwestern Australia.

A small to medium-sized shrub with pink, cupped flowers that are sweetly scented. Once established, it will only live for around ten years, with a profuse display of bright flowers over a long season.

I'm—here. I'm—here. I'm—here.

Alice listened to her heart, the only way she knew how to steady herself and calm her emotions. It didn't always work though. Sometimes hearing things was worse than seeing them: the dull thud of her mother's body hitting a wall; the nearly silent, tiny exhalation of breath from her father when he hit her.

She opened her eyes and looked around for help, clamouring for air. Where was the storyteller from her dreams? Alice was the only person in the room, alone except for the machines beeping frantically at her side. Panic stung her skin.

A woman came rushing in. 'It's okay, Alice. Let's sit you up so you can breathe better.' The woman reached over her and pushed something on the wall behind her. 'Try not to panic.'

The top half of Alice's bed rose until she was propped up in a sitting position. The pains in her chest began to ease.

'Better?'

Alice nodded.

'Good girl. As deep breaths as you can manage.'

Alice breathed, as fully as she could, willing her heart to slow. The woman leant against the side of the bed, holding two fingers lightly against Alice's wrist while she studied a little watch clipped to her tunic.

'My name's Brooke.' Her voice was kind. 'I'm your nurse.' She glanced at Alice and winked. Her cheeks disappeared into deep dimples when she smiled. Ripples of blue and purple eyeshadow glittered in the folds of skin above her eyes, just as Alice had seen mother-of-pearl shimmer between the crags in oyster shells. The beeping slowed down. Brooke let go of her wrist.

'Is there anything you need?'

Alice tried to ask for a glass of water, but couldn't form the words. She gestured for a drink.

'Easy-peasy. Back in a tick, love.'

Brooke left. The machines beeped. The white room filled with a hum of strange noises: distant pinging; staticky voices, some calm, others urgent; the whoosh of doors opening and closing; squeaky footsteps, some running, others ambling. Alice's heart began to knock against her ribs again. She tried to slow it down with her breathing, with her eyes closed, but it hurt to breathe too deeply. She tried to call out for company, for help, but her voice was no more than vapour. Her lips cracked; her eyes and nose burned. The weight of her accumulating questions hung from her ribs. Where was her family? When could she go home? She tried to speak again but her voice would not come. Her mind filled with an image of white moths flying from her mouth in the ocean of fire. Was that a memory? Did that really happen? Or was it a dream? And if it was a dream, did that mean she'd just been sleeping? How long had she been sleeping?

'Easy, Alice,' Brooke said as she hurried back into the room with a jug and cup. She put them down and took Alice's hand as she wiped the tears from her cheeks. 'I know it's a shock waking up, love. But you're safe. We're taking good care of you.' Alice looked into Brooke's mother-of-pearl eyes. She wanted so much to believe her. 'The doctor's on her way to see you.' Brooke rubbed slow circles on Alice's hand with her thumb. 'She's lovely,' she added, studying Alice's face.

Soon after, a woman in a white coat came into Alice's room. She was tall and willowy with long silver hair swept off her face. She reminded Alice of seagrass.

'Alice, I'm Dr Harris.' She stood at the foot of Alice's bed and flipped through papers on a clipboard. 'It's very good to see you awake. You've been a very brave girl.'

Dr Harris walked around the bed and took a little torch out of her pocket, which she clicked on and shone back and forth between Alice's eyes. Alice instinctively squinted and turned her face away.

'Sorry, I know that's not nice.' The doctor pressed the cold pad of her stethoscope on Alice's chest and listened. Would she hear the questions inside? Was she suddenly going to look up and give Alice answers she wasn't even sure she really wanted to hear? Tiny holes of fear widened in her belly.

Dr Harris took the buds of the stethoscope out of her ears. She murmured a few things to Brooke and handed her the clipboard. Brooke hung it on the end of Alice's bed and closed the door.

'Alice, I'm going to talk to you now about how you got here, okay?'

Alice glanced at Brooke. Her eyes were heavy. She looked back at Dr Harris and nodded slowly.

'Good girl.' Dr Harris smiled briefly. 'Alice,' she began, pressing her hands together as if she was praying, 'you were in a fire on your property, at home. While the police are piecing together what happened, the most important thing is that you're safe and recovering so well.'

An awful pause filled the room.

'I'm so very sorry, Alice.' Dr Harris's eyes were dark and damp. 'Neither of your parents survived. Everyone here cares about your well-being and will look after you until your grandmother arrives ...'

Alice's ears stopped working. She didn't hear Dr Harris mention her grandmother again, or anything else she said. She thought only of her mother. Her eyes, filled with light. The songs she hummed in her garden, their haunting sadness. The turn of her tender wrists; her pockets filled with flowers; her warm, milky breath in the morning. Being in the nest of her arms, on cold sand under hot sun, feeling the rise and fall of breath in her chest, and the rhythm of her heart and voice as she told stories, spinning the two of them into their warm, magical cocoon. *You were the true love I needed to wake me from a curse, Bun. You're my fairytale.*

'I'll see you on my next round,' Dr Harris said, and, after glancing at Brooke, left the room.

Brooke stayed at the end of Alice's bed, her face sombre. A hole was burning through Alice's middle. Couldn't Brooke hear it? Roaring like fire, hissing and raging, swallowing everything inside? A question repeated over and over in her mind. It hooked through Alice and tore bits of her away.

What had she done?

Brooke came around her bed and poured a cup of pale juice, handing it to Alice. At first she wanted to smack it out of Brooke's hand, but once she tasted the cold sweetness, she tipped her head back and swallowed. It hit her stomach, cold. Panting, she held her cup up for more.

'Easy does it,' Brooke said, hesitantly pouring more.

Alice drank so fast some juice dribbled down her chin. She hiccupped as she held the cup out for more. More. More. She shook the cup in Brooke's face.

'Last one.'

Alice nearly gagged swallowing the last mouthful. She lowered her cup shakily. Brooke grabbed a sick bag and flicked it open just in time as Alice vomited up streams of juice. She fell back on her pillow, heaving.

'That's it.' Brooke rubbed Alice's back. 'Nice and steady. Good girl. One breath at a time.'

Alice never wanted to breathe again.

Alice slept fitfully. Dreams of fire left her drenched in cold sweat. When she awoke her heart was so hot she felt it might melt her chest right open. She scratched at her collarbone until her skin bled. Brooke clipped her nails every few days but it didn't stop; Alice clawed at her skin night after night until Brooke brought fluffy gloves for her to wear to sleep. And still, her voice would not come. It was gone, evaporated like a salt puddle at low tide.

New nurses came to visit her. They wore different pinafores from Brooke. Some walked her around the hospital, explaining that her muscles had weakened while she was sleeping and needed to remember how to be strong. They taught her exercises to do in bed and around her room. Others came to talk to her about her feelings. They brought picture cards and toys. Alice didn't hear the storyteller's voice again in her dreams. She grew paler. Her skin cracked. She imagined her heart was withering of thirst, drying out from its edges to its raw, red centre. Every night she fought her way through waves of fire. Mostly, she lay in her bed and stared out the window at the changing sky, trying not to remember, trying not to question anything, and waiting for Brooke to arrive. Brooke had the best eyes.

Time passed. Alice's voice was lost. She could not eat more than a few forkfuls at each meal, no matter how much Brooke fussed over her. Her unasked questions took up all the room in her body; the same one frightened her the most.

What had she done?

Though she hardly ate, she drank jug after jug of sweet juice and water, but nothing washed the smoke or sorrow away.

Soon dark purple smudges appeared like storm clouds under her eyes. Nursing staff took her for walks out in the sun twice a day, but the glare of the light was too much to bear for more than a few moments at a time. Dr Harris visited again to explain that if she didn't start eating, they were going to have to feed her through a tube. Alice let them; her unasked questions hurt more than any tube ever could. She had no room left inside her to care.

One morning Brooke squeaked into Alice's room in her pink rubber shoes, her eyes twinkling like the summer sea. She had something in her hands, hidden behind her back. Alice looked at her with weak interest.

'Something's arrived.' Brooke grinned. 'Just for you.' Alice raised an eyebrow.

Brooke made a drum-roll noise.

'Ta da!'

In her hands sat a box tied with strands of brightly coloured string. Alice propped herself up in bed. Her body tingled with faint curiosity.

'It was at the nurse's station this morning when I started my shift. Nothing but this tag, with your name on it.' Brooke rested the box on Alice's lap with a wink. It was delightfully heavy.

Alice untied the string bow and opened the top of the box. Inside, nested under swathes of tissue paper, was a pile of books. Their spines faced upwards, the way flowers in her mother's garden turned their faces towards the sun. She ran her fingertips over the lettering of their titles, gulping when she spotted one she knew. It was the book she first borrowed from the library, about selkies.

In a surge of energy Alice heaved the box upside down. The books tumbled onto her lap. She sighed with pleasure, scooping them into her arms. Thumbing through the pages, she breathed in their musty paper-and-ink fragrance. Stories of salt and longing fluttered around her face, beckoning to her. When she heard the squeak of Brooke's shoes on the linoleum outside her room, Alice looked up in surprise; she hadn't heard her leave.

Later, Brooke silently wheeled a table into Alice's room and angled it directly over her bed. It was laden with colourful dishes. A pot of yoghurt and fruit salad. A cheese and salad sandwich, all the crusts cut off, and a small pile of crunchy chips. They glistened with oil and salt. To the side, a box of sultanas and almonds. And a carton of cold malted milk with a straw.

Alice met Brooke's eyes. After a moment, she nodded.

'Attagirl,' Brooke said, locking the wheels of the lunch table before leaving the room.

Keeping the selkie book close, Alice riffled through the other books and picked one. She opened the cover, shivering with delight when she heard the spine crack. She reached for a triangle of sandwich and closed her eyes as she sank her teeth into the soft, fresh bread. Alice couldn't remember the last thing she'd eaten that was so good. The creaminess of salted butter and tangy cheese. Crunchy lettuce, sweet carrot and juicy tomato. Ravenous, Alice stuffed the rest of the triangle into her cheeks, struggling to chew around bits of bread and carrot poking out of her mouth.

After taking several sips of malted milk to wash down her lunch, Alice let out a loud burp. She smiled to herself in satisfaction and, with her belly full, turned her attention to her book. Though she was sure she'd never read it before, she somehow knew the story. She ran her fingertips over the embossed cover. It showed a beautiful young girl sleeping, holding a thorny rose in her hand.

The next day, when she was nearly finished *Sleeping Beauty*, Alice glanced from her book to see Brooke and Dr Harris hovering outside her room with two strange women. One was in a suit with heavy square glasses and bright lipstick. She had a folder thick with paper in her arms. The other woman was in a khaki buttoned-up shirt, trousers the same colour, and solid-looking brown boots, like those her father wore to work. Her hair was threaded with grey. Whenever she moved it sounded like little bells were chiming; a collection of silver bracelets hung from her wrists, tinkling against each other as she used her hands. Alice couldn't stop staring at her.

The group turned to enter Alice's room. Alice focused on her book. When they came in she didn't look up. The little bells tinkled and chimed.

'Alice,' Brooke started. Her voice was too high. Alice didn't understand the tears in Brooke's eyes.

The woman in the suit stepped forward. 'Alice, we've come to introduce you to someone special.'

She kept her eyes on her book. Briar Rose was about to be saved by love. When the lady in the suit spoke again, her voice was too loud, as if Alice was hard of hearing.

'Alice, this is your grandmother. Her name is June. She's come to take you home.'

Brooke pushed Alice in a wheelchair through the hospital and out into the bright morning. Earlier, she'd disappeared from Alice's room while the woman in the suit was talking. June had just stared at Alice and fidgeted a lot. Alice had read enough about grandmothers to know that in her King Gees and Blundstones, June did not look or behave like one. While her bracelets didn't stop chiming, she hardly said a thing, not even when the woman said it was June who'd sent Alice her box of books. Dr Harris said June was Alice's guardian. She and the suit lady used that word a lot. Guardian. Guardian. To Alice, it conjured images of lighthouses. But June didn't look like she was full of guarding light. Her eyes were the most distant Alice had seen, the kind of horizon so far away that you can't tell the sea from the sky.

Outside, June was sitting in an old farm truck in the visitor car park, waiting for them. Beside her was an enormous, panting dog. Classical music poured from the open windows. When the dog spotted Brooke and Alice it leapt to its feet, barking, filling the truck's cabin with its bulk. June started and turned the volume down, wrangling herself around the dog.

'Harry!' June yelled, tried to hush him. 'Sorry,' she called, fussing as she clambered out of the truck. Harry kept barking. Before she could stop herself, Alice lifted her arm to signal 'quiet' to Harry – Harry, not Toby. When he didn't respond and Alice realised her mistake, her chin quivered before she could stop it.

'Oh no,' June cried, misunderstanding the expression on Alice's face. 'I know he's big, but you don't have anything to fear. Bullmastiffs are gentle.' She crouched by Alice's wheelchair. Alice couldn't look at her. 'Harry's got special powers. He looks after people when they're sad.' June stayed there, waiting. Ignoring her, Alice busied herself with her hands in her lap.

'Let's get you in the truck now, Alice,' Brooke said.

June stepped back to let Brooke help Alice out of the wheelchair and up into the passenger seat. Harry leapt up to sit beside her. He smelled different from Toby, sweet and earthen, not salty and damp. And he didn't have long, fluffy fur either, nothing for her to curl her fingers into.

Brooke leant through the window. Harry panted happily at her. Alice sucked on her bottom lip.

'Be a good girl, Alice.' Brooke touched Alice's cheek gently, before abruptly turning her back to the truck. She went to June who was standing a short distance away, and together they talked in low voices. Any minute Brooke would turn back, march over to the truck in her pink rubber shoes, throw open the door and declare it was all a mistake. Alice didn't have to leave. Brooke would take her home to her desk and her mother's garden, and Alice would find her voice somewhere down by the sea among the scallop shells and soldier crabs, and she'd bellow loud enough for her family to hear her. Any minute now, Brooke would turn around. Any minute. Brooke was her friend. She wouldn't let Alice go off with someone she didn't know. Even if she was a lighthouse.

Alice watched them intently. June touched Brooke's arm and Brooke returned the gesture. She was probably comforting June, explaining it was all a big mistake – Alice wouldn't be leaving. Then Brooke handed June Alice's bag of belongings, which consisted entirely of books, and turned back towards the truck.

'Be good,' Brooke mouthed to Alice, lifting her hand in a wave. She lingered by the entrance with the empty wheelchair. After a moment, she pushed it towards the automatic doors and disappeared through them.

Alice was struck by dizziness, as if Brooke had walked away and taken all the blood in her body with her. She'd left her with this stranger. Alice rubbed her eyes to push the tears back in, but it was no use. She'd made the mistake of thinking her tears disappeared to the same place as her voice. But now they streamed down her cheeks as if they ran from a broken tap. June stood at the passenger window, her arms hanging at her sides as if she didn't know what else to do with them. After a few moments she opened the passenger door, stowed Alice's bag behind her seat and shut the door gently. She walked around the truck and climbed into the driver's seat to start the engine. They sat together in silence. Even Harry the enormous dog.

'Let's head on home then, Alice,' June said. She put the truck into gear. 'We've got a long drive.'

They pulled out of the car park. Exhaustion tugged on Alice's eyelids. Everything hurt. A few times Harry tried to nose her leg but she pushed his face away, turned her back to both of her companions and kept her eyes closed to shut out her new world.

Brooke jabbed the elevator down button and rummaged through her handbag until her fingertips grazed her emergency packet of smokes. She gripped them in her fist. When the elevator pinged, Brooke walked in and punched the button for the car park harder than she meant to. Again she recalled the happiness on Alice's face at the sight of that box of books; the light that filled her eyes made the lie Brooke had told about where they'd come from worth it. Alice was with her grandmother now. Her family, Brooke reminded herself, was what Alice was going to need most.

In her whole life, Brooke had never witnessed anything like the aftermath of what had happened at the Hart property. Police were calling it a perfect storm: dry lightning, a child left alone with matches, and a family trapped in the cycle of a man's violence against his wife and daughter. Brooke hovered nearby when the police approached June to explain: Clem had beaten his child unconscious in her bedroom then, realising there was a fire, dragged her outside before going back in to rescue Agnes. But by the time the fire brigade and ambulance arrived, Agnes couldn't be resuscitated, and Clem died at the scene shortly after from smoke inhalation. At that point June was such a sickly colour that Brooke had intervened and suggested a break.

The elevator reached the car park with another nauseatingly cheery ping. Brooke took deep lungfuls of fresh air, holding off from lighting her smoke. That poor woman, Agnes. Only twenty-six years old, and in such fear of her husband that she'd made a will for guardianship of her children, one of whom would never know her. Brooke pressed a hand to her stomach at the thought of him, the baby boy, pulled from Agnes's dying, beaten body. She swallowed a rising wave of bile. How could a husband do that to his pregnant wife, to his young daughter, to his unborn son? What would become of Alice, the daughter who survived fire?

Images of Alice unconscious, beaten and inhaling smoke overwhelmed Brooke. She threw her smokes and lighter into a bin, got into her car and left the hospital in a squeal of tyres on concrete, desperate to put as much distance as she could between herself and Alice's empty room.

The summer dusk was thick and balmy. Along the seafront the Norfolk Island pines teemed with parrots screeching drunkenly, singing their sunset song. Brooke pulled over and wound down the windows to inhale the heavy fragrance of salt, seaweed and frangipani. Alice had mumbled incessantly about flowers when she was in the grip of her night terrors. Flowers, phoenix birds and fire.

'C'mon,' Brooke muttered to herself. 'Get your shit together.'

She wiped her eyes, blew her nose, and turned the key in the ignition. Speeding away from the sea, she cut the corners of the empty streets in her neighbourhood, pulling hard into her driveway. Once she was inside, Brooke went straight to the phone, lifted the receiver and began to make the call she'd been dreading all day. She willed herself to press the last digit of Sally's phone number, which she'd known since she was twelve.

Blood pulsed in her ears as the dial tone turned to a ring.

And her light

stretches over salt sea

equally and flowerdeep fields.

Sappho

6

Striped mintbush

Meaning: **Love forsaken**
Prostanthera striatiflora | Central Australia

*Found in rocky gorges and near outcrops. Very strongly mint-
scented. Narrow leathery leaves. The white flower is bell-shaped
with purple stripes inside the bloom and yellow spots in the
throat. Should not be ingested, as it can cause difficulty in
sleeping. Vivid dreams are also symptomatic.*

The drive was long, hot and filled with yellow dust. There was
no hint of the sea on the breeze. The air from the truck's vents
was hot on Alice's face, like Toby's panting breath. At the thought
of his face, his drooling, wolfish smile, she sucked on her bottom
lip, staring hard out the window at the strange and unfamiliar
surroundings. No silver seagrass or salt pans, no soldier crabs or
sea tides to read, no seaweed necklaces to wear, and no skies filled
with ghostly wisps of virga, warning of storms out at sea.

On either side of the flat highway the land was thirsty, dry
as a cracked tongue. Somehow, though, the strange landscape
teemed with life. It hummed in Alice's ears, the clicking buzz
of cicadas, the occasional wild cackle of kookaburras. There was
the occasional blur of colour where wildflowers grew at the base
of gum trees. Some had trunks as white as fairytale snow while
others were an ochre colour, as glossy as if covered in a slick of
wet paint.

Alice squeezed her eyes shut. Her mother. Her unborn brother
or sister. All her books. The garden. Her desk. Toby. Her father.
She rubbed the heel of her palm over the left side of her chest.

Opened her eyes. In her peripheral vision June reached a hand out towards her but, seeming unsure of where to rest it, let it hover before eventually putting it back on the steering wheel. Alice pretended not to have seen. That seemed as good a way as any to manage the situation. She angled herself away from June, turning more directly towards her window. Stretching an arm behind her seat, she reached into her bag for her books, choosing to ignore that they'd come from June and focusing instead on them belonging to her. Alice tugged from the bag the first one her fingertips touched and almost smiled at the sight of it. A perfect comfort. Clutching it, Alice took solace from its solid, sturdy shape, its reliably straight edges, its papery smell, its beckoning story, and its hard cover bearing an image she'd spent countless hours studying, of a girl with her name, who fell into a strange and wonderful land but still found her way home.

June kept her eyes on the road and both hands firmly on the steering wheel for fear of what would happen if she glanced away or slackened her grip. She couldn't stop the tremors in her limbs. Only a nip of whisky from the flask in her side pocket would do that. But she didn't dare. Not today. Not with the child in the truck, sitting so close June could have reached out and touched her. Alice. Her granddaughter, who she'd never laid eyes on. Until today. In sidelong glances June observed the girl pressing her book to her chest like it was the very thing keeping her heart beating. She'd agreed to go along with the nurse's suggestion that they tell Alice the box of books came from her grandmother. Apparently Alice loved them so much, it seemed the simplest way to establish a connection between them. *The most important thing right now is that Alice is protected from any further stress*, the nurse had said.

Looking across at Alice, June felt ridiculous for believing any untruth might help to alleviate the situation. She chided herself for her stupidity. She should have just bloody well sat down and talked no nonsense with the child. *Hello, Alice, I'm June, your grandmother. Your father is* – June shook her head – *was my son, who I hadn't seen for many, many years. I'm going to take you home, where you'll never feel unsafe again.* June blinked her tears away. Maybe it only would have taken a few words. *I'm so sorry, Alice. I should have been a better mother. I'm so, so sorry.*

When the local police knocked on the front door at Thornfield, June had hidden in the pantry to take a long guzzle of whisky from her flask before answering. She let them in, thinking they'd come about one of the Flowers. Instead they removed their hats and told her that her son had been killed in a house fire, along with his wife. They were survived by their children, a newborn son and a nine-year-old daughter. Both of June's grandchildren were receiving medical care, and she was listed as their next of kin. She should know, it was clear Clem was responsible for the serious abuse of his wife and daughter. After they left, June barely made it to the toilet in time to vomit. Her deepest fear about her son, which she'd kept at bay for years, had become reality.

Taking another sidelong look at Alice, June was nauseous again. The girl was so much like Agnes. Wild hair, thick lashes, full lips, and big eyes, deep with curiosity and yearning. They both wore vulnerability like it was a vital organ, on the outside of their body. If Alice looked like her mother, did she take after her father in her personality? Was she like Clem? June couldn't tell yet. Alice's silence was deeply unsettling. *Selective muteness is common in children processing deep trauma,* Dr Harris had reassured her. *Usually it's not permanent. With proper counselling and support, Alice will speak again when she's ready. Until then, we won't know how much she remembers.*

June gripped the steering wheel, her bracelets tinkling. She glanced at them. Five yellow petals set in silver charms, each dangling from one of five silver bracelets. Butterfly bush flowers all had the same slightly unequal five yellow petals. A red mark appeared on the upper petal of every bloom, and at the centre of each flower were three stamens, the largest of which was shaped like a little paddle boat. June had made the bracelets for today specially. Every time they chimed on her wrists, they repeated their meaning to her like a secret prayer. *Second chances. Second chances. Second chances.*

Alice gasped, twitching in her sleep. Her head was bent back at a painful-looking angle. June thought about reaching out to reposition her, but after a moment Alice coughed and shifted on her own.

June focused on the road. Pressed her foot harder to the accelerator. Hoped that whatever dreams the child was wading through, they were gentle.

Late afternoon sunlight poured into the cab. Alice started. She'd fallen asleep without realising; dried tears cracked in the corners of her eyes and there was a kink in her neck. She straightened up and stretched. Harry licked her hand. She let him; she was too tired to push him away again. No longer on the highway, they were bouncing noisily along a rough dirt track. A pink bruise had formed on her knee where it had knocked against the door handle as the truck jostled over bumps and dusty pockmarks. Alice craved salty sea air.

June had her window down, one tanned elbow resting on the open sill. Her greying curls moved gently in the wind. Alice studied her profile. June didn't look anything like her father, but felt so familiar. When she tucked a curl behind her ear, the silver bracelets jangled on her wrists. From each one a small charm dangled, with a pressed yellow petal inside. She glanced at Alice, who was too slow at acting asleep.

'You're awake.'

Through the blur of her pretend-sleep eyelashes, Alice saw June smile and shake the bracelets on her wrist. 'Like them? I made these myself. All the flowers, they come from my farm.'

Alice turned her head away to look out the window.

'Each flower is a secret language. When I wear a combination of flowers together, it's like I'm writing my own secret code that no one else can understand unless they know my language. Today I thought I'd wear just one flower.'

A muscle twitched in Alice's cheek. June changed down gears, the bracelets chiming in response. 'Want to know what they mean? I'll tell you the secret.'

Alice ignored her, focusing hard on the tinder-dry bush streaming past the window. Her stomach lurched as they drove over a cattle grid. The noise of cicadas drowned out her thoughts. June was still talking. 'I could teach you.' Alice glared at the strange woman beside her. For a while, June didn't speak. Alice closed her eyes. She wanted to be left alone.

'You just missed town. Never mind. Plenty of time for exploring later.' June worked the truck's pedals and gears; the engine grumbled as it slowed. 'Here we are.'

They turned off the dirt track onto a smaller, smoother driveway. The ruckus that had filled the truck while they were on graded dirt dissolved to a hum. The air changed; it was sweet and green. Flowering grevillea bushes appeared alongside the truck. Monarch butterflies hovered – flap, flap, swoop – over wild cotton. Alice couldn't stop herself sitting up straighter. The droning of bees came from a cluster of white hives by twisted, silver-green gums that all pointed towards the biggest house Alice had ever seen. One she realised she'd seen before.

The house was more vivid than in the old photo she'd found in her father's shed, the photo that had shared a hiding place with a lock of hair, blue-black, tied with a faded ribbon. Alice checked June's hair. Though it was silvered it might have been that dark once.

When they reached the end of the driveway, June swung the truck around and parked it by a garage blanketed in thick vine. Harry sat to attention, his tail beating Alice's side in unison with her heart. The trees were dense with birdsong. At home, this was close to Alice's favourite time of day, when the world was dusted blue by the approaching dusk, and the air was pungent with whatever the tide brought in. Here, it was different. Drier and warmer. No hint of the sea. No pelicans drifting, no call of the currawongs. Alice dug her fingers into her thighs, steadying herself. A monarch butterfly tapped at her window. It hovered, almost as if it could hear all the things Alice couldn't say, before it fluttered away.

'Welcome, Alice.' June had hopped out of the truck and was standing at the top of a short stack of wooden steps that led onto the verandah. She held one hand out.

Alice stayed in the truck. Harry kept to her side, and her fingers found their way to his ears and scratched the place Toby had loved most. He groaned in appreciation. No one else had come for her at the hospital. No one but June, a stranger she'd been given away to like a lost dog. June's smile was starting to falter. Alice closed her eyes. She was tired, so tired she felt she could go to sleep and not wake up for a hundred years. She made a bargain with herself: she'd go inside just to get to bed.

Avoiding June's eyes, Alice climbed down out of the truck with Harry. She took a deep breath, squared her shoulders, and trudged up the steps.

The house had a wide wraparound timber verandah, strung with glowing kerosene lanterns. Birds and crickets sang the sun down. The wind rustled through the trees, releasing the cool scent of eucalyptus. Alice followed June across the verandah, stopping when she got to the front door. The screen opened and closed behind June, without Alice. Harry stayed by her side.

'Alice?' June walked back to the screen door. 'I've made up a room for you. I know it's not the one you're used to but it's a place you can make all your own,' she said through the screen, gently pushing it open.

Alice's nose was running. She wiped at it with the back of her hand.

'Why don't you come in, wash your face, and lie down. I'll bring you something to eat.'

Alice's vision swam.

'Would you like a hot facecloth? The bathroom's just here, at the end of this hall.' June walked out to Alice.

Too tired to protest, Alice allowed herself to be guided through the front door. Her head bobbed like a drooping flower. Harry sauntered alongside them.

The sheer size of the house loosened Alice's jaw. The long hallway, pale as a seashell, was lit with lamps, all different sizes, throwing shades of soft light. They followed a runner mat down the hall. Potted plants sat in every nook. Books lined the shelves, interrupted by jars of white stones, vases of feathers, and dried bouquets of flowers. Alice wanted to touch everything.

June led her into a spacious timber and white-tiled bathroom. She ran warm water in the hand basin. Opening a mirrored cabinet she took down a small brown glass bottle, unscrewed the cap, and shook a few droplets from it. A warm and calming scent rose from the water. Alice's eyelids drooped. June doused a facecloth in the sink and offered it to Alice, who covered her face and inhaled deeply. The heat dismantled some of the aching behind her eyes. When she finished wiping her face, she saw June hadn't moved.

'I won't leave you. I'm not going anywhere,' June whispered.

After they were done in the bathroom, Alice and Harry followed June up a lamp-lit flight of winding stairs. At the top was a little door. Alice hung back as June opened it, then trailed in after her. As June flicked the light switch, the sharpness of the light made Alice gasp and cover her eyes. June quickly turned it off.

'Here, I'll help you,' she offered. Alice stiffened as June put an arm around her and they crossed the room. She scurried away from June and climbed into the soft bed, pulling the sheet up in the dark. It settled like feathers on her skin. She waited for the sound of June's departure. Instead, she felt the weight of her grandmother sitting on the edge of the bed.

'We'll just do this one step at a time, Alice,' June said quietly. 'Okay?'

She rolled away, silently willing June to leave. After a time she felt her rise; the door clicked softly as it closed behind her. Alice exhaled. The last thing she heard before sleep was the tapping of Harry's nails as he turned in circles before thudding to the floor at the foot of her bed.

Downstairs in the hallway, June held a hand against the wall to steady herself. She hadn't had a drink all day.

'Is she here?'

She started at the sound of Twig's voice behind her. She didn't turn around. Nodded.

'Is she okay?'

A pause.

'I don't know,' June answered. Cricket song filled the pause between them.

'June.'

She stayed as she was, hand pressed to the wall.

'She deserves no less than any of the other Flowers. As you well know,' Twig said, stern and resolute. 'If anything, she deserves more. From you. From us. From this place. She's your family.'

'She's his,' June retorted. 'She's his, and I don't want to care.'

'Good luck with that,' Twig said, her voice softening. Another pause. 'You're shaking.'

June nodded.

'Well, are you all right?'

'It's been a big few days.' June pinched the skin over the bridge of her nose. She sensed what was coming.

'Where's the baby?'

June sighed deeply.

'You really didn't bring him home?' Twig's voice shook.

'Not now, Twig. Please. We can talk about it in the morning.' She turned, only to find the hallway empty and the screen door slamming shut. June let her go. She knew better than anybody that sometimes words did more damage than good.

She went around the house and switched off all the lights. At second thought, she retraced her steps and switched a lamp back on in case the child woke through the night. June paused at Candy's closed bedroom door but there was no light beneath. Maybe she was across the field in the dorm with the Flowers. The scent of pouch tobacco wafted through the house; Twig was smoking on the verandah. June went back down the hall, into the lounge room. She reached through the open window and snapped a blossom from the bottlebrush tree. Back down the hallway, she slid it into the keyhole of Twig's bedroom door. *Acknowledgement.*

Once June was in the privacy of her bedroom, she turned a lamp on and let herself fall onto her bed. She flung an arm over her eyes, pretending for just a little longer that the full flask in her pocket wasn't growing heavier with temptation by the minute.

After eighteen-year-old Clem found out that June had excluded him from her will, he took Agnes and left Thornfield in a fury. June had only heard from him once since. Nine years ago, when June now guessed Alice was born, a package arrived at Thornfield, addressed to June in her son's handwriting. She'd done the same thing then as she did now; retreat to her bedroom with her whisky flask.

June sat on her bed, took the flask from her pocket, unscrewed the top and took a deep swig. She drank until the whisky stopped the tremors in her limbs and numbed the tension in her neck. When her hands were steady, June reached under her bed for the tattered, over-handled package and drew it out. She unfolded the lid of the box and gingerly lifted out the hand-carved wooden ornament, cradling it in her hands. A new baby, with the same rosebud mouth and big eyes as the child asleep in the room above her, nestled in a bed of leathery leaves and bell-shaped flowers. There were stripes inside each bloom and yellow spots on the throat of each.

'Love forsaken,' she said tearfully.

7

Yellow bells

Meaning: Welcome to a stranger

Geleznowia verrucosa | Western Australia

*A small shrub with great yellow flowers. Sun loving, drought
tolerant and requiring a well-drained soil. Will grow in a
little shade, but sun for most of the day is essential. Makes a
wonderful cut flower, although fickleness in propagation and seed
germination make this a rare plant.*

At first light, June rose from bed, slid her feet into her Blundstones
and went silently through the house to the back door. Outside
the world was cool and blue. She held herself in it, breathing it
in. She hadn't slept well, not even after draining her flask. The
truth was she hadn't slept well in decades. Especially not since
Clem left. June dropped her chin. She studied the nicks and scuffs
on her boots. She hadn't exactly helped herself last night, keeping
the carving of the baby and mint bush on her bedside table. She'd
gone looking for penance and insomnia was it.

As the sky lightened, June went around the side of the house
to the work shed, where she collected clippers and a basket before
making her way through the fields towards the native-flower
greenhouses. The morning was filled with the low drone of bees
and occasional magpie song.

Inside, the greenhouse was rich and damp. June breathed easier.
She went to the back, where yellow bells were already flowering,
and took her clippers from her apron pocket.

Thornfield had always been a place where flowers and women
could bloom. Every woman who came to Thornfield was

given the opportunity to grow beyond the things in life that had trampled her. After Clem left, June had thrown herself into making Thornfield a thriving place, a place of beauty, peace and refuge. It was all she could do to validate her decision not to bequeath her flowers, the lifeblood of the women who came before her, to her volatile son.

Twig had been the first Flower to arrive, a shell of a woman after the government had taken her children. *Everyone needs somewhere and someone to belong to*, June said to her on her first night at Thornfield. And Twig had remained steadfast by June's side through everything life had thrown at them since. As she had the night before, reminding June that the strange and silent child asleep in the bell tower deserved just as much as any of the women who worked in June's flower fields. Even if she was Clem's daughter.

June knew Twig was right. But fear had her in its chokehold. There were some things she could not unearth. Some things she was happy to let lie, and rot. Just the thought of talking to Alice about her father made June feel parched, as if the mere threat of being spoken reduced her words to dust.

The sensation of walking on eggshells around Alice, of being vulnerable, of perhaps ruining this second chance, was foreign to June. She was used to being in charge. She planted seeds, and they bloomed when and as she expected them to. Her life had its cycles of sowing, growth and harvesting, and she relied on that rhythm and order. A child coming into her care now, when life was slowing down and she was thinking about retirement, was deeply unsettling. But when June had laid eyes on her granddaughter lying in that hospital looking as if she was fading, she'd pressed a hand over the ache in her chest, realising how much she still had to lose.

As the sun gathered strength outside, June wandered among the native flowers, clipping those in bloom. She might not know where or how to begin talking to the child, but she could do the next best thing. Teach her the ways of speaking through flowers.

Alice woke up gagging. The sickening screech and hiss of fire echoed in her head. She wiped the cold sweat from her face and tried to sit up. Her knickers were wet; her legs were tangled in sodden bed sheets, coiled around her as if they were living things. Kicking hard, she fought her way out to sit on the edge of the bed. The heat of her dreams began to fade. Her skin cooled. Beside her, Toby woofed. Alice shook her head. It was not Toby. He was not there. Her mother wasn't coming for her. Her voice would not tell another story. Her father wasn't immersed in fire. He wouldn't ever be anything other than what he was. She would never meet the baby. She was not going home.

Alice gave up trying to wipe her tears away and let them flow. Everything inside her felt as charred as the seagrass in her dreams.

Slowly, she became aware she wasn't the only one in the room. She turned to find Harry sitting neatly at the foot of the bed, gazing at her. Almost as if he was smiling. He walked to her, his size reminding Alice more of a small horse than a dog. What had June called him? A bull-something? Harry rested his head in her lap. His eyebrows twitched with expectation. Alice was hesitant, but he didn't scare her; she lifted her hand and stroked his head. He sighed. When she scratched behind his ears he sat and groaned in pleasure. He sat with her for a long time, his tail sweeping the floor in a slow side-to-side arc.

Her arrival the night before was far away, as if it was at one end of a long, dark tunnel and she was at the other. Moments clacked against each other. The sound of June's bracelets. Her own skin coated with yellow dust.

Harry stood and gave one sharp bark. Alice kept her head down, her shoulders curled inwards. Harry barked again. She glared at him. Again, another bark. Louder this time. She couldn't stop herself crying, but eventually her tears subsided on their own.

Harry's tail wagged. Though he could hear perfectly well, Alice held her thumb up to him anyway and wagged it side to side. He cocked his head, studying her. He came forward and licked her wrist. Alice patted him, yawning deeply as she took a half-hearted interest in her surroundings.

The room was hexagonal. Two walls were panelled in long white shelves, each crammed with almost more books than could fit. Three walls were floor-to-ceiling windows covered by thin curtains. In front of one sat an intricately carved desk with a matching chair, drawn as if in invitation. She turned to look at the last wall, behind her. Her bed folded outwards from it like a page unfolding from a giant book. Someone had gone to a lot of effort to set up this room. Did June do this for her? June, the grandmother Alice never knew she had?

She swung her feet to the floor and pushed herself up to stand. Harry turned a circle, panting and ready. Her head spun so intensely that she stumbled. She closed her eyes to wait out the dizzy spell. Harry steadied her. When the dizziness passed, she went to the desk and sat in the chair, which felt as if it was made to fit her body. Alice ran her hands over the surface. The wood was smooth and creamy, its edges carved with suns and moons bound together by butterfly wings and star-shaped flowers. She traced the carvings with her fingertips. Something about the desk was familiar, but why was yet another question Alice couldn't grasp the answer to. On the desk sat an inkpot beside jars of pens, coloured pencils, crayons, tubes of paint and paintbrushes. A pile of notebooks sat in a neat stack. Alice riffled through the pencils, which were every colour she could think of. In another jar she discovered a fountain pen. She took the cap off and drew a small black line on the back of her hand, relishing the glossiness of the wet ink. She flicked through the notebooks; page after blank page beckoned.

'This used to be a bell room once.'

Alice jumped.

'Sorry. I didn't mean to scare you.'

Harry yapped at the sight of June, who stood stiffly in the doorway with a plate of honeyed toast and a glass of milk. The buttery sweetness filled the room. Alice hadn't eaten since a few bites of a stale Vegemite sandwich at a petrol station the day before. June came into the room and set the plate and glass on the desk. Her hands were shaking. A yellow petal was stuck in her hair.

'A long time ago, when Thornfield used to be a dairy farm, this was one of the most important rooms in the house. The bell in here rang out across the property to let everyone know when the day began and ended, and when it was time to eat. It's long gone, but sometimes when the wind blows the right way I think I hear it ringing.' June fidgeted, adjusting the plate this way and that. 'I've always thought being up here feels a bit like being inside a music box.'

June looked around, sniffing. She went to the windows and drew the curtains. 'You open them like this.' She pointed to a latch that opened the top third of each window.

Alice's cheeks were hot. She couldn't watch as June approached her bed. In her peripheral vision she snuck glimpses of June stripping the sheets, bundling them in her arms without fuss and turning for the door. 'I'm downstairs when you've finished eating. A shower might be a good idea. I'll get you some fresh clothes. And sheets.' She gave a small nod. Her eyes were still far away.

Alice exhaled. She wasn't in trouble for wetting the bed.

Once June's footsteps faded, Alice pounced upon her breakfast plate. She closed her eyes as she chewed, savouring the sweet, oily flavours. She opened one eye. Harry sat watching her. After a moment's consideration she tore off a piece of toast, a good bit with a dollop of butter, and held it out to him. A truce. Harry delicately took the toast from her fingertips, smacking his jowls. Together they finished the plate and the glass of milk.

A whiff of something sweet caught Alice's attention. She cautiously approached the window June had opened and pressed herself to the glass, her hands splayed. From the top of the house she had a circular view of the property. From one window, she saw where the dusty driveway ran from the verandah steps towards the gum trees. Alice ran to the next window. Alongside the house was a large timber shed with a rusty corrugated-iron roof, up one wall of which grew a thick vine. A path cut between the shed and the house. At the last window, Alice's heart started racing. Behind the house and the shed, row upon row of different bushes and blooms stretched into fields for as far as she could see. She was surrounded by a sea of flowers.

Alice undid the latches on all the windows. The fragrant air that swept in to meet her was more pungent than the sea and stronger than burning sugar cane. She tried to identify the scents. Turned sod. Petrol. Eucalyptus leaves. Damp manure. And the unmistakable smell of roses. But it was the next moment that Alice would always remember, when she saw the Flowers for the first time.

They could have been mistaken for men, dressed in their thick cotton work shirts, trousers and heavy work boots, just like Alice's father. Their hats were full-brimmed and their hands were gloved. They emerged from the work shed in a V formation, carrying buckets, clippers, bags of fertiliser, rakes, spades and watering cans, and dispersed among the flowers. Some cut and filled buckets with flowers, ferrying them back to the work shed before re-emerging with buckets ready to be filled again. Others were pushing wheelbarrows full of new soil along the rows between the flowers, pausing to shovel it onto the beds. A few more were spraying sections of the fields, checking leaves and stems. Occasionally one would laugh with another, the sound ringing out like a little bell. Alice used her fingers to count them. There were twelve in total. Then she heard the singing.

Off to the side, near a cluster of greenhouses, one woman sat alone, sorting through a box of bulbs and seed packets. When she paused to take her hat off and scratch her head, Alice gasped as her long, pastel blue hair fell down her back. She gathered it back up, tucked it into her hat and continued to sing.

Pressed to the window, Alice watched her intently. The blue-haired woman made thirteen.

Alice stayed up in her room that morning, watching the rhythms of the women working. The watering, the tending, the planting and cutting of flowers. The buckets of brightly coloured blooms that almost seemed bigger than the women who carried them from the field to the work shed.

Her mother could have been any one of them, any one of those women whose faces were obscured by big hats and their bodies protected by heavy work wear. Alice could see her mother's profile, hat pulled low over her brow, wrists wearing bracelets of dirt, reaching for the bud of a flower. As long as she stayed in her room, that was possible.

Harry scratched at her door, crying. Toby used to do the same thing when he needed the toilet. Alice tried to ignore him. She wanted to sit by the windows all day. But when he started scratching with both paws she was worried someone might come up. And, she really didn't want to make him wee himself. Alice opened the door and Harry galloped downstairs, barking. She watched from the window as he bolted outside, running up to each of the women, sniffing here and there. They all patted his flanks affectionately. He didn't need to wee at all. Traitor.

Alice counted the women again. This time there were only nine working outside. She searched for the blue-haired woman but, unable to distinguish her from the others, she gave up and wandered away from the window. She sat on her bed. The sun was high and her room was hot. How lovely it must be downstairs, outside, running through the rows of flowers. Her legs twitched. She drummed her fingers on her thighs.

A sharp bark at her door interrupted her thoughts. Harry moseyed over to lick her hand. Though Alice ignored him, he sat close and stared at her. Not panting. Not wagging his tail. Just staring. After a while Alice shook her head. Harry stood and started barking. Gesturing with her hands, she tried to hush him, but he wouldn't stop. When she got to her feet, Harry finally fell quiet. He went to the door and waited. As Alice followed, he went downstairs. She stopped at the top step in hesitation. A succession of barks came up the spiral stairwell. With a huff, she descended.

The hallway at the bottom of the stairs was empty. At one end, Alice saw the bathroom where she'd washed her face with June. She tiptoed in and stopped short. On a shelf in front of her, next to fresh towels, sat a stack of new clothes. Knickers, a pair of khaki trousers, and a work shirt just like the women outside were wearing. And a pair of baby-blue boots. Alice ran her fingers slowly over the shiny patent leather. She'd never owned such beautiful shoes. She held the shirt up to her body. It was her size. She pressed it to her face, inhaling the clean scent of the cotton. Hurriedly she closed the bathroom door, turned the shower on and peeled off her old clothes.

Back in the hallway, Alice brushed her wet hair with her fingers, shivering from the light and airy sensation of the new clothes, and the pleasure of being so clean; the shower water had run brown from dust. The scent of the soap lingered on her skin. She glanced up and down the hall. There was no one around. Self-conscious and unsure of what to do next, Alice was about to scurry back upstairs, when the sounds of cutlery and plates and women's voices caught her attention. She pressed herself against the wall and followed the babble of conversation and the occasional squawk of laughter. At the end of the hallway, sprawling behind the house, a screen door opened onto the wide verandah. Safe in the shadows, Alice peeked through the screen.

Clusters of women sat around four large tables on the verandah. Some had their backs to Alice; the faces of others were blocked from her view. But several of them faced Alice's direction. They were all ages. One had a delicate tattoo of bluebirds covering her throat. Another wore glamorous black-framed glasses. One had speckled feathers braided through her hair. Another wore perfect, bright red lipstick despite her face being filthy with sweat and dust.

The tables were covered in white cloths, laden with green salads, sweating jugs of iced water with sliced lemon and lime, plates of grilled vegetables, deep dishes of quiche and pie, pots of sliced avocado and small bowls of strawberries. Harry's tail poked out between two chairs, wagging back and forth. Alice inched closer. In the middle of each table sat a vase bursting with flowers. How her mother would have loved them.

'There you are.'

Alice jerked in fright.

'New clothes look good,' June said, behind her in the hallway. Alice didn't know where to look so kept her eyes on her baby-blue boots. 'Alice,' June started, reaching out as if to touch her cheek. When Alice flinched, June snatched her hand back, bracelets tinkling.

Laughter rang out from the verandah.

'Well.' June looked through the screen door. 'Let's get some lunch. The Flowers are waiting to meet you.'

8

Vanilla lily

Meaning: **Ambassador of love**
Sowerbaea juncea | Eastern Australia

*Perennial with edible roots found in eucalyptus forests,
woodlands, heaths, and sub-alpine meadows. Grass-like leaves
have a strong scent of vanilla. Flowers are pink-lilac to white,
papery, with sweet vanilla perfume. Resprouts after fire.*

June swung the screen door open. A hush fell over the seated women. She turned and gestured for Alice to follow.

'Everyone, this is Alice. Alice, these are the Flowers.'

Their murmured greetings fluttered over Alice's skin. She pinched her wrists, trying to distract herself from the uneasy feeling in her belly.

'Alice is,' June paused, 'my granddaughter.' A few cheers rose from the Flowers. June waited for a moment. 'She's come to join us here at Thornfield,' she stated.

Alice was curious about whether the woman with blue hair was among them, but that wasn't enough to make her look any of them in the eye. No one spoke. Harry sidled up and sat on her foot, leaning his bulk against her. She patted him gratefully.

'Okay,' June broke the silence. 'Let's eat then. Oh no, hang on, wait.' She scanned the women. 'Twig, where's Candy?'

'Finishing up. She said to go ahead and eat without her.'

Alice followed the voice to a willowy woman with a halo of dark hair and a clear, open face. She smiled at Alice in a way that warmed her skin, as if she was standing in full sun.

'Thanks, Twig.' June nodded. 'Alice, this is Twig, she looks after the Flowers, and she keeps Thornfield running.'

Twig smiled and waved. Alice tried to smile back.

June continued around the table, introducing the Flowers. Sophie wore the glamorous glasses. Amy had the feathers in her hair. Robin wore the red lipstick. And Myf was the one with bluebirds tattooed across her pale throat; when she smiled and nodded at Alice, their wings moved. The names of the other Flowers flowed over Alice. Some – Vlinder, Tanmayi, Olga – she'd never heard before. The rest – Francene, Rosella, Lauren, Carolina, Boo – she'd come across in stories. Boo was the oldest person Alice had ever seen; her skin was papery, crinkled and folded as if she was a living page from a book.

Once June was done with the introductions, she showed Alice to her seat. Around her place setting was a wreath of yellow flowers, each one like a little crown.

'Yellow bells offer welcome to a stranger,' June said stiffly as she sat beside Alice. Her hands didn't ever seem to stop shaking. Alice swung her feet under her chair. 'Dig in, Flowers,' June said with a wave, her bracelets chiming.

At her command, the verandah came to life. Bowls were passed, and glasses clinked together in iced relief. The clatter and din of spoons scooping dips, and tongs pinching eggplant slices, met with the occasional excited bark from Harry. The volume of the talking women rose and fell between mouthfuls. In Alice's mind, a flock of seagulls cawed over a feast of yabbies on wet sand. She kept her chin down, vaguely aware that June was speaking to her as she served a little bit of everything onto Alice's plate. Alice was too preoccupied with the wreath of yellow bells to think about eating. *Welcome to a stranger.* June was her grandmother and her guardian, but she was a stranger. Despite the heat, Alice shivered. When she was sure no one was looking, she tugged a few of the yellow bells free from the wreath and slipped them into her pocket.

She studied the women seated around the tables. Some of them had sad eyes that welled when they smiled. A few had hair like June's, streaked with silver. When they caught Alice's eye they all waved at her like she made them happy, like she was something they'd lost and found. Watching them, the way they interacted, so in sync with each other, it seemed as if they were doing a dance they'd done a thousand times before. Alice recalled a story she and her mother had read together, about twelve dancing sisters who disappeared every night from their castle. Sitting among these women who each wore sadness as if it were the finest dancing gown, Alice felt like she'd fallen asleep and awoken in one of her mother's stories.

After lunch was cleared away and the Flowers went back to work, June and Alice stood together on the back verandah. The mellowing afternoon was layered with the scent of hot-baked earth and coconut sunscreen. In the distance magpies warbled and kookaburras cackled. Harry sprawled out beside them, full of leftovers.

'C'mon, Alice,' June said, stretching her arms wide. 'I'll show you around.'

Alice followed her down the back steps towards the rows of flowers. At eye level, they were taller than they appeared from upstairs. It was so much like being between sugar cane stalks that Alice stopped in momentary confusion.

'These are our cutting gardens.' June pointed ahead. 'We mostly grow native flowers. That's what Thornfield has always been built on, our native flower trade.' Her speech sounded stiff and sharp, like she was talking with a slice of lemon on her tongue.

June walked to the far side of the field, pointing out the hoop houses and greenhouses towards the back, and the workshop opposite, where the Flowers worked in the afternoons to avoid the heat.

'Beyond the farm is wild bushland until you get to the river. The river is …' June faltered.

Alice looked up.

'The river is another story altogether. I'll tell you another time.' She turned to face Alice, who was distracted by the thought of water being close by. 'All of it is Thornfield land. It's belonged to my family for generations.' She paused. 'Our family,' she corrected herself.

One hot afternoon in the kitchen at home, Alice had sat at her mother's feet reading a book of fairytales while Agnes made dinner. Fairytales taught her that when it came to family, things weren't always as they seemed. Kings and queens lost their children like they were odd socks, not finding them again until they grew very old, if they ever found them at all. Mothers could die, fathers could disappear, and seven brothers could turn into seven swans. To Alice, family was one of the most curious stories of all. Overhead, the powdery flour her mother was sifting drifted down onto the pages of Alice's open book. She'd caught her mother's eye. *Mama, where's the rest of our family?*

Agnes dropped to her knees, holding her finger over Alice's lips. Her eyes darted past Alice towards the lounge room where Clem snored softly. *It's just us three, Bun*, she said. *It always has been. Okay?*

Alice nodded quickly. She knew the look on her mother's face, and she knew not to ask again. But from that day on, when she was alone down on the beach with the pelicans and gulls, Alice loved to imagine what it would be like if one of the birds suddenly turned into her long-lost sister. Or aunt. Or grandmother.

'Why don't I take you into the workshop?' June asked. 'You can see the Flowers at work.'

As they walked among the rows of flowers, Alice didn't recognise many at all. But then, in front of her, she spotted a bush of scarlet kangaroo paw. And ahead of her, bindweed flower. Alice spun around, searching the rows. There they were, to her right: the fluffy yellow heads of lemon myrtle. Alice could almost smell the air, full of sweetly rotting seaweed, and green sugar from the cane fields. Her fingers twitched at the memory of the glossy surface of her desk under their tips. The smell of wax and paper when she lifted the lid, revealing her boxes of crayons, pencils and exercise books. Her mother, gliding past the window, her hands running over the heads of her flowers, speaking her secret language. *Sorrowful remembrance. Love returned. Pleasures of memory.*

Questions tangled with memories. The anxiety of waking up every morning and not knowing who she would find in the house with her: her spirited mother full of stories or the ghostly heap that couldn't get out of bed. The fear as oppressive as humidity in the moments waiting for her father to come home, his behaviour as unpredictable as a westerly storm. Then, Toby's smiling face. His big eyes, fluffy fur, and perky ears that couldn't hear. A question she hadn't thought of before hit her suddenly.

Was Toby dead?

Nobody mentioned Toby. Not Dr Harris, nor Brooke, nor June. What happened to Toby? Where exactly was her dog? What happened to animals when they died? Was there anything left of everything she loved? Was she to blame? By lighting that lamp in her father's shed ...

'Alice?' June called, shading her eyes from the afternoon sun.

Flies swarmed around Alice's face. She swatted them away, staring at June, the grandmother neither of her parents ever told her about. June, her guardian, who took her from the sea and brought her to this strange world of flowers. She hurried towards Alice and crouched down to her level. Galahs screeched in pink streams overhead.

'Hey,' June's voice was warm, sweetened with genuine concern.

Alice took great gulps of air, trying to breathe normally. Her whole body hurt.

June opened an arm to her. Without any hesitation Alice stepped forward, into her embrace. June picked her up. Her arms were strong. Alice tucked her head into June's neck. Her skin smelled salty, laced with the scents of tobacco and peppermint. Fat tears rolled down Alice's cheeks from a place inside her as deep and frightening as the darkest parts of the sea.

As June carried her up the steps and onto the verandah, Alice glanced back over her shoulder. Leading from the flower field up to the house was a trail of picked flowers, fallen from her pocket.

The Thornfield kitchen was full of cicada song and twilight. Candy Baby stopped washing the dishes and leant towards the window to breathe in the autumn air. It carried the watery scent of moss and reeds from the nearby river. Goosebumps covered her skin. June had explained that it was around this time of year Candy had been born, but where, and to whom, no one knew. The date she celebrated as her birthday was the night June and Twig found her abandoned, swaddled in a blue ball gown, floating in a bassinet on a waterlogged heath of vanilla lilies between the river and the flower field. They'd been in the house putting two-year-old Clem to bed when they heard her cries. When June's torch beam found her and Twig crouched to pick her up, Clem cooed and clapped his hands. The air was so dense with the scent of vanilla, the women called her Candy Baby. By the time June and Twig became her legal guardians, the name had stuck.

She plunged her hands back into the dishwater as she studied the streaky indigo sky. Within the wood and mortar of Thornfield's walls the pipes groaned as the shower turned on. Candy emptied the sink and dried her hands on a tea towel. She went to the kitchen door and peeked down into the hall. June sat waiting against the closed bathroom door, her head leant back, her eyes closed, her arms resting on her knees with her fingers interlaced. In the low and pale lamplight, her wet cheeks shone silver. Harry sat at June's feet, one paw on her foot, as he often did when she was upset.

Candy stepped back into the kitchen. She polished the countertops until they gleamed. While the others tended the flowers outside, the kitchen was her garden, where feasts and banquets bloomed. At twenty-six, she couldn't imagine ever loving anything as much as cooking. Nothing fancy though; no big white plates and tiny morsels. Candy cooked to feed the soul. Flavour and quantity were of equal importance. She had become Thornfield's resident cook when she dropped out of high school and convinced June she was safe with knives. *It's in your blood*, Twig said after a bite of her first cassava cake, fresh from the oven. *These are your gifts*, June said when Candy served her first platter of spring rolls with mango chutney, made from homegrown vegetables and herbs. It was true; when she was cooking or baking, it was almost as if a deeper, hidden knowledge took over her hands, her instincts, her tastebuds. She thrived in the kitchen, spurred by the idea that maybe her mother was a chef, or her father a baker. Cooking soothed the incision-like cut she felt inside whenever she thought that she might never know.

The house shuddered as water pipes shut off. Candy stopped polishing. She leant against the counter, listening. There was a shuffling in the hall and, after a moment, the sound of the bathroom door opening.

It was always hard when someone new arrived: another woman needing a safe place to sleep stirred up dust and memories for everyone at Thornfield. But this was different. This was Clem's child. Who wouldn't speak. More so, this was June's family, when the story everyone knew best about June was that she had none. *Flowers are my family*, she was often heard to say, with a sweep of her arm towards the fields and the women at her table.

But now the myth surrounding June's family had crumbled. A child had returned.

To Alice's great relief, June left her alone to shower. She let the water run over her face. She wished for depths she could immerse herself in, water to dive into and under, salty enough to sting her lips and cool enough to soothe her eyes. There was no sea she could run to here. She remembered the river and itched to find it. First chance she got, she decided. Something to look forward to, no matter how small.

Alice waited until her fingers pruned before she turned the shower off. Her towel was fluffy and plump. She put on the pyjamas June gave her and brushed her teeth. Her toothbrush was pink with cartoon princesses on it. The toothpaste was filled with sparkles. They were so pretty that for a moment Alice wasn't sure if they were playthings or real. She remembered her clear plastic toothbrush with the frayed bristles standing in a Vegemite glass next to her mum's on the bathroom counter. That deep and dark place swelled again, and down the tears came. The more she cried, the more Alice believed she really did have some of the sea inside her.

After she'd finished in the bathroom, Alice followed June upstairs. Harry pushed past them to gallop ahead.

'I know he can seem like a bit of a clown, but don't let Harry fool you.' June winked at Alice. 'He's got a very special magic power. He can smell sadness.'

Alice paused at the door, watching Harry settle at the end of her bed.

'Everyone works here, and that's Harry's job: to look after anyone who's sad, and help them to feel safe again.' June's voice softened. 'Harry has a secret language too, so that if for whatever reason he's not aware you need his help, you can tell him you'd like some. Would you like to learn it?'

Alice picked at the skin on the edge of her thumbnail. Nodded.

'Excellent. That's your first job, then. To learn how to "speak" Harry. I'll get Twig or Candy to teach you.'

Alice's spine straightened the tiniest bit. She had a job.

June walked around her room closing the curtains; they billowed like dancing skirts.

'Would you like me to tuck you in?' June asked, gesturing to Alice's bed. 'Oh,' she exclaimed. Alice followed her gaze.

On her pillow sat a small rectangular tray holding a glittering white cupcake, decorated with a pale-blue sugared flower. Dangling from the cupcake was a paper star that read, *EAT ME*. Next to it sat a cream-coloured envelope bearing Alice's name.

A smile squeezed through the tangles and hurts inside, warming her cheeks. She ran to her bed.

'Goodnight, Alice,' June said, standing at her door.

Alice gave a small wave. Once June was gone, she tore open the envelope. Inside was a handwritten letter on matching cream-coloured paper.

Dear Alice,
Here are three things I know for sure:
1. *When I was born, someone — I like to think it was my mother — wrapped me in a blue ball gown.*
2. *There is a colour in this world that was named after a king's daughter, who always wore gowns that were made of exactly the same shade of blue. The stories about her make me wish sometimes I could have been friends with her; she smoked in public (at a time when women didn't), once jumped fully clothed*

into a swimming pool with the captain of a ship, often wore a boa constrictor around her neck, and another time shot at telegraph poles from a moving train.

3. *My favourite story goes like this: once, on an island not far from here, there was a queen who climbed a tree waiting for her husband to return from a battle. She tied herself to a branch and vowed to remain there until he returned. She waited for so long that she slowly transformed into an orchid, which was an exact replica of the pattern on the blue gown she was wearing.*

Here's one more thing that I know for sure is true.

On the day June told us she was going to hospital to bring you home, I was in the workshop pressing blue lady orchids. I've always loved them best because their centres are my favourite colour: the colour of the gown I was once wrapped in. The colour a king's wayward daughter favoured. A colour called Alice blue.

Sweet dreams, sweetpea. See you at breakfast.

Love,

Candy Baby

Alice's mind filled with images of newborn babies, wild women, and blue gowns that turned into flowers. Suddenly ravenous, she picked up the cupcake, peeled back the patty paper, and sank her teeth into the rich vanilla sweetness.

She fell asleep with crumbs on her face, clutching Candy's letter to her heart.

Candy filled an old tomato can to water the herbs in the alcove behind the sink. The fragrance of fresh coriander and basil rose in the air. She set four mugs by the kettle for the morning. June's soup bowl that she liked to call a coffee cup, the chipped enamel camping cup Twig insisted on drinking her tea from, and her own porcelain teacup and saucer, hand-painted in vanilla lilies for her by Robin. The fourth cup was small and plain. At the thought of the child's grief-stricken face, Candy looked up at the ceiling, wondering if Alice had found her cupcake yet.

She was hanging up the tea towels when June came downstairs and into the kitchen. The pool of light falling from the range hood cast her face in deep shadows.

'Thanks, Candy. For the cupcake. That's the first time I've seen her smile.' June rubbed her jawline roughly. 'It's uncanny,' she said, her voice pinched by tears, 'how she can look so much like both of them.'

Candy nodded. It was for that very reason she hadn't been ready to meet Alice yet. 'Tomorrow you can start over. That's what you always tell us, right?'

'Not so easy, is it?' June muttered.

Candy gave June's arm a squeeze on her way out of the kitchen. As she went into her bedroom, she heard the liquor cabinet squeak open. Candy had never known June to drink as heavily as she had been since the police came with the news about Clem and Agnes. People searched in all kinds of places for an escape; June found it at the bottom of a whisky bottle. Her own mother, Candy imagined, found it in a heath of wild vanilla lilies. Candy had learned the hard way that her escape was Thornfield's kitchen.

She closed her bedroom door and switched on her bedside lamp, casting her room in diffuse light. Nearly everything she loved was here. The wide window seat with the big windows. Twig's framed botanical sketches on the wall, all of the vanilla lily. Each one was dated, the first from the night she and June had carried Candy home from the heath. In the corner, her chair and desk, topped with her recipe books. Her single bed covered by the blanket of gum leaves that Ness, a past Flower, had hand-crocheted for Candy's eighteenth birthday. A postcard had arrived a few years back, from a small banana plantation town up north where Ness said she'd bought a house. Some women, like Ness, came to Thornfield, took what time and strength they needed, and then left. Others, like Twig and Candy, knew they'd found a permanent home.

She sat and opened her bedside-table drawer, reaching inside for the necklace she always took off when she cooked. Slipped it over her head and held the pendant to the light. A fan of vanilla lily petals, preserved in resin, edged by sterling silver on a cob chain. June had made it for her sixteenth birthday, just before Candy had opened her bedroom window to a moonless sky and slipped out into the shadows, trying to outrun a loss that cut her to the core.

June had named her son after clematis, a bright and climbing star-shaped flower, and that's exactly what Clem was to Candy growing up – a boy as beguiling as a star, a boy she was besotted with. She was always following him around, which he scowled about, but he still checked over his shoulder frequently to make sure she was there.

Candy went to her window and let her eyes rest upon the path at the bottom of the fields, which curled into the bush and led to the river. She was about Alice's age the first time June allowed her to go to the river by herself. Candy thought she was alone running the winding path through the trees but, of course, she should have known better than to think Clem would let her have an adventure on her own. When she reached the river he swung from a rope tied to the river gum overhead and dropped screeching into the water, making her scream. After she'd recovered, Clem took Candy into the secret cubby house he'd built from branches, sticks and leaves in a clearing near the giant gum. Inside he had a sleeping bag, a lantern, his pocketknife, river stone collection and favourite book. They sat together, their knees touching while he read to her, tracing his finger around the illustration of Wendy sewing Peter Pan's shadow back on for him.

We're stitched together, like this, Candy, he said. *And we'll never grow up.* He flicked open his pocketknife. *Swear it.*

She offered the tender centre of her palm to him. *I swear*, she said, gasping at the quick, piercing pain.

Blood promise, he crowed as he sank the knife tip into his own palm and pressed his hand to Candy's, lacing his fingers between hers.

Candy rubbed the tiny, faint scar on her palm with her fingertip.

As she grew up, Clem was indeed the bright and ever-climbing star in Candy's sky. But when she was fourteen years old, and Clem was sixteen, everything changed the day the Salvation Army brought Agnes Ivie to Thornfield. Clem turned pale, moody, and his eyes no longer fully focused on Candy; he was fixed upon Agnes. She was the same age as Candy, and an orphan too. Arrived with sprigs of wattle in her hair, a copy of *Alice in Wonderland*, and big, deep eyes that followed you wherever you went, like a painting. June set her straight to work and Agnes took to her tasks as if she had a fight to win. Out in the flower fields from dawn to dusk, she worked until her hands blistered, and then until they split and bled. She worked until her spindly arms gave out, carrying buckets of fresh cuts from the flower fields into the workshop. She studied the Thornfield Dictionary with a furrow in her brow. At night she sat in the bell room and sang what she had learned of the language of flowers to the moon. Candy started following Agnes around Thornfield, hovering in long shadows as she worked, studying the girl Clem loved more. She followed her to the river and hid in the bushes watching as Agnes took a pen and wrote stories on her skin, down each forearm, up each leg, before she undressed and swam in the green river water until she was washed clean. When a twig snapped nearby, Candy saw Clem hidden, watching Agnes in the river too, with a look upon his face as if he'd found a star fallen to earth. When Candy saw he'd carved his and Agnes's names into the trunk of the giant gum, she knew she'd lost him. All she could do was watch on, helpless, as everyone at Thornfield fell under Agnes's spell, most of all Clem. Agnes seemed to wake something inside him, something entitled, something cruel. He was never the same with Candy again.

When Clem and Agnes left Thornfield, the wake of his violent rage and the totality of his absence tore the belly out of Candy's world. She had splinters for a month after she scratched Agnes's name from the giant gum in a grief-stricken frenzy. Nothing eased the pain. Not even leaving Thornfield herself.

Her memories of the night she ran away were still visceral: the burn in her legs as she ran in the moonlight through the bush to the road, lured by a lover's promise to be there waiting for her. Candy had been sneaking into town to meet with him ever since the afternoon he'd pulled up in his car alongside her on her walk home from school. He gave her vodka and smokes. Told her stories about where he'd come from, a place like paradise on the coast. He was passing through town on his way back there. Did she want to go with him? He'd teach her how to ocean-swim, and get them a place with her own garden. The sense of freedom Candy had felt the night she met him on the highway was intoxicating. She got into his car, he put his foot down and they launched into the pale silver night, headed for a place where the haunting pain of Clem's absence wouldn't find her. But, only a few months later, Candy walked up Thornfield's driveway with no more than the cotton dress she was wearing and the vanilla lily pendant hanging from her neck. June and Twig had been sitting on the front verandah. They took her in, set a third place at the table, and didn't say a word. Her bedroom was exactly as she'd left it; she was crushed to find it unchanged. June and Twig knew Candy had acted a fool and would be back. They'd seen her mistake before she'd made it. Candy had thought she could escape grief.

Candy looked at the ceiling again, thinking about Alice, Agnes and Clem's silent daughter, caught in her own world of memories, sifting through them, trying to understand what had happened to her life. Candy had overheard June telling Twig the story: Clem had beaten Alice unconscious, and Agnes's pregnant body wore bruises that told a similar story. What sort of coward did that? What kind of beast had he become? And what now of Clem's baby son, Alice's brother?

She pushed the questions away. Ran the pad of her thumb over the pendant, focusing on the language of the vanilla lily: *ambassador of love*. Since June's great-grandmother Ruth Stone created a flower farm from drought-stricken land in the nineteenth century, Thornfield's motto had remained the same: *Where wildflowers bloom*. It was the one thing Candy and every other woman who came to June for safety knew to be true.

As she readied herself for bed, Candy wondered if Alice knew yet, in even the smallest way, that no matter where she'd come from, or what had happened to her, she had come home.

9

Violet nightshade

Meaning: **Fascination, witchcraft**
Solanum brownii | New South Wales

A member of the nightshade family, often toxic. Commonly associated with death and ghosts in folklore. Latin name comes from 'solamen' meaning to quieten or comfort, and refers to the narcotic properties of some species. Used as food plants by the larvae of some butterflies and moths.

Alice bolted upright in bed, dry retching. Her skin was covered in cold sweat. In her dreams ropes of fire were choking her. As the heat began to fade from her face, she lay back on her damp pillow, squinting in the glare of the morning light. Candy's letter lay crumpled beside her. Alice picked it up and traced a fingertip over the curls of the handwriting. The dream fire had been different this time. It was blue. The colour of her name, of Candy's hair, and a woman's gown turned into an orchid by grief.

She tried to stop the tears, but they came anyway, signalling Harry like a whistle. He padded into her bedroom, his collar tinkling, and nudged her bare knee with his wet nose. His vast size made her feel safe.

Alice closed her eyes and pressed her fingers over them, hard, until it hurt. When she opened them her vision was full of black stars. As they cleared, she noticed someone had been into her room and set out clothes and a tray of breakfast on her desk. Harry licked the side of her face. Alice half-smiled at him and got up.

Laid over the back of the chair was a clean pair of shorts and a T-shirt. Socks and knickers were folded on her desk, and her boots sat neatly on the floor. There was also a broad-brimmed hat, and a little apron just like the one the Flowers wore. Someone had embroidered her name in azure thread on the pocket. Alice ran her fingertips over the stitched lettering. It was the colour she imagined the queen's gown in Candy's favourite story. The thought of waiting so long for love to return that you could turn into something else made Alice's head hurt.

She reached for a slice of peach from the tray and popped it in her mouth. Her cheeks ached from its sweet juice. After another slice, she wiped her hands on her pyjama bottoms and picked the T-shirt up. It was the kind of cotton that felt like it had been worn a thousand times already. Her mother used to have one just like it. Alice loved to wear it to bed after Agnes had worn it long enough for it to smell of her.

'Morning.'

June stood at the door. Harry snuffled happily. Alice's hair hung over her face. She made no move to push it behind her ears as June stripped the bed again and left the room wordlessly. She came back up the stairs moments later, slightly out of breath, carrying a clean set of sheets. Shame burned Alice's cheeks. Leaning against her, Harry licked the tears from her face. June's knees popped as she crouched next to Alice.

'It won't always feel this strange, Alice,' she said. 'I promise. I know you're hurting, and I know everything is new and frightening. But this place will look after you, if you'll give it half a chance.'

Alice lifted her head to look at June. For the first time, her eyes weren't far away, on the horizon. They were right there, close and full, focused on Alice.

'I know everything seems pretty awful now, but it will get better. You're safe here. Okay? No more bad things are going to happen.'

The longer Alice looked at June, the faster her heart beat in her ears. She squeezed her eyes shut. It grew hard to breathe.

'Alice? Are you okay?' June's voice started to sound like she was far, far away. Harry paced around them, barking.

Alice shook her head. Memories broke apart inside her. Before Thornfield, before the hospital, before the smoke and ash. Back further, before.

Inside her father's shed.

The carved wooden figures of a woman and a girl with flowers.

June's lips were moving but Alice couldn't hear her properly. Everything sounded as if she was underwater, sinking and floating at the same time, looking up at June through the filter of the sea. Her face swam in Alice's vision, except for a fleeting moment when she was perfectly clear.

Finally, Alice recognised her.

June: her expressions, her hair, her posture, her smile. Alice had seen them before.

She struggled to breathe.

June was the woman her father carved over and over again in his shed.

June whipped her Akubra off the hook by the front door, jammed it onto her head, and grabbed her keys from the sideboard. She raced outside and down the front verandah steps, squinting against the glare of the morning as she strode to her truck. Yanking the door open, she yelped in surprise to see Harry inside. He'd just been upstairs with Alice, but there he was sitting to attention with his tail curled around his feet, staring at her.

'You bloody escape artist,' June muttered. 'You never fail to amaze me.' She ruffled his big ears. As she climbed into the truck, she broke out in a cold sweat recalling the look on Alice's face upstairs; the recognition deep in her eyes. June tried to settle her shaking hands, having to make three attempts before she got her key into the ignition. She patted down her pocket and pulled out her flask for a quick swig.

'June,' Twig called from the front door.

She quickly slipped her flask back into her pocket. The whisky burned as it went down.

Twig hurried to the truck and stood at June's window, waiting. They hadn't exchanged more than clipped sentences since Alice arrived. June braced herself for another flare-up in their ongoing argument, which was becoming the kind that either ends old friendships or makes them stronger. They'd had some doozies over the decades, but here they were in the middle of another, still pulling together. As family was meant to do.

When June rolled her window down, Twig took a pointed step backwards and she cursed herself for not having any breath mints.

'She's okay,' Twig said after a moment, keeping her voice even. 'She's resting in the lounge room with Candy.'

June nodded.

'I rang the hospital –'

'Of course you did,' June scoffed.

Twig ignored her. 'The nurse, Brooke, said it sounded like a panic attack. Alice needs rest, company and a close eye. She also needs counselling, June.' Twig stepped forward and put both her hands on the windowsill. 'She needs to see someone.'

June shook her head.

'Everyone needs someplace and someone to belong to.' Twig's voice was barely audible over the truck's engine.

June smirked; Twig knew what she was doing, repeating the very words June herself had said, years ago when Twig first came to Thornfield. June threw the truck into gear. She would not be manipulated.

'I'm going to enrol her in school. Where she belongs,' she snapped. Twig leapt back, stung.

As June drove away, her skin crawled as the full weight of Twig's words settled. What the hell was she thinking, taking responsibility for her son's daughter? Who was she, other than Next of Kin on a form? The flicker of recognition in Alice's eyes that morning played over and over in her mind. The same question nagged at her: how did Alice know her face?

Alice lay on the couch by the windows and listened to the rumble of June's truck fade into the distance. She was trying to connect pieces of information. The statues in her father's shed were of June. June was her grandmother, but was also her father's mother. Why hadn't Alice ever met her before? It couldn't be that her father didn't love June; why else would he spend so much time carving statues of her? Alice sighed, snuggling deeper into the couch. A magpie's song drifted through the window. She closed her eyes and listened. The ticktock of the grandfather clock. The slow beat of her heart. The evenness of her breath.

After June had carried her downstairs into Twig's care, she'd disappeared out of the house and hadn't come back again. Twig had made Alice a cup of something sweet, which made her body feel like chocolate left in the sun. Her eyes drifted closed and when she opened them again Twig was gone. But sitting in front of her was Candy Baby, her long blue hair like waves of unspooled fairy floss.

'Hey, sweetpea,' Candy said, grinning.

Alice drank in the sight of her hair, the sparkling gloss on her lips, her chipped mint-coloured nail polish and the enamel cupcake studs in her ears.

'Good to see colour in your face, little flower.' Candy took Alice's hand and gave it a squeeze. Unsure of how to respond, Alice just continued to stare. 'I'm baking biscuits,' Candy went on.

'They're for morning tea, but I need someone to taste them before I give them out. Wondered if you might help me out?'

Alice nodded so vigorously that Candy laughed, suddenly and deeply from her belly.

'Well, would you look at that?' Candy tucked a piece of Alice's hair behind her ear. 'Loveliest smile I've seen at Thornfield,' she said. Only her mother had ever told Alice her smile was lovely.

While she waited for the biscuits, Alice drummed her fingers on her belly. Sunlight fell in thick, bright beams through the patchwork of giant tropical leaves at the window. The scent of tobacco mixed with sugary wafts from the kitchen. Every now and then Candy's humming floated into the lounge room.

Eventually, footsteps approached from the kitchen, bringing a gust of syrup-scented air with them. Alice struggled to sit up.

'No, sweetpea. Rest.' Candy dragged a little side table to the couch and set a plate of Anzac biscuits and a chilled glass of milk on top of it. 'Rest. With a treat.' Alice took an Anzac biscuit warm from the oven. She pressed its edges between her thumb and index finger. Firm. She pressed its middle the same way. Doughy. Alice looked at Candy in astonishment.

'Oh, totally. Crunchy edges, chewy middle. Only way they should ever be eaten,' Candy said with a firm nod. In that moment, Alice loved her. She took as big a bite as possible.

'Your cheeks are bulging like a possum's,' Candy snorted.

The screen door swept open and the sounds of someone stomping and scuffing their boots on the welcome mat filled the hall. A moment later Twig came into the lounge room, her brow knotted in worry. When she saw Alice and Candy, her face relaxed.

'Perfect timing, Twiggy Daisy.' Candy offered the plate. Twig looked at Alice with an eyebrow raised in question. Alice nodded with a shy smile.

'Who am I to say no, if Alice says so?' Twig took a biscuit

from the plate and groaned as she bit into it. 'You're an alchemist, Candy.'

Alchemist. Alice promised herself she'd look it up in the dictionary later.

'Reckon that chamomile and honey tea worked a treat, Alice. Feeling a bit better?' Twig smiled warmly at Alice. Alice nodded. 'Good. That's really good.'

'Where's June gone?' Candy asked, immediately looking like she wished she hadn't.

'June's, uh, had to run a few errands in town.' Twig shot Candy a pointed look and briskly changed the subject. 'Ready for the Flowers to come up for morning tea?'

Candy nodded. 'Coffee and tea urns and biscuits are out on the back verandah ready to go.'

'Great. I'll –' Twig was interrupted by the beep of a car horn as tyres crunched up the driveway. She craned her neck to look out the window.

'Boryana's here to get her pay. Can I take her a biscuit?' Twig pinched two biscuits from the plate, then took a third, which she held between her teeth, smiling. She disappeared into the hallway, only to come back a moment later with her boots on. 'God, they're sinfully good, Candy.' Twig turned to leave then stopped. 'Why don't you show Alice around the workshop if she's up to it? Good chance while the Flowers aren't in there. I'll see you ladies later.' Twig waved and walked outside.

'Boryana's a Flower too, the only one who doesn't live here,' Candy explained. 'She and her son live on the other side of town. Bory comes every week and keeps Thornfield clean and tidy. She's Bulgarian and totally lovely.'

Alice wondered what 'Bulgarian' was. A type of flower, maybe?

'So listen, I'm going to run up and get your boots and stuff, and maybe once you're dressed we'll check out the workshop?' Candy asked. 'If you're up to it I'll introduce you to Boryana.'

Alice nodded. She would have been up for anything as long as it was with Candy Baby.

While Candy was upstairs, Alice went to the window to see what a Bulgarian looked like. Outside, talking to Twig by an old and battered car, was a woman with strong, tanned arms, long black hair and bright red lipstick. They laughed heartily together. But it wasn't the women that captured Alice's attention. It was the boy sitting in the front seat of the car.

Alice had never been so close to a boy.

She could only see his profile, most of which was hidden by shaggy wheat-coloured hair. It hung over his face, just like hers did. He was looking down, at something in his hands. She wondered what his eyes were like. He shifted his weight and lifted the book he was reading to rest it on the window. A book!

As if he could hear her heart drumming, the boy looked up and straight at her. Something strange shot through her body. Her limbs wouldn't work, as if she was frozen to the spot. Alice stared back at him from behind the window. Slowly, he raised his hand. Waving. He was waving. Bewildered, Alice lifted her hand and returned the wave.

'Ready?'

Alice spun around. Candy had her farm clothes under one arm, and was dangling her blue boots by the shoelaces. She shook her head. Her insides felt all wrong, like they'd been taken out of her body and put back in different places.

'What is it?' Candy asked, coming to her side. Alice turned back to the window, pointing, but Boryana had driven off in a dust cloud with the boy.

'Oh, don't worry sweetpea, you'll meet her another time, soon.'

Alice pressed her hands to the glass, watching where the dust settled.

Alice followed Candy past the dormitory where the Flowers lived. When they reached the workshop, they stopped at a doorway covered in thick vines. Candy held the vines aside, took keys from her pocket and slid one into the keyhole.

'Ready?' she asked, grinning. The door swung open.

They stood at the entrance of the workshop together. The morning sun warmed their backs, but the air conditioning inside gave Alice a sudden chill. She rubbed her arms, recalling the boy raising his hand to wave.

'That was a big sigh.' Candy raised an eyebrow at Alice. 'You okay?'

Alice wanted so much to speak, but all that came out was another sigh.

'Words can be totally overrated sometimes,' Candy said, taking Alice's hand in her hers. 'Don't you think so?'

Alice nodded. Candy gave her hand a squeeze before letting go.

'C'mon.' She held the door open. 'Let's take a look around.'

They walked inside. The first half of the workshop was filled with benches, stacks of buckets, a row of sinks and a line of fridges set against the wall. Shelves held tools, rolls of shade cloth, and all sorts of bottles and sprays. From hooks on the wall hung broad-brimmed hats, aprons and gardening gloves, below which stood pairs of gumboots lined up, like a row of invisible flower soldiers standing to attention. Alice turned towards the benches. Each had more shelving underneath, filled with tubs and containers. The workshop smelled like rich soil.

'This is where we bring flowers after they've been cut from the fields. Every single flower is checked before it goes out. They have to be perfect. We get orders from buyers all over the place; our flowers are shipped near and far, to florists and supermarkets and petrol stations and market sellers. They're carried by brides and widows and –' Candy's voice wavered, 'new mothers.' She smoothed her hands over one of the benches. 'Isn't it a magical thing, Alice? The flowers we grow here speak for people when words can't, on pretty much every occasion you can think of.'

Alice mimicked Candy's movements, running her hands over the worktop. Who were the people that sent flowers instead of words? How could a flower possibly say the same things as words? What would one of her books, made of thousands of words, look like in flowers? No one had ever sent her mother flowers.

She crouched to inspect the tubs of cutting tools, balls of string, and small buckets of markers and pens in all colours under the bench. She took the lid off a blue marker and sniffed it. On the back of her hand she drew a straight vertical line, an *I*. After a moment, she wrote next to it, *'m h-e-r-e*. As Candy came towards her, Alice rubbed the words off.

'Pssst. Alice Blue.' Candy popped her head over the bench Alice was squatting beside. 'Follow me.'

They wove between the benches, past the sinks and fridges, into the other half of the workshop, which was set up as an art studio. There were desks covered in blank canvases, dotted with tins of paint and jars of brushes. In one corner stood easels, stools and a box filled with tubes of paint. At another desk sat coils of copper foiling, pieces of coloured glass and jars of tools. By the time Alice reached the closed-off area at the back of the studio, she'd forgotten about the boy. She'd forgotten about June and her father's statues. She was too absorbed by what was right in front of her.

'X marks the spot.' Candy chuckled.

From a frame overhead hung dozens of flowers in various stages of drying. One long bench ran alongside the makeshift wall. Sat upon it were tools and cloths, all blackened from use, and dried flower petals, scattered, discarded like clothes left on shore. Alice pressed her hands to the wooden surface, remembering her mother's hands floating over the heads of the flowers in her garden.

At one end of the bench a velvet sheet was laid out, adorned with bracelets, necklaces, earrings and rings, all decorated with pressed flowers in resin.

'This is June's place,' Candy said. 'This is where she makes magic out of the stories Thornfield was built on.'

Magic. Alice stood in front of the jewellery, each piece catching the light.

'June grows every flower here.' Candy picked up a bangle; the pendant hanging from it contained a pale peach-coloured petal. 'She presses every one and casts it in clear resin, then seals it in silver.' Candy returned the bangle to its place on the bench. Alice inspected the rainbow of other flowers pressed in necklace pendants, earrings and rings. Each one was sealed forever, frozen in time while still coloured with life. They would never turn brown or waste away. They would never decay, or die.

Candy came to stand beside her. 'In Queen Victoria's time, people in Europe talked in flowers. It's true. June's ancestors – your ancestors, Alice – women who lived a long time ago, they brought that language of flowers all the way over the ocean from England, down the generations, until Ruth Stone brought it right here to Thornfield. People say that for a long time she didn't use it. It wasn't until she fell in love that she started talking in flowers. Except, unlike the flower language she'd brought from England, she only used flowers that her lover brought her.' Candy stopped, her face flushed. 'Anyway ...' she trailed off.

Ruth Stone. Her ancestor. Alice's cheeks tingled with curiosity. She wanted to slide a ring onto every finger, press the cool silver pendants against her warm skin, slip the bracelets onto her wrists and hold the earrings up to her unpierced ears. She wanted to wear this secret language of flowers, to say for her all the things her voice wouldn't.

At the other end of the bench sat a small handmade book. Alice inched towards it. The cracked spine had been repaired many times, bound together with multiple red ribbons. The cover was hand-lettered in faded gold calligraphy, with an illustration of red flowers that looked like spinning wheels. *The Thornfield Language of Australian Native Flowers.*

'Ruth Stone was your great-great-grandmother,' Candy said. 'This was her dictionary. Over the years, women who descended from Ruth have grown the language as they've grown the flowers here.' She ran a hand down the edges of the musty pages. 'It's been in June's family for generations. Your family, actually,' she corrected herself.

Alice hovered a fingertip over the cover. She so wanted to open it, but wasn't sure if she was allowed. Its pages were yellowing and stuck out at odd angles. Snippets of handwritten words were visible on the outer margins. Alice turned her head to the side. She could only read a few complete words. *Dark. Branches. Bruised. Fragrant. Butterflies. Haven.* It was the best book Alice had ever seen.

'Alice.' Candy bent down so she was at eye level with Alice. 'Have you ever heard this story before? About Ruth Stone?'

Alice shook her head.

'Do you know much about your family yet, sweetpea?' Candy asked gently.

A sense of shame Alice didn't understand made her look away. She shook her head again.

'Oh, what a lucky girl.' Candy smiled sadly.

Alice looked at her, confused. She wiped her nose on the back of her hand.

'You know Alice Blue, the woman I told you about in my letter, the daughter of a king?'

Alice nodded.

'Her mother died when she was young, too.' Candy took her hand. 'She was heartbroken and sent away to live with her aunty in her book-filled palace. Later, when she was all grown up, Alice

Blue said it was the stories her aunt told her and those she read in her books that saved her.'

Alice imagined Alice Blue, a maiden in her signature-coloured gown, reading in pale light falling from a window onto the pages of her book.

'What a lucky girl you are to have found this place, and with it your story, Alice. What a lucky girl you are to get the chance to learn and know where you come from and who you belong to.' Candy turned her face away. After a moment, she wiped her cheeks. The air conditioners clicked and hummed in the background. Alice studied the old book, daydreaming of women who might have bent over it through time, maybe holding a bunch of native flowers in their fist as they added a new entry in their secret language.

Alice's legs started to twitch from idleness. Candy turned back to her and asked a question that flooded Alice's body with longing.

'Want me to show you the way to the river?'

10

Thorn box

Meaning: **Girlhood**

Bursaria spinosa | Eastern Australia

*Small tree or shrub with furrowed dark grey bark. Smooth
branches are armed with thorns. Leaves yield pine-like fragrance
when bruised. Sweetly scented white flowers bloom in summer.
Provides nectar to butterflies and safety to small birds. Intricate
architecture of thorns is much sought after by spiders for
constructing webs.*

Alice shielded her eyes from the sun. Although autumn had
cooled the nights, the days were still broiling. Candy lifted the
vine, locked the workshop door behind them, and let the vine
fall back over the doorway. On the back verandah the Flowers
had finished morning tea and were ferrying their cups and plates
from the tables into the kitchen. Candy called out to Myf, with
the bluebird tattoo at her throat, to ask for the time. After Myf
replied, Candy turned to Alice, her face filled with dismay. Alice's
heart sank.

'Oh sweetpea, I'm sorry. It's later than I'd realised. I have to
get lunch ready I'm afraid, or else we'll have neglected Flowers, in
every sense. I'll have to take you to the river another time.'

Alice searched her face.

'No, don't give me that look. Please. I just can't let you go by
yourself.'

Alice kept her eyes on Candy's face.

'Dammit,' Candy muttered under her breath. 'Listen, only as
long as you promise to be more careful than you've ever been.

In. Your. Life.' Candy frowned. 'And as long as you promise to come back as soon as you've had a quick look at the river. Straight back. I mean it.'

Alice nodded vigorously.

'And one last thing: you cannot tell June or Twig I let you go off by yourself the very first time they left me to look after you.'

Alice raised her eyebrows.

'Oh. Right. That won't be a problem.' Candy folded her arms. 'Okay, Alice Blue,' she surrendered, smiling despite herself. 'You can go to the river by yourself and explore. But don't let me down, okay? Second chances aren't easy to come by around here.'

Alice ran to Candy and threw her arms around her waist. *I trust you.*

For the next ten minutes Candy repeated the directions to the river: go to the path at the end of the flower fields. Follow it through the bush to the river. Do not leave the path. Do not go into the river. Do not try to cross the river. Do nothing at all other than follow the path to the river.

After Alice had nodded along to every word three times, Candy was satisfied.

'Okay, then,' she said. 'I'm going to prep lunch. See you soon, sweetpea.'

Alice hesitated, not quite believing that she was allowed to leave. At the back steps Candy turned. *Go,* she mouthed with a grin, shooing Alice away with her hands.

She took off around the flower field with Candy's directions ringing in her ears. She didn't stop, look back or falter. If her voice was working she would have thrown back her head and crowed. She didn't let her eyes stray from the chalky path at the bottom of the garden that cut away into the forest. *To the river,* Alice sang to herself. To the river.

Once she was within the arms of the bush, Alice slowed to walking pace. Streams of light fell through the canopy and pooled at her feet. Crickets and bellbirds sang together, joined by the occasional whump-whump of a tree frog. She gazed at the gum trees overhead, their branches and leaves hushing each other in the wind. Monarch butterflies flap-flap-swooped over wild cotton bushes. She stopped to study lichen-covered rocks, the hairy curls of tree fern buds, and patches of sweet-smelling purple wildflowers. The air was rich with the smell of dry earth, vanilla and eucalyptus.

She'd almost forgotten why she'd come until she heard it. She stopped and listened. There it was, faint, but unmistakable; water called to her as vividly as if it were her mother's voice. Alice bolted for the river, her hair streaming behind her.

The path came to an end at a clearing on the banks of a wide, green river. It didn't curl, roar or crash like the ocean; it was calm, one flowing constant song. Alice was drawn to it the way everything else around her also seemed to be: tree roots reached into the river, as did long and wispy strands of moss that clung to half-submerged rocks.

Do not go into the river.

Alice made a silent apology to Candy as she kicked off her boots. She'd just peeled off her socks when she noticed a thin trail leading off along the riverbank.

She strained to see where it led. Candy had made no mention of another trail. *Second chances aren't easy to come by around here.* Alice crept towards it. She'd just take a peek. But, to her disappointment, the trail didn't lead anywhere. It ended abruptly, almost as soon as it began, at a tiny circular nook in the shade by the river, big enough for maybe two people. Alice scuffed her feet in the dust, sighing in disappointment. But as she turned to go back to the river, something caught her eye: the gilded edge of something big enough to block the sun. Her eyebrows shot up as she took in the size of the giant river red gum. Its trunk was wider than she was tall. Alice looked into the arms of the tree that reached so high she couldn't see its top. The thought of climbing it made her hands clammy. Its branches were heavy with flowering blossoms and fragrant, crescent-shaped leaves. Its roots ran into the river, creating pockets that were filled with gum nuts, leaves and flowers. It was a king of trees. But more mesmerising to Alice than anything else was the spot on its trunk where a list of names was carved. Although they started above her eye level, when she stood on tiptoe with her head leant back, Alice could read them all. She recognised Ruth Stone's name but didn't know any others, until she got to the last two.

June Hart.

Beside June's name was a deep cut, where Alice guessed another name was once carved. Below was Alice's father's name: *Clem Hart.* And next to it was a similar scar, where yet another name must have been. Alice tried to make sense of the list, as if it was maybe a secret language like the flowers, but she couldn't. *Ruth Stone, Jacob Wyld. Wattle Hart, Lucas Hart. June Hart. Clem Hart.* Plus the two gouged from the wood.

The harsh screech of a cockatoo made her jump. Something about the missing names and the smallness of the cleared space made her nervous.

When the cockatoo shrieked again, Alice scurried back to the clearing by the river and stood panting, willing her heart to slow.

The smooth and even flow of the river calmed her. Heat and humidity pressed on her skin. A bead of sweat rolled down her spine. *Promise to come back as soon as you've had a quick look at the river. Straight back.*

Alice couldn't stop herself. She whipped her T-shirt and shorts off, left them by her already discarded boots, and stepped down the bank onto the sandy shore. When the cool water lapped at her feet she shuddered from the familiar comfort of it. The last time she'd gone for a swim felt so far away and so long ago, she could barely remember the taste of salt water. She walked in up to her knees, lulled by the gentle current, then up to her waist, fanning the surface of the water with her open hands. Her shoulders loosened. The forest around her ticked and buzzed.

She glanced towards the gum tree, thinking about the names carved into its trunk. *The river is another story altogether*, June had said when they'd been in the flower field together. *It's belonged to my family for generations. Our family.* Alice looked down through the water, at her feet on the sandy bottom. Was a river a thing that could ever be owned? Wouldn't that be like someone trying to say they owned the sea? Alice knew that when you were in it, the sea owned you. Still, the thought that she was somehow a part of this place filled a small space inside her with warmth. Overhead a kookaburra burbled. Alice nodded. Enough thinking. She took a step forward and sank into the swirling green water, leaving all her unasked questions on the surface.

The sweet and absolute absence of salt shocked her. Her eyes didn't sting. She exhaled bubbles and watched them rise and pop. The heart of the river beat in Alice's ears. Her father told her once that all water eventually ran to the same source. A new question bloomed: could she swim down river, through time, all the way home?

Alice pondered the question for so long that she stayed underwater until her lungs were burning. She pressed her feet firmly on the riverbed and pushed herself to the surface, coming up spluttering. It hadn't hurt so much to breathe since the fire. Suddenly the light in the bush didn't seem as welcoming, nor did the water feel as soothing. She staggered out of the river, coughing hard as she scrambled up the bank and onto dry ground. She coughed and coughed, bent over, hands on her knees.

'Are you all right?'

She spun towards the voice.

There he was. On the other side of the river. The boy from the car.

Alice doubled over coughing again, her nose and eyes running. She couldn't stop. The more she tried the harder she coughed. When she started to cry, coughing turned into retching. Behind her, a loud splash was followed a few moments later by water dripping on her feet. The boy was at her side, sopping wet.

'Breathe in, think "in". Breathe out, think "out".' He rested his hand between her shoulder blades. She glanced at him and followed his instructions.

In. Out.

In. Out.

Slowly, her coughing receded.

When she stood, she realised too late that she was wearing nothing but her knickers. Her face burned as she grabbed her T-shirt and shorts and, before she could look at his face again, tore off down the path.

'Hey!' he called. Alice would not look back.

Only when the bush met the boundary of the flower farm did she stop to put her clothes on. It wasn't until she noticed her bare feet that she realised she'd left her boots by the river.

As she ran along the edge of the flower fields towards the house, the early afternoon sun warmed her skin. Her face had cooled. She didn't know what she would do about her boots other than try to sneak out later to get them.

Across the fields the workshop air conditioners hummed. The Flowers were inside, tending to their cuttings from the morning. Alice sprinted lightly up the steps of the back verandah. The tables were clean, the chairs all neatly pushed in. She didn't know how long she had been gone. Had she missed lunch? Her stomach growled loudly in response. Alice tiptoed towards the screen door.

Inside, there didn't seem to be anyone about. Maybe Twig and Candy were in the workshop too. Alice relaxed. She went into the kitchen looking for food and found bread, butter and Vegemite to make herself two sandwiches.

'You must have an appetite the size of Harry's today!'

Alice froze, then turned, forcing herself to smile calmly at Twig, who stood in the doorway.

'Candy said you ate your lunch upstairs earlier, after such a tough morning. She said you polished off your plate.'

Unsure of what to do, Alice nodded. She'd missed lunch. She must have been gone for much longer than she thought, and was queasy at the idea of getting in trouble, or worse, getting Candy in trouble. But Candy had covered for her. The thought made her genuinely happy.

'A good appetite is as important as a good attitude, I like to say,' Twig said as she walked away, down the hall. 'Listen, speaking of Harry, when you finish your sandwiches, come on into the lounge room, will you?'

Alice exhaled the breath she'd been holding; Twig didn't seem to have noticed her dusty bare feet or damp hair.

As she stood in the kitchen, chewing her sandwiches, Alice couldn't stop herself from smiling. She had one thing now, one thing at Thornfield that felt like it was her own. Her first visit to the river would always be hers alone. Except, of course, for the boy. At the thought of him, Alice's cheeks burned anew. She put her sandwich down. It had suddenly lost all flavour.

The lounge room was airy and bright. Twig sat on the couch with Harry at her feet, who occasionally sighed as she scratched his ears. Alice joined them, sitting in the same spot as earlier that morning, after June carried her downstairs and disappeared. That felt like days ago. Outside, Alice noticed June's truck was parked by the workshop. Would she be joining them? The thought made her nervous. She rubbed her eyes. They were suddenly very heavy.

'I think June's mentioned to you that our Harry here has special powers?' Twig asked.

Alice nodded, yawning.

'I thought I might teach you the ways we talk to Harry, whenever we need help.'

Hearing his name, Harry's ears half-heartedly perked under Twig's massaging fingers. He slouched against Twig's legs, slack-jawed and occasionally drooling. *Hardly a super-dog*, Alice thought.

'Harry's what's called an Assistance Dog. Have you heard of Assistance Dogs before, Alice?'

She shook her head. Before Harry, the only dog she'd ever known was Toby, and he wasn't her assistant. He was her best friend.

'Assistance Dogs are specially trained to help people when they're afraid. Dogs like Harry can pick up on people's emotions. They can comfort you and distract you when you're sad or scared or upset.' Twig smiled as Harry licked her hand. 'Maybe Harry's brought you a little bit of that comfort and distraction already, since you arrived?' she asked, looking over at Alice.

Alice thought about Harry staying by her side in the truck after she and June pulled up at Thornfield. He'd been there when she'd woken from her bad dreams, and even managed to get her to come downstairs yesterday. She took in his big toothy smile, his black-tipped ears and golden face. He wasn't Toby, but Twig was right; there was something about Harry that made her feel better.

'Harry's assistance is usually most needed when we have someone new join us here at Thornfield. So, any time you need him, Alice, anytime you're upset, scared or panicked, remember Harry is here for you. As we all are.' Twig smiled. She smoothed Harry's ears down, gave his flanks a pat. 'Most of Harry's commands are spoken, but we use visual commands too. I'll teach you those, okay?'

For the rest of the afternoon, Alice learned how to speak to Harry. She got the hang of it quickly. Clicking her fingers in front of her body directed Harry to stand before her, creating a barrier between Alice and anything else. Clicking her fingers behind her told Harry to position himself there. Clapping her hands told him to enter a room and turn the lights on, so that Alice didn't have to go into the dark. That was her favourite command. Seeing Harry canter into the lounge room and press the button on the floor to switch on the standing lamp made her laugh.

'He knows every room in the property, Alice, and where all the light switches are.' Twig nodded seriously, but her eyes were smiling.

The last command, sweeping her open palm over her head from left to right, cued Harry to enter a space and search for people or intruders, barking if he found anyone. She didn't like the thought of using that one.

'Good, Alice. That's great. You're a quick learner. If you're ever alone again and you feel faint, like this morning, remember you can call on Harry.'

By the time the workshop door opened and the sounds of the Flowers finishing up for the day drifted through the windows, Alice had the knack of Harry's commands. She flopped on the couch, too tired to practise anymore.

'June will be in soon for dinner,' Twig said. 'How about a bath beforehand, then early to bed? It's been a big day.'

Alice nodded. She didn't really want a bath, but Twig's gentle voice made everything she said sound like perfect sense. As she followed Twig down the hallway towards the bathroom, Alice clicked her fingers behind her, though she didn't need to. Harry was right at her heels.

Twig swung the screen door open and sat on the back verandah steps in the last light of the day. She rolled herself a smoke, lit it and took a deep drag, listening to the crackle of the burning tobacco, feeling the smoke fill her lungs. She blew a plume up to the first stars. Across the flower fields yellow light fell from the workshop windows. June had been in there ever since she'd come home earlier that afternoon. Twig had been doing paperwork in the office, waiting for Alice to return from the river, when June's weary footsteps came up the front steps. She'd gone to greet her in the hall. June had held her hand up in protest.

'Twig,' she'd said, before Twig got the chance to speak. Her eyes were red-rimmed. Harry bounded between them, nearly knocking them over.

'She's at the river,' Twig had said. 'I'm going to teach her basic cues with him when she gets back.' Twig patted Harry's head. 'She needs something to help her cope when she has another panic attack.'

'*If* she has another panic attack.' June had sighed. 'I've enrolled her in school. She starts next week. I'll tell her tonight.'

Twig clenched her fists. June wasn't ever this stubborn raising Candy Baby. Twig knew the difference though: Candy was a blessing. Alice was blood.

'And enrolment took all morning?' Twig had looked out the front screen door, at June's truck. The corner of a hand-carved hazelwood box poked out from under a tarpaulin on the tray. Twig raised an eyebrow. She knew exactly where June had been: digging up old ghosts in her storage shed in town.

'Easy, Twig. It's not what you think. It's been one helluva day.'

'Yes. Yes, it has been,' Twig had hissed. 'For your granddaughter most of all, but hey, who knows about your grandson? Since you cast him aside like some kind of weed.'

The words smashed to splinters at their feet. When she saw June's face, Twig had wanted to sweep them up and swallow their serrated edges one by one. June had stomped out of the house, into the workshop, and slammed the door behind her. She hadn't emerged since.

Twig lit another smoke. She was grateful June had the grace not to throw her own pain back in her face. Her anger wasn't just about June separating Clem's children. Of course it wasn't. It was about her own babies. It was about the day thirty years ago when welfare officers pulled up in their shiny Holden and came into her home with a court order accusing her of child neglect. Because she didn't have a husband. Because she often left Nina and Johnny with Eunice, her sister, while she went out looking for work. Because she was poor. Because the Child Welfare Department decided the only chance her children had of being proper Australians was if they grew up with a proper Australian family. A white Australian family. One of them had held Twig down while the other wrenched Nina and Johnny from her arms. They were screaming. Twig sang, trying to calm them, but they were inconsolable, tearing fistfuls from the daisy bush in the front yard, reaching for anything to hold onto as they were taken away. Twig had crumpled by the torn daisies browning and dying in the sun; the last things her children touched. She was still there, singing in the harsh northwesterly wind, tending the dead flowers as if she might be able to replant them, when Eunice came home after work. Twig had tried to carry on, believing Nina and Johnny would somehow find their way back to her, but after Eunice went missing a few years later, she had fled. Drifted up the coast, and then inland, hitchhiking from town to town. Until one day when, walking along the highway, she was lured down Thornfield's driveway by curiosity, then the sound of a crying baby.

A peal of laughter from the dorm interrupted her memories. Twig wiped her eyes on her shirt. She'd asked Candy to serve dinner to the Flowers in the dorm; if June was going to explain to Alice that she was going to school, they needed privacy. That was, if June ever planned on coming out of the workshop.

As if on cue, the workshop door opened. Twig hid the lit end of her cigarette and sat perfectly still in the shadows as June made her way towards the front of the house. If she saw Twig, she didn't let on. The front door opened and closed. The hinge of the crockery cabinet in the dining room squeaked open as June set the table. Further down the hall the bath gurgled as it emptied. The bathroom door opened. Light footsteps travelled down the hall into the kitchen. The sigh of the oven being turned off. The murmur of June's voice. Chairs dragging on the dining room floorboards as June and Alice sat down. The clink and scrape of steel on china as they ate.

Alice must have been starving for a proper meal after her run to the river and back. Twig knew exactly where she'd been when she came upon Alice in the kitchen earlier that afternoon. Her shirt was buttoned up wrong, her wet hair was full of leaves, and her feet were sandy. But there was a light in her eyes and a colour in her cheeks that kept Twig silent. She knew as well as anyone that Thornfield found all sorts of ways to mend the broken souls that came to call it home. For now, it was the river that would hold Alice together. For Twig, ever since she came to Thornfield, the fix was always June.

Alice lay in bed, her head spinning from the news June had given her at dinner. She was enrolled in the local school. She started class next week.

'I went and spoke to the principal myself today,' June had said. 'He suggested Harry goes to class with you so you have a friend right from the beginning.'

School. She'd read about it. Teachers and classrooms, desks, pencils and books. Children, playgrounds, cut sandwiches, reading, writing and homework. And she could take Harry with her.

Alice rolled onto her side. She turned her thoughts instead to the river. How it sounded below the surface, and the strange feeling she got when the boy put his hand on her back to help her breathe.

A breeze tickled under her chin. Alice sat up. One of the white curtains in her room twirled in the darkness. She didn't remember opening a window. Alice reached over to switch on the lamp, squinting in the light.

There, sitting on the floor by her bed, were her baby-blue boots. In one of them was a bunch of vanilla-scented wildflowers.

Twig was rolling a third smoke when she heard the thud at the side of the house. She held her breath to sharpen her hearing. Footsteps crunched down the dirt path to the flower fields until the young boy came into view. Twig narrowed her eyes. She exhaled slowly. Held her unlit rollie in one hand and her lighter in the other, waiting to see if he'd look back. Just before the path went into the forest, he turned, his face in full moonlight.

There he stood, Boryana's boy. With his eyes so locked on Alice's lamp-lit window, Twig doubted he'd have noticed her on the back steps even if she was lit up in flames.

When he turned back to the path and disappeared into the forest, Twig lit her smoke with shaky hands. She'd seen this all happen before. When Agnes Ivie was the child in the bell room. And Clem Hart was the one sneaking through her window to give her flowers.

11

River Lily

Meaning: Love concealed

Crinum pedunculatum | Eastern Australia

*Very large perennial usually found on the edge of forests,
but also at the high-tide level close to mangroves. Fragrant,
white slender star-shaped flowers. Seeds sometimes germinate
while still attached to the parent plant. The sap has been used as
a treatment for box jellyfish stings.*

Alice spent the rest of the week following the Flowers around the farm while they worked. At morning tea, she and Boo did the newspaper crosswords; Boo knew a lot of words. Later she collected honey from the hives with Robin, who let her wear some of the red lipstick she kept in her apron pocket, and showed her how to eat honeycomb fresh from the hive. She tagged along behind Olga, Myf and Sophie as they went up and down the rows of flowers cutting new blooms. She helped Tanmayi make rosewater from fresh rose petals, enchanted by her stories about Sita, the princess who surrendered herself to the earth after being accused of sorcery, and Draupadi, the princess who cursed one hundred men for mistreating her. In the afternoons, Alice hung around the workbenches in the workshop, making necklaces out of petals, stems, leaves and string, while Francene, Lauren, Caroline and Amy filled flower orders, wrapping bouquet after bouquet in brown paper and twine. She hummed along with Rosella in the seedling houses, and helped Vlinder water the wild cotton bushes; monarch butterflies swooped in to feed and fluttered over them.

On Friday, Alice, Twig and Candy joined the twelve women on the back verandah at the end of the day. They all untied their aprons, took their big straw hats off and fanned their faces. June brought an Esky filled with frosty bottles of ginger beer and handed them around like amber treasures. The Flowers sat with their heads leant back and their eyes half-closed. The rows of blooming flowers, the hoop houses, the white beehives and the thick silvergreen bush in the distance wavered in the twilight like a dream.

While Alice sipped her drink she snuck glances at their faces. Most of the time the Flowers were jovial and hardworking. But that afternoon on the verandah, something changed. Everyone fell silent. As the sun went down, all the stories the Flowers lived, loved and left behind crowded in on them. The women's shoulders sagged inwards. Some of them cried. They turned to comfort each other. And June sat in the middle, her face composed and her back straight.

Alice had realised she wasn't so different from any of the Flowers. Even June. Everyone needed silence sometimes. And that was the magic of Thornfield; it was a place where it was possible to say the things you could not speak. And, in her own way, Alice was beginning to understand the power of a language spoken in flowers. Ever since her trip to the river, every night after dinner when she went to her room, a new flower sat in her baby-blue boots at the end of her bed.

June sat on the back verandah, watching the sun rise over the flower farm while she blew the steam off a cup of strong black coffee. The morning held a faint crispness, a first hint of winter. She took the flask out of her pocket and poured a splash into her cup. Pressed the rim of the cup to her lips and took small sips, savouring the warmth.

As the flower fields absorbed the light, it occurred to June that she could be watching the sun come up on any day when Thornfield was in bloom. It could have been eighty years earlier. Ruth Stone could easily have come around the corner from the workshop, backlit by the copper wash of dawn, her hands deep in her pockets and her eyes not yet lined by sorrow.

June finished her coffee, picked up her gardening gloves, and stuffed them into the pocket of her vest. She walked into the brightening morning, through the fields towards the seedling houses her mother had built. Sometimes her longing to have just one more conversation with her mother made her feel as if she might splinter to bits if she breathed too hard. Knowing that Alice was aching for Agnes in the same way tormented June. History's inclination to repeat itself was nothing but cruel.

The air inside the seedling houses was dense with the promise of new beginnings. June closed her eyes for a moment. They'd spent hours in there together, gathering the longings of people's hearts in fistfuls of shoots and seeds while her mother told her Thornfield's stories. *Pay attention now, Junie*, Wattle Stone used to say. *These are Ruth's gifts. These are the ways we've survived.*

As a child June's imagination was captured by stories of her grandmother. She spent hours down by the river, running her fingertips over Ruth's name carved into the trunk of the giant gum, and Jacob Wyld's name carved beside it.

When she first appeared in town, rumours about Ruth Stone were rife. Some said she was born to a woman on the last convict ship sent to Australia. Others said she was the descendant of a Pendle Hill witch who escaped fate. Reportedly, her only possession was a small notebook filled with a strange language. Some argued it was a spell book. Others swore they'd seen the inside of it; filled with flowers, they said. The only thing unanimously agreed upon was that Ruth Stone had been traded by Madame Beaumont, owner of a roadhouse brothel in the next town, in exchange for the last dairy cows from Thornfield, a crumbling farm on the outskirts of town. The reclusive owner, Wade Thornton, watched helplessly as his farm turned to dust during the worst drought in the town's history. He had his own share of town gossip to contend with. Wade Thornton was known for trying to drown his demons in rum; once Ruth Stone arrived, helping himself to her body became his preferred method of exorcism.

It didn't take long for Ruth to figure out when to flee the house. After Wade finished whatever gruel she'd been able to make for dinner, she would slip out for more stove wood before his fourth drink, and run to the drought-stricken trickle of a river. There, Ruth found a place to hide until Wade inevitably drank himself into oblivion. At the base of a giant river gum, Ruth sat and let herself sing and cry. Books and singing were all that kept her mind strong. She sang stories her mother had taught her, about flowers that spoke things words could not. She was singing by the giant gum the night an out-of-work drover, with nothing but seeds in his pockets, wandered into the cracked riverbed spellbound, as if her song led him right to her. At the sight of Ruth, singing and crying in the moonlight, they say Jacob Wyld crouched wordlessly and planted seeds at her feet, in the earth between the roots of the gum tree. What grew from that night, where Ruth's tears fell to the earth, was a heath of wild vanilla lilies, and an equally heady love affair between Ruth and Jacob.

They met at the river whenever Ruth could get away. He brought her flower seeds and she brought him whatever meagre food scraps she could sneak from the house.

Soon Ruth had enough seeds to till a small, shaded corner of dirt near the house, where a nearly dead, lone wattle tree stood. The dirt was so dry it took her a month to soften it with whatever water she could carry from the river. Eventually, the wattle tree exploded into flower, a winter blaze of sweet yellow. Ruth fell to her knees at the sight. The scent floated all the way into town. Bees droned around the tree, drunk on its nectar. Beneath the wattle were circles of green shoots. Ruth sketched each one in her small notebook. As they bloomed, so different to the foxgloves and snowdrops of her mother's songs, Ruth noted down what they meant to her, adapting the Victorian language of flowers. The strange and beautiful native flowers, able to flourish in the harshest conditions, enchanted Ruth; none more so than the deep scarlet flowers with red centres the colour of the darkest blood. *Meaning*, Ruth wrote in her notebook, *have courage, take heart.*

In the grip of an extreme drought, farms were dying, farming families were going bankrupt and nothing would grow from the earth; when the town looked set to be scorched off the map forever, Ruth Stone started a native flower farm.

News spread quickly. People came to see for themselves the shock of colour among the dust and cow bones. Soon they returned bringing cuttings from their dying gardens. Ruth planted them and under her care, they grew rampant. Wade Thornton stopped drinking. He opened the doors to Thornfield and let people in. They brought their hoes, their water drums, their precious seeds. Ruth told them where to go and what to plant. They constructed greenhouses. They worked from sunup to sundown, tending new shoots. The air was heavy with the green smell of expectation. When Thornfield bloomed, people came together with Ruth to harvest the flowers, make bouquets, and drive through the night to the biggest fresh flower markets in the country; every bunch was tied with a handwritten card explaining Ruth's meaning for each flower. They'd sold out before lunch. And took orders back to Thornfield for more of the native flowers that spoke the language of Ruth's heart. The townspeople began to hope.

Days passed. Winter flowers bloomed. Plans were made for more flower market trips. As Wade Thornton stood sober in the shadows of his house and watched Ruth's flushed and smiling face among the locals, something bitter grew inside him.

One night, not long after Ruth's first successful harvest, Wade drank enough rum to convince Ruth he'd passed out, then waited until he heard her footsteps fade on the dirt outside. Under the cold and starry sky he followed her along the path he'd long ago hand-cleared to the river. There, behind the bushes, he waited. When a man rose from the riverbed to take Ruth in his embrace, Wade's vision was blurred by rage. Every time he forced himself upon Ruth he had to spit on his fingers just to get inside her, and she turned her face away, her eyes empty, her body lifeless. But in this man's arms Ruth was alive, silver and luminous. In the pale winter moonlight, Ruth took the man's hand and pressed it to her stomach. She smiled. Her eyes glittered. With a roar Wade Thornton lunged from the bushes and knocked Jacob Wyld unconscious with a river stone. He gagged and tied Ruth to a tree and made her watch as he drowned her lover with his bare hands.

June shuddered, rubbing her arms against the damp air of the seedling house. The weight of Thornfield's legacy pressed as heavily upon her as when she was a teenager, when she'd been devastated by the story of what happened to her grandmother. *Pay attention now, Junie*, her mother would say when she was teaching her about the flowers. *These are Ruth's gifts. These are the ways we've survived.*

What would her mother tell her now, June wondered as she set about scarifying new seedlings so they could grow. Wattle Stone would say to her daughter, *Junie, Thornfield is Alice's birthright. Which she should learn about from you.*

'Alice, let's get this show on the road.' June's voice spiralled up the stairs.

Alice sat on her bed in her stiff and starched uniform. Harry licked her knee. Alice sighed. She hauled her new schoolbag off her bed, and dragged her feet downstairs.

'Now, don't be like that,' June snorted as she crossed the kitchen, holding Alice's lunchbox out to her. 'You're going to have a great time. You'll make new friends.'

Outside, June opened the farm truck. Harry leapt inside. Alice stood at the top of the verandah. Her feet wouldn't work. June held a hand out to her.

'Harry's going to be with you.' June gestured for her to join him. Alice stomped down the front steps, just to be clear. June helped her up into the truck. Harry yapped. Alice huffed. June shut the door, her bracelets chiming.

'Off we go,' she said, jogging around the truck to get in. As she drove away from the house a chorus of squawks and hoots erupted behind them. Alice turned to look through the back window. The Flowers ran after them, crowing and catcalling, throwing spools of streamers, and popping confetti bonbons.

'You'll be great, Alice!'

'Go Alice!'

'Have a great first day at school, Alice!'

Alice leant out of the truck, waving madly. June pressed on the horn as they drove away. Alice saw her wipe her eyes.

When they reached the road into town, June put her foot down. Alice hung on to Harry's collar so tightly her fingers ached.

The town primary school was a cluster of small weatherboard cottages, canopied by gum trees. Leaves and gum nuts crunched under June and Alice's feet, releasing their lemony scent. Harry strained against his lead, sniffing everything, nearly pulling Alice over. Outside the main building June squatted down to straighten

Alice's collar. Her breath smelled minty. Alice studied her face, so close. June's eyes were just like her father's. June stood and squared her shoulders.

'Come on, now. You can do this.'

Walking into reception, Alice wasn't sure which one of them June was talking to.

Alice sat waiting with June and Harry. The receptionist said Alice's new teacher would come and meet her soon, at little lunch. June chewed on her peppermint gum like a cow with its cud. Her leg jiggled nonstop. Alice held Harry's lead, stroking his smooth flanks. June checked her watch.

A bell shrilled.

'Any minute now, Alice,' June muttered. Harry reached forward to lick her hand reassuringly. June rubbed his ears. He arched his back to stretch, and released a long, loud fart. June coughed but kept her expression deadpan. Alice's cheeks flamed. The receptionist cleared her throat. When the smell hit them, June got the giggles. Her eyes watering, she coughed again as if she might mask the smell with sound, and stood, hurriedly fumbling for the window latches. While Alice tried to help her, Harry sat panting, smiling.

'I'm so sorry,' June croaked at the receptionist. 'So sorry.' The woman nodded, holding a handkerchief to her nose. They got the windows open and sagged in relief. Alice peered at children of all ages pouring from the school rooms. She turned and sat back in her seat. Imagined Harry farting beside her in class. After a moment she leant forward and gave him a big hug, then handed June his lead. June looked at it and then at Alice, her eyes softening.

'You can do this on your own, Alice,' she said, smiling. Alice nodded.

The door opened. A young man with a streak of white chalk on his cheek walked in.

'Alice Hart?'

As he approached, his nose twitched. He sniffed a couple of times, then glanced at Harry. June stood to meet him. Alice hung back. One of the man's knee socks was falling down. His legs were covered in fine blonde hairs, not dark coarse ones like her father's.

'Well, Alice,' he said, smiling. 'I'm Mr Chandler. Your new teacher.'

He dusted his hand on his shorts and held it out. Alice glanced at June. She nodded encouragingly. Mr Chandler's hand hovered, outstretched. June mumbled something to him, out of Alice's earshot. He dropped his hand. After a moment, he rubbed his chin, the same way Alice had noticed Twig sometimes did when she was deep in thought.

'Tell me, Alice, do you happen to like books? I need a helper with our class library and I think you might have come along at the right time.'

After another moment, Alice offered him her hand.

The hours until the three o'clock bell went by as slow as cold molasses.

'See you all tomorrow,' Mr Chandler called as Alice's classmates surged outside.

Alice dawdled, packing her schoolbag.

'How did you go, Alice? First day okay?'

Alice nodded, keeping her head down. She didn't make any friends. Because she didn't talk. Because everyone acted like she smelled as bad as Harry. She should have kept him with her after all. Then she would at least have had one friend.

'Are you being picked up?' Mr Chandler asked.

'I'm here to pick her up.' Candy Baby stood in the doorway, chewing pink bubble gum, as startling and out of place as a spring flower in winter. Harry sat beside her, his tail wagging. Alice sniffled, beaming at the sight of them.

On their way out to the car park, as Candy asked Alice questions about her day and Harry excitedly licked her face, they passed a group of girls Alice recognised from her class.

'There she is. The Spaz,' one called.

'I'm sorry, what was that?' Candy asked.

Alice wanted to go home, to her room with her books, overlooking the Flowers. As she fidgeted with her schoolbag zipper, she heard someone whimpering. She stopped to listen. Heard it again. Wandered away from Candy and Harry. Behind one of the school cottages, she found the boy from the river, lying in a patch of bindies. One of his cheeks was bruised and his lip was split. His legs were covered in fine, bleeding scratches.

'Alice?' Candy called, alarmed. 'Oggi!' she exclaimed as she came up beside Alice. 'Oggi, what happened?'

'I'm okay,' he said as they helped him sit up. He looked Alice in the eye. 'You're not the only one that gets picked on for being different.'

'Spazzos love each other!' A snigger came from nearby bushes. Candy lurched at them, shaking the branches, sending Alice's classmates scattering. Alice didn't care; whatever Oggi was, she didn't mind a bit if everyone thought she was the same.

He winced as Alice helped him to his feet. She picked up his schoolbag and swung it over one shoulder then offered the other to Oggi to lean on. He was easier to support than her mother when she was hurt; he was Alice's size.

Together they hobbled to the front gate. Candy opened the truck, stowed their schoolbags, clipped Harry onto his lead in the back, and helped Alice get Oggi up onto the passenger seat.

'Let's get you home, mate. Put some calendula on those scratches and bruises, and you'll soon be right as rain. Can't say the same for whoever did this to you, though. God help them when Boryana finds out.'

'Which is why we won't tell her,' Oggi begged.

Candy shook her head as she put the truck into reverse. They rode silently while Harry paced the tray, occasionally sticking his head into the wind. As they drove down Main Street, Alice drank in the pastel colours of the shopfronts. In her mind's eye she emerged from the sugar cane again, taking in the dress shops, the cafe with the yellow flower on the table, and the library across the street, with the librarian who had a kind smile and gave her the book on selkies. Sally. Alice tried to see her more clearly, but Sally's face drifted away.

Just past the town limits sign, Candy angled the truck onto a dirt track.

'How beautiful are these old giants?' Candy said, leaning forward over the steering wheel to look up. Alice admired their white and silver trunks, thinking of her mother's stories of places so heavily covered with snow that trees and earth and sky were the same thing. 'Here we are.' Candy pulled up at a small clearing by the river. Alice watched it flow. So that's how he'd found her; the river had led Oggi right to her.

Oggi eased himself out of the truck and limped towards a small timber house with a wide, low-set front verandah, red cotton curtains and an open front door.

'Oggi?' A voice called from inside. The black-haired woman with the red lipstick emerged from the house. 'What's going on?'

'Oggs had a bit of trouble at school,' Candy said as she got out of the truck.

Boryana spoke a torrent of words in a language Alice didn't understand. She fussed over Oggi's purpling bruises and spinifex cuts. He held his hands up as if in surrender and replied in the same bubbling language. Harry barked from the back of the truck until Candy let him off his lead. He sailed off the tray and ran to Boryana's side, yapping at her hands as she gesticulated.

'Sorry, sorry, Harry.' Boryana patted Harry's head to reassure him. 'Everything's all right. Ognian here is a big boy who can take care of himself, apparently, and won't tell me who did this.' Boryana crossed her arms.

'We'd better get going, Bory, and leave you two to it,' Candy said, nodding. 'C'mon Harry.'

'What? No! You have to come in. For a quick tea. June won't mind.'

'She bloody well will,' Candy said. 'It was this one's first day at school' – Candy put her arm around Alice – 'and June will be keen to hear all about it. Bory, this is Alice. June's granddaughter. Our newest Flower.'

Alice smiled shyly, though couldn't take her eyes off Oggi.

'Well, now, how lovely it is to meet you.' Boryana's words sounded like they were coated in something thick and rich. She took Alice's hand and pumped it up and down.

'You and my Oggi are friends?'

'We go to school together.' Oggi stepped forward.

Boryana nodded. 'Very good.' She glanced at Candy. 'You really won't stay for a quick cuppa? Looks like there's a lot to catch up on.' Boryana raised an eyebrow. Alice looked pleadingly up at Candy.

'All right, all right. A quick one,' she surrendered.

Candy and Boryana walked arm in arm into the house, their heads bent together, gossiping. Oggi and Alice stood awkwardly.

'I'll show you around.' Oggi gestured to the river. Alice nodded. She clicked her fingers behind her. Harry licked her wrist as he followed.

Behind the house was a small, well-kept rose garden and a coop holding three fat chickens. Alice sat under a paperbark tree as Oggi opened the coop to let the chickens roam. Harry sniffed after them but then curled up, uninterested.

'This one's Pet, she's my favourite,' Oggi pointed out a fluffy black chicken, wincing when he stretched his bruised arm too far. Alice squeezed her eyes shut but could still see her mother's naked body, covered in bruises, coming out of the sea.

'Are you okay, Alice?'

She shrugged. Oggi went to his mother's rose garden and gathered a collection of fallen petals and leaves. When his hands were full he carried them back to Alice and placed them on the dirt around her. Back and forth he went, between the rose garden and Alice, until his circle was complete. He jumped inside it and sat down.

'After my dad died I did this to make myself feel better.' Oggi wrapped his arms around his knees. 'I told myself, anything inside the circle is safe from sadness. I'd make the circle as big or as little as I'd like. Once when Mum wouldn't stop crying I made a circle around the whole house. Except I had to use all of the petals on her roses to do that, and she didn't react the way I thought she would.'

Yellow butterflies fluttered over the roses. As Alice watched their wings, tiny lemon flames, she remembered how they hovered over the sea in summer, basked in the casuarina trees, and tapped against her bedroom window at night.

'The mine Dad was working in collapsed. For a while Mum sat on the verandah every day waiting for him to come home. Always with a rose.'

Just like the queen who waited for her love to come home for so long she turned into an orchid. Alice rubbed a shiver from her arms.

'Are you cold?' he asked. She shook her head. They both sat looking at the river.

'That's why I pick you flowers and leave them in your boots at night,' Oggi said, quietly.

Alice let her hair fall down over her face.

'I know how it feels. To be sad and alone.' Oggi turned a rose petal over in his hands. 'We were only meant to be here for a little while, until Dad made enough money for us to move on, but since he died we have to stay here now. Mum doesn't have the papers to do anything else.'

Alice tipped her head to one side.

'We're not Australian. I mean, Mum wasn't born here. So we're not officially allowed to be here. If we try to leave town or go anywhere else, Mum says we could be arrested and separated; she could get sent home and never be allowed to come back again. Which Mum doesn't want, because this is – was – Dad's country. That's why we keep to ourselves and Mum doesn't work anywhere too much, and I'm not allowed to have friends at school. Besides, no one wants to be my friend. They call my mum a witch. Like they call all the women at Thornfield.'

Alice's eyes widened.

'No, no, don't worry,' he said. 'It's not true.'

She sighed, relieved.

Oggi picked at a stone in the dirt. 'Mum dreams about going back to Bulgaria one day, so that's what I'm going to do when I grow up. Make enough money to take her home to the Valley of the Roses.'

Alice lifted a rose petal to her nose. The fragrance reminded her of dreams of fire.

'That's where Mum says I was born. In the Valley of the Roses, back in Bulgaria. Not that it's a place. Mum says it's more a feeling. I don't really know what that means, though. Except kings are buried there, and the roses grow as sweet as they do because there's gold buried in the ground with their bones.'

Alice raised an eyebrow.

'Okay, so I made up that last bit about the gold and the bones. But wouldn't that be cool? If the bones of kings and treasure were buried underneath these magic valleys of roses?'

Footsteps approached.

'We gotta get going, sweetpea,' Candy called.

Alice and Oggi stepped outside the rose petal circle and followed Candy to the front of the house where Boryana was waiting for them.

'Here, Alice. A little something to say welcome.' Boryana handed her a small glass jar topped with cloth and tied with ribbon. Inside glistened pink jam. 'It's made from roses,' she said. 'It does magic things to toast.'

'Bye, Alice,' Oggi called. 'See you at school tomorrow.'

Tomorrow. Alice waved back at him as Candy drove towards Main Street. She'd see him tomorrow.

As they headed home, she touched her fingertips to her hot cheeks. Sunbeams, she imagined, were shining out of her face.

12

Cootamundra wattle

Meaning: I wound to heal
Acacia baileyana | New South Wales

*Graceful tree with fern-like foliage and bright golden-yellow
globe-shaped flower heads. Adaptable, hardy evergreen, easy to
grow. Profuse flowering in winter. Heavily fragrant and sweetly
scented. Produces abundant pollen, favoured for feeding bees in
the production of honey.*

June shuffled down the hall in the dark, switching a few lamps on.
The grandfather clock struck two in the morning. Come sunup,
she had the big drive to the flower markets in the city. But that was
a couple of hours away. Just one nip.

For weeks now the nights had stretched on, empty and restless.
June's bed was weighed down with too many ghosts, sitting at
her feet, holding boughs of wattle in bloom. Winter was always
the hardest season. Flower orders dropped right back. Old stories
turned where they lay under early frosts in the earth. And this
winter Alice had come home.

Although she wasn't speaking, Alice was smiling more often.
Something at school had awakened her in some way, stirring her
from the deep paralysis of grief. She hadn't wet the bed for weeks.
There hadn't been another panic attack. Twig had eased off on
her push for counselling. Alice always had a book open in her lap,
with a pressed flower between the pages. Or she was at Candy's
side in the kitchen or the herb garden, helping her concoct a new
dish. Or she traipsed around in her little blue boots, following
Twig like a second shadow through the workshop.

But no matter how much June tried to keep an eye on her, and even with the temperature cooling every day, Alice still managed to vanish and come home with wet hair sometimes. June knew she'd found the river. And likely, the river gum. Yet, June couldn't bring herself to tell Alice Thornfield's stories, of the women from whom she was descended. Once June spoke Ruth's name, there was only one direction that story could flow: to Wattle, then June, and then straight to Clem, Agnes and the choice June had made.

June stood at the kitchen counter with the open whisky bottle and poured herself another glass. She was tired. Tired of bearing the weight of a past that was too painful to remember. She was tired of flowers that spoke the things people couldn't bear to say. Of heartbreak, isolation and ghosts. Of being misunderstood. When it came to telling Alice about her family, June struggled with the thought of bearing any more blame for the secrets that grew among Thornfield's flowers. There had to be another way for the child to heal than to be accosted with the truth about her family, which, despite the morning when Alice seemingly recognised her face, June was fairly sure she didn't know. Nothing indicated that Alice knew why her father took her mother away from Thornfield, or that June could have changed her mind, surrendered to Clem, and maybe saved Agnes. But she'd let her son go, and he'd taken Alice's mother with him. Because June would not yield to his rage. Because Agnes loved him more than she knew how to love herself.

She took the whisky into the lounge room, drinking straight from the bottle. On Alice's first day at Thornfield, when she'd curled into June's arms and tucked her face into the curve of her neck, June had felt her body fill with a love she hadn't dared to let herself remember. She couldn't risk losing that. She couldn't bear Alice thinking badly of her. Day after day, the stories remained unspoken. She kept moving the mark. When Alice starts school, I will tell her. When Alice smiles, I will tell her. When Alice asks,

I will tell her. *Be careful, June,* Twig warned. *The past has a funny way of growing new shoots. If you don't treat them right, these kinds of stories have a way of seeding themselves.*

June sank into the couch, the whisky bottle lolling in her hand, the past gathering around her. Thornfield's stories were never far from her thoughts.

Jacob Wyld's murder broke Ruth's mind. She gave birth to his baby alone by the river, and named their child after the wattle tree that first flowered during the drought. It was all that was left of Ruth's garden, and all she could give her daughter: a name that might embolden her to survive growing up in a house with Wade Thornton and his abuse. *I was determined not to let him do to my mind what he did to my mother's. Her eyes were as empty as the cicada shells in the dust where her flowers once grew, Junie,* Wattle used to say.

The townspeople became willfully blind to Thornfield after Ruth stopped selling flowers and let her garden wither and die. When they saw Wade in town, no one challenged him about rumours of his violence, and they mostly ignored Wattle, the girl some said had been raised more by the birds than by her own mother. But not Lucas Hart, who first saw Wattle when he was a boy walking alone along the river. He'd thought she was some kind of river mermaid then, the way her skin shone green under the water and her long black hair was tangled with leaves and flowers. Though he never saw her at school, or in the shops, or at church, she irrevocably captured his imagination. Whenever he went to the river he hoped to see her swim. It always struck him that her sinewy limbs cut through the water as if she had a score to settle. Over time, they both grew up. She became a reclusive young woman, hardly ever seen in town, and he went away to finish his medical studies. Neither city life nor an education could distract him; thoughts of Wattle ran through his veins like a fever. He moved home, took up the local GP residency, and walked the river path nightly. He'd heard the rumours about Wade Thornton.

No one seemed to have intervened, though; family business was kept private between a man and his wife. Except, Lucas always wanted to say, Ruth Stone never was Wade Thornton's consenting wife, nor, as the story went, was Wade Wattle Stone's father. Every night that Lucas walked the river he promised himself he would go up the steps to the front door at Thornfield, knock and introduce himself. Inevitably, every night, he got as far as Thornfield's boundary and turned on his heels. Until the night he heard a woman scream, followed by a single gunshot. Then silence.

Lucas ran down the path from the river into Thornfield's dusty yard, where Wattle Stone was holding a rifle, crumpled over Wade Thornton's body, soaked in blood so dark it could have been ink. *Are you hurt?* Lucas cried. *Is it you bleeding, Wattle? Are you hurt?* Wattle sat up, rigid and frighteningly pale, her eyes as dark as the blood around her feet. *Wattle?* Lucas yelled. Slowly, she shook her head. *It's not me*, she whispered, the gun shaking in her hands. They searched each other's eyes, each making a silent vow.

News of Wade Thornton's death sent an overnight fire of speculation through town. Some said Ruth bewitched him and made him suicide. Others said it was Ruth's daughter who murdered him. The Stone women and the language of their flowers were decried as bad luck; a curse on the town since Ruth's failure to maintain the flower fields had taken away people's incomes and hopes. Fishermen at the river were quick to join in, claiming they'd seen Ruth at night, talking to something in the shallows. When the sighting of a Murray cod was reported, it caused further uproar. The River King shouldn't have been anywhere near a waterway that far north; she'd conjured a bad omen. That Ruth Stone and her flower farm once saved the town from drought was forgotten.

The slander didn't stop until Dr Lucas Hart went public with his testimony: he witnessed Wade Thornton stumbling around in a drunken stupor, firing off his hunting rifle as he tried to clean it, and ultimately shot himself dead. The police wrote his death up as accidental, and the town turned its eye in another direction. Wattle Stone married Lucas Hart, carrying a bouquet of wattle down the aisle. They lived together at Thornfield, with Ruth.

Then we had you, Junie, her mother would always say at that point in the story, looking directly at June, her eyes brimming. *And people started to be kind again; you broke Thornfield's curse.*

With June in her bassinet by her side, Wattle blew the dust from Ruth's notebook. While Lucas was at his clinic, she methodically went about gathering books from the town library, reading them aloud, naming Ruth's sketches and writing lists of the seeds she would need to order from the city, while June cooed along. Over a dozen seasons, Wattle cajoled her mother's flower farm back to life. People started to nod approvingly at the bouquets that appeared for sale at the town markets. *Return of happiness*, spoke one bouquet of waratahs, each the size of a human heart. *Devotion*, rose boronias said, a bunch of fragrant cupped flowers. Soon the buckets were empty. Once again Thornfield's flowers were in demand.

Although Wattle revived her mother's beloved garden, she couldn't settle the madness in Ruth's mind. Wattle doted on her mother the way she did on her own child, trying to make her happy, but Ruth still crept out of the house every night. Wattle lay awake listening to the floorboards creak, until one moonlit evening, with June snug against her chest, she decided to follow her mother to the river. She watched as Ruth laid flowers in the water, talking the whole time.

Mama, Wattle stepped onto the sandy river bank in the silver starlight. Her mother's eyes were lucid and bright. *Who are you talking to, Mama?*

Your father, my love, Ruth replied simply. *The River King.*

Bubbles burst on the surface of the river as a flower was dragged under, but by what, Wattle didn't see. She turned and fled, back to her husband, warm in bed.

Ruth died in her sleep when June was just three years old. The morning Wattle found her, Ruth's hair was damp from the river, filled with gum leaves and vanilla lilies.

Her will left everything to Wattle. Ruth asked only one thing of her daughter: to ensure Thornfield was never bequeathed to an undeserving man. And in the generations since, it never was. To Clem Hart's unforgiving fury.

Pay attention now, Junie, her mother's voice rang in her mind. *These are Ruth's gifts. These are the ways we've survived.*

June sighed deeply as first light appeared in the sky. She stumbled from the couch into a standing position and staggered towards her bedroom, the last of the whisky sloshing in the bottom of the bottle.

On the first day of the winter holidays, Alice stood at her window, gazing at the chalky white path that cut away through the bush to the river. She and Oggi were meeting there the next morning, as soon as they woke up, for her tenth birthday. Oggi was the best friend Alice ever had, which she reasoned was fair because Toby was a dog, and Candy was much older, and Harry was also a dog, and a book wasn't actually a person.

She turned from the window to her homework, which was spread out on the floor. Harry wagged his tail as she sat down. She had a holiday assignment to do: write a review of a book she loved, and why she loved it. Although the other kids groaned, Alice twitched with excitement when Mr Chandler handed out the assignment sheet. She knew straight away which book she would choose: the selkie stories Sally picked out for her in the library, the book June gave her at hospital before they'd met.

Alice went to the bookshelves, walking her fingers along the spines until she found the selkie book. When she slid it off the shelf another book came with it, falling to the floor. Alice picked it up, a clothbound hardcover with gilded lettering and a faded illustration on the cover. It was the story about the girl with her name, and the wonderland she fell into.

Alice opened the front cover. As she read the inscription, her body went cold.

'Hey, sweetpea, I brought you some hot cocoa.' Candy appeared in the doorway carrying a steaming mug. 'Alice? What is it?' She put the mug down. 'Let me see.' Candy prised the book out of Alice's hands. Alice watched as Candy read the inscription. 'Oh …' she trailed off.

Anger propelled Alice into action. She pushed Candy out of her room, slamming the door after her. Harry ran to Alice's side, barking. Alice opened the door and shoved him out too.

She didn't come down for the rest of the day. Candy brought her roast dinner, which she left untouched. After trying to talk to her through the bedroom door, Twig retreated to the back deck where she sat chain-smoking.

It was after dusk when the headlights of June's truck bounced along the driveway. Alice sat on her bed, gripping the book. Downstairs the front door swung open. June's keys landed in the glass dish on the bureau. Weary footsteps went down the hall into the kitchen. The kitchen tap whooshed on, then off. Bracelets tinkled. The bubbling hum of the kettle on the stove, followed by its whistle and the sigh of steaming water over a teabag. The chime of a teaspoon tapping against the lip of a china cup. A moment's quiet, before June's weary footsteps came through the hall to the staircase.

'June.'

'Hang on, Twig.'

'June, I –'

'Hang on, Twig.'

Her footsteps on the stairs. Up. Up. A knock at Alice's door.

'Hey, Alice.' June opened the door. Harry bounded in with

her, barking. Alice didn't look up. She kicked her feet hard against the frame of her bed.

'How was your day?' June walked around Alice's room, one hand in a pocket and the other nursing her cup of tea. She stepped over Alice's homework on the floor and went to the bookshelves. Alice watched June's boots. When June turned to face Alice she stopped short.

Alice held the book up with both hands, open to the inscription page, where her mother had written her name, over and over again, making love hearts of every 'a'.

Agnes Hart. Mrs A. Hart. Mr and Mrs C & A Hart. Mrs Hart. Mrs Agnes Hart.

And underneath it, her father's handwriting.

Dear Agnes,

I found this book in town, and thought of you. I know it's the one thing you came to Thornfield with, and I hope you won't mind having a second copy, from me.

Before I bought it for you, I hadn't read this story. But I have now, and it reminds me of you. How being around you feels like I'm falling, but in the most wonderful way. Like I'm in a maze I never want to find my way out of. You're the most magical, puzzling thing that's ever happened to me, Agnes. You're more beautiful than any of the flowers that grow at Thornfield. I think that's why Mum loves you so much too. I think you might be the daughter she never had.

I just wanted to say thanks too for telling me your stories about the sea. I've never seen the ocean, but when you look at me I feel like maybe I understand what you've described. The wildness and the beauty. Maybe one day we'll go. Maybe one day we'll swim in the sea together.

Love,

Clem Hart

June rubbed her forehead roughly. Harry panted hard, his tail flicking back and forth anxiously.

'Alice,' she started.

Alice watched as if she was outside of herself, like when she was in hospital and saw the snakes of fire coil around her body, turning her into something she didn't recognise. She stood from her bed. Swung her arm back. And with all her might, hurled the book at June. It hit her square in the face, and clattered to the floor, its spine cracking as it landed.

June barely flinched. An angry bruise began to bloom on her cheekbone. Alice glared at her grandmother. Why wasn't June reacting? Why wasn't she angry? Why wasn't she fighting back? Alice's vision was blurry. She pulled on her own hair, wanting to scream. When was her mother at Thornfield? Why hadn't anyone told her that her mother was here? Why hadn't anyone told her that it was where her parents had met? What else didn't she know? Why would anyone hide this from her? Why did her parents leave? Alice's head ached.

June came towards her, but Alice kicked her away. Harry growled, pacing. Alice ignored him. He couldn't protect her from this.

'Oh, Alice, I'm sorry. I know you're hurting. I know. I'm sorry.'

The more June tried to comfort her, the angrier Alice got. She kicked and bit and scratched at June's hands. She fought hard against June's strong body, against her life at Thornfield, against being so far away from the ocean. She fought against the bullies at school and how they still picked on her and Oggi. She kicked and screamed against why people had to die. She fought against needing Harry's help, and against tasting sadness in Candy's cooking, and hearing tears in Twig's laughter.

All Alice wanted was to break free and run down to the river, dive into the water and swim, far, far away, all the way back to the bay. Home to her mother. To Toby's warm breath on her cheek. To her desk. Where she belonged.

As she began to tire, Alice started to cry. How she wished she'd never come to Thornfield, where nothing was as it seemed. How she wished she'd never, ever gone into her father's shed.

13

Copper-cups

Meaning: **My surrender**

Pileanthus vernicosus | Western Australia

*Slender woody shrub found in coastal heathlands, sand dunes
and plains. Magnificent flowers ranging from red to orange
and yellow. Flowering occurs in spring, on twiggy branchlets
densely covered in small hardy leaves. Young floral buds bear
a glossy oily coating.*

Of all the ways Alice might have learned about her parents' history at Thornfield, the last June expected was that they would tell her themselves. But there their handwriting was: Agnes practising her future name, Clem writing what would be into being. Before Alice arrived, June thought she'd packed all evidence of both Agnes and Clem into boxes, which she took into town and kept in a rented storage shed. She hadn't once thought to scour the bookshelves in the bell room.

After Alice thoroughly exhausted herself, June carried her downstairs to the bathroom, where Twig was waiting with a hot bath. June tried to avoid Twig's eyes. She would never have said the words, that wasn't Twig's style, but June heard them nevertheless. *The past has a funny way of growing new shoots.*

June hurried past the kitchen where Candy was at the stove warming milk for Alice, and went wordlessly into her bedroom. She closed her door firmly behind her. The hazelwood box sat on her bed where she'd left it. She eyed it warily.

The morning Alice had her panic attack and June took off in her truck, it was true, she did go and enrol Alice in school. But she'd spent most of the time in the storage shed, taking comfort from memories and relics of her past. And when she left to head home, she took the hazelwood box with her, telling herself it was because what she needed for Alice's birthday was inside.

She sat beside the box and considered its detailed woodwork, imagining the hours Clem must have laboured over it. Second to the desk he carved for Agnes, which was in Alice's bell room, the hazelwood box was Clem's proudest work. He was good with seeds and flowers, but he was exceptional at whittling felled trees into dreams. He finished the box just before he turned eighteen, a time when a boy thought he could carve his soul into hazelwood and become a man.

Around one border of the lid were images of Ruth. One with her hands full of seeds, and flowers growing at her feet. Another, a side view of her swollen belly, and lastly, much older, her back hunched, and a serene look on her lined face as she sat by the river, with flowers in her arms and the faintest shadow of a giant cod in the shallows beside her. Around the other border was Wattle, carrying baby June in her arms, a crown of flowers on her head, the house and a field of flowers sprawled behind them. In the centre of the box, Clem carved himself, with a faceless man standing behind him. To one side of Clem stood June, smiling, in full view. On the other side a girl approached, carrying sprigs of wattle.

That was how Clem saw himself: the centre of Thornfield's story. Which was why, June reminded herself, he'd done what he'd done: left the farm with Agnes after he'd overheard June telling her she'd decided not to bequeath Thornfield to him. In essence, her own son had heard his mother tell the girl he loved that she deemed him undeserving.

June reached for her flask and took a long swig. And another. And another. Her head stopped pounding.

Looking at Agnes's face carved by her son's hand, June was loath to admit how much Alice was like her. The same big eyes and bright smile. The same light step. The same big heart. Giving Alice something of her mother was the least June could do. She lifted the brass hook from the latch and opened the lid. Memories flooded her senses before she could stop them. The honeyed scent of winters by the river. The bitterness of secrets.

June was eighteen years old when she stood beside her mother to scatter her father's ashes around the wattle tree. Afterwards, when the town gathered in their house to share tales of the babies her father delivered and the lives he saved, June fled to the river. She hadn't run the chalky path much, not since she was a child when she began to learn stories about the bad fortune doing so brought to the women in her family. June craved an order to things and it frightened her that love could be so wild and unfair; she hated the sight of the gum tree her mother and grandmother had carved their names into, bearing the blessing and curse love had dealt each of them. That day, however, her body parched by grief, June was drawn through the bush by the thought of the water.

When she reached the river, her face tear-streaked and her black stockings full of holes, she found a young man swimming naked in the tea-green water, staring up at the sky.

June quickly wiped her cheeks, and drew herself together. *This is private property*, she announced in her haughtiest tone.

His calm expression was disarming. As if he was expecting her. He had dark hair and pale eyes. Stubble covered his chin.

Get in, he said. His eyes rested on her black clothes. *Nothing hurts in here.*

She tried to ignore him. But watching him watch her, heat started to rise to her skin; the relief of feeling something other than death and grief was sweeter than the honey from her father's beehives.

June started unbuttoning her dress; slowly at first, then in a frenzy until she'd shed her dark mourning clothes and thrown her pale body into the water. She sank to the bottom, blowing the air in her lungs up to the surface. Sand and grit rubbed between her toes. River water filled her ears and nose and eyes.

He was right. Nothing hurt in there.

When the pressure in her lungs pinched she sprang to the surface, hungry for breath. He stayed his distance, looking across the green water at her. Before she understood fully what she was doing, June swam straight to him.

Later that afternoon, with a small fire crackling in a sandy pit on the riverbank, they lay curled into each other. Her body stung from pain and pleasure. She'd fumbled around with boys in the bushes at high school but it was the first time she'd wholly shared herself with a man. She traced her fingertips over a mottled red scar on his chest. There was another at the same point on his back. June kissed each, on either side of his body, tasting the sweet river water on his skin.

Where do you live? she asked.

He disentangled himself from her limbs.

Everywhere, he replied, pulling his boots on. She watched him, realisation sinking through her like a stone. He meant to leave.

She gathered her clothes to her body. *Will I see you again?*

Every winter, he replied. *When the wattle blooms.*

June fell into love like it was the river: steady, constant and true. She told herself this was nothing like her grandmother Ruth's ill-fated love affair with the River King, nor the safety of her mother and father's union. The way June saw it, she was in control; she would not lose her heart to a man and have to engrave her name in a tree to bear witness to her pain. Her love wouldn't be an unfinished story. He would be back. When the wattle bloomed. And the wattle always came into bloom.

The months following her father's death were slow, dusty, and arduous. Wattle Hart wouldn't get out of bed. The house smelled of rotting flowers. June turned to the farm, spending long days tending the flower fields and running deliveries to the surrounding towns. At night, after she'd cooked a meal that Wattle barely picked at, June tucked herself into the workshop, where she taught herself to press flowers into jewellers' resin. She stayed there until her eyes started to blur. Sometimes she slept at her desk, waking with a crick in her neck and flower petals stuck to her cheek. She avoided her mother's pain wherever and however she could; she couldn't bear to witness the wreckage love left behind.

The following May, June kept a close watch; at the first sign of wattle blossom buds in bloom, she ran to the river. She held her breath as she ran. *I'll breathe when I see him. I'll breathe when I see him.*

She went back day after day. The end of winter drew near. Wattle blossoms began to drop. June's clothes hung from her hips and collarbone. Purple half-moons appeared under her eyes. While her skin became feverish and her fingers were stained with dirt, the flower fields thrived. One afternoon at the end of August, when she walked through the clearing to the river bank, a small fire was burning, with a billy of tea boiling above it. He looked at her, the gaze of his pale eyes piercing her centre.

Where have you been? she asked.

He glanced away. *I'm here now,* he said. A new scar, blue and jagged, under his right eye.

June fell to him, gathering his arms around her, feeling his heartbeat through his flannel shirt pressed against her own.

She didn't go back to the house for three days.

They camped by the river, eating tinned pea and ham stew with damper, making love by the fire and daisy chains in the sun. He didn't tell her where he'd been. She didn't tell him how much she needed him to stay.

A few months later, articles about a series of bank robberies far away in the city appeared in the papers. They alleged the thieves were veterans, returned from war. They warned rural towns to be on vigilant watch. *These criminals will be armed, dangerous and looking for somewhere to hide.*

Through the spring, summer and autumn, Thornfield yielded a blaze of blooms, the result of June's relentless work. She was so absorbed, turning her torment into flowers, that she didn't notice how frail her mother was until Wattle was a mere wisp of the woman she'd once been.

Pay attention now, Junie, Wattle used her last words to warn her daughter. *These are Ruth's gifts. These are the ways we've survived.*

While June wasn't paying any attention, disease had eaten what was left of her mother's heart. For the funeral, June cut down all the flowering wattle at Thornfield.

Their third winter together by the river was nearly wordless. He didn't ask her why she cried. She didn't ask him where the scars on his knuckles came from. Just like him, she didn't want to hear the answers.

By the time spring came, June knew she was pregnant. She gave birth alone on a windblown autumn day and named her son Clematis, a bright and ever-climbing star. When the wattle was next in bloom, June knew before she reached the clearing by the river with the swaddled baby in her arms that he would not be there. Nor would he ever come again.

On the farm, bereaved, alone and with a new baby, June spent nights crying guilt and terror into her pillow, fearful that her neglect caused her mother to die, fearful that her son would have the same callous nature as his father. Night after night was the same, until the warm day when unexpected friendship walked up her driveway.

June riffled through the hazelwood box until she found them: a bunch of dried twiggy daisies. She cradled them between her palms, turning them over in her hands.

It was a clear spring morning when Tamara North arrived at Thornfield with one small bag and a pot of blooming daisies to her name. June answered the knock at the front door, unwashed and stinking of sour milk, with Clem screaming in her arms and a farm of dying flowers at her back. She offered Tamara a job on the spot. Doing what, she wasn't sure; farmhand or friend, June needed both. Tamara put her bag and pot plant down and took Clem from June's arms.

You put a fussing baby in water, she said. *Water calms them*.

Tamara walked confidently to the bathroom, as if she was utterly sure of where she was going and what she was doing. June stayed in the hall, bewildered by the sounds of running bath water, Tamara's soothing song and Clem's subsiding wails.

On Tamara's first night at Thornfield, after she'd put Clem to bed and settled herself into her new bedroom, June clipped some of the daisies from her pot plant. She hung a small bunch to dry upside down by her window and pressed a few more into the Thornfield Dictionary with a new entry beside them.

Twiggy Daisy Bush. Your presence softens my pains.

Tamara had answered to Twig and softened June's pains ever since. Even when June wouldn't listen.

She put the dried flowers back into the box. Ran her fingertips over its whorls. It was the last thing Clem gave her before he found out Thornfield would never be his. Before the temper that simmered just below his skin ever since he was a baby tore through him irrevocably. *I wish it was you I never knew and I was raised by my father instead*, he screamed at June before he grabbed Agnes and took off in his truck. The hoarseness of his voice and his sickly pallor were still vivid in her memory, as was the emptiness in Agnes's eyes through the passenger window.

June's gut twisted as she wondered if her son chose hazelwood intentionally, though he couldn't possibly have known how its meaning would haunt her in years to come: *reconciliation*. Before a sob could escape her, June hurriedly dug through the box until she found what she needed to make Alice's birthday present.

She slammed the lid shut and reached a shaky hand for her flask. After a few long glugs, she left her room and went through the house, outside and across to the workshop.

Long after everyone went to bed, June worked at her desk, under her jeweller's lamp, until her eyes burned and her flask was dry. Once her letter to Alice was written and her gift was finished and wrapped, June switched the lamp off. She left the workshop, stumbled through the dark into the house, and up to Alice's bedroom.

Alice stirred in her sleep. She sat up. In the thin moonlight falling through her windows she saw June at her desk, but, unable to keep her eyes open, she sank back to sleep onto her pillow. When she awoke it was light. Her tenth birthday. Remembering her vision in the night, she leapt up. On her desk sat a present and a letter.

She tore at the wrapping, opened the jewellery box inside, and gasped. A large silver locket hung from a silver chain. Encased in resin, the lid of the locket held a cluster of pressed red petals. Alice slid a fingernail into the clasp. The locket sprang open. Looking up at her from behind a thin sheet of glass was a black and white photo of her mother. Hot tears rolled down Alice's cheeks. She put the necklace on and picked up the letter.

Dear Alice,

Sometimes, some things are just too hard to say. I know you understand this better than most people.

When I was about your age I started to learn the language of flowers from my mother, your great-grandmother – who in turn learned it from her mother – using the flowers that grow from this land, our home. They help us to say what words sometimes cannot.

It breaks my heart that I can't fix what has been taken from you. Just like you've lost your voice, I seem to have lost part of mine when it comes to talking about your mother and father. And that's not okay, I know that. I know you need answers. I'm figuring this

out as we go along, just like I know you are too. When I find the
part of my voice that's missing, please know I will give you every
answer I can to every question you have. I promise. Maybe we'll
find our voices together.

I am your grandmother. I loved your parents very much. And I
love you. I will always love you. We are each other's family now.
And will be, always. Twig and Candy, too.

This is the one photo I have of your mother. It now belongs to
you. I made this locket using pressed petals from Sturt's desert peas.
To the women in our family, they mean courage. Have courage, take
heart.

Thornfield is your mother's home, your grandmother's home,
your great-, and great-great-grandmother's home. Now, it can be
yours too. It will open its stories to you just like this locket. If you'll
let it.

Your loving grandmother,
June

Alice closed the letter and ran her fingers along the fold. She
tucked it into her pocket and held the locket open in her palm,
staring at the photograph of her mother's face. Maybe June was
right. Some things were too hard to say. Some things were too
hard to remember. And some things were just too hard to know.
But June had promised: if Alice could find her voice, June would
find answers.

Alice tugged on her blue boots and crept out of the house into
the cool purple morning.

Downstairs in the office, Twig kept the phone to her ear even
though the conversation had ended. Her heart drummed loudly.
It had been too easy: the state's adoption services department was

in the Yellow Pages. She'd simply picked up the phone, dialled the number, said her name was June Hart and that she wanted to register an enquiry about the adoption of her grandson. Gave her postal address care of Tamara North, Thornfield Farm Manager, and was told the forms she needed would arrive in seven to ten working days. It took no more than five minutes. Then the line went dead. And Twig just sat there, listening to the dial tone hum in her ear. It was the sound of fate set in motion, a sound she never succeeded in hearing in her search for her own children. On paper, there was no record of Nina and Johnny's existence. But Twig marked their birthdays every year, planting a new seedling. There were over sixty such plants and trees around Thornfield now.

Outside, the sun shone down on the Flowers, who were busy cutting branches of flowering wattle and gathering them in buckets. One of them was singing an old hymn. Twig thought about humming along but didn't. She stopped going to church years ago.

No sounds came from June's bedroom. Twig knew she'd been up until the early hours, making amends the best way she knew, through flowers. But guilt was a strange seed; the deeper you buried it, the harder it fought to grow. If June wouldn't tell Alice about the baby, Twig was prepared to. And that meant she needed information.

As she leant forward to put the phone receiver back in its cradle, something glinted in the sunshine outside. Twig narrowed her eyes, following the light. Alice's new necklace caught the sun as she tiptoed past the Flowers to scurry into the bush. Twig knew who Alice was going to meet at the river. She didn't have any interest in stopping her either. That child needed all the solace and comfort she could get.

Alice scampered through the flower fields. The dead winter grass crackled underfoot and the cold air burned her lungs. At the bottom of the farm the wattle trees blazed yellow, radiant with their sweet scent. The Flowers were already out and working; Alice ducked from their view as she cut away from the flower fields onto the path through the bush. She ran to the beat of the locket bouncing against her chest.

Have-courage—take-heart. Have-courage—take-heart.

When Alice reached the river, she stopped to catch her breath and watched the green water gush over stones and tree roots. She stood there for a while, remembering the sea. It felt so far away, almost as if it was never real, almost as if it was the same as her dreams. She hated that thought, that her life by the sea and everything she loved there would never again be more than the fires she fought in her sleep. That Toby, his paw on her leg when she read to him even though he couldn't hear, was no more than the flicker of a flame dream. Or her mother, in her garden, her feet bare and her hands tender, no more than a wisp of smoke. Did her mother come to this river? Did she stand where Alice was standing, watching the water gush over the stones and roots? Was her name one of those cut from the river gum? She could almost feel her mother's skin, the warmth of her arms.

Alice tugged June's letter from her pocket and unfolded it. *When I find the part of my voice that's missing, please know I will give you every answer I can to every question you have. I promise. Maybe we'll find our voices together.*

She folded it up and put it back in her pocket. Sweat beaded on her forehead as her memories shifted to her father. She remembered him coming out of his shed with his arms trembling under the weight of her new desk, his eyes filled with hope. How quickly they darkened. Smashing his way through the house, throwing her mother's body against the wall before roaring towards Alice.

Squeezing her eyes shut, Alice clenched her fists by her sides, took a deep breath and screamed. It felt so good she screamed again, imagining her voice might flow with the river and run all the way to the sea, where it could reach the edge of the ocean and sing her mother, the unborn baby and Toby home. All the way home, where they could emerge from her fiery dreams and keep each other safe.

When her throat started to ache, Alice stopped screaming. She undressed and kicked off her boots. Fearful of it being damaged, she unclasped her desert pea locket and tucked it into her clothes. The dark green water rushed by. She dipped a toe in, shuddering at the cold. Dilly-dallied for a while, until she felt brave enough. *On the count of three.* She threw herself into the river. The cold shock of the water made her splutter to the surface, where she found herself coughing up rose petals the colour of fire. Confused, she looked down. Another petal stuck to her shivery skin. And then another, and another. She glanced upstream. Oggi was crouched by the river bank, setting loose petals onto the water. A thick blanket and a backpack sat on the bank beside him. She sent a splash towards him with a smile.

'Hi, Alice.'

She waved, scrambling to the rocks.

'Here.' He stood to offer her the blanket, turning his head away. 'I had a feeling you'd swim today, even though it's freezing.' Shivering, she took the blanket and wrapped it around herself. 'Happy birthday,' he said. His smile warmed her with its brightness. They walked together back to her boots and clothes. He sat and unpacked his backpack. 'Did you know, in Bulgaria, you get to celebrate being you twice a year? Once on your birthday, and again on your name day. That's when everyone with the same name all celebrate on the same day. I don't know if there's a name day for Alice, though. Anyway, the tradition is that people come uninvited to celebrate, and the person celebrating gives them treats to eat and drink.'

Alice frowned.

'But I've never really liked that idea, so I brought treats with me for you.'

At that, Alice beamed. She sat down beside him. From behind his back Oggi revealed a cloth-covered parcel, patterned in roses, each corner tied in a knot. He gestured for Alice to untie it. The cloth fell away, revealing a pot of fiery-coloured jam and a flat, rectangular wrapped present. She smiled. Oggi took a box of buttered bread, a bread knife and a small, battered flask out of his backpack.

'I bet you didn't know that in Bulgaria your birthday falls at the end of rose-picking season. It lasts from May to June, when the Valley of the Roses is covered in roses of every colour. They're cut one by one, and put into willow-baskets to go to the distilleries. That's where they're turned into whatever they're going to be next. Jam. Oil. Soap. Perfume.'

Alice turned the jar of jam over in her hands. It shimmered in the cold light. Oggi unscrewed the lid of the flask and used it as a cup.

'This is what we drink when we celebrate.' Oggi poured something clear from the flask. 'It's called rakija.' He handed her the flask and raised the lid in a toast. 'We say, "nazdrave".'

Alice nodded. Following his lead, she raised the flask to her lips, took a sip, and swallowed. They both coughed and spluttered. Alice spat and wiped her tongue on the blanket repeatedly.

'It's gross, I know, but grown-ups love it,' Oggi croaked. Alice pulled a face in disgust, shoving the flask back at him. He screwed the lid back on, laughing. 'Open your present.'

First she tore open the corner, then in a rush of excitement yanked the brown paper away from the book. It had a cracked spine and yellowed pages, and smelled like the Thornfield Dictionary. Alice ran her fingers over the lettering of the title.

'I thought you might like it. One of the stories is about a girl from the sea who loses her voice.'

Alice looked at Oggi.

'And how she finds it again,' he said.

Without thinking, she leant forward, kissed Oggi's cheek and sat back before she realised what she'd done. Oggi's fingers flew to the spot her lips had touched. Desperate for distraction, Alice reached for the boot that her locket was inside. She tipped it out into her palm and held it up by the chain.

'Wow,' he said, holding his hand up to touch it. Alice opened the clasp. Oggi studied the photograph of Alice's mother.

'Oggi, this is my mother,' she said, carefully forming her words.

Oggi dropped the locket and sprang back as if she'd pinched him. 'What …' His face was frozen in surprise. 'Alice, you spoke? You're speaking? What? You can talk?'

Alice giggled. She'd forgotten how good it felt to laugh.

'She speaks!' Oggi stood up, running in circles around them. Alice closed the locket and slipped the necklace over her head.

When Oggi came to a stop, he doubled over, his hands on his knees. 'Time for birthday breakfast?' he gasped.

'Yes, please,' she said, shyly.

'She said "Yes, please"!' Oggi laughed. 'The crowd goes wild!' He cupped his mouth with his hands and cheered. 'Alice, this is the best birthday ever and it's not even mine.'

'Thank you so much for my presents,' she said slowly, getting used to the shape of words again. She hugged the book.

'You're welcome,' Oggi smiled. He opened the pot of jam. 'Mum made this batch specially for your birthday.' He dipped the butter knife into the jar and spread a thick dollop of jam onto a piece of bread. 'From her garden, made of roses with my name.'

'What do you mean?' She took the bread he offered her.

'Oh, that's what colour they are,' he explained, making a slice for himself.

'Ognian is a colour?' Alice asked in surprise. Her name was a colour too.

'It can be,' Oggi replied, taking a big bite of his jammy bread. 'Iph-meams-pire,' he said.

'Pardon?'

Oggi laughed and swallowed. 'My name, Ognian,' he said. 'It means fire.'

'Oh,' Alice said. The babble of the river intermingled with a bellbird's call. Winter light broke through the trees.

'Say something else,' Oggi said after a while.

'Something else,' Alice said, her cheeks flushed with the joy of making him laugh.

When Alice got home, June was in the kitchen, watching over sizzling frying pans. Candy and Twig were at the table, reading. Harry sat at Twig's feet. His tail thumped at the sight of Alice. The three women looked up.

'Happy birthday,' June said, her eyes on Alice's locket.

'Happy birthday, sweetpea.' Candy closed her recipe book.

'Hi, Alice. Happy birthday.' Twig folded up the paper.

June's frame was hunched. Candy's face was pale. Twig's movements were slow and heavy. All three tried to smile but none of them had happy eyes. No one mentioned Alice's wet hair or her sandy feet.

'I'm making birthday pancakes. Would you like some?' June's voice shook.

Alice gave June the kindest smile she could.

'Coming right up.' June poured more batter into a pan.

Alice angled herself onto one of the chairs.

'How about some sparkling birthday juice, Alice?' Twig offered, sliding her chair back. Alice nodded. Twig went to the cupboard to get a champagne flute, giving June's hand a squeeze as she passed. Harry curled at her feet with a thud. Alice watched the women. The way June's shoulders always shook a little. Twig's sad eyes. Candy's blue hair, which, no matter how bright it was, couldn't hide her sorrow. Alice wasn't the only one who was sad and missed people she loved.

June served pancakes with butter and syrup. Twig set a flute of apple juice and fizzy water beside Alice's plate.

'Thank you, June. Thank you, Twig,' Alice said.

June dropped the spatula covered in pancake mix. Twig's mouth gaped open. Candy shrieked. Harry, unable to decide between licking the pancake batter off the floor or turning in circles, decided to do both.

The women descended upon Alice, wrapping her in a group hug.

'Say that again, Alice!'

'Alice, say Candy Baby!'

'No, Alice, can you say Twig?'

Standing in the centre, Alice looked up at their faces, gathered around her as tightly as petals in a new bud. Although it was her birthday, sharing her voice felt like a gift for them all.

She smiled to herself as the women danced around her. She'd found her voice. Now June had to keep her promise to find Alice answers.

How do I yearn, how do I pine
For the time of flowers to come

Emily Brontë

14

River red gum

Meaning: Enchantment

Eucalyptus camaldulensis | All states and territories

Iconic Australian tree. Smooth bark sheds in long ribbons. Has a large, dense crown of leaves. Seeds require regular spring floods to survive. Flowers late spring to mid-summer. Has the ominous nickname 'widow maker', as it often drops large boughs (up to half the diameter of the trunk) without warning.

Alice gripped the steering wheel, white-knuckled. She kept her eyes on the traffic light, waiting for it to turn green. Her left leg shook from the strain of pushing the clutch.

'Okay, Alice, we're going to proceed to the end of Main Street, where you'll execute a U-turn, please.' The police sergeant kept his head down, scribbling on the clipboard in his lap. It was early, that hour before the school run started and the shops unlocked their doors and flipped their signs over to OPEN. Overnight spring showers had turned the road quicksilver in the morning light. Alice narrowed her eyes. The light turned green.

She eased her left foot off the clutch. *Wait until you feel it take*, Oggi had told her dozens of times, sitting beside her in the old farm truck. The thought of him calmed her. When the clutch engaged, she pressed her right foot on the accelerator. Not so much as one kangaroo-jump. Exhaling, she reclaimed her grip on the steering wheel, smiling to herself. She glanced at the sergeant. His face was unreadable.

Through the traffic lights and down Main Street, mindful of the speed limit. The road stretched flat ahead of them, a black ribbon leading out of town, curved into bushland. Alice kept her eyes on the exact spot where the road disappeared between the scraggly gums. She yearned to follow; the possibilities of where it might lead made her feel faint.

'Pull over here, do a U-turn please, and we'll head back to the station.'

Alice nodded. She slowed down and flicked the indicator on but spotted double lines in the middle of the road. She turned the indicator off and kept driving.

'Alice?'

She kept her eyes on the road. 'Double lines, Sarge. Illegal.' Alice willed herself to stay calm. 'I'll be turning left up here at Fatty Patty's. We'll head back to the station that way.'

The sergeant tried to stay deadpan but Alice caught the flicker of a smile cross his face. She turned at the fish and chip shop and drove the quiet streets back to the station.

June and Harry were in the car park when Alice pulled in. She beeped repeatedly as she parked.

'Attagirl!' June clapped her hands together. Harry yapped huskily. He was an old dog now.

'I'm driving home!' Alice screeched, punching the air as she followed the sergeant into the station. A short while later Alice walked out with her licence in her pocket. No matter how many times the sergeant had cautioned her to hold a more serious pose, her licence photo was filled with a wide grin.

Alice angled the truck onto Thornfield's driveway and did a careful U-turn in front of the house. She pulled the handbrake up but left the engine running.

'You going somewhere?' June undid her seatbelt, an eyebrow

raised. Harry's eyes darted back and forward. 'Everyone's waiting to see you.'

'I know, I'm just going to pick up Oggi,' Alice said, beaming, 'since I passed and everything.'

The slightest shadow flickered across June's face. 'Of course. Plenty of pancakes for everyone.' She smiled, but her eyes were cold.

Alice drove through town, taking long, cooling breaths until all the things she wished she could say to June stopped burning inside her. Harry panted at her side. The more kilometres she put between herself and Thornfield, the calmer she grew. The closer she got to Oggi, the happier she was. As she'd been ever since she was nine.

When Alice took the last left onto the dirt road just before the town limits sign, Harry started to bark.

'Nearly there.' Alice laughed. Sometimes she thought Harry loved Oggi even more than she did.

She pulled up in front of Oggi's house; he was waiting for her on the verandah. Emotion surged through her with such intensity that she almost expected sparks to fly from her fingers when she reached for the door handle.

'I got it,' she sang, grinning as she swung out of the truck with her licence in her hand. Harry followed.

Oggi's face lit up. Alice wanted to drink it down, that look, the light in his eyes because he loved her.

'I knew you'd pass,' he said, taking her face in his hands, kissing her deeply. Hair fell across his eyes and she drew back to brush it away, the bracelets on her wrist chiming. She'd deliberately picked them from her jewellery box to wear today. *River red gum. Enchantment.*

'Wanna take a ride with me?' she asked, smiling coyly.

'Definitely,' he replied, kissing her again. 'But first, I've got something for you.'

She raised an eyebrow at him before he put one of his hands over her eyes, resting the other on the small of her back.

'Ready?' His lips brushed her ear.

'What are you up to?' She held on to him tightly as he guided her off the verandah.

'Okay. Open.' Oggi took his hand away from her eyes. Alice gasped.

The peeling, mint-green Volkswagen Beetle had a rusted bonnet and was missing one hubcap. Around the rearview mirror was a lei of fiery petals.

'Oggi,' Alice exclaimed. 'How did you do this?' She opened the door and sat in the spongy driver's seat, running her hands over the big, thin steering wheel.

'I worked extra shifts at the timber yard.' He shrugged. 'And ... I might have gotten it for a good price over the bar.'

She burst into laughter. Earlier that year Oggi had picked up night work at the local pub.

'You swindled a drunk out of a car for me?' She leapt up.

'The very least I would do,' he said with a half-smile as he pulled her close.

'But what if I didn't pass my test?'

He ran a fingertip along the bare skin peeking between her singlet and skirt, hooking his finger over her waistband to graze the top of her knickers. Warmth tingled the inside of her thighs.

'I just knew you would,' Oggi replied.

Alice kept her eyes open while she kissed him, wanting to remember everything she could about this moment, wanting to keep it in its wholeness forever; the bright, lucid light, the sound of the butcher birds singing, and the green river flowing behind them. The heat and hunger spreading through her body for the boy, the person, she loved most in her world.

Alice drove home in her new Beetle with Oggi and Harry following in the farm truck. She couldn't believe she was driving a car Oggi had bought for her. It was perfect. The peeling mint-coloured paint, and the solid *thunk* of the doors when she closed them. The big steering wheel, bouncy little seats and springy pedals. Most of all, the rumble and vibration of the engine, so loud she almost couldn't hear the stereo. All the hours of work it must have taken for him to save enough money. All for her. A thrill rippled through her body as she relived moments from the hour they'd just spent by the river. She couldn't get enough of him.

When she pulled up at Thornfield Alice pressed the middle of the steering wheel, laughing at the cheery beep of the Beetle's horn. Oggi pulled up beside her. The Flowers hurried down the path between the house and the workshop to greet them.

'You did it, sweetpea!' Candy squealed, a streak of batter on her chin, wrapping her in a cinnamon-scented hug. The others huddled around, exclaiming over the Beetle.

Twig came up behind them. 'Hey, you did it,' she said. 'Congratulations, Alice.' She kissed Alice's cheek.

'Thanks,' Alice said uncertainly. She searched Twig's eyes. 'What is it, Twig?' she asked.

Twig looked at Oggi and then to Alice. 'June's, um, she's –'

A backfiring motor interrupted them. June drove a restored Morris Minor truck out from behind the house. It was painted a bright and glossy yellow, with white inner rims on polished hubcaps. As June turned to park, Alice read the lettering on the door.

Alice Hart, Floriographer. Thornfield Farm, where wildflowers bloom.

Her heart sank. When Alice turned seventeen, June had started talking about her taking a managerial role at Thornfield once she'd finished school. It wasn't the idea that bothered her as much as the fact that June never asked if it was what she wanted. And it wasn't lost on Alice that June always ignored Oggi in any talk of her future.

'A gift from us all,' June said as she got out of the truck. 'Everyone chipped in.'

'Oh, it's … it's …' Alice faltered. 'It's amazing, June. Everybody. Everyone, thank you so much.'

June met her eye. 'And what's this?' she asked, gesturing to the Beetle.

'You won't b-believe it,' Alice stammered. 'Oggi saved up and bought it for me.'

June's smile didn't waver. 'Oggi,' she snorted. 'What an extraordinary gift for you to give Alice, when you can't afford a car of your own. How lucky we both had the same idea! So, Alice can have the Morris, and Oggi, you can keep the VW. Everyone wins.' She clapped her hands together. 'Well, Candy's spent all morning making a veritable feast …'

'Yes,' Twig said, too loudly, rushing forward. 'Yes, everyone, let's eat.'

As the group turned towards the path, Twig sidled up to Alice. 'Just give her some space,' she cautioned. 'She's been planning that surprise for six months, and she's just taken aback a bit, that's all.'

Alice forced herself to nod. *But why is it always about her?* She wanted to scream.

When Oggi came to her, Alice couldn't bear to look at him. He took her hand and gave it a squeeze. Kept squeezing until she looked up. Despite the humiliation she knew he must be feeling, he winked at her. After a moment, she squeezed his hand in return.

Following a tense brunch, Alice and Oggi slipped out of the house and ran to the river. They sat on the bank. She made a chain out of wildflowers. He polished white river stones on his shirt and skipped them across the water. She felt the intensity of his sidelong glances but she couldn't bring herself to speak. She didn't know what to say. How to apologise for June's behaviour. How to apologise for not standing up for him and his beautiful gift. How to apologise for not standing up for herself. Eventually, he broke the silence.

'She can't get away with it, treating you like this. Like you're just something in her garden that she can tell when to bloom or not.' Oggi didn't look at her.

Alice knotted daisy stems together.

'Sometimes it feels like that,' she said. 'Like I'm just one of the seedlings in her glasshouse. I'll never get out from the protection of her ceiling. My future is written.'

'What do you mean?'

'It feels like my destiny is decided. You know? Like, this is it. I'm where I'll always be.'

'Is that what you want?' He studied her face.

She snorted. 'You know it's not.'

After a long time, he cleared his throat. 'So, I've got another surprise for you.'

Oggi reached into his pocket and took out a dog-eared postcard. Offered it to Alice. She took it from him, and recognised a scene from his stories. The Valley of the Roses.

'The thing is, by the time you turn eighteen next year, we'll have enough saved up for our flights.' He rubbed his thumb over her ring finger, sending warmth up the underside of her arm and into her heart. 'We could fly into Germany and catch the train to Sofia. We could camp under the stars. Drink rakija to keep us warm, and make pear stew from the tree in my grandmother's garden. I could farm roses and you could sell them at the markets.

We could be different people and live different lives. We could be together, just us.' He held both of her hands in his. 'Alice.' His eyes searched her face for her answer.

Alice's lungs expanded with longing for lands covered in snow, cobblestoned cities, and rose gardens that grew from the bones of kings. She didn't understand why Oggi was laughing until she realised she was nodding.

'Yes,' she said as he drew her close. 'Yes,' she laughed, into his ear. He wrapped his arms around her, shaking slightly. The sun speckled Alice's face with warm light. Oggi kissed her forehead and her cheeks and her lips. He named more places they would go and things they would do in their new life. Together.

Candy put the last of the brunch dishes away and made herself a black coffee. She drank it watching the Flowers milling in the fields, checking the new blooms. Their usual babble and laughter was thin. Something frosty had settled over Thornfield. After brunch, Oggi and Alice had slipped away, thinking they'd gone unnoticed. June had stalked into her workshop, slamming the door behind her. Twig went to the seedling houses to tend her trays of desert peas. And Candy scrubbed the dishes with steel wool until her knuckles were raw.

It was no longer ignorable: the days of Alice's childhood were long gone. Neither Twig, Candy nor June talked about how difficult it was to see Agnes's hopefulness and Clem's wildness in the depths of Alice's eyes. Sometimes, when Alice passed her in the house or in the fields, Candy's first instinct was to look to the sky for smoke; she could swear she smelled something catching alight.

Even though she'd never heard from Clem after he'd left with Agnes, Candy had never broken their promise. She was there, her life sewn to his, only now through his daughter, who was fast becoming a woman with her own mind. A woman who didn't seem to have inherited Clem's demons, who seemed to be breaking free of Thornfield's story. Something Candy had never managed.

She drank the last of her coffee, grimacing as she swallowed the bitter grinds. She might be thirty-four, but she was still nine, the girl in a cubby house made of sticks, bound to a shadow that was never coming home.

When the afternoon began to soften, Alice ran home from the river. Her fingertips tingled for her pen and journal. How would she write about this day? Everything was luminous: the yellow wings of Cleopatra butterflies as they fluttered over the bushes and flowers; the air sharpened by the smell of lemon-scented gum leaves crushed under her footsteps; the golden quality of the light. Oggi's voice rang in her ears. *We could be different people and live different lives.*

As she ran, June's face filled her thoughts. What would her leaving Thornfield do to June? Guilt pinched hard between her ribs.

Alice slowed to catch her breath and tried to push June's face away. When she picked up her pace again, her heartbeat and footsteps were back in sync.

15

Blue lady orchid

Meaning: **Consumed by love**
Thelymitra crinita | Western Australia

> *Perennial spring-flowering orchid. Flowers are intensely blue and form a delicate star shape. Does not need a bushfire to stimulate flowering, but can be smothered by other vegetation, so periodic burns to restrict taller-growing shrubs are beneficial.*

That year, leading up to Alice's eighteenth birthday, Twig saw what no one else at Thornfield did. Night after night she sat in the shadows and watched as the back screen door swept open and Alice, with her long hair streaming behind her, crept across the verandah, down the steps, and into the blooming flower fields under the moonlight. Twig sat smoking long after Alice's silvered silhouette disappeared into the bush. Although she knew June wanted Alice to be different, to be immune, the truth was on the path that led to the river for anyone to see: Alice was deeply, wildly, blindly in the thick of first love.

The night Alice turned eighteen, after the fancy roast and second helpings of the tiered vanilla lily cake that Candy baked, everyone went to bed tipsy from the crate of Moët that June ordered in specially. Twig sat on the back verandah rolling a smoke, grateful for the silence of the winter stars. Things were changing. You could smell it in the air like a new season. Alice was unsettled. As was Twig over the lies she'd told Alice every time Alice had asked about her family. Although she'd fought against June's dishonesty,

Twig was complicit; she too had kept secrets from Alice for nearly as long as June had.

When the form Twig had filled out and returned to the state adoption services led to nothing, she'd gone back to the Yellow Pages and picked up the phone. She gave the first private investigator to answer her call the name of the woman Agnes noted in her will, and the name of the town where Alice grew up. Not long after Alice had started school the investigator's report arrived by mail. Twig had to walk all the way to the river before she calmed down enough to read it. Alice's baby brother was healthy and well, in the care of the woman Agnes instructed should be the guardian of her children if June was not fit or able to raise them. Alice and her brother were living without each other, unaware – were Nina and Johnny the same? Contrary to common belief, Twig knew that not even Thornfield could save a woman from her past. She'd made a good life there, raising Candy, and she'd done her best with Clem. She'd cared for Agnes and the rest of the Flowers, managing the farm and running a good business. But the truth was that no amount of second chances, not even at Thornfield, could change the past, no matter how much June wished it were so. Twig's relationship with June had never been the same since June came home with only Alice in the truck. *I'm the executor of the will, Twig,* she'd drunkenly hissed over the years, more times than Twig could count. *I made the hard choice that was in everyone's best interests.* Twig hid the investigator's report and a secret copy of Agnes's will in the seedling house. She'd waited nine years for the right moment to give them to Alice. Still they stayed hidden, among desert pea seedlings.

When the screen door opened, Twig shrank into the shadows, watching Alice creep into the flower fields, a faint trail of champagne in the air behind her. Alice had drunk flute after flute at dinner. Something was brewing in her life, Twig could sense it as well as any shift in the weather. She counted silently, waiting a whole minute to be sure Alice wouldn't hear her footsteps, before she hurried down the path to the river, following her.

Oggi was waiting on the riverbank, with a small fire burning by the giant river gum. He'd been especially quiet at dinner. Twig crouched behind a cluster of skinny iron bark trees. Alice flung herself at him as if she'd not seen him for years, their skin painted bronze by the firelight. They kissed tenderly. The look on Oggi's face at the sight of Alice caused Twig's eyes to well. She'd loved someone like that once. She remembered how it felt to be so clearly seen by another person, to be so unbroken.

They drew apart and Alice sat leaning against him, cradled in his arms. 'Tell me the plan again.'

He kissed the top of her head. 'We meet tomorrow at midnight, right here. We bring one suitcase each. That's it. We travel light.' He kissed her temple, her cheek, her neck. 'We catch the first bus to the city airport, and pick up our tickets. We fly for so long you'll think we're never going to land, but we will, in Sofia, where we'll go to my grandparents' house, drink rakija, eat shopska salata, sleep off our jet lag, wake up and catch the cable car up Mount Vitosha, to stand on the lake of stones and look out over the world. We'll walk the goats in the mornings. The bells on their collars sound better than Christmas Day. On the weekends, we'll take my grandfather's truck and drive across the border to Greece, where we'll swim in the sea, and eat olives and grilled cheese.'

'Oggi,' Alice whispered dreamily, turning to him. 'Do you have your pocketknife?'

They carved their names into the trunk of the gum tree, then fell into one another, kissing with the hunger of adolescence. The child who came to Thornfield, so silent, so wrought with horror, was more alive than Twig had ever seen her.

Twig stood silently and shook out the cramps in her legs, then crept back to the path and followed it home. Inside the seedling house, she unearthed the plastic pouch of yellowed papers holding the truth of Alice's life, then went into the house to wait for Alice to return.

She sat on the couch. Thought about making a coffee. Closed her eyes for just a minute.

It was a regret Twig would carry from that day on, sinking into a sleep so deep that she didn't hear the floorboards creak when Alice came in.

The next morning, Alice was out running a delivery into town when June came downstairs. Twig was in the kitchen making her mid-morning cuppa and turned to offer June one, but stopped short. June stood in the doorway, Alice's journal dangling open in one hand.

'June?' Twig eyed the journal, its pages filled with the loops and curls of Alice's handwriting.

June walked slowly out the back. For a while she sat on the verandah staring into the flower field. Twig set a cup of tea down beside her. Cockatoos screeched overhead. June didn't speak.

For the rest of the morning Twig busied herself with the Flowers, keeping them all out of June's way. Even Harry gave her a wide berth. Every now and then Twig would glance at June on the back verandah. Whether she'd made her peace with it or not, June had been changed forever by Alice's arrival as a child. Now Alice was grown, on the cusp of independence, and in love; as June herself knew, there wasn't much in the world more threatening than a woman who knew her own mind.

It was mid-afternoon when June moved. Twig hovered, expecting June to go to the workshop or get in her truck. Instead she walked inside, into the study, and closed the door behind her. Twig followed and pressed her ear to the door. She could hear June's voice but couldn't make out what she was saying. After a long pause, Twig knocked. Once, then again, harder. She tried the doorknob and it twisted open. As she walked in, June hung up the phone. The look on June's face stopped Twig mid-stride.

'What have you done?' Twig asked flatly.

Behind her desk, June turned to look out through the window as Alice's truck puttered into the driveway. They both watched Alice and Oggi get out of the truck, and come together by the workshop, talking and laughing.

'What I had to do,' June replied. A tear rolled down her cheek.

It was years since Twig had seen June cry. The absence of the smell of whisky in the room only caused her more alarm.

June roughly wiped her cheeks and stood. 'What I had to do,' she said again. 'All right, Twig?' She stood, as if trying to hide something from Twig's view.

'What's going on?' Twig asked, taking a step forward.

In a fluster, June tried to sweep the stack of letters on her desk into a drawer, but only managed to scatter them across the floor. She swore under her breath. Twig crouched, gathering letter after letter and photo after photo, all of the same little boy. She turned to face June. 'How could you keep these from her?' she whispered.

'Because I know what's best for her,' June snapped. 'I'm her grandmother.'

Twig stood and glared at June, the letters shaking in her fists. Without another word, she threw them at June and left, slamming the door after her. Outside, it was windy. Twig leant against the verandah, taking long, cooling breaths. Alice and Oggi were mucking about by the workshop, teasing each other.

As she watched them, Twig braced her arms over her chest where the wind cut through her clothes. She could feel it in her bones; a northwesterly had blown in.

Alice eased her bedroom door open and stood at the top of the winding staircase, listening. The only sounds in the house were the rhythmic ticking of the grandfather clock and the muffled snores from June's bedroom. A sudden heaviness weighed on Alice's body. She remembered the night she arrived, unable to speak and barely able to hold her head up under the weight of sorrow. June had washed her face with a hot facecloth. *I'm not going anywhere*, she'd said. And that was the truth. She'd always been right there. At the end of a school day, over flowers in the garden, at the head of the dinner table, in the workshop overseeing Alice's bouquet arrangements. Alice thought of June's hands, their tough calluses, holding the steering wheel, waving at the gate, ruffling Harry's ears, holding Alice tight. Too tight.

With one last glance around her room, Alice picked up her suitcase and crept down the stairs as if she were made of the same ghostly vapour as the Thornfield memories from which she was so desperate to disentangle herself.

Alice tiptoed down the hall. Harry's collar tinkled in the lounge room as he twitched on his bed. She knelt down to kiss his head. Even in slumber he kept her secrets.

Her hands shook as she opened the screen door. She took a deep breath of the fragrant night. When she stepped off the verandah onto the dirt, Alice broke into a run.

The scrub scratched her bare ankles as she stumbled in the dark through the bush. Tears streaked from her eyes, but she pushed on. The night was cold, dry and full of cicada song. Light from the moon cast the world in milky light. Her future glowed ahead of her, an ember waiting to be breathed to life.

Alice reached the river. She put her suitcase down. Wiped her brow. In the moonlight she studied the names etched into the gum tree of the women in her family, who'd sat at that very spot and cast their dreams into the river. She ran her fingers over her own name, and Oggi's, and smelled the scent of cut wood on her fingertips, remembering when she was a child and first came to the river, thinking she might follow it all the way home. Instead, the river had brought Oggi to her. He was her home now. He was her story.

She arranged herself neatly on the smooth grey rock at the base of the gum and listened for Oggi's footsteps. Lifted her locket from under the neckline of her shirt. 'I'm here,' she whispered, looking at her mother's face. She wrapped her scarf around her body, and propped herself up against the trunk of the gum tree.

Alice leaned her head back, watching for falling stars.

She waited.

A squawk of galahs woke her. She had a pain in her neck, and her skin was damp. Wincing, she straightened herself, shivering. The river churned in the cold light of morning.

His name sprang to her lips. Alice stood and scrambled over the grey rocks and tree roots by the riverbank. No notes wedged between the stones, nothing tied in the low branches of the tree. Maybe he was waiting for her at the flower farm. A cackle rose from the trees as kookaburras started their early morning chorus. Alice left her suitcase and ran, cutting through the long grass and trees, trying to outrun the pit of fear in her stomach.

When she got back to Thornfield, the Flowers were in their aprons, dotting the fields as they tended to the plants. Alice began to weep. She went up the back steps and into the kitchen. June was standing at the counter, drinking coffee.

'Morning, love. What can I get you? Toast? Cuppa?'

'Is he here?' she asked, her voice breaking.

'Who?' June asked calmly.

'You know who,' she said, exasperated.

'Oggi?' June put her mug down, frowning. 'Alice,' she said, coming around the counter to embrace her. 'Alice, what is it?'

'Where is he?' she cried.

'At home, I expect, getting ready for work as you should be,' June said, looking Alice up and down in her crumpled dress. 'What's going on?'

Alice wrenched herself out of June's arms, grabbed her keys off the wall hook and ran to her truck.

Panic coiled around her body as she sped through town. She pulled hard left down Oggi's driveway, her truck fishtailing on the loose dirt track until she lurched to a stop at the house.

On the porch were two chairs, either side of the small table, with a fresh rose in a vase on top, as if any moment Boryana might swing open the door and come out offering a pot of tea.

Alice ran to the front door, expecting it to be locked. It opened without resistance. Inside, nothing was out of the ordinary. No sign of trouble. No evidence of chaos, crisis or any reason that would have stopped him from meeting her at the river. She wandered through the house. It looked lived in and welcoming but something wasn't right. It was too neat. Or maybe she just didn't want to admit the deeper truth and most obvious answer. He'd taken Boryana home to Bulgaria; he'd changed his mind and gone without Alice. The wind was hollow as it whistled through the house.

Around the back, the rose garden was resplendent. Alice thought of rose valleys grown from gold and the bones of kings, a sea of petals the colour of fire. She snapped rose heads off their stems and tore them apart, scattering the petals at her feet.

He left without her.

Alice was standing among torn petals when June pulled up. She didn't feel her knees give out. When she came to she was crumpled on the dirt, cradled in June's arms. The smell of June's skin, freshly tilled earth, whisky and peppermints.

'You fainted, Alice. You're okay, I've got you,' June soothed.

'He left without me.' She began to sob.

June tightened her embrace, rocking back and forth.

The two of them sat that way for a long time, until Alice's cries quietened to hiccups.

'Let's go home.' June rubbed Alice's arms gently. Alice nodded.

They helped each other up, dusted themselves off and walked around the house, each to their truck. Alice drove slowly back to Thornfield. June followed at a close distance.

When they got home Alice ran straight upstairs to her room. June let her go. *She must be exhausted.* June pushed the thought away of Alice waiting all night for Oggi. What was done was done, to keep her granddaughter safe. It was for the best. *It was for the best*, she repeated more firmly to herself. She opened the screen door and let it sweep shut behind her. It was done. Alice was here. She was in pain, but it was the kind of pain she was young enough to get over. She was safe. She was close enough for June to keep her safe.

June went to the fridge and poured herself a glass of cold soda water. She took a lemon from the chiller drawer and sliced it into wedges, dropping two into her drink. She went quickly to the liquor cabinet and took down the whisky, unscrewed the cap and filled the glass. After stirring it with her pinky she stood at the sink, gulping it down.

Soon Thornfield would be under Alice's care. That was the next step. A heartbroken young girl was as vulnerable as a timber house without a firebreak in bushfire season; any spark could consume her. Just as June saw Agnes, an orphan, consumed by

Clem. And there was Alice, made of them both. When a look crossed Alice's face that was so like Clem's, it drove June to her flask before breakfast. Other times her gentle and whimsical nature made it seem as if Agnes had arrived at Thornfield all over again.

June couldn't bear it. She would not make the same mistake twice; she would not lose her family again. She'd done what was necessary to make sure of that. What Alice needed now was distraction and independence. A sense of worth, purpose and freedom. Which was exactly what June planned on giving her.

Alice dug and cut at the trunk of the river red gum until her wrist ached from the effort. She'd returned to the river every night for a week. The more days that went by without answers, or Oggi himself turning up to deliver them, the more Alice felt cursed by the river and all its secret stories. Starting with the name at the top of the list on the tree trunk, Ruth Stone.

Over the years Alice had learned barely anything about Ruth beyond what Candy told her when she was nine: Ruth Stone brought the language of flowers to Thornfield and grew it from the earth with the Australian native flower seeds her doomed lover gave her. Whenever Alice asked Twig and Candy about Ruth, they told her to ask June, but then when Alice did that, June was evasive. *Ruth Stone is how Thornfield has survived*, she'd say, or something equally cryptic, like, *It's because of Ruth that you'll one day own this land*. Alice always wanted to retort what a ridiculous thing it was, anyone thinking they owned dirt or trees or flowers or the river. But she'd always been distracted by a more niggling thought. *What about my father?* she asked June once. *Shouldn't he have taken over Thornfield from you?* June didn't answer.

Even though June had written in Alice's tenth birthday letter that if Alice found her voice, June would find answers, she never offered to talk about Clem. Or Agnes. Or how they'd got together or why they'd left. Everything Alice pieced together about her parents and what happened between June and her father was through half-truths. She knew her family's story was buried in the earth from which June grew flowers to say the things that were too hard to speak; if only Alice knew where to dig. Only by pestering the Flowers for hours on end was Alice able to cobble together one simple truth: not even June was immune when it came to fate and love. Both had eaten parts of her life whole, and spat out what remained to make the woman she was today. June's father died when she was young, and both her lover and their son had left her. Every time June had loved a man it had broken her heart. Alice was bound to June by blood and grief, and now, by the fate of waiting on a promise, only to be left broken by the river.

Alice hacked at the tree trunk with her pocketknife, scratching Oggi's name from the bark. She cut into the letters of his name, his smile, his good heart and kind nature. When she was done she threw her pocketknife and any stones she could find into the river.

She dropped to the dirt and curled into a ball, sobbing. She would never let love make such a fool of her again.

June watched Alice through the window as she returned from the river. She walked heavily, carrying her sorrow, her face as haggard as when she was nine years old and June had brought her home from the hospital. But at least she was there. June hadn't lost her.

Alice came in the back door. June busied herself making a cup of tea.

'June,' Alice started, but didn't finish her sentence.

June turned to face her. Opened her arms. Alice studied her, as if she was weighing something up in her mind, before stepping forward into June's embrace.

While she held her granddaughter in her arms, June thought about her most-loved Thornfield Dictionary entry, Sturt's desert pea, and its meaning. *Have courage, take heart*, Ruth Stone had entered in her spidery handwriting. June had learned everything she could about Sturt's desert pea from her mother, and her books. How fragile and difficult it was to propagate, despite growing wild in some of Australia's harshest landscapes. But how, under the right conditions, it always came into blazing bloom.

Landscape is destiny

Alice Hoffman

16

Gorse bitter pea

Meaning: Ill-natured beauty

Daviesia ulicifolia | All states

*Spiny shrub with stunning yellow and red pea flowers. Blooms
in summer. Easy propagation from seed, following scarification.
Seed retains viability for many years. Unpopular with gardeners
for its very prickly habit, but beneficial to small birds as
a refuge from predators.*

Alice stood on the back verandah watching the afternoon sky
darken over the flower fields. She burrowed her face into the folds
of her scarf. Storms frightened her at twenty-six as much as they
had when she was nine.

February was a scatty month for everyone at Thornfield. Hot
summer windstorms blew in from the northwest and caused
havoc, threatening to tear up the flower fields and batter the
hoop houses and vegetable garden. Days on end of dry heat and
raging winds were almost unbearable; they stirred up the dust
and ashes of things long forgotten, and roused old hurts and
unspoken stories from where they slept in forgotten corners,
dreams and unfinished books. On sweltering nights, nightmares
were rife. By mid-February, no woman at Thornfield was left
unshaken.

For Alice, the worst thing was the wind that howled through
the flower fields calling her name. The erratic weather always
brought back the fateful day she snuck into her father's shed.

She lifted her locket from beneath her work shirt. Her mother's
eyes looked up at her in grainy black and white. Alice could still

remember their colour: the way they changed in the light; the way they lit up when she told stories; how far away they were when she was in her garden, filling her pockets with flowers.

Alice kicked her boots together as she watched the flower fields shaken by the crosswinds. She told herself she could never have left Thornfield, the place where her mother found safety and solace, where she learned to speak in flowers. The place where her parents met and, Alice liked to believe, for a time loved each other the way she loved Oggi.

As had become instinct, Alice buried the thought of Oggi. She didn't allow herself to think what if? What if she went after him when he didn't show up at the river that night? What if she made her own way to the Valley of Roses? What if she found him, and what if they made completely new plans? What if she studied at university overseas, somewhere like Oxford – where she'd read the buildings were made of sandstone the colour of honey – rather than by correspondence at June's kitchen table? What if she'd said no to June, back when she turned eighteen, and didn't agree to take over Thornfield? What if she never went into her father's shed? What if her mother had left her father and raised Alice at Thornfield, with Candy and Twig and June? With Alice's younger sibling?

What if, what if, what if?

Alice checked her watch. June and some of the Flowers had gone to the city flower markets the day before and were due back that afternoon, but if Alice waited any longer to help them unload, she would miss the post office. Business was picking up again after Christmas, and there were crates of mail orders to send out; June's jewellery was as popular as ever.

Alice went through the house and stopped by the front door to put her Akubra on. A funnel of ochre dust whirled at the bottom of the steps. She pushed the screen door open slowly.

'Dust devil,' she whispered.

It swayed for a moment, almost a man's broad shape and stature, then dispersed and scattered. Alice exhaled roughly, reminding herself it was February, a time when the past blew in and ghosts were everywhere.

She climbed into her truck, relieved at the calm inside. She glanced at the passenger seat, wishing for Harry's company. While Alice was still adjusting to the enormity of his absence, Harry's death had driven June to the blatant comfort of her whisky bottle, without restraint or secrecy.

It was the latest tipping point. As June got older she grew increasingly agitated, set off by the smallest thing, whether it was the mail arriving, a westerly blowing or the Cootamundra wattle coming into flower. Occasionally Alice heard her muttering Clem's name, and she'd taken to making jewellery only from flowers that told stories of loss and mourning. More and more often June's eyes focused on something far away, something Alice couldn't see. What was she remembering? Was she finally grieving Alice's father? Every time Alice thought about asking June such things, silence was easier. Silence, and flowers. Sometimes she'd leave them on June's workbench. A handful of mauve fairy flowers: *I feel your kindness*. June would always leave her reply on Alice's pillow. A bunch of tinsel lilies: *You please all*.

Alice sat in the truck, looking at the spotted gums, the house, the vine-covered workshop, the wheaten grass, the wildflowers growing in the cracks between rocks. Thornfield had become her whole life. Speaking through flowers had become the language she most relied on.

She sighed heavily and turned the key in the ignition. The sky was darkening. As she drove off Alice watched Thornfield shrink in the distance in her rearview mirror.

Thunder rumbled as Alice pulled up and began unloading the mail order crates. She trolleyed them into the post office and collected her mail. When she came back out the afternoon light had turned eerily green. A flash of lightning sent Alice scurrying into the driver's seat. She started the engine and distracted herself from the jitters in her stomach by shuffling through her stack of mail. Bank statements, phone bills, invoices, advertising junk. And a handwritten envelope. Addressed to her personally. Alice flicked it over. The return address was Bulgarian.

She tore the envelope open. Scanned the inky black scrawl too fast, taking in only every third or fourth word. At the bottom was his name, written by his hand. *Oggi.*

She started from the top, forcing herself to read slowly, to take in every word.

Zdravey Alice,

I've lost count of how many times I've tried writing this letter to you. I could probably fill a box with my attempts, letters full of things I don't have the courage to tell you. But the cliché is true: time does something to pain that nothing else can. Enough years seem to have passed now. This is the letter I'm going to write to you and actually send.

If I'm honest, ever since the night we were meant to meet at the river, you have always been on my mind. I've seen on the internet that you've taken the reins of Thornfield and under your care business is flourishing. I've seen your profile picture update over the years. I can see the girl I remember, in your eyes.

But that was a long time ago. We are different people now. We have different lives.

I live and work in Sofia with my wife, Lilia. Five years ago, we had a daughter. Her name is Iva. She's a lot like you were when we were kids. She's wild and adventurous, dreamy and sensitive, and she loves books. Especially fairytales. Her favourite is a famous Bulgarian story about a good, naïve wolf, and a cheeky, cunning fox. The moral is that tricky people will always try to abuse your weaknesses if you let them. Iva asks me to read it over and over. I read it as many times as I can stand to; Iva always cries for the wolf. She always asks me why the wolf can't see how cunning the fox really is. I never know how to answer her.

After so many years, I'm writing to you now to close the wound. I want you to be happy. After everything that happened, I wish you a good life.

Take care of yourself. Take care at Thornfield.

Vsichko nai-hubavo, Alice. All the best.

Oggi

Alice bit her bottom lip, hard. Dropped the letter and leant over the steering wheel to watch lightning ripple through the storm clouds. A flock of galahs screeched from the silver-green crown of a gum. The road ahead beckoned, leading out of town. How she longed to know where it might take her. What if she followed it right then and didn't stop? The burden of her unrealised dreams hung heavily from her ribs, flattened by the weight of her sighs. She imagined them like pressed flowers, each one squashed while it was still blooming, a keepsake of what might have been. Kicking the door hard, she wiped her tears away and threw the truck into gear. The truth was she had only herself to blame. For not going after Oggi. For not leaving when she had the chance. Why had she stayed? This was the life she'd made, throwing herself into the tending of land that grew secrets and flowers alike. That she would own one day, that she didn't want a square inch of.

She picked up his letter again, groaning in distress as she skimmed over the lines.

I can see the girl I remember in your eyes. But that was a long time ago. We are different people now. We have different lives.

Before she fully understood what she was doing, Alice flattened her foot on the accelerator, her tyres spitting up stones. On a whim, instead of turning home, she went in the opposite direction, down Main Street. Pulled sharp left onto the dirt track almost obscured by bushes. Pushed through the dense overgrowth down the avenue of gums until she reached Oggi's old house. She hadn't been back for eight years.

When she drove into the clearing Alice gasped. She swung out of her truck, into the brewing storm. Ognian roses had consumed the house. They crept up the sides, covering the walls and the roof. Everywhere Alice looked, the wild bushes were in full bloom, a house smothered by a fire of roses. The fragrance was overpowering.

Alice shouted his name, to no one. The wind stung her face. She paced back and forth. For eight years he'd known where she was and what she was doing with her life. Eight years it had taken him to write to her. But still he didn't give her answers. Why didn't he come to meet her that night by the river? What happened to him? Why did he wait so long to contact her? What didn't he have the courage to tell her? How could he bear living the life they'd planned together with a different woman? Why did he use so much of his letter to tell Alice about his daughter's favourite fairytale? He'd known where she was, all of this time, while she'd known nothing of him, not even if he was okay; over the years she had searched for his name on the internet but found nothing. For Alice, it was as if Oggi was something she had dreamed.

The wind tore roses from their stems, scattering them at Alice's feet. She scooped up a handful of petals and ripped them to pieces. She lunged at the rose-covered house, tearing at the vines, cutting herself on thorns. She tore and grabbed and cried, swept into a rampage of rage and grief and humiliation.

A sudden downpour of cold rain broke her trance. Alice stood stunned as she came back into her senses. Ran to her truck, drenched. The rain splattered heavily on her windscreen. She sat catching her breath. Watched the house through the wipers.

A spear of lightning struck the bush nearby, followed by a huge crack as a gum bough crashed to the ground. Alice shrieked and spun her truck around. She drove off, rose petals clinging to her wet skin.

When Alice got back to Thornfield, everyone was in a frenzy, securing the house, dorm and workshop, tying things down and ferrying anything untethered inside. The rain had eased but the gale was cutting. She pushed through the wind, up the front steps to the verandah.

'What's going on?' Alice asked June, shielding her puffy eyes.

'The storm,' June yelled. 'We raced it the whole way back from the city. Weather report says cyclonic floods.'

'Floods?' Alice looked in dread at the flower fields.

'That's what they're saying. We need to move, Alice. Now.'

The rain didn't let up. They worked hard to secure the farm, but there was only so much they could do to protect the garden beds from the whim of the wind and rain sobbing down. The power cut out not long after sunset. The dorm windows were filled with the light of lanterns and candles, as was the dining room in the house. Candy, Twig, June and Alice sat at the table eating leftover cassava curry Candy reheated on the gas camping stove.

'You all right, sweetpea?' Candy asked, offering Alice a bowl of chopped coriander. 'You're very quiet.'

Alice declined with a wave of her fork. 'Just the storm.' Oggi's words circled in her thoughts. Something about the fairytale his daughter loved niggled her. She threw her cutlery on the table in frustration, its clatter louder than she intended. 'Sorry,' she said, pressing her fingers to her temples. The wind sucked under the doors and rattled the glass in the windows. The storm was strengthening. Was Thornfield in danger? 'God, I feel like I can't breathe.' Alice pushed her chair back. She stood and paced the floor.

'Alice?' June's face was lined with worry. 'What is it?'

'Nothing,' Alice said sharply, waving June's concern away. She squeezed her eyes shut before tears could well. Tried to push the image of fire roses smothering Oggi's house away.

'It's not just the storm, and it's not nothing, Alice. What's the matter?' Twig asked.

Alice recalled the falling bough crashing to earth at Oggi's house. 'What aren't you telling me?' she blurted. 'What don't I know?'

'What?' June's face paled.

'I don't know. I just, I don't …' Alice shook her head. 'I'm sorry.' She exhaled and closed her eyes briefly. 'I got a letter out of the blue from Oggi today and I'm upset.' She glanced up. Candy's eyes darted between Twig and June. Twig's stayed calmly on Alice. June's face was unreadable.

'What did he say?' Twig put her fork down.

'Not a lot.' Alice shook her head. 'Just that he wanted to close "old wounds" with me. He's married and a father. He wants me to "have a good life".' Alice's voice cracked. 'But he didn't say why he left me here, or what happened to make him go. And I just don't understand … I don't know how I got here, how my life has come to this.' She took a deep, ragged breath. 'I don't know who I'm meant to be or where I'm meant to belong …' she trailed off. 'And now there's fucking cyclonic floods coming, and I'm scared. I don't know who I am without this place. What's going to happen if we lose the flowers? Why don't we talk more? About anything? I'm so sick of everything we don't say to each other. I want to know stuff. I want to have an actual conversation rather than get a bouquet of flowers every time I get too close to the bone. I want to know, June,' she begged, turning to face her grandmother. 'I want to hear it from you. All of it. About my parents. And where I come from. I just have this enormous sense of, of ...' she trailed off in frustration, making empty circles in the air with her hands. 'Of waiting, for something that's just never going to come. You said that if I found my voice, June, you'd find your answers ...' Her shoulders sagged in despair.

Shadows hung from June's cheekbones. 'Alice,' she said, standing to take a step towards her. Alice searched her eyes, hopefully. The rain howled outside.

'I'm not going anywhere. You've got me,' June said in a small voice.

Alice's disappointment was stinging. 'That's your answer for everything, isn't it,' she said bitterly. 'Sweep it all away, because I've got you.' Watching the sharp edges of her words cut into her grandmother, Alice winced. 'I'm sorry,' she said, regaining her composure. 'I'm sorry, June.'

'No,' June mumbled. 'No, you're quite right to be angry.' She folded her napkin and left the room. After a moment Twig slid back her chair and followed.

Alice put her head in her hands. June only ever tried to look after her. Why couldn't she just let her and leave it be? But another question rose. Why couldn't June just tell her what she wanted to know? For that matter, why couldn't Oggi? If he was going to go to the effort of writing her a letter after eight years, with a well-established life and family of his own, why would he hold anything back from her?

Candy started to clear the table.

'I'm sorry,' Alice said again.

Candy nodded. 'It's no one's fault, sweetpea. Everyone's got their sad stories. Sure is the case here, always has been. It's what our flowers grow from.' She fidgeted with the cutlery. 'June's got so many stories tangled up inside her, I believe she doesn't know where to start.'

Alice groaned. 'With the simplest things? With, "Alice, this is how your parents met", or "Alice, this is why your father left", or "Alice, this is who your grandfather was".'

'I get that. But she probably thinks that if she tells one story, she's got to tell ten that are connected. Pull one root up and the whole plant is at risk. The thought must terrify her. Can you imagine? Being faced with those odds, when you're someone who loves control as much as June?' Candy paused at the doorway with the bouquet of forks in one hand and a kerosene lantern in the other. 'It must be awful carrying around the burden of wanting so much to tell someone something, something they should know, but that frightens the pants off you because you have to go somewhere inside you don't want to go, to find that story you damn well know you can't rewrite.'

'But where does that leave me? The one person I have left in my family won't tell me about our family. I've only got secondhand stories, and as much as I cherish anything you, or Twig, or even Oggi told me about this place and my parents, it's not the same as hearing it from June. You don't have the same stories she does.'

'No, we don't,' Candy said. 'But like I've always said to you, at least you have a story, sweetpea. At least you can know where you come from. Don't overlook what a gift –'

'I don't,' Alice interrupted, struggling to keep her voice steady. 'I know you mean well, Candy, but I'm getting pretty sick of being palmed off with advice to be grateful for the story I have, as a way of avoiding the stories I don't. Stories that June promised when I was a kid that she'd tell me. And never has.'

The room filled with the sound of heavy rain. After a while Candy cleared her throat.

'I'm really sorry about Oggi.'

Alice didn't respond.

As she walked out of the room, Candy took most of the light with her.

That night, Alice tossed and turned in a fiery sea of dreams. Over and over again, she tried to scream for her mother who'd left her clothes on shore. Over and over again, the sea of fire would not yield her. On the scorched beach a wolf and fox chased each other through the dunes, their tails on fire. In the shallows a boy sailed a paper boat, its edges charred and burning. After starting awake in a cold sweat, Alice got up. Her temples pounded from anxious exhaustion. She clicked on her torch and went downstairs to make a cup of tea.

In the hallway she came to a halt. Voices drifted from the kitchen and the air was thick with whisky. Alice inched closer.

'You are this close to losing her, June,' Twig hissed. 'Is that what you want? You have to tell her the truth. You have to tell her.'

'Shufth up, Twig,' June slurred.

Alice crept along the wall.

'You think you know iss all buts you don't know shit. You're juss another one who knows all the stories and think you know erryfink.'

'I can't talk to you like this. You need to go to bed.'

'I see how much you love her, you think I don't? You thinks I dunno she's one of the chil'ren you couldn't raise?'

'Be careful, June.'

'Oooooh, "be careful, June".' June hiccupped.

Alice stood at the doorway.

'I saved that girl,' June hissed, drawing herself together. 'I saved her. Oggi would only have stolen her future, and broken her heart. We've seen it all before, Twig. Don't say we haven't. That day I called Immigration was the best thing I've ever done for her.'

The shock of June's betrayal went through Alice as though she'd been physically struck. She would remember that night as if she had been watching through the windows rather than embodied in the moment. The way she flew into the kitchen, her eyes aflame and her hands shaking. The horror and regret in Twig's eyes when she realised Alice had overheard them. June's drunken smile as she tried to keep her composure. Alice's shouting. Twig's attempts to comfort her. June's crying. The deep sorrow in Twig's eyes as she told Alice the truth.

'He was deported.' Twig's voice wavered. 'He and Boryana were sent back to Bulgaria.'

Seething, Alice turned to look at June. 'You reported them?' she shrieked. June squared her chin, her eyes unable to focus.

'What's going on?' Candy asked as she hurried into the kitchen, her face creased with sleep.

A surge of adrenalin jolted Alice into action. She fled from the kitchen, up the stairs and into her room. She lunged for her backpack and stuffed it with anything she laid eyes on that she cared about. Ran down the stairs, pushed past the women in the hallway and wrenched her keys and hat off their hooks. Alice threw open the front door and was knocked back by the force of the wind and rain. She stumbled to regain her balance. Twig and Candy pleaded with her not to leave. The next scene always played out in her mind the same way, slow and distorted: she turned to see their faces, so full of worry. Behind them, June swayed in the shadows.

Alice glowered at the three women. After a moment she turned and pushed herself into the storm, slamming the door behind her.

The windscreen wipers couldn't keep up with the torrential rain. Alice gripped the steering wheel as her truck aquaplaned on the muddy, flooded road, her arms shaking from the strain. She kept her foot down on the accelerator, fearful that if she let up she might get stuck or, worse, lose her nerve and turn around.

She planned to go straight through town. Past the town limits sign and into the bushland, heading east. But only a few kilometres down the road she slammed her foot on the brake: in the beam of her headlights a low-lying dip in the highway was lost under rising floodwater. The river had burst. Alice hung her head. The flower fields would be destroyed; the seeds washed clean out of the beds.

She studied the blackness of her rearview mirror. What if she didn't go east towards the coast, but went inland? Away from water. She revved the engine. Another moment passed. Alice wrenched on the steering wheel and sped back the way she'd come. At the turn-off to Thornfield her foot faltered on the accelerator. She pressed it to the floor, tightening her hold on the steering wheel, racing west into the darkness.

No matter how much Twig and Candy cried and begged, June refused to come back inside. She swayed on the spot, in the dark, lashed by the weather. Alice would come back. June kept her eyes fixed straight ahead, so she'd be right there the minute she saw Alice's headlights. Alice would come back. And then June could explain.

The whisky in her blood was thinning; she was beginning to feel the needling cold. When the next gust hit, June fell to her knees. The front door swung open and Twig rushed out with a coat.

'Get up, June,' she yelled over the wind. 'Get up and get your sorry arse inside.' Twig threw the coat around her and helped her to her feet.

'No. She's coming back, and I'll be right here when she does.' June trembled. 'Alice will come home, and then I'll explain everything.'

Twig glared at her. June braced for a scathing reply.

They stood that way for a while, close but separate from each other, until Twig put her arm around June. And, as the sky sobbed down on them, turned with her to face the driving rain.

17

Showy banksia

Meaning: I am your captive

Banksia speciosa | Western Australia and South Australia

Small tree that has thin leaves with prominent 'teeth'.
Cream-yellow flower spikes appear throughout the year, which
store seeds until opened by fire. The flowers attract nectar-feeding
birds, particularly honeyeaters.

Alice drove through the storm for the rest of the night. At dawn she stopped for petrol at a roadhouse not far beyond the state border. After filling up she parked under a gum and propped her head against the window to sleep. When she awoke the sun was burning her face and her mouth was dry. She got out of her truck and went into the roadhouse, emerging ten minutes later with a paper cup of burnt black coffee, a stale bun with thick pink icing, and a map. She managed a sip and a few bites before tossing the lot into the rubbish. Her wheels spun on grit as she drove onto the highway following the signs west, her map open on the seat beside her. Alice pushed away thoughts about anything other than what was right in front of her. All she would allow herself to focus on was driving as far as she could from water.

The further inland she drove, the thirstier and more unfamiliar the landscape grew. Wide, flat fields of yellow grass were dotted with rocky outcrops and gullies of twisted gums. Alice spotted the occasional corrugated-iron roof of a farmhouse, or a silver water tank squatting by a creaking windmill. All under the upturned bowl of endless blue sky.

Her mobile ran out of battery on the first day. She didn't bother fishing her charger out of her bag. When she was tired she pulled up on the side of the road wherever she was, locked her doors, and slept. Deeply, and without dreams. When she passed through one-street towns that seemed to shoot up out of the yellow dust like wildflowers after rain, she stopped for fuel and salad sandwiches or tins of peaches that she ate with her fingers. Sometimes she'd buy a cup of milky tea to swill as she pondered her map; the name of a town had caught her eye. It was at least a few more sweltering days of driving away but she wasn't dissuaded. At her next roadhouse stop she bought a spray bottle, filled it with tap water and used it during the following stretch of driving, spraying her face to cool herself down. The harsh sun beat down on her without mercy.

On her third night on the road, sweat still trickling down her backbone after sunset, Alice spotted a neon sign flashing on the outskirts of a mining town. She pulled into the motel parking lot and paid extra for an air-conditioned room with a kitchenette. In a convenience shop nearby she found pancake mix. Alice bought a box along with a stick of butter and tin of golden syrup, and fried them up before she'd even taken off her boots. Lying sprawled in her knickers across the floral polyester bedspread, Alice tore the pancakes into strips, slathered them with butter and syrup, and ate the stack while the rattling wall unit belted out stale, cold air. The lullaby of twenty-four-hour movies on the cable television sent her into another empty sleep.

The next morning Alice left her motel room key on the bureau and closed the door behind her. The sun was only just up but already creating a heat haze. At first she thought it was a trick of the eye, but looking around, Alice stopped mid-stride. The night before, in the dark, she hadn't realised that the colour of the earth had changed so dramatically. Though she'd heard people talk about the Red Centre, it wasn't the kind of red she'd expected. It was closer to orange. Like rust. Like fire. Overwhelmed, Alice closed her eyes and listened. Birdsong, the humming air conditioners behind her, the desert wind, a small yap. She opened her eyes to look around. Walked towards her truck, searching for the source of the yapping.

Crouching under a nearby shrub was a tawny-coloured puppy with one white patch of fur in the middle of its back. Alice glanced around. There were no other cars in the car park, or coming in either direction down the flat highway. The puppy yapped again. It didn't have a collar, and clumps of fur were missing along its flanks. While Alice was looking it over, fleas surfaced and burrowed again into the white patch. The puppy belonged to no one, or if it did, to someone who didn't care for it. Alice checked behind its tail. A girl. She scooped the puppy under one arm, opened the door and plonked her on the passenger seat. They gazed at each other.

'How do you feel about Pippin?' Alice asked. The puppy panted. 'Too formal?' Alice put the truck into gear and turned onto the highway, continuing to follow signs to the town she'd picked on her map.

'Come on, then, Pip,' she said. 'Less than half a day's drive to go.'

The town of Agnes Bluff sat at the base of the towering red outcrop it was named after. Main Street was lined with spotted gums and dotted with Victorian shopfronts the colour of sugared almonds. A newsagency, a few desert art galleries, a library, a couple of cafes, a grocery store and a petrol station. Alice pulled in and was about to fill up when Pip cried as she weed on the passenger seat. Her urine was bloody.

'Oh, Pip,' Alice said. The puppy whimpered.

Alice raced inside and came back with directions scrawled on a scrap of paper. She sped off, praying she had enough fuel to get to the nearest vet.

Pip cried forlornly in her arms while Alice pounded her fist on the clinic door. She cupped her hand around her eyes and peered through the glass. A clock on the wall said it was three minutes past one. A sign on the door said the clinic closed at one on Saturdays. Was it Saturday? She didn't have a clue. She kept banging until a man about her age appeared with a stethoscope around his neck behind the reception desk. He unlocked and opened the door.

'Can I help?'

'Please,' Alice pleaded.

She followed him into the surgery. He put a pair of gloves on and took Pip from Alice's arms. He bent to inspect her skin where fur was missing. Shone a light in her eyes, then into her mouth. When he stood up, the warmth was gone from his face.

'Your dog has severe mange.'

'Oh, she's not mine. I mean, she is, I, I, just found her this morning. I mean, we found each other. At a roadhouse.'

He considered her for a moment. 'You'd best wash your hands,' he said more gently, nodding towards a sink in the corner. Alice washed her hands with warm water.

'That's what that odour is,' he said.

Alice looked at him blankly, drying her hands with paper towel.

'You can't smell it?'

She shoved her hands in her pockets. 'I, uh, didn't notice.'

'That's why she can't stop scratching.'

He was right, Alice realised. The puppy hadn't stopped scratching since Alice found her. 'There's blood, too, I just saw, in her urine ...' Alice trailed off.

'She's got a nasty urinary tract infection, which causes the blood. She's also got a high fever, no doubt from malnourishment.' He peeled off his gloves and threw them into the bin. 'Sadly, it's pretty common for strays out here.'

The vet picked Pip up and put her in an empty cage. She immediately started to howl.

'Hey!' Alice stepped forward.

'She needs immediate medical care,' he cut in. 'I'm just helping her.' It took a second but Alice backed off. Pip huddled into the far corner of the cage, her tail between her legs.

Out at the reception desk, the vet asked for Alice's details.

'I don't, uh ...' she trailed off.

'You've just arrived in town?'

Alice nodded.

'Literally?'

'Yep.'

'Are you a FIFO worker?'

She frowned.

'Fly in, fly out?'

Shook her head.

'Have you got a place to stay?'

Alice didn't answer. He scribbled something on a notepad and tore the top sheet off.

'Go to the Bluff Pub. Ask for Merle. Tell her I sent you.' He handed her the note.

'Thanks.' Alice took it, her eyes drifting over the letterhead. *Moss Fletcher. Agnes Bluff Veterinarian.* Moss. She remembered a page of the Thornfield Dictionary. *Moss. Love without exception.* She mumbled some parting remarks and left as quickly as she could.

When Alice walked outside, the dry heat hit her like an invisible wall. Nothing about this place was familiar. The sky was a bleached blue, empty and stretching without end. There was no hint of river water, or flower fragrance. Her head spun and her pulse quickened.

Alice stumbled towards her truck, overcome by the rapid sound of her beating heart. She struggled to breathe as she reached for her door handle but couldn't grasp it. Her hands cramped and clawed inwards. Memories came back to her; the ocean and the fire roared indistinguishably.

She tried closing her eyes. Tried breathing through the panic. Tried to protect herself, before everything turned black.

Moss did a last check on the animals before he closed up. Alice's puppy was medicated and sleeping. He walked out into the blazing afternoon, which was heavy with the scent of diesel fumes and takeaway chicken from the fast food shop next door. The smell reminded him of what lay ahead: another night at home, alone.

He crossed the car park to his van, noticing a bright yellow truck. *Alice Hart, Floriographer. Thornfield Farm, where wildflowers bloom*. There was no one inside. Rounding the tail-end he found Alice collapsed on the bitumen, her nose bleeding.

Moss rushed to her, repeating her name. She didn't move. Her skin was frighteningly pale. He checked her breathing and her pulse. Pulled his mobile out of his pocket and punched in the speed dial for the medical centre. He was careful not to move her. When the doctor answered, Moss responded to her questions robotically, his heart racing.

Please, not again.

It wasn't an ocean of fire; Alice floated on a river. A river made of stars. They painted her skin silver-green. She lay on her back watching as they rained down from the night sky. Some got caught in the tallest branches of the silhouetted gum trees. Others stuck in her eyelashes, and between her toes. She swallowed a few. They tasted sweet and cool. She gathered an armful, surprised by their lightness, and carefully set them around her. A circle of stars. Inside which, nothing hurt.

Alice spluttered as she came to consciousness, thinking she was spitting out stars.

'Oggi,' she slurred.

'Yes, Alice, you'll be a bit groggy. Easy does it.'

Alice looked up. A woman smiled at her as she shone a light in each of Alice's eyes. The sensation agitated her memory; she was in a hospital bed in a white room. There was a needle in her arm. She winced and rolled her head away. A man sat stiffly in the chair beside her bed, staring at her. He raised his hand. Alice lifted her fingers to wave back. The vet. He was the vet. Moss Something. *Love without exception.*

'You're on a saline drip, Alice. You were quite badly dehydrated. It's something we see often in visitors not used to the desert heat. That's probably why you fainted.' The woman wore a white coat with *Dr Kira Hendrix* sewn above the pocket. 'Routine questions now. Do you have a history of low blood pressure in your family?'

Alice didn't know. She shook her head.

'What about anxiety, or panic attacks?'

'Not since I was a kid,' she answered quietly.

'And what brought them on?'

The wind blowing? The sight of a flower? The lingering flame of a dream?

'I don't know,' Alice answered.

'Are you on any prescribed medication?'

Alice shook her head again.

'Luckily your nose isn't broken and will heal in good time. Plenty of rest, for now. Lots of fluids. At the sign of anything worrying, come back and see me. Moss said you've just arrived in town today?'

Alice nodded.

'Where are you staying?'

Alice glanced over at Moss. He held eye contact for a moment before speaking.

'At the pub, doc. A room at the pub.'

'Hmmm,' the doctor said again. She patted Alice's shoulder, then turned to look at Moss with an eyebrow raised. 'A word?'

They huddled in the opposite corner. Alice glanced sidelong at them. Dr Kira was gravely serious while Moss looked taken aback.

'Great,' Dr Kira said brightly, ending their discussion. She returned to Alice's bedside. 'Let's get that drip out of your arm now, Alice, and see you on your way. Eat small meals. Plenty of sleep.'

Alice nodded, her eyes downcast.

Moss unlocked the passenger door of his van and held it open, closing it after Alice climbed wearily inside. The interior was immaculate. A cardboard tree hung from the rearview mirror, scented with an imitation of eucalyptus.

They rode in silence. Moss cleared his throat a few times.

'I, uh, found you in the car park after I'd closed up,' he said, not looking at her. 'I didn't move you, I called Dr Kira and she came and got you in the ambulance. I followed in my van.'

Alice kept her eyes straight ahead as she played through the image of him finding her unconscious. A deep sense of shame made her eyes hot. *You will not cry right now.*

'Here we are,' Moss said, pulling up at the clinic. He reached into his pocket and took out her truck keys. 'They were in your hand when I found you.' He sounded apologetic, as if he was responsible for her blackout.

'Thanks,' she said quietly. 'For everything.' Alice grabbed her keys from him, noticing him flinch as a sharp edge scraped his finger. 'Sorry,' she muttered, covering her face with her hands. She sighed, shaking her head at herself. 'Thanks,' she said again and got out, headed for her truck. But when she saw the lettering on her door panels, she came to an abrupt stop. There it was, laid bare, everything she was trying to leave behind.

Alice Hart, Floriographer. Thornfield Farm, where wildflowers bloom.

'So, uh, Alice?'

She turned, trying to block the door from Moss's view.

'You'll be okay?'

'Yep,' she nodded. 'Thanks. I'll get a room at the pub.'

He glanced away, then back at her. 'Dr Kira asked if I'd check in on you over the next twenty-four hours.' He cleared his throat. 'Would that be okay with you?'

Alice forced herself to smile. 'Rest. Fluids. Food. Pretty sure I can manage.' She just wanted to crawl into a bed, pull the covers over her head and not come out again. 'Thanks, though.'

'Yeah. Okay.' Another long pause. 'Well, Merle's got my number at the pub if you need anything,' he said, putting his van into gear. Alice nodded, relieved when he drove away.

She got into her truck and drove straight to the petrol station. After filling up, she scoured the shelves inside, stopping when she found the touch-up paint. The only colour available was turquoise. She picked up a tin, and a brush. On her way to the till, a stand of bright decals caught her eye. She grabbed a bundle, paid, and left.

In the pub car park she took to her truck in a fury with the brush and paint. In the fading light of her first day in the central desert, Alice painted who she'd been and where she'd come from into turquoise oblivion.

Merle wasn't at the pub when Alice arrived. A young girl with a thick accent checked her in, explaining the dinner menu with relentless enthusiasm while Alice pretended to listen. The girl had a map of the world tattooed on the underside of her forearm. Tiny stars dotted the map. What must that feel like, to be somewhere so far flung from all you knew, somewhere you'd willingly chosen to go, to explore? What was that like, to have no other purpose than to travel and collect experiences so vivid and meaningful that you permanently marked them on your skin? Each star taunted Alice. *I haven't been there. I haven't been there. I haven't been there.*

'Miss?' The girl waved a menu in Alice's face, smiling brightly.

'Sorry.' She shook her head. 'Can I order up to my room?'

'For a good tip.'

After ordering, Alice went upstairs with her backpack, unlocked the door to her room and locked it behind her.

She sat on the bed, unlaced her boots, and dropped sideways onto the pillow, letting go of the sob that had been pressing against her ribs for days.

18

Orange Immortelle

Meaning: Written in the stars

Waitzia acuminata | Western Australia

Perennial with long, narrow leaves, and papery orange,
yellow and white flowers. Spring blooming after winter rain.
En masse these flowers are spectacular. Have been found in their
millions across much of the scrub and desert in the west, with
people often travelling long distances to see them.

Alice was woken by the sunrise. She kicked the sweaty sheet off her legs and sat up, rubbing the salt crust from her eyes. Her room was bathed in an orange glow. She went to the window and pushed back the curtains. Unfettered light flooded in, reflected off the Bluff towering over the dusty town. Alice looked beyond the buildings and streets to the undulating red sand dunes and gullies of spinifex and desert oaks, stretching as far as she could see. She remembered soldier crabs, sea breezes, green sugar cane, silver river water, and fields of bright, blooming flowers. The desert air was so dry and thin that the perspiration on her body evaporated before it could bead. She was further than she'd ever been from anyone, anything and anywhere she knew.

'I'm here,' she whispered.

After a coffee and a fruit scone at the bar, Alice walked out of the pub to her truck. She checked the turquoise paint on her doors was dry, and went to the glove box for the decals. She covered both doors with them, then stepped back, folding her arms. She'd never have thought anonymity could come as easily as a coat of paint and some monarch butterfly stickers.

Later she went to the grocery store, and filled the freezer of her bar fridge with lemonade ice blocks. She ate three in a row lying on her bed, watching through the window as the midday sun blanched the trees. In the afternoon, when it started to cool, she went out to wander the strange red landscape.

She walked along the base of the bluff, studying the squat emu bushes, clumps of spinifex, and spindly desert oak trees. She stopped to notice the wildflowers that grew among the rocks, and picked a couple for her pockets. A charm of finches flew overhead, singing into the vivid afternoon sky. Alice swallowed roughly; the otherworldly feeling of the desert landscape saturated her senses.

Days and nights passed. The split on her nose healed. Occasionally a memory would rise, and Alice would let it. But if she found herself drawn back to the night she left Thornfield, she did whatever it took to distract herself from thinking through the depths of June's betrayal, or what had happened to Oggi and Boryana. Were they arrested? Were they scared? Did they know it was June who had reported them? She knew how to push the unanswered questions down.

To give structure to her days, Alice developed a routine around the sun; she was insatiable for the desert light. Every morning, she sat on her windowsill, above the corrugated-iron roof of the hotel. As the sun came up, it painted the rocky outcrops and ranges in varying hues: rich wine-coloured burgundy, bright ochre, shimmering bronze and butterscotch. Beholding the seemingly endless expanse of the sky, Alice tried to breathe more deeply, as if she might inhale the space, as if she might create a similar kind of vastness inside herself.

After sunrise, she would take a walk. The town was set in an ancient, dry riverbed, filled with pebbly sand from which tall and thick ghost gums grew. She strolled among their cream to white and pink-tinged trunks, stopping to inspect a pale grey stone or a fallen gum nut. It was hard to believe water had ever flowed there, as if the river was no more than folklore, something that long ago took to the sky on the wings of black cockatoos.

Through the middle of the day, when it was hottest, Alice stayed in her room with the air conditioning on high, flicking through the cable channels. As the afternoons cooled, she went back out to wander again. At night, after dinner, she found refuge in shadows and watched the stars.

Two weeks passed. She didn't go back to see the vet. She didn't check her emails. She took the SIM card out of her mobile phone and threw it away.

To her surprise, there were things in the desert that brought her such comfort, they felt almost medicinal. The fiery colour of the dirt, and the feel of it cupped in her hands, soft as powder. The melodic songs of the birds. The light at the beginning and end of each day. The warm wind, the silver-green-blue of the gum leaves, the endless, cloud-tufted sky, and, most of all, the wildflowers growing in the riverbed, among roots and stones. She had started to pick and press them, without fully admitting to herself that it was the familiarity of the flowers that brought her the most solace.

One morning, Alice discovered she'd filled a whole notebook with pressed wildflowers. After she finished breakfast at the bar, she headed into town to buy a new one.

Walking along a quiet street by the dry riverbed, Alice found the town library. She smiled at a faded mural on the library wall, evidently an attempt to make the small boxy building look like a stack of books. Inside was cool respite from the searing heat.

Alice wandered between the shelves contentedly. She remembered the library from her childhood, filled with pastel light and stained-glass windows that told stories.

'Sally,' she mumbled.

'Can I help you?' the librarian asked from the next shelf over.

'Where are your fairytales?' Alice asked.

'By the back wall.'

Alice ran her fingers along the spines of the stories she remembered reading as a girl. Her writing desk, her library bag, her mother's ferns. She searched for one book in particular and when she found it she let out a small cry.

Later, after she'd joined and tucked her library card into her pocket, Alice borrowed the maximum number of books allowed and lugged them back to her hotel room. She spent the afternoon flicking through their pages, running her fingertips over stray sentences, intermittently stopping to rest an open book on her chest while she watched the lacy patterns of gum tree shadows dancing across her wall. That night she bought pad thai takeaway with extra chilli, and a six-pack of cold beer, then lay on her bed under the air conditioner while she read the book she'd treasured as a girl, full of stories about women who shed their seal skins and left them and the sea behind for the love of a man.

One afternoon, when Alice was on her way back from the riverbed with a fistful of wildflowers, Merle, the owner of the pub and hotel, intercepted her at the bar.

'Alice Hart,' she announced. 'You've got a phone call.'

Alice followed Merle into a small office behind the bar. Her palms were sweaty. Had June found her?

The phone receiver sat on the desk. Alice waited until she was alone, wiped her sweaty hands on her shorts and picked it up.

'Hello?' she asked. She pressed her other hand over her ear to drown out the noise of the pub at knock-off time.

'I thought you'd want to know your dog is all better,' Moss said on the other end of the line.

Alice exhaled.

'Hello?'

'Hi,' she exclaimed, giddy with relief.

'Hi there.' Moss chuckled.

'Sorry.' Alice inwardly kicked herself. 'Thanks for letting me know. That's wonderful news.'

'I thought you'd think so. When can you come and pick her up? She's fat, happy and fluffier than Merle's perm.'

Laughter took Alice by surprise. As did the warmth in his voice.

'Tomorrow,' she heard herself say.

'Great.' A pause. 'How have you been?' he asked.

'Fine,' Alice said, fidgeting with her picked flowers. 'Sorry I haven't …'

'Not a problem. You've been busy. Getting rest. Borrowing the entire catalogue of the town library.'

'What?'

'Small town.' Moss laughed easily. 'It's not hard to make news around here. Apparently, you like to read.'

Merle cleared her throat at the door.

'Sorry, I have to go,' Alice said.

'So, I'll see you tomorrow.'

'Where?' Alice asked.

'The Bean on Main Street. Eleven?'

'Sure.'

Alice hung up.

'Sorry,' she muttered to Merle as she left her office.

'No problem.' Merle smiled curiously, an eyebrow raised. 'Fancy a beer, love? It's happy hour.'

'Maybe I could take it to my –'

'Nope.' Merle cut her off with a hand held up. 'No one drinks alone on my watch. Come and sit at the bar. Tell me what you're doing here, holed up alone in my pub in the middle of nowhere. I love a good story.'

The thought of telling anyone anything about her life before she drove into Agnes Bluff made Alice nauseous. Moss's words rang in her ears. *It's not hard to make news around here.*

Moss hung up the phone, staring at it as if it might offer him answers to his questions about Alice Hart. Questions that had nagged at him for days. He'd waited and waited for her to come back for the puppy, but she hadn't. Regular chats with Merle kept him updated. She was still there. She was okay. She hadn't blacked out again as far as anyone knew. *Why do you care so much?* Merle asked him. *You of all people should know you can't save every stray.* Moss changed the subject. He couldn't tell Merle he cared because Alice was the first person who made him feel like he had anything to offer, anything to give, in the five years he'd been in town. After losing Clara and Patrick, he never expected to feel any such thing again. And yet. There she was. Alice Hart. A woman who knew how to speak through flowers.

He went to the fridge, got a beer and returned to his desk. A nudge of the mouse brought the computer screen back to life. Moss's pulse quickened at the sight of her photo he'd found earlier. It was top of his search results. *Alice Hart. Floriographer. Thornfield Farm.* Her profile was on the About Us page. In the photo she was standing deep in a field of flowers, surrounded by gnarled gum trees, holding a bouquet of natives so large it nearly dwarfed her body. She looked sidelong at the camera. A barely there smile. Eyes clear. Her hair piled on her head, fastened with an enormous red heart-like flower.

> *Alice Hart has lived at Thornfield for most of her life and grew up on*
> *the farm's language of native flowers. She is a skilled floriographer*
> *and can help you to create the perfect arrangement to speak from your*
> *heart. Available for consultation by appointment only.*

He'd Googled *floriographer* next: a person fluent in the language of flowers, a craze that was at the height of its popularity in the Victorian era. He'd hoped that Googling her might quash his fascination, but her enigmatic story only fuelled it.

Moss leaned back in his chair, reading the Thornfield contact information. He sipped his beer. Picked up the phone and put it down. Hesitated for a few moments, then reached forward and picked up the phone again. Dialled the number on the website, gripping his beer bottle as he listened to it ring.

He was just about to hang up when a woman answered, her voice thick with tears.

Alice settled herself at the bar. The sunset filled the pub with a kaleidoscope of colour.

Merle set a fresh coaster down and sat an icy pint of beer on top of it. 'Cheers,' Merle raised a shot of bourbon. 'So now, Alice Hart, tell me what you're doing here all alone? Where've you come from? Where're you going?'

Alice wrapped both hands around her beer.

'Oh now, don't clam up. Everyone here's got a story. You think you're the only whitefella who's run away to the desert to become someone else? Forgive me, darlin', but you're not that special.' Merle tapped her acrylic fingernails on the bar. A loud shout came from the beer garden outside. 'Oi! Cut that shit out!' Merle bellowed, making Alice jump. 'Don't go anywhere, pet, just gotta sort out this kerfuffle.'

Alice exhaled in relief. Around her the noise rose steadily as the pub filled. Carrying her flower pickings and beer, she squeezed herself off her stool and wriggled her way outside into the cooling blue dusk. She took a sip of her beer and opened her fist. The flowers were crushed. As she was looking them over, Alice became aware someone was behind her.

'Sorry, didn't mean to startle you,' a woman said, raising a pouch of tobacco in explanation. Her voice was kind. Alice nodded, gripping her beer. The woman rolled a smoke, lit a match and bent her head towards the small flame. She was wearing a uniform but in the dim light Alice couldn't make out the insignia. She waved the smoke away from Alice as she exhaled.

'It's the only pub for a hundred clicks. Gets pretty busy.'

'Yeah, I know,' Alice said. 'I'm staying here.'

'Oh, right. Been in town long?' the woman asked.

'A month today.'

'Lived in the Territory long?' She raised an eyebrow at Alice.

'A month today,' Alice said, feeling herself smile.

'Aha. You've got about two months to go then.'

'Until?'

'You start to feel like you're not on another planet. I'd guess a classic newbie to the desert, from the city or the coast. You've got that telltale deer-in-the-headlights look about you.'

Alice stared at her. 'How do you know this isn't just how I look?' she heard herself say.

The woman was quiet for a moment, before chuckling. 'Shit, you're absolutely right. Sorry. That was rude of me.'

Alice nodded, studying her beer fizz.

'I live down the road. Grew up in the red dirt,' the woman said, smiling. 'Which might explain my highly evolved social skills.'

Alice couldn't help but look up and return her smile.

'I'm Sarah, by the way.'

'Alice.'

They shook hands.

'What do you do out here, Sarah?' Alice gestured at her uniform.

'I manage the park,' she replied, poking a thumb in an obscure direction over her shoulder.

'The park?'

'Kililpitjara. The national park? You haven't been yet, I take it.'

Alice shook her head.

'A very special place.' Sarah stubbed her smoke out. 'How about you, what do you do?'

'I, um …' Alice trailed off. 'Sorry,' she said, rubbing her forehead. 'I'm in communications.'

'Communications?' Sarah repeated.

Alice nodded. 'I got a business communications degree through Open Uni. I used to,' she stopped. Tried again. 'I used to run a flower farm. But not anymore.' If Sarah noticed her fumble, she didn't let on.

'Bloody hell. The way this place works will never fail to amaze me.' Sarah laughed, shaking her head. Alice looked at the pub, not understanding. 'No, no,' Sarah said. 'Not the pub. The desert. The people that blow through here. The timing and craziness of it all.'

Alice smiled politely.

'We've just had a job opening for a visitor services ranger in the park. That's why I'm in town, to talk to a few people about finding someone to fill the role.' She grinned at Alice. 'It's a tricky one because we need someone who can do the hard yakka but is also qualified in communications.'

Alice nodded slowly, beginning to understand.

'The pay's good. You get housing,' Sarah said. 'If I give you my card and you're interested, how about you email me and I'll send you more details?'

Alice's palms were clammy. It was a long time since she'd felt hopeful. 'That'd be great,' she said, brushing invisible things from her arms.

As Sarah took a card out of her shirt pocket and offered it to Alice, she got a better view of the badges on Sarah's shirt. They read *Kililpitjara National Park* and adapted the design of the Indigenous Australian flag: the top half was black and the bottom half was red, with a yellow circle in the middle. In the centre of the yellow circle was a cluster of Sturt's desert peas.

'Thanks,' Alice said, taking the card.

Sarah checked her watch and began to walk away. 'I've got to go, but it was great to meet you, Alice. I'll keep an eye out for your email.'

Alice raised the card in farewell as Sarah disappeared into the crowd. She held it to the light. It bore the same emblem as Sarah's shirt. Alice didn't need the Thornfield Dictionary. She'd memorised the meaning of Sturt's desert peas the morning of her tenth birthday, when she opened her locket and read June's letter.

Have courage, take heart.

The next morning Alice was waiting at the library when the doors opened at nine o'clock. She hurried to the computers with Sarah's card, which she'd already dog-eared. She typed the national park's website into a search engine and waited for it to load. Checked the clock. She was meeting Moss in two hours.

The web page loaded slowly, filling the screen with the national park's homepage. At the top was a landscape photograph. Alice leant forward, as if she might will it to load faster.

A pale mauve sky. A few smoky wisps of cloud. A smudge of apricot light above the violet line of the horizon. An aerial view of green foliage on luminous red dirt.

It took Alice a moment to realise that she was looking at a crater from above; she didn't grasp its size until the whole photograph uploaded and she saw a tiny dirt road and the white dots of vehicles. Her eyes were drawn to the centre of the crater, which was filled with red wildflowers. She drummed her fingers on the desk, waiting as an inset photo of the flowers loaded. She stopped drumming. The heart of the crater was a circle of Sturt's desert peas in mind-blowing, blood-red bloom.

She gripped her locket as she scrolled down.

While Kililpitjara, or Earnshaw Crater, was only 'discovered' by non-Indigenous people in the early fifties, it has been a living cultural landscape for Anangu for thousands of years. Geologically, the crater is the impact site where an iron meteorite hit hundreds of thousands of years ago. In Anangu culture, the crater was caused by a great crash that also came from the sky, but not an iron meteorite; it is where a grieving mother's heart fell to Earth. Long ago, Ngunytju lived in the stars. One night, when she wasn't looking, her baby fell from its cradle in the sky to Earth. When she realised what happened, Ngunytju was inconsolable. She took her heart from her celestial body and flung it to Earth, to be in and of the land with her fallen child.

Alice stopped. She sat back, letting the images of the crater's creation story settle. When she was ready she continued reading.

In the middle of Kililpitjara grows a wild, concentric circle of malukuru, Sturt's desert peas, which bloom for nine months each year. Visitors come from around the world to see Ngunytju's heart in flower. It is a sacred site of deep spiritual and cultural significance to Anangu women. They welcome you here and invite you to learn the story of this land. They ask that when you walk into the crater you do not pick any flowers.

Alice scrolled back up to the photo. She quickly opened another tab. Created a new email address, grateful for the sight of a blank inbox. She hurriedly wrote an email, typed in Sarah's address and clicked send before she could overthink it. The computer responded with a cheery ping. Sent.

Alice slouched in her chair, staring at the celestial crater. The caption caught her eye.

In Pitjantjatjara language, Kililpitjara *means* belonging to the stars.

19

Pearl saltbush

Meaning: My hidden worth

Maireana sedifolia | South Australia and Northern Territory

*Common in deserts and salty environments, this low shrub
creates a fascinating ecosystem of almost hidden treasures: geckoes,
fairy wrens, fungi and lichen colonies. Drought-tolerant, with
silvery grey evergreen foliage that forms a dense groundcover
that is fire-retardant.*

Alice hurried down Main Street, her head full of colliding stars and blood-coloured flowers with dark red centres. She checked the name of the cafe she'd written on the back of her hand, along with Merle's directions. Down Main Street, turn left. Look for plants and mismatched tables. She was fifteen minutes late.

The Bean cafe was in a small alley, an array of colourful chairs paired with knocked-about tables speckled with paint. Between each table was a small jungle of pot plants. It was a lush haven in the desert.

Moss was sitting at a table under a potted umbrella tree, running his fingers along the metal grate of a small pet cage.

'Morning,' Alice said, glancing at Moss. He straightened, his face awash in relief. Pip leapt at the grate, wriggling at the sight of her. She was plump, her coat was fluffy and her eyes were clear. A lump swelled in Alice's throat.

'I wasn't sure you'd come,' he said.

A young girl with dreadlocks arrived in a cloud of patchouli to take their order. 'Coffee?'

'Flat white, please,' Moss said. The waitress nodded and turned to Alice.

'Same, thanks,' Alice replied. The girl took their menus and disappeared inside.

'So,' Moss said. Alice busied herself fussing over Pip. 'How have you been?'

She pressed her lips together, nodding like a dashboard toy. 'Good,' she said. Pip nibbled at her fingers.

'No more blackouts?'

She sat back and met his gaze. He looked genuinely concerned. She shook her head. The waitress returned with their flat whites.

Moss smiled and changed tack. 'So, Pip's right as rain. I put her on some pretty strong antibiotics.'

Alice nodded. 'Thank you.'

'You want to hold her?' he asked.

'Yes, please.' She beamed.

He opened the cage door. Alice squealed as the puppy leapt into her arms, licking the underside of her chin, snuffling at her ears.

'There's no way she would have survived if you didn't pick her up when you did,' Moss said. 'Animals' needs are no different from ours sometimes. TLC can be as powerful as medicine.'

Images rose in Alice's mind before she could stop them: Candy's mischievous smile; Twig's calm, measured gait; June's shaking hands.

'This hot, dry air is hell,' Alice mumbled as she wiped her eyes. She closed them for a moment, imagining herself from an aerial view, an indistinguishable dot overwhelmed by the expanse of desert.

'Alice?' Moss leant forward, touching her arm. Alice jumped, clutching Pip to her. She wasn't weak. She didn't need help.

'I don't need saving,' she said quietly.

A strange expression flickered across Moss's face. He looked past her, out to Main Street where markets were being set up under the shade of trees.

'I didn't think you did,' Moss said slowly. 'I just know what it's like to turn up here alone.' He folded his hands on the table. 'I don't know if you've heard it, but there's a saying around here, Alice. Whitefellas end up in the Red Centre for one of two reasons: they're either running from the law, or running from themselves. It was certainly true –'

'I'm not running,' she cut him off, indignation setting her cheeks aflame. 'From anything.' She struggled not to let her chin quiver. She didn't want him to see her cry. 'You don't know me, Moss. I don't need protecting. I don't need –' she stopped herself before she said June's name. 'I don't need help,' she said.

Moss held his hands up in surrender. 'I meant no offence.' His eyes had dulled. Why wasn't he fighting her? Why wasn't he arguing? She was ready for a fight.

'I didn't ask for help,' she said, her voice brittle. Pip yelped in her arms; Alice realised how tightly she'd been holding her.

'I don't understand what you're accusing me of, or why you're so angry. You turned up at my clinic and passed out in the car park, Alice. What kind of person *wouldn't* help you?'

Pent-up emotion left Alice's body in a single sigh. Depleted, she ran a finger along the patterns in the Formica tabletop, following the marbled white through the blue, each rivulet like a wave. A memory: her father, zigzagging on his windsurfer towards the horizon.

Without another word, Moss put a ten-dollar note on the table, and pushed his chair back. Alice didn't look up as he walked away, but when he was almost at the end of the alley, she couldn't stop herself from calling out his name. He turned.

'What was it for you?' she asked. 'The law, or yourself?'

Moss looked down for a moment, his hands deep in his pockets. When he looked up there was a sadness in his face that hit Alice in her chest. He gave her a half-smile and walked away without answering.

Alice stayed where she was, staring at the space he'd left behind. It wasn't until Pip nibbled her finger that Alice realised Moss hadn't charged her for Pip's treatment.

That afternoon, Moss pushed his legs to run faster until his muscles had no more to give. He eased off, slowing to a jog as he pressed on up the trail that scaled the spine of the Bluff.

He had been determined to tell Alice, and honour his promise to Twig. But when Alice had arrived at the cafe, at first so cautious and then so fragile, he just couldn't do it. He couldn't be like the doctor who walked out to him in the waiting area at the hospital and spoke the words that made Moss's legs buckle. He couldn't bring himself to be that person to Alice, the person she'd remember forever as the one who told her that her only blood family was dead.

Twig's words came back to him. *June's own heart killed her. It was a massive heart attack, after the floods.* Although he didn't know June, the words stung. *June and Alice had a troubled relationship, but they were each other's only family.* Twig's voice had cracked. *Is Alice okay?* Moss didn't hesitate to assure Twig that Alice was safe. And yes, given the circumstances, of course he'd tell her to call. Of course he'd tell her that Twig needed her to come home.

Moss came to a stop at the summit, heaving for breath as he surveyed the town. What had he set in motion by calling Thornfield? Why had he involved himself in a stranger's life?

He leaned forward, trying to breathe through his mouth as the hospital counsellor suggested all those years ago. It was their first family holiday. Lucas sat in his car seat, clutching his bucket and spade. Clara wore a new, bright summer dress. Moss took his eyes off the road for seconds. Mere seconds. The tyres veered onto loose gravel and at the speed he was doing, their four-wheel drive flipped. He got a few stitches and a neck brace. *You're very lucky to be alive*, the doctor told him. *What about Clara and Patrick?* Moss had screamed until he was sedated.

Right or wrong, Moss would not – could not – be the bearer of that kind of news in Alice's life.

The phone call came two days later.

'Phone's for you,' Merle said, leaning against Alice's door jamb.

'Who is it?' Alice took a step back.

'Pet, I do most jobs in this place, but personal secretary isn't one of them.'

'Right,' Alice said. 'Sorry.' She closed Pip into her room and followed Merle downstairs. 'Thanks for letting me have Pip here, Merle,' Alice said as they entered her office.

'No worries. Moss owes me one,' Merle said. She nodded towards her desk. Once Merle was gone, Alice went to the desk and picked the phone up.

'Hello?' she asked nervously.

'Alice, Sarah Covington. I got your application for the ranger job. Thanks.'

Alice exhaled, relieved again it wasn't Thornfield calling.

'Alice?'

'Yes, sorry, I'm here.'

'Good. So, your application was impressive. Running a flower farm is no small feat. Since our vacant role here is a temporary contract we don't have to go to interview, which means, Alice, I'd like to offer you the job.'

She smiled widely.

'Hello?'

'Sorry, sorry, Sarah, I'm nodding. Yes. Thank you! Yes,' Alice said giddily.

'Great. When can you start?'

'What day is it today?'

'Friday.'

'Monday?'

'You sure? You don't need more time to pack up and get organised?'

'No.'

'Monday it is. I'll meet you at park headquarters when you arrive. I'll get the Entry Station to radio me when you come through, so I know to expect you.'

'Entry Station?'

'It'll make sense when you get here.'

'Okay. Entry Station. Park headquarters. Kililpitjara. Monday. See you then.'

'Looking forward to it, Alice.'

The line went dead. Alice hung up the phone.

For once she didn't will her heart to slow.

Monday dawned clear and hot. Alice and Pip walked the dry riverbed of the Bluff for the last time. Seizing the chance, Alice pocketed leaves from the bat's wing coral tree. *Cure for heartache*, she later wrote from memory into her notebook after she'd taped all but one to the page. She packed her few things into her backpack and, after a cursory glance, left the pub room that had been her home.

'Will we be seeing you again?' Merle asked Alice as they waited for her bankcard to clear. She tore the receipt from the machine and handed it and Alice's card across the counter. Alice took them with a nod of thanks and tucked them into her pocket. She'd never imagined she'd eventually spend the money she'd saved to see the world with Oggi on creating a new life alone in the desert.

'You never know,' Alice said as she walked out to the car park, not looking back.

She put her things into her truck, whistled for Pip to leap in, and followed. From her pocket she took the last coral tree leaf and stuck it to the edge of her rearview mirror. *Cure for heartache.* As she drove off, Pip sat to attention, barking, causing a thought to nag at Alice. At the next set of lights she turned down the street the vet clinic was on. But when his van came into view, Alice lost her nerve and put her foot down.

The highway shimmered in the morning heat. Behind her Agnes Bluff disappeared in the distance. When the road intersected, Alice drove west, further into the desert. She wound her window down, rested her elbow on the sill, and leant her head back against her seat. Imagined the heat might blanch her memories, much like the central Australian sun had done to cattle carcasses littering the barren land. Leaving nothing but white bones and dust behind.

Alice drove for three hours through empty desert before she came to a roadhouse. She pulled in to fill up and gave Pip a long drink. A menagerie of camper vans, four-wheel drives and tourist buses trundled by. Alice thought back to her conversation with Moss. Whitefellas went into the desert either to outrun the law, or themselves. Alice ushered Pip back into the truck. She'd committed no crime, but was no exception.

Glancing around, she wondered what someone looking in her direction saw. A girl in her truck with her dog, who knew where she was going? She hoped it wasn't obvious that she didn't have a clue what she was doing. She hoped no one could tell how hard she was trying to believe she could outrun anything if her desire to leave it behind was strong enough.

As she idled through the families and backpackers and tourist groups, Alice felt a surge of hope for where she was headed. If she could make a life for herself in a place where a grieving heart once hit the earth and grew into flowers, maybe everything she'd left behind could be transformed into something meaningful too.

The rocky red landscape rolled slowly into clean sand dune country. Less than a hundred kilometres to go until she reached Kililpitjara. To distract herself Alice studied the pristine patterns on the dunes. The nearest loomed, an untouched pyramid of fiery red sand, rippled by wind. She wiped the sweat from her face with her T-shirt. Her legs stuck to the vinyl seat. The sun was high, the glare was white-hot. Pip jumped onto the floor and curled in the shade. Alice pressed her foot down on the accelerator.

'Nearly there, Pip.'

Finally, after she drove over a slight rise in the highway, a purple shadow appeared ahead of her, far away on the horizon. Alice blinked a few times to be sure it wasn't a mirage. As she got closer, she leaned forward, her thighs peeling from the seat. Behind undulating sand dunes, the tops of buildings appeared. A few white sails. Tour buses. A road that turned off the highway, with matching signs either side: *Welcome to Earnshaw Crater Resort*. Alice kept driving until the Kililpitjara National Park Entry Station came into view. She pulled up at the gate by the window of a brick and corrugated-iron building, where a woman greeted her in a park uniform like the one Sarah had been wearing.

'Hi.' She leant towards the intercom grille below the window. 'My name's Alice Hart.'

The woman ran her finger down a clipboard before looking up, smiling.

'Go right ahead, Alice. Sarah's waiting for you at HQ.' Her voice crackled through the intercom as she pressed a button to raise the boom gate.

Alice drove through, mesmerised by the sight of the crater ahead. It was as elaborate as a dream, changing shape and form with every bend the road took. Its beauty was strange and mystifying, rising like a textured ochre and red painting against the blue sky. The sand dunes, dotted with spinifex and clusters of mulga and desert oaks, were seemingly endless, and all-consuming. After weeks in the desert, there was something about feeling small, unfamiliar and out of place that Alice enjoyed. It was as if she could, at any moment, recreate herself entirely, and no one would notice. She could be whomever she chose.

Twenty minutes later, Alice pulled up outside a timber-framed building that blended in with the surrounding trees and bushes, under the towering presence of the crater. She turned the engine off. Listened to it tick and cool. Wiped her face on her T-shirt again. After spotting a tap on the side of the building, Alice clipped Pip's collar onto her lead and got out of the truck. She knotted Pip's lead loosely to the tap, turned it on to a drip and left her to slurp, tail wagging. Behind Alice a screen door opened. She turned to see Sarah walk out, smiling.

'Alice Hart. Welcome.'

'Thanks,' she exhaled. Having a dog in a national park suddenly struck her as problematic. 'Sarah, I didn't mention this, but I have a dog ...'

'Other rangers have dogs here too. Your yard has a fence.' Sarah nodded. 'Come in. Contracts to sign and uniform fittings and so on, then I'll show you to your house.'

Alice's step lightened as she followed Sarah inside. Maybe sometimes it really could be as easy as leaving everything behind to begin again.

With a pile of green ranger uniforms beside her, Alice followed Sarah out of the headquarters car park and onto a ring road that encircled the crater. The enormity of the outer wall was deceiving, as if it were the side of a mountain range; a line of peaks rather than a circular rock formation. Something about it made Alice shiver: its size, its age, what the impact must have been when the meteor hit the earth. How long ago that was. Pip yawned on the seat beside Alice.

'Quite right, Pip,' Alice mumbled. Her mind was too tired. The day was too hot. She was in no shape to be contemplating celestial geology.

Sarah turned off the ring road and onto a smaller, unmarked track that curved between mulga trees. Alice peered through them, spotting a few buildings and a dusty oval. They came to a roundabout that forked in three directions, and took the first turn, driving slowly past a fenced work yard, inside which was a large aluminium shed, petrol bowsers, and lockable cage garages full of machinery and vehicles that bore the park logo. As Alice drove by she caught sight of two rangers inside. One was wearing a slouchy hat and sunglasses, talking over the roof of his ute to another. Though she couldn't see his eyes, his head turned to follow her truck as she drove past.

They went over a dune and around a bend to the edge of the cluster of staff houses, where they stopped in front of a squat, brick house painted white, with a cage garage and padlocked fence. Alice wondered what all the security and fencing was for, what or who there could be to lock out. Sarah got out of her ute and gestured for Alice to pull into the empty garage.

'Is this all you've got?' she asked, carrying Alice's backpack and box of notebooks. Pip leapt out to explore.

'My new bedding and kitchen stuff is in the back. I went shopping before I left the Bluff.'

Sarah took a key off the ring clipped to her work belt and unlocked the front door. Pip ran in ahead of them.

The house smelled freshly disinfected and was full of light. Alice set her belongings on the dining table, distracted by the view through the rear sliding glass door. The backyard was full of wild acacia, spinifex and thryptomene bushes.

'There's a kettle and tea on the counter, and long-life milk in the fridge,' Sarah said. 'Main thing to know is where the air con switch and your power box are.' Sarah pointed at the switch by the front door and flicked it on. A low noise hummed through the house as air gushed from the ceiling vents. 'You've got a swampy system, so it's water cooled, which means it's never going to get lower than around twenty-five, but it does the job.'

Alice nodded.

'Your power box is out the back by the water tank, so if anything shorts, that's where you'll reset it. And that's where your power card goes. There's five dollars' worth in there to get you started. You can top up at the Parksville store.'

'Parksville?'

'Where we are,' Sarah chuckled. 'Staff housing and community.' She gestured around them. 'On this side of the dune,' she pointed to the red sand dune rising behind Alice's back fence, 'is where park staff live. On the other side of the dune is a small general store, oval, hall and visitor housing. Twenty clicks away is the resort, where all the tourists stay. That's where you'll find the supermarket, post office, bank, petrol station, and a couple of pubs and restaurants.'

Alice nodded again.

Sarah's face filled with compassion. 'One step at a time, mate. Soon it'll be second nature. I've arranged for one of the rangers to come by this arv and give you a tour.'

'Thanks,' Alice said.

'I'll leave you to get settled. See you bright and early tomorrow.'

'Thanks,' Alice repeated. 'For everything.'

As Sarah's ute faded into the distance, Alice pressed her back against the door and closed her eyes. The house filled with a silence that made her temples pound. *I'm here*. She breathed in. And out. *I'm here*.

Pip licked her ankle. Alice opened one eye and peeked at the puppy. Pip cocked her head to one side. Alice nodded. She faced her new home.

Against the wall stood a tall wooden bookshelf. Beside it, a bulky grey desk and chair. Alice sat and splayed her hands on the desk, thinking of her flower notebooks. She looked into the backyard, taking comfort from the wild native plants. This is where she would write, she decided. Memories of writing at her desk as a girl gathered in her fingertips: the cool, creamy wood, the smell of crayons, pencil shavings, paper. The velveteen green ferns in her mother's garden. Alice shook her head, refocusing on the desk in front of her and the view ahead. Red dirt, green bushes, and a wire fence that sectioned off the yard from the surrounding dunes, all under a jewel-blue sky.

Next to the desk was an archway that led into the main bedroom. Alice left her new desk and went to make her new bed.

Afterwards she stood at the bedroom window. In the distance the red rock wall of the crater shimmered in the heat like a fiery dream.

20

Honey grevillea

Meaning: Foresight

Grevillea eriostachya | Inland Australia

Kaliny-kalinypa (Pitjantjatjara) is a straggly shrub with long narrow silver-green leaves that produces bright green, yellow and orange flowers. Commonly grows on red sandhills and dunes. The flowers contain thick, honey-like nectar, which can be sucked from the flowers; a favourite treat for Anangu children.

At five o'clock that afternoon a horn beeped outside. Alice peeked through her kitchen window and saw the profile of a woman sitting in one of the park utes. She set down fresh water for Pip, gave her a rub behind the ears, grabbed her house keys and hurried out the front door. Her thongs kicked up little clouds of red dust in the late afternoon light.

'Alice!' The woman pushed her sunglasses off her face and greeted Alice like an old friend. 'I'm Lulu.' Her eyes were the colour of eucalyptus leaves: pale green and hazel brown. Around her neck a silver star-shaped pendant hung from a thin piece of leather.

'Hi,' Alice said shyly as she got in.

'Let's check out the sunset, chica,' Lulu said, as if they'd been mid-conversation. She put her foot down and the ute bounced over the graded dirt track, away from Alice's house. Pink and grey galahs streaked overhead.

'So where are you from, Alice?'

The crater loomed ahead of them, its edges gilded by the light.

'Uh, east coast, then inland. On a farm. Kind of all over the place.' She gulped. 'You?'

'Down south. The coast, not the city.' Lulu glanced over, smiling. 'So, we're both girls from the sea.'

Alice nodded silently. Dunes and gullies of red sand and brownish-green bushes passed her window in a blur. The passenger mirror was caked in red dust. It had begun to calm her somehow, the searing colour of it, the way it stuck to everything. She turned her hands over. The tiny creases in her fingers were filled with it. Alice folded them together in her lap.

Lulu turned onto the ring road. 'Sarah suggested I point out who lives where but there's no point really since you don't know anyone yet. So, I reckon I'll just take you straight to the sunset viewing area.' She peered at the violet underbellies of a few stray clouds. 'It should be a corker.'

The red wall of the crater rose in the distance. Above, the chopping sound of helicopter blades. Camera flashes caught Alice's eye.

'Tourist flights,' Lulu said. 'Sunset circus, chica.'

Alice watched the helicopters circling. 'Sunset circus,' she repeated curiously.

The car park was full of coaches, rental cars, camper vans and four-wheel drives. There was a rising cacophony of tourists' chatter, cameras clicking, the hum of coach generators, and the erratic opening and closing of car doors and camper-van hatches. Lulu pulled up by another park ute and put on her hazard lights.

'Welcome to your first Kililpitjara sunset.' Lulu whistled as she got out.

Alice swung her door open to follow, stopping short. Lulu was talking to the ranger with the slouched hat and sunglasses.

Her cotton dress felt suddenly flimsy. She crossed her arms over her chest, wishing for the obscurity of Lulu's unisex park uniform and the sturdiness of her work boots. Though it was warm, Alice shivered. She tried to look anywhere other than at him, until Lulu gave her no choice.

'Alice, this is Dylan Rivers. Dylan, Alice Hart. Our newest comrade.'

She forced herself to look up at him. Her reflection was small in the mirrored lenses of his sunglasses.

'G'day,' he said with a nod, tipping his hat at her. 'Welcome to Wonderland.'

A thrill rippled through her body. Alice willed herself to stay calm. 'Thanks.'

'First time down the rabbit hole?' Dylan gestured to the crowds.

'Yeah. I start tomorrow.'

'Let the baptism of fire commence,' Lulu said.

Alice raised her eyebrows.

Lulu laughed. 'Don't worry, chica, you'll be fine. We all go through it. It's the nature of the place.'

Dylan was about to respond when his attention was diverted by tourists.

'I'm going to have to ask you to come behind the barrier please.' He corralled a group back from the low fence they'd jumped, trampling plants and wildflowers to get a photo with the crater. When he returned to Alice and Lulu, he stood close enough to Alice for her to smell his cologne.

'Sometimes I wonder, if they didn't have their photos, would they even remember being here?' He shook his head.

'It's like this every day?' Alice asked.

Dylan nodded. 'Sunrise and sunset. Two years ago guide books started listing this place as 'one to see before you die'. Since then, our visitor numbers have doubled.' He turned suddenly to Lulu. 'Hey, did Aiden tell you about last night?' he asked.

Lulu straightened up, as if on guard, and shook her head. 'I haven't seen him yet; he was on sunset last night, I was on sunrise this morning.' She shot a glance at Alice. 'Aiden's my boyfriend,' she said. Alice nodded, noting the hint of tension in Lulu's voice.

'Yeah, so,' Dylan went on. 'At the end of her patrol yesterday arvo, Ruby went into the crater and found a group of minga off track. They were inside Kuṯuṯu Kaana. Naturally, she asked them to get out of the desert peas, and the same old argument flared up: "We've got as much right to these flowers as anyone else, I'm an Australian, this place is as much mine as it is yours, you can't stop us from being here." All that bullshit. Ruby had to radio Aiden for backup.' Dylan shook his head. 'When I got to work this morning, Ruby was in Sarah's office absolutely giving it to her. I heard Sarah say something about her hands being tied, incident reports and a park staff meeting.'

'Christ,' Lulu muttered under her breath. 'Have you seen Ruby today?'

He shrugged. 'She's been out on the homelands, I think.'

'I'll bet,' Lulu nodded.

Alice tried to follow their conversation. Minga? Homelands? Dylan and Lulu looked at Alice as if they'd just remembered she was there.

'Sorry,' he said. 'None of this will make sense to you yet.'

'But it will soon enough,' Lulu said resolutely.

'Right.' Alice smiled. 'What's that place you mentioned?' she asked.

'Kuṯuṯu Kaana. The circle of desert peas inside the crater. Means Heart Garden,' Lulu explained.

'Heart Garden,' Alice murmured.

Lulu nodded. 'The problem's with the walking track. It follows the outer circumference of the crater and climbs the wall to a visitor viewing platform, which was built after Handback, when this place was recognised as Aboriginal land. From the platform the track goes into the crater and around the desert peas, following a path that's existed for thousands of years. Traditionally, it's a ceremonial walk for women. Anangu have been asking for years for the park to close it to tourists. There was talk of it for a while, but since the tourist boom, that's stopped.'

'Why?' Alice asked.

'Tourists are money, right? They pay the park entry fee to get up close to the desert peas. So the walk into the crater and Kututu Kaana stays open. Tourists inevitably pick the desert peas as souvenirs to take home with them. And for the women whose ancestors have always been here, like Ruby, it's dire. Every flower is a piece of Ngunytju's heart.'

'"Oong-joo"?' Alice repeated.

'Ngunytju,' Lulu said, nodding. 'Mother.'

Mother's heart. Alice's stomach lurched.

'The major concern is the threat they pose to desert peas. If tourists don't stop picking the flowers, it could cause mass root disturbance. If the desert pea roots are wrecked, the flowers, which quite literally are the heart of this place, its story and its people, will be destroyed.'

Alice tried to hide her filling eyes. She couldn't understand why she was getting so upset.

'You'll see for yourself on your orientation tomorrow,' Dylan said.

Alice nodded, watching as hordes of tourists continued to arrive. Some spilled out of coaches, while others mingled, drinking champagne from plastic flutes and eating salmon canapés. Families unpacked picnics and unfolded camp chairs, staking their claim to front-row views of the crater wall's sunset colour changes. Couples sat on the roofs of their four-wheel drives, watching the sky. There was a nervous energy in the air. *Be still*, Alice felt the urge to yell. *Pay attention.*

Around them, the willowy needles of desert oak trees swayed in the pale orange light. Wafts of yellow butterflies fluttered low over acacia and mulga bushes. The crater wall slowly changed colour as the sun sank, from flat ochre to blazing red to chocolate-purple. The sun slipped under the dark line of the horizon, glowing like an ember as it threw its last light up into the sky. Something about the vastness reminded Alice of how she felt, long ago, a girl looking out over the sea.

As she watched the sky, a telltale cold sweat sprang from her skin. Her vision started to blur and her hands started to claw. She tucked them under her arms. Squeezed her eyes shut. *Please*. Her breathing was short and shallow. *Breathe*, she told herself. But her heart wouldn't slow.

'You okay?' Dylan's voice sounded far away. As he came towards her, he took his sunglasses off.

The next moment became the memory Alice would later slow in her mind, panning for the glimpse of gold: the simmering sky behind him, the dry air on her skin, and the drone of flies, like the bees at Thornfield. The rustling through the mulga trees, and the hum in the earth beneath her feet, as if every feeling she'd ever felt was practice, readying her for this, the first time she made eye contact with him. It wasn't being put under a spell, or being hit by a truck, or getting an electric shock, or any of the other ways that the Flowers had described it to her when she was young.

For Alice, falling in love was nothing else but feeling her insides set on fire. The feeling consumed her, as if she'd somehow always known him and had been searching for him just as long.

Here he was.

As her knees gave way, she held his gaze, staring at him as she sank to the ground.

A sea of light rippled across her eyelids.

Alice, I'm right here, can you hear me?

Lulu's face came into focus above her.

'Sally?' Alice asked.

'Who?' His voice. Dylan. Dylan was crouched by her side.

'Alice Blue,' Alice said, looking into his eyes.

'She's all right, just talking nonsense. She's all good.' Lulu cradled Alice's shoulders and eased her up. 'Slow and steady, chica.' She opened a water bottle and gave it to Alice. The car park was empty. The sky was nearly dark. They sat in a pool of light spilling from Lulu's ute.

'Like making an entrance, hey?' Dylan asked.

Embarrassment stung her cheeks. 'Sorry,' she said.

A small smile played on his face. 'Reckon you're going to keep us on our toes, Alice Hart.'

'When was the last time you ate something?' Lulu asked, her brow furrowed.

Alice thought back to the sandwich she had that morning at the roadhouse. She shook her head.

'Okay. Dinner at mine, then. Let's go.' Lulu helped Alice to stand. The silhouette of the crater rose against the starry night sky. Alice looked around. The place felt entirely different emptied of crowds. Her eyes met Dylan's.

'You two going to be okay?' Dylan didn't take his eyes off Alice's face.

'All good,' Lulu said firmly. She walked around her ute to the driver's side. Dylan shut the passenger door, brushing Alice's elbow. Her skin burned where his fingers had touched.

'Thanks,' Lulu called curtly as she started the engine.

'Look after her,' Dylan called, walking away with a wave. *Look after her.* A wave of pleasure curled through Alice. She strained to follow him in the low light.

As they headed back towards Parksville, Alice watched the star-soaked sky. 'Thanks, Lulu,' she said quietly.

Lulu reached over and squeezed her arm. 'It's a bit intense for everyone when they arrive. Like I said, baptism of fire, chica.'

Lulu stood in the dark at her back fence, watching the beam of the torch she'd given Alice bounce down the dirt road between their houses. When Alice's torchlight waved, Lulu clicked hers on and waved until she saw Alice's flick off. She walked back through the yard to her house. The splatter of water came from the bathroom. Aiden was in the shower. She cleared away the dirty dishes and empty Corona bottles with soggy slices of lime at the bottom, waiting for him to finish before she filled the sink.

There was nothing left of dinner. Lulu had made fish tacos using her abuela's recipe, which had travelled around the world from Puerto Vallarta in Mexico with her when her abuela fled an arranged marriage. The secret to her spices was fresh cocoa. Always. Even if only a pinch. And it worked. Alice ate like a hungry dog, cleaning her loaded plate three times and necking beers until she wore the dozy smile of satisfaction that Lulu strived for whenever she cooked. Just one of the things her abuela taught her.

It was also Lulu's abuela who taught her she had prevision. *Just like me*, she'd say knowingly. Foresight ran in the women of their family, an unbreakable thread through generations, to see danger before it arrived; to see trauma when it was hidden; to see love before it bloomed. *Trust yourself, Lupita*, her abuela used to say, looking deep into her eyes. *This is why we named you 'Little Wolf'. Your instincts will always guide you, like the stars.*

Lulu was twelve when her abuela died. Afterwards, Lulu's grief-stricken mother banished their traditional ways. She cleansed their home of shadow boxes and rosary beads. No chilli chocolate, no sugar skulls. No fire, no spice. No folktales. No monarch butterflies. No foresight. But Lulu's visions didn't stop. Her mother took her to a doctor in the city. *Overactive imagination*, the doctor said with a smile as he gave Lulu jelly beans, and her mother a referral to an optometrist. Lulu was prescribed glasses. *Are they gone?* her mother asked, eyes brimming with desperation. Lulu pushed her new glasses up her nose and nodded. She never again told anyone about her visions. Instead she spent nights by her window, whispering to her abuela in the sky.

As Lulu grew up, the visions grew stronger. At the sound of someone's laugh, the smell of rain, the way light fell, or the sight of a flower, a curtain in Lulu's mind drew back and there it would be, a slice of someone else's life. *Don't be afraid*, her abuela told her. *This is your gift, Lupita.*

Years later, Lulu's visions continued though rarely made sense – a strange woman running along a beach, an unknown boy setting a paper boat into the sea, a house of flowers engulfed in fire – but Lulu experienced them as vividly as any memory of her own.

Three weeks before Alice arrived, Lulu had been on her back patio, potting seedlings, when the curtain drew back and a torrent of monarch butterflies swarmed through her, the sensation of their wings fluttering so strongly in her body she lost her balance. That afternoon, when Lulu pulled up outside Alice's house and saw up close the monarch butterfly stickers on the sides of Alice's truck, she'd heard her abuela's voice. *Guerrero del fuego.* Fire warrior. Lulu had never been able to connect a vision to someone she knew. Until she met Alice Hart.

'Lu?' Aiden came down the hall, towelling his wet hair.

'Sorry?' She turned to look at him.

'I asked if Alice got home okay?'

Lulu nodded. While she talked to Aiden often about her abuela, Lulu never told him, or anyone else, about the foresight. She'd tried a couple of times but could never find words that felt true, so in the end she outright lied. Aiden consequently thought vertigo was hereditary in Lulu's family and often asked if she was getting enough rest, or eating enough to keep her blood sugar up.

He slung his towel over the back of a dining chair and went to the cupboard.

'Alice seems pretty great,' he said. 'Sounds like Dylan made his classic impression, though.' He took down a wine glass, and the bottle of red they'd opened the night before.

'Yeah,' Lulu agreed. Dread spread through her as she thought of the way she'd seen Alice looking at Dylan.

'Does she know he's got a girlfriend?' Aiden poured a glass of wine.

Lulu ran the sink, added too much dishwashing liquid. 'I'm not sure.'

'Maybe you should mention it?' Aiden asked.

'It's not my place, mi amor.' Lulu turned the taps off. Kept her back to him.

'Reckon it's precisely your place, my love,' he replied. Lulu sunk her hands into the hot, soapy water, washing a plate clean. If only past mistakes were as easy to wash away.

'She seems a bit sad though,' he said, gently nudging Lulu away from the sink to take over. He gestured towards the glass of wine. Lulu dried her hands and took a sip.

Their conversation lulled. Lulu wandered to the back door with the wine glass. Put her hand on the latch.

'Say g'day to your grandmother for me,' Aiden called. She smiled at him gratefully.

Outside, the night was warm and silver, the sky thick with stars and the light of a waning moon. Dogs howled in the distance. Lulu sat on the dune at the back of their yard and sipped her wine. The red dirt was cool and fine. She picked up a handful and let it run through her fingers as she looked through the silhouettes of desert oaks towards the lit windows in Alice's house. Flames fluttered through her mind; fire-coloured butterflies.

After a while she swivelled slowly in the other direction until she was facing Dylan's house. Its shadowy bulk sat dark and silent. A movement in the shadows caught her eye. Lulu watched, taking a shaky sip of her wine. The memory of his cologne flooded her senses.

21

Sturt's desert pea

Meaning: Have courage, take heart

Swainsona formosa | Inland Australia

Malukuṟu (Pit.) are famous for distinctive blood-red, leaf-like flowers, each with a bulbous black centre, similar to a kangaroo's eye. A striking sight in the wild: a blazing sea of red. Bird-pollinated and thrives in arid areas, but very sensitive to any root disturbance, which makes it difficult to propagate.

In the pre-dawn light Alice and Pip wound through the bushes to the back gate. Pip wagged her tail, her nose bent to the ground, following scents. They headed up, over the sand dune, and down the other side to the fire trails, as Aiden had told her the tracks around Parksville were called. *They're breakers*, he'd said. *To stop the flames jumping if there's ever a bushfire.* Alice had nodded, trying to look interested, but her insides went cold. She'd taken a long slurp of beer to wash away memories of smoke and fire.

Talking with Aiden while Lulu cooked, Alice had been transfixed by their company and home: Lulu's husky laugh, the sizzling tacos, the brightly painted pots of aloe vera and green chilli, shelves of books, framed prints of Frida Kahlo self-portraits. Alice was consumed by a sense of longing, though for what exactly she wasn't sure. Going back to her mostly empty, bleach-scented house was sobering. She'd gone to bed yearning for coloured walls, glossy pots, and books to fill her empty shelves.

Alice and Pip walked through a huddle of desert oaks and reached the ring road. They crossed and slipped into the bush, joining the trail that zigzagged up the wall, disappearing over the top.

'C'mon, Pip.'

The sky was starting to lighten. Her boots crunched loudly on the grit.

By the time the two of them reached the viewing platform, the neck of Alice's T-shirt was ringed with sweat. Pip flopped onto her side, panting hard. Black flies buzzed around Alice's face. She swatted at them as she took in her surroundings. On either side of the platform, ochre walls peeled up and away, a circular wave of rock gouged from the earth by violent impact. At the centre of the crater, in a perfect circle, was a wild garden of blooming desert peas, a mother's heart, a rippling sea of red. There was a surprising covering of lime-green grass on the crater floor. Kuṯuṯu Kaana was more staggering than Alice had imagined; it was every story she had ever read or heard or imagined about an oasis in the desert.

Have courage, take heart.

The force of her yearning for her mother, for her grandmother, and the women she'd left behind tore through her without warning or mercy. She gasped from the pain, biting hard down on her lip until she tasted blood.

Later, back at home, Alice showered and got herself ready for her first day in her new job. She took great care dressing in her green ranger uniform, studying the circular badges on the sleeves of her shirt in the mirror. She traced her fingertips over the desert peas in the centre of the Indigenous flag. How different from her Thornfield apron; she'd never felt the pride of wearing a uniform she'd earned on her own merit before.

She laced up her stiff new boots and gathered her backpack and hat. 'Do not play with a snake, okay?' Alice kissed Pip's nose, locked her in the garage cage, and got into her truck. As she drove through Parksville she marvelled at the day. The sky was lapis lazuli, the morning light citrine.

When she parked her truck at headquarters Alice's heart started to pound. She breathed steadily, trying to slow it down.

'Wiṟu mulapa mutuka pinta-pinta,' a soft voice spoke at her window.

'Sorry?' Alice shaded her eyes. A woman stood by her truck, wearing the same shirt as Alice. Her hair was wrapped in a black, red and yellow headscarf, under a full-brimmed Akubra. Around her neck hung strings of glossy, blood-red seeds. Her trousers were white, covered in green, yellow and blue watercolour budgerigars, such a random and joyful sight Alice couldn't help but grin.

'I'm Ruby.' The woman held out her hand. Alice got out of her truck and took Ruby's hand in hers. 'I was just saying, I like your butterfly truck.'

'Oh.' Alice laughed nervously, glancing over at the butterfly stickers on her doors, thinking about everything they were hiding. 'Thanks,' she said.

'I'm the Senior Ranger here, and I'm training you this morning. You're out in the field with the other rangers this arv.' Ruby walked off towards a park ute. 'You can drive.' She tossed the keys back to Alice.

'Oh. Right.' Alice hurried to catch up. She got into the ute and leant over to unlock the passenger door.

Ruby got in. 'Head out onto the ring road.'

'Sure.'

Ruby's demeanour reminded Alice strongly of Twig. She tried to think of something to say but her words dried up, red dust on her tongue.

'I'm a senior law woman,' Ruby stated after a while. 'I train new rangers like you. Teach you the stories that can be publicly told here. I'm also a poet and artist. I chair the Central Desert Women's Council, and live between here and Darwin. My family –'

'That must be such a huge contrast,' Alice interrupted, leaping at any chance to contribute to the conversation. 'Going between here and the city.' She tried to pause, tried to take a breath. 'So, you're a poet? I love books. I love to read. I've always loved writing stories. But I haven't done much of that since I was a teenager.' To her horror, nerves were making Alice uncharacteristically talkative; she couldn't shut herself up.

Ruby gave a polite nod but didn't speak again. She turned her back. Alice bit her bottom lip. She shouldn't have interrupted. Should she apologise? Should she try changing the subject? Was Ruby waiting for her to ask questions about Kililpitjara? What should she ask? Were there things she couldn't ask?

Alice tried focusing on not changing the gears too roughly or going too fast. As they neared the main visitor car park, the radio crackled to life.

'National parks nineteen, nineteen, this is seven-seven, over.'

Dylan's timbre shot through her bloodstream into her bones. Alice gripped the steering wheel. Very casually, Ruby leaned forward and turned the radio off.

'Pull up here,' Ruby signalled to the car park. Self-doubt wormed through Alice's mind. Was she that obvious? Did Ruby think she was more interested in Dylan than she was in doing a good job on her first day? Wasn't that kind of true? *Please stop*, she begged herself.

Ruby opened her door and got out. Alice followed. At the beginning of the trail Alice stopped to read a group of information signs. Ruby came up beside her.

'So tourists know the Heart Garden at the centre of the crater is sacred, and that you ask them not to pick any flowers, to make sure the site is protected?' Alice asked.

Ruby nodded. 'It's in all the guide books, pamphlets and visitor information. We invite visitors to come and learn the stories of this place, but please, don't pick our flowers.'

Alice remembered the conversation she'd heard the night before. 'But they still do it?'

'Uwa. They still do it,' Ruby said as she wandered off, her hands behind her back.

They walked in silence. The red dirt trail followed the outer wall of the crater, passing fields of low-lying spinifex, emu bushes and buffel grass, through clusters of tall wattle trees and skinny desert oaks. After a while they came to a giant red boulder that sat like an open door at the entrance of a small cave. Ruby went around it, inside. Alice followed, panting from the heat.

'You got kapi?' Ruby looked at her in the dim light with an eyebrow raised.

Alice gawked blankly in response, her eyes adjusting.

'Kapi. Water.'

Alice's face fell as she realised she'd left her backpack with her water and hat in her truck at headquarters. She swore at herself under her breath, and shook her head.

'You're gunna want to carry that with you everywhere here in future.' Ruby shook her head and turned away to look up at the ceiling of the cave. Alice rolled her eyes at her own stupidity. What sort of idiot went into the desert without water?

After a while, Alice's thoughts quietened enough for her to realise Ruby was speaking in a whisper. Overhead, all around them, were ochre, white and red rock paintings. Alice listened as Ruby explained the symbols women had painted thousands of years ago, telling stories of desert peas, mothers, children and stars.

'This land is where the women in my family have always brought their stories. To bear witness. To grieve. To honour what they have loved. It's a sorry place. That's why we don't live here.'

Alice stepped closer to the paintings.

'The trail into Kililpitjara follows the ceremonial path around Kututu Kaana, where malukuru grow from the star mother's heart.' Ruby's voice was still low. 'That's why we ask people not to pick any of the flowers. Each one is a piece of her.'

Neither of them spoke. Ruby gave a closing nod, turned, and left. But Alice lingered, spellbound by the rock art, and overcome by gratitude for her chance meeting with Sarah in Agnes Bluff.

After she'd caught up to Ruby, Alice wondered what it was like for Ruby, constantly fighting to protect a place and its story, which had been central to her family's culture for longer than anyone could know. Where did she find the strength to keep fighting? And who were the people that ignored her family's stories of the place, and helped themselves to the desert peas, denying that they were tearing up pieces of the star mother's heart? The signs were literally everywhere around them. No one could plead ignorance.

Ruby walked ahead, and Alice followed. Unsure of herself or her place, Alice left all of her questions unasked.

The walking track met the ring road at a site called Kuṯuṯu Puḷi, where a sheltered bench and water tank offered a close view of the crater wall jutting dramatically from the earth: a cascade of red rocks and boulders covered in silver and mint-coloured lichen. For a moment, Alice was spellbound. But then she remembered the water tank and fell to it, drinking until she was full.

'This is a thirsty place,' Ruby nodded. 'Where Ngunytju's heart caught fire and burned as it hit the earth. That's what the rocks are, pieces of her heart in flames. The lichen is where the smoke still rises from the embers, staining the crater wall.'

Alice couldn't look at Ruby, fearing she'd see the tears in her eyes and decide once and for all she was hopeless.

'Do you live in Parksville too?' Alice had seized the first thing she thought of. Why didn't she ask more about the crater story, which she was here to learn for her job? She cursed herself under her breath.

'Uwa,' Ruby nodded. 'But only when I'm here for training. I come to teach you fellas about culture. Like I said, my family doesn't live here. It's a sorry place. Not a place to live.' Ruby dusted her hands off. 'You right to keep going?'

'Yep,' Alice replied, burning to ask why any of them were there if it wasn't a place for living.

They walked the rest of the way around the crater in silence. A large tour group passed them in the opposite direction, heading back to the main car park. Alice eyed them suspiciously; had any of them picked desert peas? Swallows swooped overhead, singing. Sunshine fell in patches through a canopy of gum trees. Eventually the trail turned out of the shade and began to climb the crater wall, the same track Alice had found that morning with Pip. She shielded her face from the glare. It wasn't even mid-morning but in direct sun the temperature felt like it must be close to forty degrees.

At the viewing platform, Ruby sat to catch her breath. Alice did the same, taking in the heart of desert peas.

'Kungka, I'm going to tell you the whole story of this place,' Ruby began.

'Oh, yes,' Alice leapt in. 'I read. On the internet. About the mother's heart that fell here, after her baby fell to Earth in another impact crater near to here.' She couldn't stop herself.

This time Ruby didn't even look at her. She set her jaw, got up and left the platform, following the trail down into the crater.

Helpless, Alice watched her go, dumbfounded by her own stupidity. *Shut the fuck up!* she screamed to herself. She'd never wanted to impress anyone as much as she did Ruby. But her nervous chatter was ruining everything.

Alice put her head in her hands. She'd never gone for a job interview, or done an orientation, or undergone training like this before. She'd never been out of June's protective gaze. This was her first real chance to make something of herself, on her own. And she was fucking it up royally.

Have courage. Take heart.

She sat up. Adjusted her uniform. Nodded to herself determinedly, and followed Ruby into Kuṯuṯu Kaana.

The temperature inside the crater was stifling. Waves of heat rose from the earth. Flocks of green birds flew overhead.

'Those tjuḻpu.' Ruby laughed, waving at the birds. 'Cheeky buggers.'

As they approached the flowers, Ruby gestured towards them, about to speak. This time, Alice kept quiet.

'Minga come because of the story, but when they get here they've got closed ears. They want the story but they don't hear it. They only hear it if they take a piece of it with them.' Ruby's voice was sad, but strong. 'So many people coming, going off track, the threat is to the roots. These maḻukuṟu, these flowers, they're strong. They grow here, and have for thousands of years. But their roots, you get down there and make their roots sick and the whole lot will die. True. We ask them not to, but people still go. Into the circle. To pick flowers. Take a piece of Ngunytju's heart away with them. They'll make the roots sick. Those roots get sick, we all get sick.'

Alice paused, waiting for a moment before she spoke. 'Root rot,' she said. 'Sturt's desert peas are vulnerable to root rot. If their roots are disturbed, they're more likely to die from that than they are from drought.'

Ruby had a mix of surprise and appreciation on her face. 'Eh?' she said, giving Alice a playful nudge. 'You're a bit ninti puḻka with our heart flowers, eh kungka?' She smiled. 'You're a bit clever, eh?'

Alice exhaled, letting her shoulders fall from where they'd been hunched around her ears.

'You're all right, kungka.' Ruby chuckled as she toed a stone with her boot. 'You just need to close your mouth a bit and open your ears a bit more. Calm those thoughts in your head that are like cheeky tjuḻpu,' she said, pointing to the budgerigars on her trousers, 'so you can take the story of this place in.'

Alice nodded, unable to meet her eyes.

Ruby tugged on Alice's sleeve. 'Listen, when you wear our flag on your arms here,' she pointed to the badges on Alice's shirt, 'you've got a responsibility to tell it true now, the story of this place, to all the minga that come from all over the world.' A gust of hot wind blew around them, rustling into the circle of desert peas. 'This is a sorry place. A sacred place, for love, sadness, rest and peace. This place holds the ceremonial stories of thousands of years of women. My ancestors, raising their babies and looking after this land, and the land looking after them. Maḻukuṟu, these flowers, they keep their stories alive. We need to work together to protect them. That's your job now too,' Ruby said, gesturing towards Alice. 'Palya, Kungka Pinta-Pinta?'

Alice looked at her.

'Okay, Butterfly Girl?' Ruby translated, smiling.

What do you think you'd like to be when you grow up, Bun? Alice's mother had her hands in a pot of fertiliser among the ferns in her garden. Her face was obscured by her gardening hat. Alice didn't have to give it much thought. *A butterfly, or a writer*, she replied, smiling. Anything that kept her close to her mother's garden, or between the pages of books.

'Palya, Kungka Pinta-Pinta?' Ruby asked again.

'Palya,' Alice replied.

Ruby gave a satisfied nod and turned, her hands behind her back as she began to walk the trail around the flowers and out of the crater. Alice took a last lingering look at the desert peas before she turned and walked away.

After sandwiches and juice from the visitor centre cafe for lunch, Ruby pulled Alice aside. She had a strange look on her face. 'Before you go out in the field this arv, there's something I want to show you.'

Alice followed Ruby up a flight of stairs to an attic-like storage space in the roof of the visitor centre. It was cramped, hot and stuffy, full of shelves holding large plastic boxes. Ruby went to a shelf and took down a box. She lifted the lid and gestured for Alice to look inside. It was stuffed with letters, some printed, others handwritten. Inside every single one was a pressed, dried desert pea.

'Sorry flowers,' Ruby said. 'From people who pick them as souvenirs, take them home to wherever they come from, then start to believe their bad luck in life is a curse for ignoring our culture.' She gestured to the shelves behind her, filled with similar boxes.

Alice leant over the open box.

'Go ahead,' Ruby said.

Riffling through, Alice reeled at the volume of dried flowers people had picked and returned. Envelopes bearing postage stamps from all over the world contained letters begging forgiveness, begging to be free of 'the curse'. A handwritten one caught her eye. As Alice opened it, a dried and shrivelled desert pea fell into her palm. She read, aloud.

'"My husband got sick as soon as we left Kililpitjara. When we got home to Italy, we found out he has cancer. A few days later our son was in a bus accident. And then our house flooded. Please accept our deepest apologies for not respecting your beautiful country on our visit. Please free us from any more tragedy. We are so deeply sorry for picking the flowers from the crater and taking what wasn't ours to take."' Alice rocked back on her heels, incredulous. 'They're all the same thing? Asking for forgiveness and freedom from "the curse"?'

Ruby nodded. '"The curse", a myth that's travelled around the world for as long as minga have been coming here.'

'But it's … not real?' Alice asked slowly.

'No!' Ruby snorted. 'It's not real. It's just a trick guilt plays on guilty people's minds.'

Alice's thoughts drifted to June's slurred confession the night she left Thornfield. 'We can't hide when we've done wrong,' Alice said, 'even if we try to bury it in the deepest parts of ourselves.' Aware that Ruby was watching her closely, Alice put the letter back in the box and brushed her hands together. 'Do you ever write back? Tell them "the curse" is something people have made up and isn't anything to do with your culture?'

'Ha!' Ruby said drily. 'I've got better things to do than run around after minga and do the work for them, teaching what they should have opened their eyes and ears to and learned when it was right in front of them.'

Alice nodded, letting Ruby's words sink in. 'I just can't believe there's so many,' she said, going through the envelopes once more.

'This is why we're so worried about malukuru becoming endangered. Worse, there's even more stories in the roof at headquarters. We've started having meetings to figure out what to do with them. There's a couple of university fellas interested in cataloguing all the stories. But they'll have to be quick. We're running out of storage.'

A childhood conversation with her mother came to mind. *A fire can be like a spell of sorts to transform one thing into another.*

'Maybe you could burn them,' Alice blurted.

Ruby studied her face appreciatively. 'Maybe,' she said.

By the time Alice got home that night she could barely keep her eyes open. She stumbled through her front door, flicked on the air conditioning, and stood under the cold shower watching as the water turned red.

She'd worked with Lulu after lunch. *Ruby showed you the sorry flowers?* she'd said when they were out in the field together, after Alice described her morning. Alice nodded. *Man, you must have done something right, chica. Ruby doesn't show anyone those flowers unless they're in her good books.*

Standing under the shower, replaying Lulu's words, Alice flushed with pleasure. She'd done something right.

Later Alice shared with Pip a veggie burger she'd brought home from the cafe, and flopped into bed before the sun set. The warm air carried the rich scent of baked earth and the sweet end of her first day.

Her dreams were filled with visions of June. Every time her grandmother opened her mouth to speak to Alice, a torrent of brown and withered dried flowers gushed out.

Ruby stood on her patio in the setting sun, watching rainbows catch in the spray while she watered her pot plants. The mineral-rich smell of the damp red dirt took her straight to the memory of her mother and aunties, like a song. The sky gathered a palette of pink clay, ochre and grey stone. Ruby's trio of dogs raced each other along her back fence, their ears flattened in joy. The mellowest part of the day always made them the silliest.

Once she'd hung up the hose she took her axe into the yard and cut down some wanari branches. Wanari was the best for cooking fires; it burned the hottest. She piled the wood in the pit, sucking the blood from her finger when she got a splinter. After she raked together dry desert-oak needles, skinny twigs and sticks, she stuffed them into the gaps between the branches. A few matches later, her fire was roaring.

Ruby sat on a log with her pen and notebook, and relaxed her shoulders. Once she was settled, she closed her eyes. The weight of her missing family settled around her. Ever since she was a child, when she was taken from her mother, the one constant in her life was the present absence of her family. It was a visible kind of invisibility; all Ruby could ever see were those not there with her.

While her dinner cooked on a skillet over the fire and the sky started to darken, Ruby uncapped her pen and opened her notebook.

She watched the flames. She waited.

The stars swirled, the dogs dozed, and the warm desert breeze blew. She waited.

The new poem came down from the stars, looking for her as most of her poems did. It tumbled over the sand dunes and fluttered across her mother's country, bringing earth, smoke, love and sorrow.

> there are always seeds that thread us
> and carried on the wind set us apart
> does the wind come from the origins
> or the mother or the father
> will my origins be blown away
> or remain in distance if I leave
> will the wind stand breathless
> shall I remain to die broken from home

Ruby put her pen down and rubbed her hands. They were shaking, as they always did when her ancestors gave her a poem. After a moment, she picked it up again and wrote *Seeds* at the top of the page.

She seasoned and turned her malu steak, and slathered more garlic butter on her fried potatoes. Sat back and watched the flames dance. Smoke plumes curled into the sky.

As Ruby served up her dinner her mind wandered back to showing Alice the shelves of sorry flowers. Ruby had seen more people come and go through Kililpitjara than she'd written poems in her notebooks. She could pick those who were lost and aimless from those who were true and searching as easily as she pulled ticks from her dogs. When she'd first noticed Sarah moving Alice in, all shaky and pale-faced, Ruby hadn't given her a second thought. But after their morning together, Ruby changed her mind. She saw something in Alice Hart, the kind of grit one survivor recognises in another. Ruby didn't know what Alice was looking for, but it burned in her brightly enough to leave fire in her eyes.

22

Spinifex

Meaning: **Dangerous pleasures**
Triodia | Central Australia

*Tjanpi (Pit.) is a tough, spiky grass dominating much of
Australia's interior red sand country, thriving on the poorest,
most arid soils the desert has to offer. Tussock-forming,
its roots go deep, often as far down as three metres. Certain
types are used by Anangu to make a resin adhesive.*

Alice threw herself into her life at Kililpitjara. She continued
training with Ruby, studying the stories of the land, and became
inseparable from Lulu, working the same roster ten days on and
four days off. Alice listened deeply and learned from both women.
With a strong voice, she guided tourists into the crater day in and
day out, telling them its story and inviting them to help protect the
Heart Garden. She got such a thrill when she saw understanding
in visitors' eyes. As the weeks passed, she felt sure no one on any
of her walks picked a desert pea.

After work, as the days began to cool, Alice and Lulu took to
walking the fire trails, or lounging on each other's patios, drinking
strong coffee and eating Lulu's homemade chilli chocolate. Under
gemstone skies, Lulu told Alice stories about her grandmother,
a woman with turquoise rings on every finger and hair so thick
she snapped combs in half trying to tame it. *What about you,
Alice? Tell me about your family.* Alice was too scared to tell her the
truth. Stories rolled freely off her tongue, about her mother and
father, her seven brothers, the games they played growing up, the
adventures they had together, their happy home by the sea. The

stories came so easily they didn't feel like lies. They were as real as real could be to Alice; they were the worlds she'd grown up in, from the pages of her books.

Late at night, when she was alone, Alice worked on her notebooks of flowers. They had become her solace and salve, her pressed and sketched flowers; her stories. Of childhood memories; loneliness and confusion; the life she'd lived without her mother; resentment, grief, fear and guilt. Her unfulfilled dreams. Her penance. Her yearning to be consumed by love.

After a few months, Alice no longer felt so glaringly incompetent. She knew everyone at the park by name, and had the vital information memorised: which days the food deliveries came in by road train and how many return trips from Parksville to the tourist resort she could make before her truck's fuel light flicked on. Kililpitjara became a place where Alice felt safe. There was no past there. No one knew about her life among the sugar cane or her life among flowers. In the desert, she could just be. Her job left her with aching muscles, blistered knuckles and a sense of bodily exhaustion so great that she no longer dreamed of fire. She was fascinated by the desert: its colours, its vast space, the staggering and strange beauty of it. When she wasn't on sunrise patrol, Alice spent her mornings with Pip hiking up to the viewing platform. Tears always sprang to her eyes at the sight of the desert peas; she relied on them to keep her centred, to keep her whole. Although Alice taught Pip some of Harry's old assistance commands, she had no reason to use them. She didn't have another blackout. The only time her heart raced was when she was near Dylan Rivers.

One afternoon, at the end of their ten-day roster, Alice and Lulu were in the work yard washing their work utes. They had music playing loudly and were dreaming up plans for their four days off together when Dylan drove through the security gate. Alice slid her sunglasses down over her eyes.

'Kungkas,' Dylan said as he drove up beside them, winding down his window. 'How's it going?'

Alice nodded. A small smile. She couldn't speak. Lulu glanced at her and then at Dylan. 'We're on day ten, so all good,' she said to him coolly.

'Jealous,' he said. 'I'm only halfway.' He didn't take his eyes off Alice. His blatancy made her uncomfortable; she felt he could see right through to her heart and what it was made of: salt, native flowers, stories, and a hopeless yearning for him. When Lulu had told her he had a girlfriend, Julie, a tour guide based out of town, Alice was sick with envy.

'Up to anything on your days off?' he asked.

She could smell his skin, the cologne he wore, fresh and sweet, reminding her of unfurling green leaves. She wanted to run, to get into his ute with him and just go, through as many sunrises and sunsets as it took to get to the west coast, where they could tumble from the red dust onto the white sand and start over by the turquoise sea. She was good at beginning again.

'Aren't we, Alice?' Lulu's pointed question interrupted her reverie. Having no idea what she was talking about, Alice nodded and smiled vacantly.

'Cool. Well, I'm off. Have a good one.' As Dylan drove away he raised his hand in a slow wave. Silver rings on his fingers and strands of leather tied around his wrist.

'Don't do that,' Lulu said, her voice low and serious. 'That's messy. There's nothing but pain there. Don't do it.'

Alice turned her face away. Out of the corner of her eye she watched Dylan's profile as he drove out of the work yard. The tail lights of his ute pierced the fading light.

'He's great as a mate, chica,' Lulu warned. 'But anything more than that? You're no safer than the girl in the fairytale who wanders into a dark wood.'

Alice was grateful for the low light, hoping it hid her face. Lulu dipped her sponge in the suds bucket and began scrubbing the windscreen.

'You've slept with him, haven't you?' Alice asked quietly.

Lulu glanced at her. Cast her eyes away. 'I just don't want you to get hurt.'

Alice's head was spinning. She couldn't bear the thought of them together, of him being with anyone but her.

Lulu wiped the windscreen down and dunked the sponge back in the bucket, sighing. 'I don't know what you've left behind but I know you've come here to put yourself back together,' she said. 'So do it, chica. You keep banging on about how much you love my place and would love yours to be like it, but you keep living like you're a nun. Decorate. Embellish. Use your weekends for adventures, go exploring. There's so much more around here than just the crater, like, there's a gorge not far from here that you have to see at sunset to believe. So, grow. Please. Grow your life here.' Lulu pointed to her heart. 'Don't give everything you've got to someone who isn't worth it.'

Alice fidgeted. She hadn't talked to anyone about what she'd left behind and yet Lulu had figured her out.

After they'd packed up they drove home together under a dusky watercolour sky. 'Wanna come over for dinner?' Lulu said too brightly. 'I'm making cheesy enchiladas. With extra guacamole.'

Alice snorted. 'No. I do not. Not at all.'

As they pulled into Lulu's driveway, their earlier conversation niggled at Alice. She nodded and laughed along with Lulu's jokes throughout the evening but couldn't stop wondering: had Lulu and Dylan slept together? Why wouldn't she answer directly?

Later, getting ready for bed, Alice told herself to just let it go. As Lulu had reminded her, she hadn't exactly been forthcoming about her life before the desert. Alice knew as well as anyone that some stories were best left untold.

Alice tried her hardest to heed Lulu's words. Went into the resort village on truck delivery day, and filled a trolley with pot plants, a hammock, a box of fairy lights, and some solar-powered garden lamps. From the park workshop she scavenged a stack of crates and leftover paint. She painted the crates green, turned them upside down, and used them as pot plant stands; hammered the garden lamps deep into the red dirt in her backyard, strung up her hammock, and wound her rope of fairy lights around the beams of her back patio. She gathered treasures like a bower bird and told herself it was all for her own wellbeing. It was all to nurture her sense of self.

She spent hours internet shopping. Bought new bed sheets with a butterfly-print doona cover, a butterfly-print shower curtain, and a tablecloth patterned in monarch butterflies. She found an aromatherapy website and bought a burner, a year's supply of tea light candles, and a blend of essential oils. After staring at her bookshelf one night, empty but for her notebooks from Agnes Bluff, Alice found an online bookshop and ordered whatever her pay cheque allowed. When the boxes came, she unpacked them and placed each book on the shelf, as gently as if they were seedlings. Especially the stories about selkies.

As he was on the opposite roster, Alice didn't have any reason to see Dylan. If they passed each other on the road or in the work yard, she ducked her head. To keep herself busy, whenever she wasn't on sunset patrol, Alice started walking Pip around the crater in the afternoons. They walked to Kututu Puli to watch the sun set on the lichen-covered red boulders. With enough determination, she could work and walk the raw burn of love out of her system. Maybe her feeling for him really was a fever. Maybe she could break it.

On her next day off Alice roamed her house restlessly. Lulu and Aiden were busy. Ruby wasn't home. Alice had been for her morning and afternoon walks, cleaned, and driven into town to buy Pip a new chew toy. By six o'clock the sky was dark enough to flick her fairy lights on and finally surrender to the thoughts of Dylan she'd been resisting all day.

Alice went outside into the smoky purple dusk. Ever since the first night she'd turned her fairy lights on, they'd been tiny secret beacons of her heart. When she lay in bed watching them shine, she was consumed by hope that the fragile little lights she'd strung in the darkness somehow reached him across the dunes, somehow spoke to him all the things she could not say.

A loud rapping knock on the front door made her jump. Pip sniffed the air, barking.

'Coming,' Alice called, rushing through the house. Could it be? She flung the door open.

'Happy housewarming!' Lulu and Aiden sang in unison.

'Oh!' Alice startled. 'You guys!' She smiled widely enough to hide her crushing disappointment.

In one arm Lulu held an oven dish of tacos oozing melted cheese and heaped with guacamole. In the other she cradled the colourful Mexican vase that Alice often commented on, filled with freshly cut desert roses. Alice remembered the handwritten entry in the Thornfield Dictionary. *Peace.* Beside Lulu, Aiden carried the Frida Kahlo print Alice always ogled most at their house, and a six-pack of Coronas.

'For you, chica,' Lulu said, grinning as she and Aiden offered their gifts. 'We know you've been working so hard to make your house a home, and wanted to celebrate with you.'

'Speechless,' Alice croaked, choking up. 'Come in, come in, you wonderful, cheeky buggers.' She sniffled, stepping aside to let them in. As she was closing the door, Pip yapped. 'What?' Alice asked her. She yapped again at the door. For a moment Alice was giddy with hope. But when she swung the door open, it was Ruby who stepped into the light.

'You need to get your outdoor light fixed, Pinta-Pinta,' Ruby said, walking inside with a fresh loaf of bread that smelled warm and garlicky. 'I baked.' She handed the loaf to Alice with a nod and went to sit with Lulu and Aiden at the table. Alice took the bread and Lulu's tacos into the kitchen, willing herself to keep smiling. Willing herself not to cry because her beautiful, kind friends weren't Dylan turning up at her door. She busied herself pouring drinks and finding plates, overwhelmed by deep gratitude, and deeper foolishness.

After the impromptu housewarming, Alice's resolve began to crumble. She wouldn't admit that she went out of her way to at least see his ute, or hear his voice on the park radio. It was a hunger unlike any she'd known. She started breaking afternoon plans with Ruby, and lying to Lulu about needing time alone. *Something's going on with you, chica. I can feel it*, Lulu said to her. Alice brushed her off.

For a long time, she'd told herself her afternoon walks had nothing to do with him. Every time Alice walked the dusty red dirt track around the crater, she inwardly denied she was driven by one thing: the moment she would come around the bend by the scraggly gums and rest her eyes on his face. She ignored that she deliberately timed her walk so she'd 'coincidentally' bump into him at sunset at Kuṯuṯu Puḻi. He held the full attention of the afternoon tourist group while he told them the story of Kililpitjara. But he always looked up just as she passed; she thrilled at his eyes drifting over her body.

And so their charade went, day by day. She would walk on, timing her pace to her best guess of how long it would take him to finish, and make his last patrol lap of the ring road. If she thought she needed to slow down, she'd amble under her favourite archway of mulga trees, which reached over the track, the fingers of their branches entwined. Or she'd gather a fistful of desert wildflowers to press in her notebook. But if she thought she needed to quicken her pace, Alice broke into a jog. She didn't stop to take in the light or the birdsong, or notice the baked scent of the earth as the day cooled. She didn't pause to wonder at the mulga archway or give a thought to wildflowers. There was only ever one thing on her mind. It was only ever him.

At Kuṯuṯu Puḷi she stopped to fill her empty-on-purpose water bottle. She always sat on the side of the water tank, facing the full light of the setting sun. She knew her legs and feet were visible from the road. It was his call whether he pulled up and stopped to see her. She stared at the red sky while she waited.

He'll be here.

No matter how many times she heard the sound, the thrill of his tyres crunching on the dirt did not wane.

His engine would cut silent. His car door would open.

He was there.

And, if anyone was watching, all they'd see was two friends bumping into each other, meeting by accident. Every day of the week.

'G'day,' he'd say with a smile.

'G'day,' she'd reply, always expressing just enough surprise to see him, never having to force her warmest grin.

As the sun set the two of them sat talking, taking their time to carefully reveal pieces of themselves to each other: they never talked about who she was before she'd arrived at Kililpitjara, or who else was in his life. Instead they talked around those things, showing each other their best half-truths.

'Have you ever been to the west coast?' he asked one day, without looking at her.

Had he heard her thoughts and daydreams? She didn't look at him. 'Not yet,' she said breezily, swatting flies away, fixing her gaze in the same direction as his, on tussocks of spinifex backlit by the sun. 'Love to though. To see where red dirt meets white sand and aqua sea.'

He laughed. 'What the hell are we doing hanging around here?'

She grinned at him. Yellow butterflies swooped over the grass, drunk on the orange light. The lichen turned black in the shadows, and the crater wall reflected the blaze of sunset colours.

Though his presence soothed painful memories she wanted to forget, every time they met, the life Alice had left behind began to creep like a vine into her heart, tendril by tendril and leaf by leaf, until she realised one day while they were talking that she was always mentally gathering him bouquets, silently telling him her deepest longings the only way she knew how: through the unspoken language of Australian native flowers.

23

Desert heath - myrtle

Meaning: **Flame, I burn**

Thryptomene maisonneuvii | Northern Territory

*Traditionally, Aṉangu women beat pukara (Pit.) with a
wooden bowl to collect dew containing nectar from the flowers.
Thryptomene, derived from Greek, means coy or prudish; this
bush appears modest but in winter through to spring produces
a cloak of tiny white flowers with red centres, blooming as if
revealing a secret.*

Alice's twenty-seventh birthday fell in the middle of her four days
off. She hadn't told anyone about it. Not even Lulu.

She lay in bed watching the winter sky and naming the
changing colours – soft navy and lilac to peach and champagne
pink – before the sun rose and lit up the red earth. She'd taken
to leaving her fairy lights on day and night. She thought of the
gossip she'd overheard in the staff kitchen at headquarters: Dylan
had taken leave to visit his girlfriend, Julie. It had hit her hard,
especially as Dylan had met her at Kuṯuṯu Puḻi the day before but
hadn't mentioned it.

Alice propped herself up in bed. Her breath puffed little steam
clouds into the air. Pip scampered out of bed to scratch at the back
door.

'Only for you, Pip,' Alice groaned, dragging herself up to let
her out. She switched the heater on, shivering while she waited for
its warmth to kick in.

On her way back inside, Pip gave Alice a lick. Alice nodded.

'Birthday drinks are an excellent idea.'

She went into the kitchen and warmed a pot of milk, pouring half into a bowl, which she set down for Pip, and the rest into a mug with a shot of espresso coffee. She took a book from her bookshelf and scurried back into bed. Pip followed, licking her milky chops.

Alice propped herself against her pillows. She sipped her coffee and opened her book, but the world outside was too beautiful a distraction. Overnight frost melted on the thryptomene flowers, glittering as it caught the sun. The sky was china blue, dotted with plump clouds. In the distance, the crater wall was luminous in the morning light. Her mind swirled with the stories she'd learned about this place, of the mother who put her baby down to rest in the stars, and lost her child to the land. The story and the landscape were one and the same; even the arcing path of the stars over the northern rim of the crater mirrored its circular formation.

She snuggled further under her doona, watching as yellow butterflies hovered over the flowering bushes; were they in Dylan's garden too? What was he doing, right at that moment, while she was at home, on her birthday, alone? Alice's eyes welled. She didn't often let herself wonder who she might be if her life had been different. Today she couldn't stop herself. If June hadn't intervened, would Alice be in Europe with Oggi now? Would she be his wife instead of Lilia, and would Iva be their daughter? If Alice hadn't found out how June betrayed her, would she ever have left the flower farm? And, underneath, the most painful question: would her mother be alive if she'd never gone into her father's shed? The next thought hit her hard, straight in her heart: Alice was a year older than her mother was when she died.

Someone knocked sharply at her front door. Alice pushed the doona back off her head. The skin around her eyes was tight from tears. Pip licked her salty cheeks. Another knock.

'Chica? It's me.'

Alice sat up and wrapped herself in her doona. She got out of bed and shuffled to the front door, opening it a crack.

'Dios mío,' Lulu said under her breath. 'Alice, what's wrong?' She pushed the door open and bustled inside, carrying an enormous pair of handmade butterfly wings and a small bag. 'These are clearly not important right now,' Lulu said, putting everything on the table. Alice allowed herself to be guided to the couch, where she curled up in a ball. Lulu flicked the heater off and flung the back door open to let warm winter sun and fresh air into the house. She made two cups of honeyed tea, and settled herself beside Alice. Pip bounded outside to chase butterflies.

'What's going on, chica?' Lulu asked gently. 'You haven't been your normal self for ages.'

The image of Dylan's face consumed her. Alice couldn't look at Lulu. 'I just miss my mother, Lu,' she whispered. 'I miss my mum,' she repeated, her voice breaking. She didn't think she had any tears left, yet a new stream flowed freely down her nose and dripped into her teacup.

'Can you call her? Or your dad? Or one of your brothers? Life out here can be hard, being so away from family, especially one as big as yours.' Lulu rubbed Alice's arm. Alice didn't understand, until she tasted the ashen lie of her fairytale family. Her face crumpled.

'Hey,' Lulu said, her eyes heavy with worry.

Alice shook her head and wiped her face. She reached under her shirt and pulled out her locket. Offered it to Lulu. She took it from Alice and ran her thumb over the desert pea inlay.

'That's my family.' Alice popped it open for Lulu. Her mother's young and hopeful face looked up at them. Alice eyed her garden of wild thryptomene flowers. *Flame, I burn.* 'The truth is, I don't have a big family. I don't really have anything left of a family at all.' Somewhere in the distance a crow cawed. Alice braced herself for anger, but after a moment Lulu smiled warmly.

'So, this is your mother?'

Alice nodded. 'Her name was Agnes.' She wiped her nose.

Lulu looked between the photograph and Alice. 'You look so much like her.'

'Thanks,' Alice said, her chin wobbling.

'Don't answer this if you don't want to, but, I mean, how did she …?' Lulu trailed off.

Alice closed her eyes, remembering the feeling of muscle and sinew under her father's skin when she held onto his legs on the windsurfer. The bruises on her mother's naked, pregnant body as she came out of the sea. The brother or sister Alice would never know. The lantern she left alight in her father's shed.

'I don't really know,' she answered. 'I don't know.'

Lulu took Alice's hand and placed her necklace in her palm. 'This locket is beautiful.'

'My grandmother made it.' Alice closed her hand around it. 'In my family, desert peas mean courage,' she said. 'Have courage, take heart.'

They sat together in silence while they drank their tea. After a while, Lulu stood with her hands on her hips.

'You can't be alone today,' she stated. 'Aiden's got the fire going and the skillet oiled up. We're having an afternoon barbecue and you're coming over.'

Alice started to protest.

'No, this one's non-negotiable, chica. Besides, I've made extra guacamole.' Lulu knew Alice's weaknesses and how to use them.

Alice sniffed and looked over at her kitchen table. With the butterfly wings splayed out, it seemed ready to take flight. She raised an eyebrow at Lulu.

'Oh, I'm making a costume for my cousin. She's in a play, and is about your size. I need to know if it fits,' Lulu stated.

'What? You want me to get dressed up? Right now?' Alice glanced down at herself.

'Yes. Although, can you shower first? Maybe wash your hair?'

'Pardon?'

'Chica, I can't send my cousin her costume with your tears and snot all over it. Besides, my abuela always said cleaning yourself up was one of the best remedies for sadness. In addition to her guacamole. Which, I may have mentioned, I have made fresh and have waiting for you at home.'

As Alice stepped under the hot shower, she listened to the sounds of Lulu clacking dishes together in the sink, humming as she tidied. Despite herself, she couldn't help but smile.

Freshly showered and dressed as a giant monarch butterfly, Alice followed Lulu down the dirt track between their houses. The burnt orange of her wings was the same fiery hue as the red dirt.

'Why have I let you convince me to wear this out of my house?' Alice asked.

'So Aiden can take photos for my cousin. I forgot to bring the camera with me to yours. Besides, who cares what you look like, chica? In case you'd forgotten, we're in the middle of fucking Woop-Woop.'

Alice snorted with laughter. She was reluctant to admit that putting on the costume did make her feel better. Lulu had spared no detail: from the wire antennae pinned in Alice's hair, to the black and white dotted dress and the carefully hand-painted monarch wings strapped to her back, she was unquestionably transformed.

They walked through Lulu's front yard into her house.

'Aiden must be out at the fire pit. Let me grab the camera and we'll go out.' Lulu scurried down the hall. Alice spotted the guacamole on the counter and darted over to it, fumbling with the cling wrap covering to dip a finger in.

'Don't even think about it,' Lulu hollered from one of the bedrooms. Alice laughed as she sucked guacamole from her finger.

'Okay, got it.' Lulu returned holding the camera. She narrowed her eyes at Alice. Alice held up her hands in innocence.

They walked outside. 'Aiden?' Lulu called.

A single paper streamer curled around the corner of the house, and then another. And another.

'Lu?' Alice asked uncertainly.

Lulu came to her side and wrapped an arm around her waist, walking her into the backyard and full view of most of their workmates.

'Happy birthday!' Ruby, Aiden, several other rangers, even Sarah, stood with plastic cups raised.

Alice's hands flew to her face. Lulu and Aiden had turned their yard into a birthday bazaar. Butterfly bunting was hung around the patio, and brightly patterned fabric awnings were strung between the trees. A fire was glowing in the pit. There was a pile of cushions and a couple of beanbags on a huge rectangular rug, with streamers tied haphazardly in the bushes. Dips and salads and corn chips were spread over a trestle table, alongside what must have been a fifty-litre cylindrical Esky, with a hand-drawn sign that read *Dangerous Punch*. And, to Alice's absolute delight, everyone was wearing butterfly wings.

'As if we didn't know it was your birthday.' Lulu grinned.

Alice gaped at Lulu, her hands pressed to her chest in gratitude.

'Come on,' Lulu urged, laughing. 'Dangerous Punch time.'

Someone put music on. Aiden manned the kebabs sizzling on the skillet over the fire pit. Alice, light-headed from the surprise and rush of booze to her head, greeted everyone with exuberant hugs and cheer. She refilled empty punch cups, stoked the fire and offered around nibblies. She did all she could to avoid focusing on the one person who wasn't there.

When the sky was dark and the punch was flowing, Alice sat with Lulu under a blanket by the fire. Flames reached for the inky sky, shooting sparks like stars.

'I don't know how to thank you,' Alice said.

Lulu squeezed her hand. 'It's my pleasure.'

The fire burned in a sea of colours: yellow, pink, orange, cobalt, plum, bronze.

'Can I tell you something?' Lulu asked.

'Please,' Alice said, smiling.

'I knew there was something special about you, chica, the first day you arrived and I saw your truck.'

Alice gave Lulu an affectionate nudge. 'Well, that's a bloody lovely thing to say.'

'I'm serious,' Lulu said as she took a sip of her punch. 'In my family monarch butterflies are daughters of fire. They come from the sun carrying the souls of warriors who fought and died in battle, and return to feed on the nectar of flowers.'

Alice watched the fire as it hissed and popped. She tightened the blanket around her, thinking about everything hidden under the monarch butterfly stickers on her truck, and whose daughter and granddaughter she was.

'When I first saw the fire warriors on your truck, I knew that you'd change everything about life here,' Lulu said.

Fire warriors. Alice didn't know how to respond.

'Dangerous Punch! Get your fresh Dangerous Punch refills here!' Aiden called across the yard. His wings were lopsided and sagging. One of his antennae was broken and flopped over his eyebrow. Lulu snorted with laughter. Relieved for the distraction, Alice joined in.

'C'mon.' She pulled Lulu's hand in the direction of the Esky. 'More Dangerous Punch.'

They drank and danced under the winter stars. As Alice twirled in the light she caught sight of her monarch wings. She couldn't shake Lulu's story from her mind. *Daughters of fire.*

He came in the early hours of the morning when the music was mellow, the fire burned bright, and everyone who hadn't passed out in their swags or stumbled home was snuggled in beanbags with blankets. Alice watched over the flames as he swung out of his four-wheel drive and headed for the Esky. Aiden clapped him on the back and offered him a cup of punch. Dylan downed it in one gulp.

'Rough trip?' Aiden raised his eyebrows, refilling his cup.

Dylan downed it again.

'How's Julie?'

Dylan shook his head. 'Not my problem anymore.'

Aiden gave him a third cup of punch. 'Ah, mate. Sorry.'

'It is what it is.' Dylan shrugged.

He turned to scan the yard. Through the fire, his eyes found hers.

When the sky started to lighten, Alice and Dylan were the only two awake.

'Is this your first desert all-nighter?' he asked.

Alice nodded, smiling drunkenly as she chewed on the lip of her plastic punch cup. His attention was hypnotic.

'Well,' he said, looking up at the sky, 'I dunno if anyone's told you, but it doesn't count unless you see the sunrise.'

They left Lulu and Aiden's swag-littered yard and, wrapped in blankets, made their way up a sand dune.

'Here comes the sun,' he said, his voice low, his eyes on her. Her skin tingled. The sky was so clear, so alive with shifting colour, that Alice flung her arms out wide as if she might soak it in.

'It reminds me of the ocean,' she murmured. 'So vast.' Her head spun with memories.

'It was,' Dylan said. 'Once upon a time, this was an ancient inland seabed.' He motioned around them. 'The desert's an old dream of the sea.'

A kaleidoscope of butterflies spun in her stomach. 'An old dream of the sea,' she repeated.

Their skin was painted by the fiery dawn light. He stood to the side of her. Though they weren't touching, he was so close she could feel the heat of his skin.

'You're so beautiful,' he whispered near her ear. She shivered.

As the world lit up, he inched closer and wrapped her in his arms. They stood that way, held together by the sunrise, until the sound of the first tourist buses broke the spell.

Lulu waited at her back door, teetering off balance as she clutched a half-empty cup of punch to her chest. The yard was littered with streamers, butterfly bunting and bottle tops. She swayed, eyes fixed on the sand dune behind Alice's house, where Dylan was hiding between mulga trees, the same place Lulu had seen him standing for months, watching Alice through her windows.

It started the afternoon Alice arrived, when she drove through Parksville in her yellow truck for the first time. Lulu was filling up at the petrol bowsers when Dylan had pulled in. He was making overtly mate-ish conversation with her, which she guessed was his way of erasing their history, until he stopped mid-sentence, staring at the road. When Lulu turned, she saw what he saw: Alice with her long, dark hair streaming out her window, dog beside her.

She'd looked straight at them. Straight at him. Lulu kept talking but Dylan wasn't listening. He was besotted by Alice. The way he'd once been by her.

Later that night, after Alice had dinner with Lulu and Aiden and walked home, Lulu was sitting outside on the dunes with a glass of wine when a movement in the shadows caught her eye. She'd remembered the smell of Dylan on her skin, and squinted to sharpen her vision in the darkness, sucking in her breath at the sight of him sneaking along the back fence line of Alice's house. Before she could stop herself, Lulu moved to the corner of her yard to better see Dylan crouched under the stars, hidden by a mulga bush, watching Alice. Inside her new home Alice went tentatively through the rooms, as if she were a guest. For a while she sat on the couch staring at the wall, cuddling her dog. Her face was so sad. Dylan waited until she went to bed and turned out the light. Then he stood, silently, and walked home. Lulu had retreated to bed, where Aiden sleepily asked why she was shaking.

At dusk the next evening, Lulu was in the kitchen grinding up chilli and cocoa beans when a passing figure caught her eye through the window. She waited until the gloaming before she slid out into the shadows of her garden. Again Dylan sat in the red sand, drawn by the open, lit windows in Alice's house. Alice was dancing in her kitchen, cooking, her wet hair hanging down her back. Blues music wafted on the thin, violet air. She shook her body around the stove, set out two plates and served dinner. Some for her, and some for her dog. Dylan stayed until she went to bed, then retraced his steps home.

Night after night, Lulu couldn't stop herself watching Dylan as he was drawn across the sand dunes by the light falling from Alice's windows, yet hated herself for it all the same. She began to wait for the hour when the shadows were long enough to look for him creeping among the trees. Protected by the darkness, he sat outside while Alice drank tea and read a book, or watched a movie on the couch with her dog. Or tended her pot plants and books, once she began decorating her house. He mostly kept his distance, until the night before Alice's birthday. Alice had returned from a walk, when Lulu saw Dylan move from the shadows to slip noiselessly through the gate in Alice's back fence. He wound through the thryptomene bushes, daringly close, nearly in the glow of her fairy lights. Watching. Seemingly waiting for something that was out of Lulu's view.

She didn't bother trying to resist following him: Lulu left her yard and took a wide arc around the dune behind Alice's house. Hid behind the thick trunk of a desert oak where she could see Dylan in the bushes watching Alice inside at her desk, emptying flowers from her pockets. She pressed them into her notebook, which she handled as gently as if it were a bird's egg. She started writing, then paused. Looked blindly into the darkness. And that's when it happened, when Lulu heard Dylan catch his breath, as though Alice was looking straight at him with her big, green eyes; as if he was what caused her face to fill with hope. Lulu had sprinted home hard and fast. Told herself that was why she retched stinging, hot bile in the sink.

At the end of the surprise party, Lulu had pretended to be asleep when Dylan and Alice left together. Would Dylan's first move on Alice be to share a sunrise with her too, like he had with Lulu?

Lulu stood at her back door watching and waiting until, sure enough, they came stumbling over the dunes. He walked Alice home, lingering long after she'd gone inside. The sun burned high into the sky before he turned to leave, a besotted, drunken smile on his face. She couldn't stop herself staring, long after he'd disappeared behind his front door.

The evening after her surprise party, Alice curled up on her couch, gazing across her yard to the gate in her back fence. Silhouetted birds tumbled through the air, a constellation of inverse stars returning to their nests. On the blackened dead tree just outside her door, the evening light illuminated a rope of silk trails left by the winter procession of caterpillars. Alice had read about them in the park's annual flora and fauna guide: they followed each other by the trails of silk they left behind, which were invisible except when they caught the light.

Her house was quiet, except for the occasional click of the electric heater, Pip's snores and the bubbling pot on the stove. Hints of fresh lemongrass, coriander and coconut made her stomach growl. She watched the gate. She waited. The light changed from gold to cinnamon. Dylan's voice rang in her ears. *I'll go home for a shower and come over. Back gate way.*

She'd been on her way home from town when she'd spotted his ute on the side of the ring road and his figure at the nearby radio repeater stations. He saw her coming and waved. She pulled over and hopped out of her car. Her body grew feverish at the sight of him.

'Pinta-Pinta.' He'd beamed, tapping his hat brim to greet her.

'G'day.' She'd grinned.

'Not too hung over?'

She shook her head. 'No, weirdly. More just sleep deprived, I think.'

'Me too.'

The air was heavy with the sweet scent of winter wattle.

'How was your first day of being twenty-seven?' he asked.

'Truck delivery day. I went food shopping.' She laughed.

'Ah.' He nodded knowingly, laughing along. 'It was a great day.'

'It was. But it's not over yet.' She paused. 'What are you doing tonight?' she blurted, looking up at him.

His eyes searched hers. 'Not much.'

'I'm making fresh Thai green curry soup. From scratch?' she offered.

'Yum.'

'So,' she said, trying to keep her voice even. 'Join me?'

'Love to.' He smiled.

'Six?'

He nodded. 'I'll go home for a shower and come over. Back gate way?'

'Sure,' she'd said, breezily.

And there it was, the beam of his torch, cutting through the spinifex, lighting his way to her. She got up and scurried into her bedroom. Stood in the shadows by her window, watching, waiting.

He came to the back gate, slid open the latch and closed it behind him. The pale light of the stars fell on his shoulders. He flicked the torch off and wound his way through the thryptomene to the patio under her fairy lights.

'Pinta-Pinta?' he called from the door.

'Hey,' she said, giving him an easy smile as she crossed the room and opened the back door. He scuffed his feet across the mat and walked inside. She inhaled the invisible curlicues of his cologne, briefly closing her eyes. He took his Akubra off and cast an appreciative glance around her house: her pot plants, her paintings, her books, her rugs, her cooking, her desk. She'd pretended it was for herself, but it had all been in hope of this moment.

'Hungry?'

'Oh yeah,' he replied, plonking down on the sofa.

'Hair of the dog?' she asked.

'Always,' he said. She opened the fridge and reached to the back for two beer bottles. The effervescence when she cracked the tops brought her such relief she wished she could open a dozen at once.

'Cheers,' she said, handing him one.

'Cheers,' he said with a nod. As they clinked bottles, a Catherine wheel of nerves spun through her body.

After soup and more beer, they slouched on her couch. Their faces were flushed, from the heating, the beers, the chilli, and something else besides. They'd been telling stories, about where they'd grown up. They knew how to do this, how to reveal certain parts of themselves and not others. They'd been doing it for weeks. But now their stories dried up like a salt flat in the sun.

'Those bloody fairy lights,' he mumbled after a while.

The heater ticked and hummed.

'What about them?' she asked quietly.

'They're all I can see from every window in my house. They've been distracting me for months.'

A thrill shot through her. 'They have?' she asked.

He turned to her. She didn't look away.

His mouth was on hers, suddenly, softly. Urgently. Alice kissed him back, deeply, unwilling to close her eyes. It wasn't a daydream; he was there.

They shed their clothes like skins on the floor. When he sat back to take in the sight of her, she covered herself with her arms. But he drew them away, pressing one of her hands to his chest. She felt it under his skin and bone, the storytelling of his heart.

He's here. He's here.

She drew him close; a sharp intake of breath; he pushed into her. Limbs entwined, indistinguishable. Raw, thrilling. Almost frightening. Sensory fragments in her mind. Wet sand underfoot, lightness in her lungs, salty skin, cawing with the gulls by the silver sea. The drift and tilt of wind through her hair between the green cane stalks. The hush and flow of the river. Fistfuls of red flowers being torn from the earth.

24

Broad-leaved parakeelya

Meaning: By your love, I live and die

Calandrinia balonensis | Northern Territory

Parkilypa (Pit.) is a succulent growing in sandy soils of arid regions, with fleshy leaves and bright purple flowers, which appear mainly in winter and spring. In times of drought the leaves can be a water source; the whole plant can be baked and eaten.

From that night onwards, they spent every spare moment together. Alice knew she was neglecting her other friends, especially Lulu, but she didn't want to be with anyone else.

As the winter wore on, they lit bonfires and slept outside in his swag, under the stars, Pip always curled up close by.

'You should change your roster,' he said one night as she lay in the crook of his arm, watching the sky. 'I miss you too much on weekends when one of us is off while the other is working. I want to see you more.'

The thrill of it: he wanted more of her. She grinned up at him, smelled the scent of his skin, earthen and green. He took his arm out from under her head and sat up. Untied his leather bracelets and turned back to her, gently taking her hands. She nodded, smiling as he bound the bracelets around her wrists and tied them in knots.

'Ngayuku pinta-pinta,' he said, his voice raw.

As he pulled her onto him, Lulu's voice shot fleetingly through her mind. *You're no safer than the girl in the fairytale who wanders into a dark wood.*

'Ngayuku pinta-pinta,' he whispered again, his hands around her wrists. *My butterfly.*

She curled her body to fit around his.

While she awaited approval to change rosters, Alice's desert life centred around Dylan. If they were both off for sunset, they took to walking the fire trails with Pip; Alice filled her pockets with wildflowers to press in her notebook, while Dylan took photos of her in the melting red light. When she was on night patrol and finished late, she drove straight to his house and often found him waiting with dinner, or a hot bubble bath. On those nights, he and Pip sat by the bath, leaning against the wall, while he read aloud to her. If they had a whole day off together they gardened in the sun until they were distracted by each other's warmed bare skin; she'd mentioned working in her mother's veggie garden as a child, and came home from work one day to find he'd made her a bed of dark earth sown through the red dirt. At night, they snuggled on the couch with the heater blazing, the television on the one regional channel with decent reception, watching BBC dramas and antique shows. On rare occasions when the winter sky was cloudy and the day didn't yield any sun, they stayed in bed. Those days became synonymous with pancakes; Alice would fry up a tower, which they'd take back to bed and devour.

One cold afternoon, after a syrupy feast, they lay watching dust motes float on the grey light falling through a crack in the curtains. Dylan sighed heavily and disentangled himself from her. He'd been agitated, restless, and hadn't looked directly at her all day, even during sleepy, languid sex. Alice didn't know what was wrong. And she didn't know why she was so reluctant to ask him.

She traced circles over his bare stomach and chest, reaching up to his neck and face. He didn't respond. 'What's wrong?' Alice whispered. Her love could fix it. Whatever it was. He didn't answer. She waited. Asked again.

'Nothing,' he snapped, shrugging from her touch. 'Sorry.' He shook his head. 'Sorry, Pinta-Pinta.' He sat up, elbows on his knees, his head hanging.

She sat up beside him. There was a familiar pit in her stomach that made her deeply uncomfortable. She chose her words carefully so as not to agitate him further.

'You can tell me,' she offered, keeping her voice light. 'Whatever it is.' She held a hand out gingerly, letting it hover for a moment before she pressed it to his back, holding her palm flat against his spine. He curled towards her touch.

'I'm sorry,' he moaned, turning to bury his face into her shoulder. 'I'm sorry. I'm not going to fuck this up this time.'

She stroked his hair. 'I know that,' she soothed. 'I know.'

'It's going to be better,' he said, as if to himself. 'I'm going to be better.' He kissed her neck, her face, her mouth, his sense of urgency growing as he gathered her into his arms.

Alice squeezed her eyes shut as she kissed him back. What did he mean, better? He was going to be different from what? How? Her chest grew tight.

'I love you,' he whispered as he lay between her legs. Whispered over and again.

She breathed in his words and banished the questions from her mind.

Winter started to wane. The mornings grew warmer, finches began to fly and leave their nests, and Alice's life with Dylan flourished. As her love for him intensified, Alice found it harder and harder to ignore the strain in her friendship with Lulu. Not long after her request to switch rosters had been approved, she saw Lulu checking the noticeboards in the tea room. From the look on Lulu's face as she read the new rosters, something was very wrong.

'Hey, Lulu,' Alice said brightly, taking two clean mugs from the sink. 'Fancy a cuppa and catch-up before patrol?'

Lulu's blank expression didn't falter as she walked right past her.

'She probably just feels left out,' Dylan said that night. 'You haven't known her that long. I have. She can be jealous and weird about shit like this.'

Alice stirred the spring vegetable risotto she was cooking. It made sense. What other reason could Lulu have to be so cold to her? But the question of Lulu's history with Dylan niggled at her. She took a sip of her white wine and shot a glance at him.

'What?' he asked.

She took another sip, not looking at him.

'Spit it out,' Dylan said, smiling. 'I can read your face like a book, Pinta-Pinta.'

Emboldened, she smiled back. 'Did you and Lulu ever ...' she trailed off.

'Me and Lulu?' Dylan scoffed, shaking his head. 'I think she might have had a thing for me way back when we first met, but it never came to anything.' He stood behind her, wrapping her tightly in his arms. 'Don't worry so much. It's all in your mind. She'll get over herself. Okay?'

'Okay.' Alice leaned back against his chest.

Once they were working on the same roster, Alice and Dylan were completely inseparable. They drove to and from work and took lunch together. She packed picnics they never ended up eating, instead sneaking off in his ute to secluded spots behind headquarters, where they could hear their radios but have enough privacy to focus only on each other. After work they shared beers, watched the sky change, cooked dinner over the fire pit and lounged with Pip to watch the stars. Alice never went home, and avoided looking across his yard in the direction of her house, which sat in the dark.

On their first four-day weekend off together, Dylan woke her early with a cup of coffee and kisses on her face.

'Come with me,' he said, wrapping her naked body in the doona and leading her to the front door. She rubbed her eyes and cradled her coffee to her lips as he swung the screen open with a flourish. Outside the morning was crystalline. She squinted in the sunshine. His battered four-wheel drive was packed, with his double swag strapped to the roof racks.

'Wanna get out of here?' He raised an eyebrow.

'We're running away to the west coast?' she asked.

'Don't reckon we'd *quite* make it there and back in four days,' he joked. 'But I know a place nearly as good.'

'Road trip,' Alice sang as she sidled up to him.

Dylan eyed her wrapped in the doona. Teased the corner of it out from under her arm so that it fell away from her body. 'Maybe not just yet.'

She shrieked with joy as he chased her inside.

A couple of hours later Alice, Pip and Dylan drove along the highway through a blur of red sand, golden spinifex and ancient desert oaks. All the windows were down. In the side mirror

Alice watched Pip's tongue lolling in the wind. Occasionally the undulating landscape plateaued, offering a view of wildflowers in spring bloom. Alice was mesmerised by fields of yellows, oranges, purples and blues. Dylan squeezed her thigh, smiling. He turned the radio up and sang along, raucously out of tune. Alice closed her eyes, blissful.

By mid-afternoon Dylan had slowed and turned off the highway onto an ungraded and unmarked road that peeled between low-lying emu bush and clusters of ruby dock. Alice wondered fleetingly how he knew it was there. He waited for the wheels to take traction before putting his foot down, kicking sprays of red dirt up behind them. They clattered over the ungraded road into a wide desert vista. The isolation thrilled and daunted Alice. Wondering where they were headed, she looked at him questioningly but he just smiled.

After a while they turned onto a thin, nearly indistinguishable track that scaled a ridge. Dylan switched into four-wheel-drive and crawled along the track, pushing through overreaching tree branches. Around them rocky red outcrops were dotted with bursts of wildflowers. Stark white trunks of giant gum trees waved their mint-green boughs. The sky was deep sapphire blue. Occasionally a hawk's dark silhouette streaked overhead.

'Pinta-Pinta.' Dylan smiled, gesturing ahead at the crest of the ridge. Driving over and down the other side, they came into a rocky red gorge, framed by acacia trees and mallee gums, with white sandy banks and a wide, green-tea-coloured creek running through it.

'What is this place?' Alice asked, awed.

'Wait until you see sunset,' Dylan said knowingly. As she watched him pull into a clearing by a cluster of desert oaks, Alice realised he hadn't needed a map to find his way.

'How'd you know this is here?'

'Before I worked for the park, I used to be a tour guide,' Dylan said, 'and one of the old fellas I guided with brought me out here. It was his grandparents' country, a happy place where family would gather and share good times. When I stopped guiding he told me I should always come back here.' He pulled up the handbrake. 'Said I should bring my own family with me.' His eyes were full of meaning.

Alice didn't trust her voice to speak over the lump in her throat.

He leaned towards her. 'How'd I ever get this lucky?' he whispered.

She answered him with a deep kiss. After a moment, he groaned. 'You render me bloody useless, Pinta-Pinta.' He shook his head. 'C'mon. Let's at least manage to make camp.' He got out and opened the back door for Pip, who went straight into the creek.

Alice hung back, watching her dog swimming and Dylan whistling as he unpacked the camp stove and Esky. Watching her little family. As she stepped into the sunlight to join them, she couldn't remember a time when she'd felt more whole.

By sunset they'd made up the swag, gathered kindling, and were playing soft music on the car radio while they drank red wine and cut up haloumi cheese, mushroom, zucchini and capsicum to grill on kebabs over the campfire. The air was a heady mix of wood smoke and eucalyptus. Black cockatoos screeched through the sky, and rock wallabies hopped nearby. Alice couldn't stop smiling. When the walls of the gorge started to change colour, Dylan took her by the hand and led her up the bank to the trunk of a gum tree where he sat, gesturing for her to do the same. She nestled between his legs, leaning against his chest.

He nuzzled her ear. 'Watch this.'

As the sun sank, its last rays filled the gorge with thick beams of toffee-coloured light.

'Stunning,' Alice murmured.

'Wait for it.'

Wrapped in his arms, Alice watched as all the colours of the sky seemed to stream down the walls of gorge and pool on the glassy surface of the creek, reflecting swirls of light back upwards again. She shook her head: the gorge and the creek were perfect bowl-like mirror reflections of each other, drenched in the fiery colours of the setting sun. The sight reminded her of her books of fairytales: the enchanted empty chalice that miraculously filled; the wishing well that held heaven in its depths.

Dylan tightened his arms around her. 'You have to see it to believe it, right?' he said.

A memory winded her like a sucker punch. *There's a gorge not far from here that you have to see at sunset to believe.*

Alice sat up, rigid. Turned to Dylan. He smiled at her.

'How many women have you brought here?' she blurted.

His eyes fell flat. 'Sorry?' he asked.

Alice's stomach lurched. She'd broken the spell.

He held his hands up. 'What sort of question is that to ask?'

'No,' Alice said, feigning lightness in her tone. 'No, I mean, women, I mean, well, did you ever bring Lulu here?' Her mind was a blur of nonsense and noise. She didn't want to upset him but couldn't stop herself asking. How else could Lulu have known about this place at sunset?

Dylan shoved her roughly away and stood over her. 'Unfuckingbelievable,' he muttered, walking back to camp.

Her body stung from the strength in his hands.

'Dylan,' she called, scrambling after him in the soft sand.

'What?' he barked, turning to face her, his eyes flashing with anger. 'I told you nothing ever happened with Lulu. Why would you ask me that and ruin our first weekend away together? You believe her and her jealousy, over me? Is that right? And what did you mean by how many women have I brought here? Who do you think I am?'

'Oh god,' Alice moaned, her face crumpling. He was right. Lulu could have been talking about another gorge, or come to this one without Dylan. She was being insecure. Why couldn't she just leave it alone?

He jabbed at their campfire, sending sparks flying.

'I'm so sorry,' she begged, reaching for him. He ignored her. 'Can we just forget it? Please? It was a stupid thing to say, I don't know why I said it. I'm so sorry. Please,' she tried again, opening her arms to him. 'Let me make it up to you. I'll cook. We'll have more wine. Let's just forget about it. Okay?'

He shot a scathing look at her, then stood and turned away.

'Dylan?' Her voice wobbled.

He walked off, into the purple shadows of the sunken sun.

Shaking, Alice prepared dinner. She grilled up all the veggies and haloumi, fed Pip, and topped up their glasses. By the time he returned, it had been dark for an hour or more. Their dinner was cold, the cheese stiff and rubbery. He sat and stabbed at his meal with a fork.

'You even ruined dinner.' He emptied his full plate into the fire and reached for his wine glass. The food Alice had managed to get down sat in her stomach like cold stone. She put her plate to the side, let Pip finish her dinner.

'I'm so sorry,' she whispered. She rubbed her knee against his. 'I'm so sorry.'

He stared into the fire, unresponsive.

She kept apologising, for hours it seemed, until, finally, he lifted his hand and ran it up the inside of her leg.

It took her most of that night and the rest of the next day, but by the time they were driving home to Kililpitjara, Alice's efforts to be as calming and compliant as she could seemed to have brought Dylan back to her.

As they pulled into his driveway, he leaned over to kiss her before leaping out to open the gates. When his back was turned Alice winced; she had chafing and bruises from their lovemaking in the gorge. He'd been rougher than usual, but now, to her great relief, they seemed back to normal.

As they unpacked the car, Dylan paused to kiss her tenderly. 'Thanks for a mostly beautiful weekend.' He searched her eyes with his.

Alice kissed him gratefully. She'd just have to be more careful in future. She'd have to be mindful before she spoke.

Spring painted the central desert in a paint box of colours. The honey grevillea flowered in masses of amber and yellow, filling the air with its thick, sweet scent. Lounges of bearded dragon lizards sunned themselves between clumps of spinifex. Alice's veggie garden at Dylan's began to sprout. The afternoons grew warm enough for ice cream and sunbathing; she lay on a beach towel on the red dirt in his yard, humming along with the music in her headphones while she read a book, until he spotted her in her bikini. He was as hungry for her as ever. Her misstep on their camping weekend was long forgotten. The days grew longer, the stars shone brighter.

'We should have a barbecue,' she suggested one night as she fried up sweet chilli tofu and tossed a green salad for dinner. 'The house is looking so good, and it's gorgeous out there by the fire pit with the honey grevillea in bloom.'

Dylan didn't respond. He was sitting at the dining table. Under the glare of the kitchen lights she couldn't read his face.

'Babe?' she asked as she lifted the frying pan off the heat.

'Sure,' he replied. 'Sounds great.'

'Great,' she chirped, as she carried their plates to the table. 'I'll put feelers out at work tomorrow.' She kissed him, and sat down for dinner. He smiled wordlessly in reply.

The next morning, Alice pulled up at headquarters full of excitement. She and Dylan had been so wrapped up in each other, it would be good for them to engage a bit more with their small community.

When she walked into the staff office, it was almost too easy. Thugger and Nicko, two rangers Alice didn't know very well, were standing together, moaning about not having anything to do on their upcoming weekend off.

'Why don't you fellas come 'round for a barbecue?' Alice chipped in.

'Hey, thanks, mate,' Thugger said.

'Yeah, cool.' Nicko nodded.

'Sorted,' Alice said, grinning. 'We'll get the fire pit at Dylan's going and he'll set up the skillet for a chargrilled feast. We can –'

'Oh,' Thugger interjected, glancing at Nicko. 'You know what, Alice? I just remembered, I've actually gotta head up to the Bluff this weekend. I'm, um –'

'That's right,' Nicko interjected. 'Shit, mate, we nearly forgot. We're gunna get our fourbies serviced.'

Alice glanced back and forth between them. It was as if she was watching a pantomime.

'Close call,' Thugger said, visibly relieved. 'Lucky you reminded us, Alice!'

'Another time, mate,' Nicko said apologetically.

'Thanks for the invite though,' Thugger called as they hurried out of the office.

After they'd gone, Alice made herself a cup of tea. Clenched her jaw. She would not cry. She would not overthink what had just happened.

Her day didn't improve. Later, she made constant mistakes out in the field, culminating in whacking her thumb with a hammer and crumpling in agony.

'Head back to HQ and get that seen to, Alice.' Thugger dismissed her from duty.

Once she'd been cleared by the first aid officer, Alice went into the tea room for a sweet biscuit and cup of tea. Her heart sank; Lulu and Aiden were standing at the boiler, talking, mugs in hand. As soon as Alice walked in, they stopped. She went to the cupboard where the teabags were kept, turning her back on them. The totality of their silence weighed on her.

Aiden was the first to speak. 'You okay, Alice?'

Before she had the chance to answer, Lulu pointedly emptied her mug in the sink and left. Aiden glanced helplessly at Alice, then followed.

'I'm fine,' Alice said in a near whisper to herself, watching them go.

The next few days unravelled in a similar way: Alice mentioned the idea of a get-together at Dylan's to other workmates, but the responses were nothing more than flimsy excuses. Dylan didn't ask about the barbecue, and Alice didn't bring it up again. By the end of the week, she'd come to realise that although he was everyone's acquaintance, Dylan didn't have any real friends at Kililpitjara. He had her. Only her. And she couldn't understand why.

When she pulled into his driveway after work and got out to open the gate, Alice recalled one of the books Dylan had read to her, a collection of Japanese fairytales. In one, a woman artist practised kintsugi, repairing broken pottery with lacquer mixed with powdered gold. There'd been an illustration of a woman bent over a pile of broken pottery pieces, laid out to fit together, with a fine paintbrush in her hand, its bristles dipped in gold. It had enchanted Alice, the idea that breakage and repair were part of the story, not something to be disdained or disguised.

She drove up to park behind Dylan's ute. Slammed the door with renewed determination. Whatever it was that made him feel he wasn't good enough, whatever reason people had for not wanting to spend time with him, wherever he thought he was broken, Alice would just melt herself like gold, and fix it.

A few days later, the Earnshaw Crater Resort sent invitations to its annual Bush Ball to all touring companies and park staff.

Dylan had been dismissive when Alice suggested they go along. 'It's just a massive piss-up,' he said with a sneer.

'Yeah, but it'll still be fun to go together, right?' she said, excited, sticking her invitation under a magnet on his fridge. They hadn't been to a party since her birthday. She'd been coveting a gold silk dress she'd found online; the thought of having an excuse to get dressed up made her giddy. As did the two of them having a reason to get out and see everyone socially.

'You really want to go?' Dylan said behind her, interrupting her thoughts.

She turned. 'I really do. It'll be so good to have a few drinks, a bit of a dance.' Alice wrapped her arms around his waist and pressed her hips to his. 'Get a bit drunk,' she said teasingly, reaching on tiptoes to kiss his neck, 'and make it count when we see the sun rise.' She decided then and there she'd surprise him with her new dress. Do her hair specially. Wear lipstick, and that perfume of hers he loved. 'We can make a date of it,' she said, looking up at him.

'You wanna be my date, Pinta-Pinta?' His eyes clouded with desire.

'Always,' she replied, squealing as he lifted her up and carried her to bed. It was going to be great, she told herself. It was going to be the best night they'd had together in ages.

The day of the Bush Ball, Alice raced home early to shower. She zipped up her new gold dress, slicked on lip gloss and lashings of mascara, and stepped into her new cowboy boots embellished with gold butterflies on the heels. When Dylan walked through the door, her cheeks flushed with excitement. She had a cold beer waiting for him, and had intentionally neglected to wear knickers, something she knew drove him mad.

His step faltered when he saw her. He stood, unmoving.

'Ready for date night?' she asked, grinning. Did a little shimmy in her dress.

Dylan slowly emptied his pockets onto the counter and went wordlessly into the kitchen.

The chill of his silence hit her between the ribs. She heard him riffling through the medicine cabinet and popping two pills from their packet.

'Babe?' she asked, trying to hide her crushing disappointment. 'You okay?'

He didn't answer. She went into the kitchen.

'Babe?' she asked again.

He kept his back to her. 'What are you wearing?' he asked stonily.

'What?' Her stomach plummeted.

'Why are you dressed like that?'

She looked down at her new dress. The gold was suddenly garish rather than magical.

He turned to face her, his eyes dark. 'Why would you buy new clothes for tonight?' His voice shook. 'Why would you want to get all fucking dolled up? Just so the blokes from work can wank over you?'

Alice went rigid as he walked around her, looking her up and down. It hurt to breathe.

'Answer me,' he said quietly.

Tears filled her eyes. She didn't have an answer. Her voice was a gone thing.

Ruby sat by the fire in her back yard with her pen and notebook open, waiting. She wasn't interested in the Bush Ball. She'd had a feeling all day a poem was coming, and didn't want to miss it.

Over the dunes, a movement in Dylan's driveway distracted her. Alice's dog scampered to hide behind a gum tree. Inside, Dylan's silhouette paced back and forth in the dimly lit windows of the house.

Ruby watched him. Inhaled deeply, and pressed her nib shakily to paper.

The season is turning.
Something bitter is in the air.

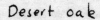

25

Meaning: **Resurrection**
Allocasuarina decaisneana | Central Australia

*Kurkaṟa (Pit.) have deeply furrowed, cork-like bark, which is
fire-retardant. Slow-growing but fast to develop a taproot that
can reach subsurface water at depths over ten metres. Mature trees
form a large, bushy canopy. Many found in the central desert are
likely to be more than one thousand years old.*

By the middle of spring, when the mint bushes had stopped
flowering and the seasonal rains came, Alice had learned to read
Dylan's moods the same way she'd learned, years ago, to read the
tides. As long as she was mindful, alert and responsive, they were
blissfully happy.

After a week of nonstop rain, the dirt roads and walking
trails around Kililpitjara turned into a sodden glue of red mud.
Notices warning against getting bogged appeared on the boards
at headquarters. Alice read them thoroughly, but that didn't help
her when she was out on patrol behind Kuṯuṯu Puḻi. She drove
straight into a bog. Her tyres were compacted and spinning. She
tried to dig a little, or idle out, but nothing worked. Eventually
she radioed for help.

Thugger was the first to respond, and pulled her ute free with
a winch. Back at headquarters, the rangers were having knock-off
drinks and nibblies.

'Come for a bevvy,' Thugger said as he got out of his ute,
covered in red mud. 'We've bloody earned it.'

'Pinta-Pinta,' Ruby called across the car park, waving from

under the desert oak where everyone was sitting, with an Esky open and a table of finger food. 'Don't be a stranger.'

Alice forced herself to smile at Thugger and wave back at Ruby. Dylan wasn't there. Maybe he was on his way. If he was on his way, she should stay, otherwise he'd be upset if she went home without him. But if he wasn't … She shook her head free of noisy thoughts, and went to join the group. She wouldn't stay for more than an hour.

Ruby handed her a beer. 'So good to see you, Pinta–Pinta.'

It was wonderful to see Ruby too. Alice couldn't stop herself from grinning when she glanced down at Ruby's budgerigar trousers.

'Yeah, mate, we haven't seen much of you about. You didn't make it to the Bush Ball?' Nicko asked.

Thugger elbowed him in the side. Silence settled over the table. Alice's cheeks flamed.

'Aaaaaanyway,' Thugger said. He raised his beer.

Cheers went around the table as everyone clinked bottles. Alice took a long swig. The beer loosened her shoulders, eased the furrow in her brow. A lightness spread through her chest. The uncomplicated warmth of the group's company was a balm.

After finishing her third beer, it occurred to Alice to check the time. She gasped when she saw she'd been there for two hours.

Hurriedly, she excused herself from the group and drove straight to Dylan's. When she got to his gate, it was locked. It was never locked. She called out to him but her voice was swallowed by the wind. Where was Pip? Was she with Dylan, wherever he was?

Alice sped around Parksville and pulled up hard and fast in her own driveway. It had been so long since she'd spent a night there it no longer felt like her home. Behind the gate, Pip turned in excited circles to see her. Dylan must have dropped her there. Alice unlocked the front door and stepped into her house.

Inside, the air was foul. Alice hunted through the house until she discovered a rat in the trap under the stove. She cleaned it up, dry retching. Threw open every window and door, washed out her oil burner, and lit sandalwood and rose geranium oil. Her bookshelves were covered in a fine film of red dust. As she wiped them clean, she ran her fingers along the spines of her neglected books. After rummaging through the pantry, Alice warmed a tin of baked beans, which mostly went to Pip; she couldn't eat. She called Dylan throughout the night, but he didn't pick up. Shivering on her back patio under her fairy lights, she looked across the dunes at the silhouette of his house backlit by stars.

The pit in her stomach widened. He was punishing her. For not going home to him. For not checking with him first if it was okay that she stayed for a beer. For not doing the right thing by him. She knew it.

Alice went inside and locked up. She took a quick hot shower, trying to loosen the knots in her shoulders, then got into bed. Pip settled beside her, snoring softly.

Just as she was on the edge of sleep, a noise outside her window jolted Alice awake. A snapping of twigs, breaking underfoot. She sprang from her bed to the window and inched the curtain back, her blood pulsing loudly in her ears. Pip barked. As Alice's eyes adjusted to the starlight she saw her backyard was full of shadows. But none that she recognised as his.

The next morning, she couldn't get more than a sip of coffee down. She shook on the drive to work. When she pulled up at headquarters he came to greet her, smiling, and held her face in his hands. She fearfully searched his eyes but they were filled with tenderness. He kissed her, stroked her cheek.

'I got a terrible migraine, took some painkillers and knocked myself out,' he said. 'I should have left a message on your machine, or a note. Sorry, sweetheart. Did you have a nice time with everyone at headquarters though?'

Alice nodded slowly, a flushing fool. What was wrong with her?

It was all in her head.

She was making the man a monster.

The days stretched longer, each twilight richer in gold than the one before. The night Alice stayed for drinks at headquarters wasn't mentioned again. Neither was the idea of them socialising with anyone else. When it was just the two of them, things were peaceful. And that was okay. Some people just weren't social. Every morning that she woke wrapped in his arms, it was exactly where she wanted to be. They'd had their ups and downs, but relationships weren't easy, she reasoned with herself. There had to be bumps every now and then as they figured each other out.

One particularly clear day, Alice was the first home from work. Earlier that morning she and Dylan had decided they'd go for a long walk together, maybe pack a couple of beers and sit on a dune awhile to watch the sun go down. She'd just taken off her work boots and laced up her sneakers when the phone rang.

'I'm gunna be late, Pinta-Pinta,' Dylan sighed. 'A diesel bore is down. I'll be as quick as I can, but I doubt I'll make it for our walk today.'

'No worries, darlin',' she said, hoping to hide the disappointment in her voice. She'd been looking forward to the fresh air after being in the office all day. 'I'll just hang here with Pip, and get something delish going for dinner.'

But, not long after they'd hung up, Pip started scratching at the screen door. Alice looked at her hopeful furry face. Outside, it was a stunning afternoon. The dunes would be nearly rose-red in the sunset light. Alice bit on the inside of her cheek. She hadn't taken Pip for a walk alone together since she and Dylan started seeing each other. An image of the desert peas, blood-red at sunset, flashed through her mind's eye. She'd said she'd wait here for him. But it was such a glorious afternoon. He surely wouldn't want her sitting inside.

'C'mon, Pip,' she cooed. 'Let's have ourselves some girl time.' Pip chased her tail in circles until Alice clipped on her lead and they headed out the door, over the dunes, towards the crater.

Alice came upon treasure after treasure: everlasting daisies in pastel pinks and yellows, trails of grey and white feathers, boughs heavy with blossom buds on the gum trees. She breathed in the warm earth and appreciated the sky, a blend of soldier-crab blue and every shade of purple in a pipi shell. *The desert's an old dream of the sea.* Alice smiled at the memory of her first sunrise with Dylan. As she and Pip climbed the crater wall, retracing the path she'd walked so often when she'd first arrived, her chest filled with nostalgia. She'd been so new to the landscape, and so unsure of what she was doing there. But now she had a job she treasured and a man who loved her like she'd never known.

When they reached the top of the crater wall and Alice saw Kuṯuṯu Kaana, Heart Garden, in achingly beautiful red bloom, she leant her head back and closed her eyes in contentment. She'd finally come home, into a life that was all hers.

Alice came over the rise in the road, mucking about with Pip and pondering ideas for dinner. She came to a halt: Dylan's work ute was in his driveway. Nerves rippled through her core. She fumbled with the gate. Tried to even her breathing. She didn't know how long she'd been gone. She hadn't left him a note. *It'll be fine. It'll be fine.* She walked up to his front door. *Don't make monsters.*

Inside, the house was dark and still.

'Dylan?' she called. 'I'm home.' She unclipped Pip from her lead, and kicked off her sneakers. 'Dylan?'

Later, when she tried to remember what happened and how, everything seemed simultaneous: Pip's agonised cries; Alice's scream as she turned to see Dylan kicking her dog in the ribs; rings of white rage around his eyes as he lunged for her.

'Where the fuck have you been?' He grabbed her. 'Who were you with? Who? Tell me.'

Black spots formed in her vision. Her throat burned as he shook her hard by the neck. Her spine clicked and popped.

'Tell me.'

He shoved her so hard her feet left the ground. There was a loud crack as the bedroom door hinges gave way from the force of her impact. Alice fell to the floor.

She lay, heaving raggedly for breath. Her mind bobbed around outside herself, as if she was a spectator, not really there in the scene. She stared at a cluster of dust balls gathered against the skirting board. They fascinated her. They were right underfoot, right in front of her and she'd never seen them before. How had she never seen them before?

A nearby whimpering made Alice look under the bed. Pip's tail poked out of the shadows.

'Here, girl,' Alice croaked. Her throat was raw. Blinding pains shot across her back. She had to cajole Pip a few times before she'd come out. Alice scooped her dog into her arms, scooting back against the wall. Rocking Pip to and fro, Alice stroked her ears and flanks, gently pressing her ribs for any reaction. Though she was shaking, Pip didn't seem to be in any great pain. As she stroked her, Pip licked Alice's chin.

She closed her eyes, trying to focus only on breathing. Her skin ached in all the tender places where she felt bruises forming.

Time passed. Around her, the house was quiet. The hum of the fridge. The tick of the roof cooling from the heat of the day.

Out in the lounge room, she heard something. Held her breath to hear better.

It was him, crying.

Alice sighed with relief. Tears meant it was over.

She stood shakily to her feet. Pip scurried back under the bed.

Dylan sat on the sofa, his head in his hands. At the sound of her, he looked up. His face was blanched and tear-stained.

'Pinta-Pinta,' he said, his voice breaking. 'I'm–I'm–I'm just so sorry.' He hung his head. 'Is Pip okay? I–I–I don't know what came over me.' He tried to catch his breath. 'I was just so worried when I came home and you weren't here.'

'I just went for a walk with my dog.' A memory of Toby came clearly to her; the sound of his body hitting the washing machine.

'You don't know,' he cried out. 'You don't get it. There are a dozen blokes here who are better than me. You don't see how they look at you. But I do. I do, Pinta-Pinta. And what if you're out walking without me and one of them sees you on the path, and you start talking after work the way we used to do?' He sniffled. 'What if that happened?'

Alice's head spun in confusion. Did he not understand how much she loved him?

'What if you start talking with one of them and they fall in love with you?' Dylan went on.

'It wouldn't ever matter, Dylan,' Alice implored him. 'Can't you see that? I don't have any room to feel a thing for anyone else.'

He clawed at his face. 'I've only ever wanted to impress you,' he cried. 'And look what loving you does to me. I just don't want to lose you. I freak out when we're apart. I just always want to be with you and I lose my shit when I'm not. You're the love of my life, Alice. The love of,' his voice cracked, 'my fucking life.'

Alice began to cry.

'I would never hit you, you know that, right?' Tears rolled down his nose. 'I would never hit you, Pinta-Pinta.'

It was true, she reasoned. He hadn't hit her. His fear had just got way out of control.

'I love *you*,' she emphasised, her voice wavering.

He pulled her close. 'I just need you to help me out by not doing things like this afternoon and setting me off like that. Can you do that for me? For us?'

She searched his face, the plea in his eyes. Nodded.

'It'll never happen again. Never again.' He leaned in close. Kissed her shakily. 'Never, ever again.'

Her lips burned where they met his.

Later that night, after hours of tearful apologies and talking, after checking Pip over again, and sweeping the floor clean of splinters, Alice let Dylan lead her into the bathroom. He turned on the hot water in the bath. Tenderly undressed her. She sat in the warm water as he washed her skin with slow, gentle strokes. Murmured his love and apologies over her body like prayers. After a while he shed his clothes and got in with her. Alice relaxed in his arms, almost renewed, almost able to forget that he had caused the very harm he was trying to heal.

The next morning Dylan left a cup of hot coffee and a scrawled note on her bedside table. He had to start early, didn't want to wake her, felt horrible after last night, but loved her more deeply than ever.

Alice winced as she sat up. Everything was sore. She hobbled through the house to the toilet to pee, stopped by her reflection in the bathroom mirror. Her neck was covered in bruises the shape and size of his fingers and hands. She turned her face away, went to the toilet and got into the shower. She didn't look in the mirror again.

When she was ready for work, Alice called Pip to put her outside. She didn't come. Alice kept calling, searching, growing more and more panicked until she found her hiding in the bushes. Alice checked Pip over. There was nothing wrong that she could see. She made sure Pip had food and water before rushing to headquarters so she wouldn't be late.

'Bit warm for a scarf, isn't it?' Thugger teased as he passed Alice in the tearoom. She forced a smile and readjusted the scarf around her neck.

Once she was at her desk, Alice did a quick Google search, opened her emails and didn't let herself think twice as she started typing.

Hi Moss,

Sorry I haven't been in touch sooner. I've been living and working as a park ranger at Kililpitjara since I left the Bluff. It's great here. I'm doing great. Trust you are too.

I'm hoping you can help me: Pip got kicked by a brumby yesterday, and though I've checked her over thoroughly and she doesn't appear to be in any pain, I'm still worried. She seems lethargic and I'm wondering if she's in shock. Is there anything you'd recommend I give her, like an anti-inflammatory? Would be so grateful for any advice.

Alice read it over once and clicked Send before she lost her nerve.

A few weeks later, Alice and Dylan drove to work separately. Sarah had asked him to check a few fences on his way in.

'Go ahead, I'll see you for lunch,' he said, as they got into their utes.

'It's a date.' She kissed him goodbye.

Alice watched him go. They'd come full circle again; she'd been particularly careful to be mindful of her behaviour, to help him as he'd asked, and they'd been peaceful. Happy.

Moss had replied the same day to her email, mentioning an anti-inflammatory he'd prescribe, insisting Alice bring Pip to Agnes Bluff for a checkup. Alice had deleted his email immediately and searched online for the medication without success. The next day an express post satchel arrived in the mail, full of antibiotics and anti-inflammatories. She'd snuck Pip the medication, and watched with great relief when she returned to her normal, happy self.

Alice was keeping it all together. Her seams of gold were holding.

When she pulled in to headquarters, her workmates were gathered in the car park. The air was charged with adrenalin.

'What's going on?' Alice asked Aiden as she swung out of her work ute.

'It's fire time.' He nodded towards Sarah who'd just come out of her office with a stack of papers in her hands.

'Wai. Palya, everyone,' Sarah called out. 'Palya.' The group settled. 'Righto. Let's get sorted. Today's weather conditions are perfect for cool burns, so our focus is paddocks around the southern rim. Let's break into groups – group leaders must be experienced burners – so Nicko, Aiden and Thugger, divide everyone up as evenly as you can. Suited in full fire gear, please. Each group takes one of the water tankers plus whatever other vehicles we have spare. Safety first, guys. Watch your drip torches, don't get trigger-happy. Pay attention to what the wind is doing. Most importantly, follow your group leader's instructions. Maps are here, take one. I want a fully charged radio on every person in the field.' Sarah handed out maps and turned to go back into her office.

As the groups came together, Alice stood on her tiptoes looking for Dylan. *It's fire time.* She battled a flurry of childhood memories. *People all over the world use fire*, her mother said that winter day in her garden. *A spell of sorts to transform one thing into another.* Alice's palms were sweaty. She continued to scan the group, looking for his face. He wasn't there. Dylan wasn't there.

'Uh, Sarah?' Alice called after her.

She turned. 'Alice?'

'Sorry. I, um, I'm just wondering if Dylan's doing fire work today?' She cringed at how childlike her voice sounded.

'No, mate,' Sarah said slowly. 'I need staff on the ground, and Dylan's already been out on plenty of burns.' She searched Alice's face. 'I can't have anyone out there today who doesn't have their head in the game. I picked you because you're a hard worker and show a deep interest in skill development. But if you're distracted …'

'No,' Alice interjected. 'No, no. I'm good. I'm good to go.'

'You sure?'

'I'm sure.'

Sarah nodded. 'Aiden,' she called across to where Aiden was standing by the uniform shed. 'Alice is with you today.'

'Palya,' Aiden called back.

'Follow Aiden's directions.' Sarah turned to walk away. 'And enjoy your first burn,' she called over her shoulder.

Alice hurried to the shed. This was fine. It was going to be fine. Sarah had chosen her to learn and diversify her skills. It was perfectly logical and understandable. Alice wasn't intentionally excluding Dylan. And he would surely understand that Sarah had given her a job she hadn't expected, so if she didn't meet him for lunch, he'd be okay with that.

But on the drive towards the southern paddocks, Alice tried to imagine cracking a beer at the end of the day and telling Dylan about the thrill of being picked for fire work. As the desert landscape rushed by in purple streaks where the parakeelya was in bloom, memories of her father awakened an old and frighteningly familiar sense of fear in Alice's body.

They parked at the southeastern rim of the crater.

'We work in a line, together,' Aiden said to the rangers as they readied their drip torches. 'Important reminder, whether this is your first or fiftieth burn: do not start fires in front of you. Do not go into the fire. Start fires behind you. Go away from the fire. Palya?'

Alice nodded. Her hands were sweaty inside her fire gloves. She gripped her drip torch tightly, but its weight made her arm shake. The sound of the fuel sloshing about inside made her queasy.

'Radios?' Aiden asked. The group checked their radios. 'Right. Let's light 'em up.'

One by one the wicks of the drip torches were lit. Alice flinched as hers ignited. It hissed like a living thing. Her hand shook.

'Make sure your breather valves are open,' Aiden called. He turned to Alice. 'Drop the flames to the ground behind you, like this,' he said, lowering his drip torch to a spinifex tussock, setting it alight and walking away. He burned and walked, burned and walked. 'Walk away from it.'

The hiss and crackle of the earth catching fire rose around them. She tried to focus on her boot-clad feet as she walked at a slow pace through the red dirt and bushes, lowering her drip torch and dropping flames behind her.

One, two, drop. One, two, drop.

I'm, here, drop. I'm, here, drop.

The memory played out in front of her: the blurred ground beneath her as she and Toby ran from her father's shed. The hot wind on her face. The lightning cracking the sky into pieces. Her beautiful mother, coming beaten from the sea.

'Alice.'

She hadn't realised she'd stopped walking.

'Keep going,' Aiden instructed the rest of the group. He called her name again across the paddock, fifty metres away.

'You're just going to take a step, towards me, now.' His face was calm and his voice was steady.

She looked down at her feet. They would not move.

'Alice, you can do this. Walk to me. Now,' Aiden said more urgently.

She was shaking; the can of fuel and drip torch wobbled heavily in her hands. Her feet would not budge. Heat from the wall of fire behind her began to radiate through her fire gear.

'Alice.' Aiden began to run to her.

She could not move.

He reached her side, bracing her. 'I'm going to take you by the arm and we're going to run together, okay?'

Alice nodded. Using his weight Aiden jolted her forward. She ran awkwardly by his side, watching her feet move out of time with his.

When they were safely away from the fire line, Aiden took his pack off and opened it, retrieving a water bottle and some jelly beans.

'Here,' he said, handing her both. Watched her carefully as she ate and drank.

'Thank you,' she muttered, handing his water bottle back once she'd had enough.

'Has it passed?' he asked.

She nodded.

'Lulu has panic attacks too sometimes. Tries to tell me they're vertigo.'

Alice glanced away. She didn't know Lulu suffered from anxiety too.

'How are you feeling now? Do you need me to radio HQ and ask someone to come and get you?'

'No,' Alice answered. 'No, I'll be fine.' She tightened her grasp on the drip torch. 'I'm fine,' she said again, willing strength in her voice.

Aiden studied her. 'Righto,' he said, nodding as he put his pack on. 'Let's work together, though. Follow my lead.'

As she and Aiden walked the paddock, working together to light a methodical line of fire, Alice felt her shoulders relax and her hand steady. With his support and watchful eye, she got the job done.

After an hour, they were collected by the pick-up team on quad bikes and driven ahead, until there was a decent distance between them and the fires. At the top of a dune they stopped to have lunch in the shade of desert oaks. Alice closed her eyes as she took a long drink from her water bottle. Her armpits were damp from the cold sweat of fear.

While the group ate their sandwiches and chatted, Alice sat to the side and kept her back turned to the distant wave of orange flames behind them. When she caught Aiden's eye, she didn't suppress her grateful smile.

At the end of the day, back at headquarters, Alice hurried to finish up and get home to Dylan. She was just about to leave when Aiden interrupted.

'Mate, I've been called out to help on sunset patrol, which leaves us short a set of hands to tick off safety checks. It shouldn't take too long. Would you mind?'

Alice swallowed her rising fear. 'Sure,' she said, masking her nervousness.

'Hey, Pinta-Pinta,' Ruby called from across the car park. 'I'll give you a hand, then you can give me a lift home.'

'Great,' Aiden said. 'More the merrier. Thanks, Alice.' He turned away but stopped and came back, his arms open wide. 'You did great today. Well done.' He gave her a short but warm hug.

'Thanks,' she said. 'I really appreciate that. And all your help today.'

After Aiden left, as Ruby and Alice walked towards the work shed, a revving engine caught Alice's attention. Her stomach plummeted as she recognised Dylan's profile in a work ute, speeding away from headquarters.

By the time Alice and Ruby wrapped up, Alice's gut was twisted in a hard knot of fear.

'Nyuntu palya, Pinta-Pinta?' Ruby asked as she climbed up into Alice's truck. 'You okay?'

Alice didn't answer. She couldn't trust her voice.

'That fire scared you today,' Ruby stated. Alice nodded again without replying. 'Uwa, fire can be scary, yes. But it is also many other things. Like medicine. Fire keeps the land healthy, and so keeps us healthy. Where we have fire, we have home. That's not so scary, is it?'

'Medicine?' Alice asked distractedly.

'That paddock you burned today,' Ruby explained, 'was covered in seedpods that need fire to split open and germinate. Without your fire today, the land gets sick. The land gets sick, our stories get sick, we get sick.'

'Fire has never been medicine to me,' Alice said quietly.

'I thought it might have been once. But I've only ever known it to be the end of things.'

In her peripheral vision, Alice saw Ruby studying her. Their hand radios interrupted, crackling to life and calling Ruby's name. Ruby unclipped hers from her belt, responded, and clipped it back in place.

They drove the rest of the way home in silence.

After Alice dropped Ruby off, she doubled back to the work yard. Dylan's work ute was parked outside the workshop. Had he seen her hugging Aiden? Would it be a problem? Surely not, she reasoned. They'd not had lunch as planned, nor been in touch through the day, but he'd understand that she'd been out on fire work. And, as Sarah said that morning, Dylan had been on burnings many times. He wouldn't begrudge her the chance to learn.

As Alice walked in, she flickered with hope that he would not be jealous, of Aiden, or her day. He'd told her she was the love of his life. What kind of disservice was she doing to their relationship if she didn't trust that and believe in him? She imagined how the scene might unfold: he'd wrap her in a hug and tell her how proud he was of her. Whisk her home, crack a beer, and ask a flurry of questions, wanting to hear all about her day.

He didn't look up from his emails when she walked in. The screen threw a sickly light on his face.

'Hey,' she said, forcing herself to smile.

His jaw was set. He didn't respond. She waited.

'Did you hear? I did my first controlled burn today,' she said. The tightness of her smile hurt her face. He still didn't look at her. A muscle twitched in his cheek.

'I heard,' he said, staring at his computer. 'No surprise there, though, the darling of the park getting chosen to do fire work.'

Fear cut through her stomach. When he turned to face her, his eyes were dark and sunken, his lips pale.

'But this is what you do, right? With your big eyes, and your butterflies, and your smile. People can't get enough of you, can they? And you play them like a fucking song.'

Her feet were root-bound.

'So, how was fire work, then?' His lips stretched in a cruel smile. 'Go on. You want to tell me all about it? Tell me all about it then. Who were you on a quad bike with? Hey?' He shoved his chair back; she flinched. 'Who'd you have your legs wrapped around on a quad bike, Alice?' He slammed his hand on the desk. 'Because I checked your training sheet and you don't have your quad bike licence. So, who the fuck were you all cosied up to? And don't you fucking lie to me.' Spittle gathered in the corners of his mouth. She couldn't speak.

'Tell me who you were with,' he screamed.

Tears slipped down her cheeks. He moved so fast she didn't have time to brace herself. He grabbed one of her arms and wrenched it behind her back.

'Tell me,' he whispered.

When he threw her into the wall, the force of his strength winded her. She couldn't breathe. She couldn't hear. She willed herself to flee.

'Yeah, that's it, run away, you fucking prick-tease. I saw you hugging Aiden. I know what you are. Go on. Run away.' His voice roared after her. 'Good fucking riddance.'

Later she would remember her body moving independently of her mind. Twisting out and away from him. Running to her truck. Turning the key in the ignition and simultaneously pressing her foot down on the accelerator. Again, her mind floated somewhere above her, disconnected, watching herself drive. She stopped at Dylan's gate to gather Pip into her arms, returned to her truck and allowed the headlights to guide her safely home.

When she drove around the bend in the road there was a dusty rental car parked in her driveway. Alice pulled up and walked shakily alongside the car, peering through the windows.

Low voices came from around the back, the rich scent of tobacco smoke. Pip ran ahead through the garage.

Her legs were leaden. She walked slowly out to the patio.

There, in the last of the day's light, stood Twig and Candy Baby.

26

Lantern bush

Meaning: **Hope may blind me**
Abutilon leucopetalum | Northern Territory

Tjirin-tjirinpa (Pit.) is found in dry, often rocky inland regions.
Leaves have a heart-shaped base. Yellow hibiscus-like flowers
appear mostly in winter and spring, but can sometimes appear
endlessly, their bright colour shining all year round. Used by
Anangu children to make small toy spears.

Candy broke down. She rushed to Alice and fussed, stroking her face and hair.

Twig hung back. She dropped her smoke at her feet and put it out under the heel of her boot. Once Candy let her go, Twig stepped forward and pulled Alice into her arms.

Alice shook as she made tea. Smoke clung to her skin, to her hair. Dylan's rage continued to play on her. The revulsion on his face. The harmful intent of his strength.

She carried three cups of tea to the table where Candy and Twig sat, so familiar but so out of context in her desert life. Set them down, trembling.

'Are you all right?' Candy reached forward, putting her hand over Alice's.

Alice sat, closed her eyes briefly and gave a nod.

'How did you find me?' she murmured.

They exchanged a glance.

Twig took a sip of tea. 'Moss Fletcher.'

'As in, the vet?' Alice exclaimed, her mind reeling. 'In Agnes Bluff?'

Twig nodded. 'He read the insignia on your truck when he took you to the doctor. Googled Thornfield, called us looking for next of kin. He rang us after you emailed him and said you were here.'

Alice couldn't look at either of them. 'He had no business doing that.' Dylan's voice: *You play them like a fucking song.*

'Maybe not,' Candy said gently. 'But we were so relieved when he rang.' She wiped her eyes. 'You just left, sweetpea,' she said. 'I texted and called and emailed you every day ...' her voice broke. 'You just left.'

Outside her fairy lights twinkled in the bruised sky. Would he call? Her head ached. The adrenalin was fading, leaving a silt of exhaustion in her body.

'You know why I "just left",' Alice said. 'What else was I supposed to do?'

'I know it's so hard to see it this way, but June was trying to protect you.'

'Oh god. This isn't ...' Alice abruptly stood and pushed her chair in. 'I can't do this,' she said, holding her hands up. She had no fight left in her. She didn't want them there. Her mind was a mess; all she could think about was Dylan. She didn't have room for ghosts and old memories. Besides, deep down she knew she was being unfair. They didn't deserve her fear, pain and anger. The best thing she could do for everyone was take some time out.

'I just need a moment.' Alice turned her back and headed for the shower. As she was about to shut the bathroom door, Candy spoke.

'She's dead, Alice.'

The words hit her like a trio of explosions. She could see Candy's lips moving, but heard only snippets.

'… a massive heart attack …'

Alice shook her head, trying to hear. Her legs were numb.

'… we were cut off from town by the floods. Day and night she sat on the back verandah, watching the water rise. We found her, eyes wide open, staring out at the ruined flowers.' Candy's face was empty.

Alice looked at them both, as if seeing them properly for the first time. Candy's eyes were bloodshot; her blue hair was dull and brittle. Twig's hair had silvered at her temples. Even under her utilitarian clothes, her frame was visibly gaunt.

June was dead.

Alice stumbled into the bathroom and shut the door behind her, pressing herself against it as her legs gave out. She sank to the floor. Desperate for comfort, she turned on a warm shower. Clambered in, fully clothed, and sat under the water. Held her face up to it. Pulled her knees to her chest, wrapped her arms around them, and let herself wail.

Alice stayed in the bathroom long after she'd showered. She wrapped herself in towels and lay in the empty bath, her eyes closed, unwilling to move, unwilling to speak.

Through the walls came the muffled sound of Twig and Candy talking in the lounge room. Sliding the back door open. Teacups being washed in the kitchen sink. The squawk of her dining chairs on the lino. Footsteps to the bathroom door.

'Alice.' Twig's voice. 'I think it's best we go and get a room at the resort. Give you some space. It was a mistake to bring you this news without any warning.' A pause. 'We're very sorry.' Another pause. Receding footsteps. At the sound of her front door opening, remorse hauled Alice out of the bath. She flung the door open. Pip rushed in, weaving herself around Alice's legs.

'Wait,' she called.

Twig and Candy were already outside. At the sound of her voice, they stepped back through the front door.

'You could stay. There's plenty of room for you here. I'm off work now for four days.' She raised her chin. 'You should stay. We should talk.' Her heart beat steadfast in her ears.

They glanced at each other. Candy was the first to speak. 'How about I rustle up something for a late dinner? We aren't of any use to each other on empty stomachs.'

While Candy helped herself to the kitchen and Twig sat out the back to roll a smoke, Alice went into her bedroom to get dressed. Every movement took monumental effort. Knickers on. Had June been in pain? One leg. Next leg. Did she know she was dying when the heart attack happened? Shirt over her head. Did she cry or call out for anyone? Was she scared? Alice's head felt too heavy for her neck to carry. She crawled into bed, just for a moment, seeking the comfort of her pillow. Curled into herself.

There he was.

The smell of his cologne on her shirt, the wending green scent and something else besides. His body, his dreams and his breath, earthen and salty.

Alice lifted the neck of her shirt over her nose, inhaling deeply. He'd been upset, he'd been excluded from the burn. He was sensitive to her attracting other men's attention. She should have been more mindful. She should go to him and apologise. He'd just lost his temper. Everyone does that now and then.

Alice tried to quell her tears. She sat up and turned her lamp off. Looked across the dunes to his house. It sat dark and unlit, a shadowy hulk under the star-splashed sky.

When she awoke the next morning to the smell of brewing coffee and the sounds of Candy and Twig in the kitchen, Alice didn't know where she was, in time or place. She could have been nine. Sixteen. Twenty-seven.

'Cuppa?' Candy asked as Alice plodded into the living room, bleary-eyed.

'Yes, please.'

'How'd you sleep?' Twig asked.

'Dreamlessly.' Alice yawned. 'You?'

'Fine.' Twig nodded.

'We felt like schoolgirls on camp. Imagine that at our ages.' Candy smiled, handing Alice a steaming cup of coffee. She nodded in thanks.

Silence settled over them. Outside, Pip chased her tail in circles.

'She needs to get out.' Alice took a sip of her coffee. 'There's a track I walk sometimes, from my back fence to the crater wall. It leads to a view I think you'd like.'

With Pip scampering ahead, Alice, Twig and Candy walked through the bush. Occasionally one of them stopped to point out a desert rose, or wedge-tailed eagle gliding overhead. Mostly they walked wordlessly as they followed the trail up the crater wall. When they reached the viewing platform, Twig was wheezing. She sat in the shade to catch her breath.

'It's those bloody durries you smoke all day long,' Candy chided. Twig shooed her away.

Alice passed water around and poured some in a bowl for Pip, who lay panting by Twig. The morning air cooled their skin. They turned to the view of the crater. The desert peas swayed bright red.

'How spectacular.' Candy sighed. 'I don't think I've ever seen so many desert peas in one place.'

'They draw tourists from all over the world.'

'They'll flower now right through summer until autumn.' Twig jutted her chin towards the crater. 'Where my family's from, down south, we call them flowers of blood,' she said quietly. 'In our stories, they grow where blood has spilled.'

'You've never told me that,' Candy said. 'Is that why you always took such care growing them at Thornfield?'

Twig nodded. 'One of the reasons. They always reminded me of the family I lost. And,' her voice cracked, 'the family I found.'

'Have courage, take heart,' Candy murmured.

Alice picked up a stick and pointed it at the desert peas. 'The story here is that this is the impact site of a mother's heart. She pulled it from her body and threw it from the stars, to be near her baby who fell to its death from the sky.' Alice snapped the stick in half, picking bits of bark from it. 'The peas bloom for nine months of the year, in a perfect circle. They say every flower is an earthbound, living piece of her.' She snapped the stick into smaller and smaller pieces until it was a pile at her feet. 'My friend Ruby says if the flowers are sick, she and her family get sick.'

'Sounds about right,' Twig said.

The three of them sat together quietly.

'Was she buried or cremated?' Alice couldn't look at either of them.

'Cremated,' Candy replied. 'She left instructions in her will to scatter her ashes in the river so she might find her way to the sea.'

Alice shook her head, remembering when she'd dived into the river and dreamed of following it all the way home.

'Maybe we could head back now, Alice. We have something to give you,' Candy said. Twig nodded.

'Sure,' Alice said. She whistled for Pip and led the way back down the trail towards home.

The sun was hot and high when they got in. Alice filled glasses with cool water and handed them around.

Candy went out to the rental car, returning with a small parcel wrapped in a piece of cloth. Alice instinctively recognised it.

'Oh, god.'

'She said in her will that you were to have it.' Candy rested the parcel in Alice's hands.

Alice unwound the cloth until the Thornfield Dictionary was laid bare. Memories rushed back to her. The first time she went into the workshop with Candy. Twig teaching her how to cut flowers. June showing Alice how to press them. Oggi, just a boy, looking up from his book and waving to her.

'It took her the best part of twenty years, but she kept her promise in the end.' Twig's voice was gravelly. 'Everything you've ever wanted to know is in there. We didn't realise, but June spent the last year of her life writing Thornfield's stories, including your mother and father's.'

Alice tightened her hold on the book.

'When you read it,' Candy said, 'you'll learn what was in Ruth Stone's will: that Thornfield was never to be bequeathed to an undeserving man.' She paused, seeming to choose her words carefully. 'Alice, when your father was young, June had a heart attack. Not major, though enough to make her write a will. But she kept it a secret,' Candy's voice caught, 'because she decided to leave Clem out of it. June saw how possessive Clem could be of your mum when they were kids. And sometimes, she saw how aggressive he was with the rest of us. Jealous if he wasn't the centre of attention. Mean-spirited if he wasn't in control. Sometimes violent when he lost his temper. When he heard June confiding in Agnes that Thornfield would one day be hers, mine and Twig's, that she'd made the choice not to leave it to Clem ... As he was leaving he vowed never to speak to June, or any of us again. Said that's all we deserved.' Her voice broke. 'That's why we didn't know you, until you were nine. We never saw or spoke to your parents again.'

'So …' Alice trailed off, as she pieced things together, 'my parents left because June made a choice she knew would anger my father?'

'It wasn't as simple as that. June felt she had good reason to do what she did. She was too wary of Clem's nature to leave everything she and the women in your family had worked for to him. He could be so volatile.'

'Yeah,' Alice retorted. 'I kind of know that, Candy.' A headache started to pound in her temples. 'Why didn't you tell me that's why they left?'

'I couldn't, Alice. I just couldn't. I couldn't betray June. Not after everything she'd done for me. It was her story to tell.'

'So that just cancelled out your own feelings? June's fuck-up became yours too?'

'Okay, that's enough,' Twig interjected. 'That is enough. Take a breather.'

Alice got up and paced the room. Tears slid down Candy's nose.

'I think it's important,' Twig said slowly, 'that we don't get caught in the past.'

'Caught in the past?' Alice shrieked. 'How can I get caught in the past when I don't even know what that means?'

'Alice, please,' Twig reasoned. 'You need to try to stay calm. We need to talk about what's at hand.'

'And what exactly is that?' Alice shot back.

'Sit down,' Twig said firmly. Her face was unreadable. Candy was the same. A sense of foreboding washed the anger clean out of Alice's body. She looked from Candy to Twig.

'What?' she asked. 'What is it? Tell me right now.'

'Alice, sit down.'

She started to protest but Twig held up her hand. Alice pulled out a chair, and sat.

'This is a lot for you to take in, and we want to spare you as much as we can.' Twig pressed her hands together.

'Just tell me,' Alice said, clenching her jaw.

'Okay,' Twig began.

Candy took a deep breath.

'Alice,' Twig said.

'Just bloody tell me!'

'Your brother survived the fire, Alice,' Twig said, sagging in her chair.

Alice recoiled as if she'd been slapped. 'What?'

'Your baby brother. He survived. He was adopted, not long after you came to Thornfield.'

She stared numbly at them.

'He was born premature, and was very sick. The doctors weren't sure if he would survive. June was worried about caring for a sick newborn, and didn't want to put you through more grief if he didn't survive.'

Alice shook her head. 'So she just left him behind?'

'Oh, sweetpea.' Candy reached out to her. 'I'm so sorry. This is such a big shock, and a huge amount to take in. It's going to take time. Why don't you come back with us, to Thornfield? Please. We'll look after you. We'll –'

Alice ran for the toilet. She retched and gagged, gripped by convulsions.

Twig and Candy's faces, full of fear, worry and love, bent over her, calling her name.

Candy slid the back door open and brought two bowls of pasta out to the patio. She handed one to Twig and sat beside her under Alice's fairy lights. For a while they ate in silence. The sky faded from blue to amber to pink. The crater wall, backlit, looked like the hull of a beached ship.

'When do you think we should wake her?' Candy asked.

'Let her sleep, Candy.'

'She's been in bed for more than a day now.'

'And, by the looks of things, she needs the rest,' Twig sighed.

'What about her phone, though? It must have rung half a dozen times.'

'Candy –'

'But where do you think she got those bruises?' Candy interrupted, whispering.

Twig shook her head. Put her bowl down and reached into her top pocket for her tobacco pouch. 'They're probably from her job here. You know how knocked about we get on the farm.'

'I feel like we've lost her,' Candy said in a quiet voice.

'You're just feeling that way because we don't know what's been going on in her life since she left. But she's not exactly had the chance to tell us, has she? We've brought too much else with us.'

Candy didn't respond. They watched the sun sink under the horizon.

'You didn't tell her June died waiting for her to come home,' Candy said after a while.

'Neither did you,' Twig replied.

'I know.' Candy rubbed her forehead. 'The last thing she needs is that kind of guilt.'

Early stars blinked in the sky.

'Did you see her notebooks?' Candy asked.

Twig shook her head again as she lit her smoke.

'They're on her bookshelves. Full of flowers and their meanings. Some pages have sketches, others have pressed flowers. Not in any order, not like they're a dictionary series or anything. They look random, but flicking through them felt like something more. Like they're a story.'

Twig took a drag, and exhaled her smoke upwards, shooting Candy a sideways glance.

'What?' Candy said. 'I was just looking. They were on her bookshelf. I was curious.' She jabbed her fork at her pasta. 'I'm worried.'

Twig took another drag. 'Me too.'

Candy put her fork and bowl down. 'We need to convince her to come home with us,' she said. 'Thornfield is a third hers now, after all.'

Twig tapped the ash from her smoke. 'All of that can wait. We're not going anywhere.'

'But don't you think she's in trouble? We're her family. She needs us.' Candy's voice wavered.

'We're not her only family,' Twig said pointedly.

Candy sat agape. 'We love her. We raised her.'

'And when she's ready, we'll be there for her. But right now, we have to give her the time she needs. To do what she needs to do.'

'Which is?'

'Live,' Twig said simply. 'You know that. Your head and heart aren't talking sense to each other about this right now. She's desperate to live her own story, and trust it enough to make mistakes and fuck up, and still know she'll be okay.'

'But,' Candy's bottom lip quivered, 'what if she's not?'

'So what, we smother her like June did, to try and protect her? You know the saying. The road to hell …' Twig trailed off, picking flecks of tobacco from her tongue.

Candy fell silent. Somewhere nearby dogs howled.

'We won't lose her again,' Twig said. 'Give her some credit.'

Candy nodded, her face creased in pain. 'Okay,' she said.

'Okay.' Twig took another long drag, the tobacco crackling in the quiet.

Alice sat on the couch drinking a cup of coffee. She'd been awake for a few hours, but her head felt as empty as the sky outside. Candy had told her she'd slept for two days. *So much for you to take in; you must have really needed it.*

Pip scurried underfoot while Candy and Twig ferried their things out to the rental car. They wanted to get back to Agnes Bluff before dark. Their return flight left early the next morning.

'I think that's everything.' Twig came inside, dusting her hands. 'I know I've already asked you twenty times, Alice, but if you want us to stay …'

Alice shook her head. 'I'm okay. Time alone to let everything sink in will be good for me.'

'Promise you'll call us,' Candy said, her face pinched. 'When you have questions, or need to talk, or just want someone who knows you and loves you.'

Alice got up and went to her.

'I hate goodbyes,' Candy wailed, wrapping her arms around Alice. 'Promise you'll come and visit. We're going to try to start over. Sowing season starts soon. Thornfield will always be your home.'

Alice nodded into Candy's shoulder, inhaling her vanilla smell.

Candy stepped back. 'Alice Blue,' she said, tucking a strand of hair behind Alice's ear before she got in the car.

It was just Alice and Twig. She couldn't meet Twig's eyes.

'You okay?' Twig cleared her throat.

Alice forced herself to look up. 'I'll be okay.'

They held each other's gaze for a moment. Twig pulled a thick envelope from her back pocket.

'When you're ready,' she said, 'everything you need is in there. I should have given this to you years ago.'

Alice took the envelope. Twig pulled her in for a tight hug.

'Thank you,' Alice said. Twig nodded.

Alice waved until their rental car had disappeared from view.

When she went back inside, everything Twig and Candy had told her was waiting. June's death. Alice's brother's life. She walked in circles, trying to make it all fit inside her somehow, but when she did that, all she had room for was Dylan. Days had passed. Where was he? Twig and Candy could have forgotten to mention that there'd been phone calls while she was sleeping. Putting the envelope Twig gave her aside, Alice hurried to her phone. Sure enough, there were messages. All from him. The first was apologetic, but his voice grew colder after the second. The last message made her sick to her stomach.

'I've been the bigger person, I've called you and apologised, and you're just ignoring me? Nice.'

Driven by guilt and her compulsion to make it right, Alice grabbed her keys and went out the back door. She walked along her fence line towards his house. She would apologise for going on the fire burn. She would apologise for not being more aware of his feelings, and for not coming to apologise sooner. She'd explain she'd had an unexpected family visit. She'd tell him. There'd been death, and life. He'd understand.

But Dylan's gate was closed and padlocked. Neither his work ute nor his personal four-wheel drive were in the driveway.

'He's not home,' Lulu said flatly behind her.

Alice turned. They hadn't spoken for months.

'He's gone,' Lulu said, burying her hands deep in her pockets. 'Said he'd been to see Sarah at headquarters and had urgent work things to take care of. Said he needed to leave suddenly.'

Alice searched her face, trying to comprehend. 'W-when?'

'I saw him yesterday at the servo when he was filling up. Did he not tell you?'

Alice couldn't suppress a wail of pain. What urgent work things? Had he talked to Sarah about what happened in the workshop? Was he hurt? Sick? Was he okay? Lulu grabbed Alice just before her knees gave way.

'What have I done?' Alice sobbed, clinging to Lulu's frame, not realising her bruises were visible.

'Qué chingados,' Lulu said under her breath, seeing Alice's arms. 'What the fuck, Alice? Has he been hurting you? Has Dylan been hurting you?'

Alice slumped in her embrace.

'Right,' Lulu said, her voice caring but firm. 'Inside, to my place. Let's go.'

27

Bat's wing coral tree

Meaning: **Cure for heartache**
Erythrina vespertilio | Central and northeast Australia

Ininti (Pit.) wood is widely used for making spear throwers and bowls. Bark, fruit and stems are used for traditional medicine. Has bat's-wing-shaped leaves, and coral-coloured flowers in spring/summer. Attractive, glossy bean-shaped seeds vary in colour from deep yellow to blood red, and are used for decoration and jewellery.

Alice walked numbly into Lulu's house, and sat at her table, staring down at her hands. Tears poured down her face. Lulu went into the kitchen, returning with two small glasses of what looked like sparkling water on ice, topped with lemon and lime.

'It'll help you calm down.' She nodded, taking a sip. Alice did the same and coughed roughly on the strong gin and tonic. 'My abuela's remedy for fever, and heart ailments,' Lulu said.

The ice cubes fizzed and cracked.

'So ... How long has it been going on?'

Alice took a longer drink, spluttering as grief closed her throat over.

'What did I do wrong?' She cried so hard that she retched.

'Oh, chica.' Lulu rushed into the kitchen. 'You didn't do anything wrong,' she said, returning to set a glass of water in front of Alice. She sat and reached across the table.

'Why are you being so kind to me again?' Alice asked, clutching Lulu's hands. 'I thought you hated me.'

'I'm so sorry,' Lulu said, her voice heavy with remorse. 'I knew you liked each other the minute I saw you two meet. I tried to warn you against him, but I didn't tell you the full story. Once it was clear you were together, I was too scared, too ashamed to tell you the truth of what happened with me.' Lulu paused and looked away, her eyes unfocused. 'I never told anyone. Aiden doesn't even know the full extent of it. Dylan fucked with my head so much. I talked it down, convinced myself it'd hardly happened. I thought it was just me, like there was something about me that didn't click well with him. That I was the reason he was so angry, so violent. It was my fault. I thought he might be different with you. If I'd had any idea that he was capable of ...' Lulu glanced at Alice's arms and let the sentence go.

As they held each other's hands, Alice's eyes fell on the strands of leather Dylan had taken from his wrists to bind around hers. She clawed and bit at them, trying to get them off.

'Chica,' Lulu exclaimed. 'Stop.' She reached for scissors from a jar on the counter. Slid the cold metal blade under the leather strands to cut each of Alice's wrists free. Alice rubbed her skin.

'Do you know what Dylan went to talk to Sarah about before he left?' she asked.

Lulu shook her head. 'I guess we'll find out at work tomorrow, though.' She gestured meaningfully at Alice's locket. 'Courage, right? I'll be there with you.'

The next morning Alice went to park headquarters with Lulu. She slid her eyes towards Dylan's house as they drove by. His gates were locked, his driveway empty. Her mind travelled through the front door. Her toothbrush was inside, on the bathroom bench next to his. Her summer dresses hung in his wardrobe. Their messy bed by the window, bathed in light. His sleepy face in the mornings. The way he cradled her head in his hands when they made love. Her veggie garden. His fire pit. The broken bedroom door. The dust balls. As they drove away, Alice's heart lingered, tangled in yearning, need and fear.

When they arrived at headquarters Alice shook her head.

'I can't do this,' she whispered.

For a moment neither of them spoke.

'Yes, you can,' Lulu whispered back.

Alice and Lulu walked in to find Sarah waiting at Alice's desk. 'Alice,' she said, her face expressionless. 'A word in my office?'

Alice nodded. As she followed Sarah, she shot Lulu a look.

'I'll be right here,' Lulu mouthed.

Sarah gestured to the seat in front of her desk.

Alice sat, remembering the day she'd arrived, sitting in exactly the same seat, signing her employment contract, filled with hope and excitement.

'I won't pussyfoot around. There's been an incident report lodged by one of the staff.' Sarah reached for a manila folder and opened it. 'Dylan Rivers has reported that an incident occurred in the workshop office after the burn last Thursday. Allegedly you demonstrated physically violent behaviour towards him.' Sarah read over the papers. 'While he's made it clear he doesn't want to take this further, he did send the incident report to me, and copied in human resources at head office.' She dropped the papers and leant back in her chair, pinching the bridge of her nose. 'I'm sorry, Alice, my hands are bound. I have to take full disciplinary action, which technically means suspension of duties, starting immediately.'

Alice shook from the effort to hold herself steady.

'I'll ask one of the other rangers to work your shifts,' Sarah said. 'I'm expecting to hear back from HR today about how long your suspension will be. They're going to send one of their staff down next week, when you'll have the opportunity to give your version of events.'

Alice said nothing.

'In the meantime you are not to have any contact with Dylan while the report is being processed. That should be pretty easy for you now because, as you're probably aware, he's taken leave.'

Alice closed her eyes.

'Do you have any questions?'

She shook her head.

'Hey,' Sarah said more gently.

Alice opened her eyes.

'Is there anything else I should know, Alice? Anything you want to share with me, in confidence?'

Alice held Sarah's eye contact for a moment, before pushing her chair back, standing and wordlessly leaving her office.

Outside Lulu was waiting in the ute, the engine running.

'Don't stay home, chica,' Lulu said when they pulled up at her house. 'Get into your civvies and come with me on the ranger walk. It might do you good, you know, to walk it out. You'll just stew in there.'

Alice looked at her house without really seeing it. He'd submitted a report against her. He'd knowingly, intentionally taken her voice. *Like the girl in the fairytale who wanders into a dark wood.*

She wiped her cheeks and opened the passenger door. 'Give me five minutes.'

Alice hung behind the group that followed Lulu along the track into the crater. It had been a mistake to come. She didn't want to hear the talk she would no longer be giving. Didn't want to think about why she wouldn't be giving it. Didn't want to hear Dylan's voice in her head. Or relive the conversation with Sarah. The humiliation. The disbelief. She wanted to fade, to blend into the desert unseen.

'You're holding up the group,' a woman called.

Alice started. 'Sorry?'

'Keep up,' the woman said primly. She stabbed the ends of her hiking poles repeatedly into the red earth.

'I'm fine,' Alice said. 'No need to wait for me.'

The woman drew her fly net down over her greying hair and pink face. 'As anyone who's read their outback guide book knows, this place,' she waved a hiking pole about, 'is more dangerous than it looks.'

'Thanks,' Alice said, bemused. 'I'll keep that in mind.'

As they walked on, the woman swatted at branches with her hiking poles. *Thwack, whip, whack, thwack, whip, whack.* Alice flinched at every beat. The intensity of her desire for solitude made her even more irritated. *Breathe*, she told herself.

But her thoughts raced. At some point over the weekend, while Twig and Candy were telling her truths that irrevocably unpicked the seams of her life, Dylan had sat down somewhere, maybe at his laptop, maybe with pen and paper, and deliberately set out to silence her. Did he drink a coffee while he did it? Or did he crack open a beer? How did it feel, as word by word he drew back an arrow aimed straight for her heart? He'd helped himself to her life, to her body, to her mind, and he'd taken his fill.

Alice's gut started to cramp.

Did he shake? Did he have remorse, even if only momentarily? Did he feel regret, as he took aim? Did he flinch or was he open-eyed when it was done? And in the days since, where was he? Where did he go? Did he have a dark and dank place he retreated to, where by lantern light he spun straw into gold, so he could reappear, transformed?

In front of Alice, the hiking pole woman came into focus. She crouched by the track. Opened her backpack and took out a small jar, leaning forward to scoop red dirt into it.

Alice took a sharp breath. 'No!' she shouted, launching forwards to whack the jar from the woman's hand. It landed in the dirt with a thud. A few tourists turned, gasping. The woman sat in the dirt, a stunned expression on her face. Alice glared down at her, fists clenched.

'Everything okay back here?' Lulu pushed through the group.

'No, it's ruddy not!' The woman got to her feet.

'Alice?' Lulu asked.

'She was trying to take some dirt. I saw her,' Alice said shakily, pointing at the jar.

Lulu squeezed Alice's arm. 'Okay,' she said, looking Alice in the eyes. She glanced at the woman then back at Alice. 'Okay?'

Alice nodded.

'Ma'am, walk with me and I'll explain why what you just did is a fineable offence in a national park.' Lulu led the woman to the head of the group, glancing at Alice, frowning in concern.

Alice walked the rest of the way in silence at the rear of the group. Unsurprisingly, no one spoke to her. Lulu kept looking back until Alice waved her on. Alice thought to turn around a few times, to go home to Pip and crawl into bed. But leaving would only make more of a scene.

When she reached the viewing platform, Alice sat away from the group. Lulu's voice drifted over to her while she kept her eyes fixed on the circular centre of flowers in blazing red bloom. Her thoughts turned to Twig, Candy and June. Then, her mother. Always her mother. Always.

She waited until her tears dried before she stood and followed the rest of the group down into Kuṯuṯu Kaana.

The crater trail was in full sun. The sea of desert peas shimmered in the heat. A wedge-tailed eagle circled above. Finches chirped in the bushes. Alice closed her eyes and listened. The timbre of Lulu's voice. The rhythm of the wind. The rustle of flowers and leaves. There was a pulse to it, the faintest heartbeat.

The sound of a zipper interrupted Alice's fragile serenity. Hiking pole woman had broken away from the group, grabbed a jar from her backpack and was crouched next to the desert peas. As Alice watched, she slowly and deliberately unscrewed the lid and reached for the flowers with an open hand.

Alice threw her full weight at the woman, who screamed as she tackled her to the ground and wrestled the desert peas from her hand.

An hour later Alice sat outside Sarah's office, her elbows resting on her knees and her face in her hands. She could smell her skin, burnt from too much sun. She remembered the scent of her mother's skin: soft, clean, cool. The delicacy of her mother's voice, the light in her eyes when she was in her garden among her fern fronds and flowers. June's scents, her whisky and peppermints. The smell of the river, and the fires Oggi burned when they were teenagers.

Flashes of Dylan merged with memories of her father. Faces white with rage. The sour scent of Dylan's breath, the mineral smell of her father's fury, her body hurt and bent, horribly cold water, hands raised about to strike. The headquarters radio squealed with interference, reminding Alice of a baby's cry. Who'd raised her brother? Did he have a good life? Was he happy? Did he know she existed?

'Alice.'

She looked up. Sarah stood in the open doorway of her office. This time, her face was pained.

Ruby was sitting by the fire in her backyard when she heard a truck pull up out the front. She peered out to the driveway. Alice's butterfly truck was packed to the hilt. Ruby refocused on the necklace she was making. She held the tip of a wire coat hanger into the flames and pushed it through the middle of an ininti seed. When it was cool she threaded it onto brown twine and reached for the next seed from the pile at her feet. She watched Alice get out of her truck, her dog at her heels. Her gait was strained and her eyes were sick. She looked exactly like a woman who'd lost her love, livelihood and home in one hit.

Alice sat at Ruby's fire, staring into the flames. Pip scampered off to play with Ruby's dogs. Three tall desert oaks sighed as the wind picked up. Ruby held her wire in the flames, waited for it to heat, and pushed the molten tip through another ininti seed. Alice stayed quiet. It took her a few tries before her voice was strong enough to speak.

'Ruby, I've come to say goodbye.'

Ruby threaded the seed onto the twine and picked up another. The wind ruffled their hair. It was a northwesterly. *That wind will make you sick*, Ruby's aunties had always said. *It's a bad one, that wind from the west. It'll make your spirit sick. You'd better have the right medicine.*

'I've been thinking about what you said the other day, Pinta-Pinta, about what fire means to you.' Ruby burned a hole through another seed and pushed it onto the string. 'I wanted to ask you where your fire place is.'

'Fire place?'

'Yeah. Your fire place. Where you gather around, with the people you love. Where you're warm, all together. Where you belong.'

Alice didn't answer for a long time. Ruby added another mulga branch to her fire.

'I don't know. But I … I have a brother,' Alice's voice cracked. 'A little brother.'

Ruby lifted the string of ininti and tied the ends together in a knot. The necklace glistened, glossy and red, scented with fire. She held it out to Alice. Alice just stared. Ruby shook the necklace, gesturing for Alice to take it. The ininti seeds clacked softly against each other as Ruby pooled them into Alice's cupped hands.

'Bat's wing coral tree seeds,' Alice mumbled. 'Cure for heartache.' Her eyes were red.

'Women in my family, we wear these for inma,' Ruby said. 'They give us strength during ceremony.' Alice rubbed her thumbs over the seeds, lifted them to her nose, and smelled their smoky scent.

'One more thing,' Ruby said, getting up and going inside, returning a moment later with a small, square cotton satchel. 'Striped mint bush,' she said, handing it to Alice. 'Put it in your pillow. It'll make your spirit better while you're sleeping.'

'Thank you.' Alice held the satchel to her nose. 'In my family,' she said, 'striped mint bush isn't for healing. It means love forsaken.'

Ruby studied her face for a moment. 'Forsaken. Healed.' She shrugged. 'Fine line, isn't it?' She prodded the fire. It crackled in response. Flames rose high into the afternoon sky. They sat together in silence.

'I'll tell you something, Pinta-Pinta,' Ruby said after a while. 'Trust yourself. Trust your story. All you can do is tell it true.' She rubbed her hands together in the fire smoke.

Alice fidgeted with her ininti seeds.

'Palya?' Ruby asked.

'Palya,' Alice answered, meeting her gaze.

Ruby smiled. The fire shone clearly in Alice's eyes.

Once she'd driven far enough to shrink Kililpitjara to a distant dream on the dusky horizon, Alice pulled over. She got out of her truck and walked on the cooling red sand with Pip by her side, through the clumps of spinifex, raising her hand to brush her palm over heads of long yellow grass.

Alice told herself she just needed a moment to get herself together, but the deeper truth was that despite everything, she still didn't know if leaving was the right thing to do. Her love for him coloured her every thought. She wiped her cheeks, remembering an afternoon not that long ago, when she and Dylan had been out for a sunset walk.

Let's say we did go to the west coast one day, he'd said to her, smiling his slow, heart-melting smile. *Let's say we packed up, got in our trucks and just drove. All the way there. What would we do once we got there?*

They'd sat together under a tall desert oak, twining their fingers through each other's.

She smiled, closing her eyes to imagine it. *We'd buy a shack, get fat on fresh seafood, grow our own fruit and veggies, and ...* She hesitated.

What?

Make babies. She exhaled. *Wild, chubby-legged, barefoot babies. Raised between red dirt, white sand and the sea.* She couldn't look at him.

He held a finger to her chin, turned her head to face him. His eyes filled with light. *Chubby legs.* He'd grinned, pulling her close to him.

I'll love you all of my life, she whispered.

All of our lives, he'd replied. Kissed her as needily as if she were air.

Alice cried out, alone with Pip in the dunes. Should she stay? Fight for her job, and try to work it out with Dylan? Surely it couldn't be over; like the Japanese artist with her gold-dusted lacquer and all the broken pieces laid out before her, Alice could remake it. Surely she could save him. Their love could save them both. How could she let it go? She could work harder, be exactly what he wanted, what he needed, make him a better man. Right from the beginning, that's all he'd wanted, to be a better man. Besides, where exactly was she going? She didn't have a home to go to. Why shouldn't she stay?

She walked slowly. Up and down the dunes.

The desert played tricks on her mind. Time had no visual meaning. A hundred years ago could have been that morning. The sun painted and repainted the landscape every day, the stars shone, the seasons turned, but signs of time passing didn't exist. Erosion and creation happened so slowly the only thing to change in a person's lifetime spent in the desert was their own physicality. It swallowed Alice into insignificance. She roamed the red sand, stopping on a tall dune. Following the road back to the crater with her eyes, she considered its silhouette. Could she go back in time? Could she undo it all and start again?

Pip nudged her. When Alice crouched down to scratch behind her ears, she noticed bruises on the back of her own legs she hadn't seen before. She didn't know how she'd got them. It must have been in the workshop with Dylan, but she didn't remember anything happening to her legs.

Her stomach plummeted; in her mind's eye she was nine, watching her mother come out of the sea, naked and covered in bruises.

Alice thought of the Japanese fairytale again, this time in an unforgiving light: she wasn't the artist with her brush, nor was she the gold. She was the broken pieces, mending and shattering, over and over again. Like her mother, who couldn't grasp life beyond the man repeatedly breaking her. Like the Flowers, who'd come to Thornfield in need of safety. All this time, she'd never allowed herself to see it.

Forsaken. Healed. Ruby had shrugged. *Fine line, isn't it?*

Pip fretted around Alice, licking her face. Alice wiped her tears away, thinking how much June would have loved Pip. As much as she'd loved Harry. A memory of June walking through the flower fields with Harry brought a string of others with it. The day June took Alice to school, and how hard they'd giggled together when Harry farted. The night before her tenth birthday, when Alice stirred in her sleep beside Harry and saw June in the dark, bent over her desk, arranging her surprise present. The morning Alice came back from her driving test to see June and Harry waiting in the police car park. Alice's smile faded as she remembered her last night at Thornfield; Harry was gone and June was a swaying, drunken mess, hopeless and stricken as Alice left. That was Alice's last memory of June. She'd never see her again.

Alice crumpled to the dirt, overcome by the stark reality that she had nowhere and no one to go to that felt safe. Distressed, Pip started to howl.

'It's all right,' Alice said, smoothing Pip's flanks. 'It's all right.' She took a few deep and slow breaths, trying to calm down so she could think straight. She needed to figure out where she was going, at least for the night.

As Alice stood up to dust herself off, a memory from the morning Twig and Candy left came hurtling back to her.

When you're ready, Twig had said, *everything you need is in there.*

Alice looked down at her truck, realisation sinking in. She took off across the dunes with Pip galloping by her side, and popped open the glove box. Grabbed the envelope and ripped it open. Tugged out a wad of folded papers.

She scanned each page, racing through the words.

She re-read the papers, again and again, shaking her head in disbelief until the words started to become real, started to become true. She ran her fingertip over them. They were definitely there, on the paper.

'Fuck,' she whispered. As if in agreeance, Pip yapped.

Alice tucked the envelope back into the glove box. She turned the key in the ignition, put her truck into gear and stepped on the accelerator, driving with the sun behind her.

Maybe sometimes it was possible to go backwards, in order to find the way forwards.

Lulu sat on the dunes, waiting for Aiden to come home from sunset patrol. She sipped her wine and wriggled her toes in the warm red sand, her arms wrapped around her knees.

Although the stars were bright, it wasn't the night sky Lulu fixed upon. Instead she stared at the rope of luminous fairy lights Alice had left behind.

After Sarah had given Alice immediate dismissal, Lulu took her home to pack up her house. She'd overheard their conversation: Sarah told Alice she was lucky; two incident reports in as many days and, with much negotiation, no pressed charges. As Lulu helped to pack Alice's life haphazardly into boxes, Alice barely said a word. She tried to give Lulu back the Frida Kahlo print, but when Alice wasn't looking Lulu packed it in her truck.

Will you let me know where you are?

Alice had nodded, staring out at the road. Her eyes were distant in a way Lulu hadn't seen before.

Why have you stayed here? Alice asked. *Why didn't you leave? After what he did to you?*

Lulu didn't answer for a while. *Because I told myself it was my fault,* she said. *That's the only way I could make sense of it.* She hunched her shoulders up to her ears as if she didn't want to hear her own answers. *And then, I met Aiden. Now we have a life here. And also,* she said, *because of the stars.* Lulu had laughed sadly. What good was foresight if you stayed blind to yourself?

After she'd watched Alice drive away, Lulu went inside and picked up the phone before she talked herself out of it. Sarah offered her the first spot in her diary the next morning. Shaking, Lulu took a wine bottle and glass straight out onto the dunes, where she poured enough to quell her nerves while she waited for Aiden to come home.

His ute soon rattled into their driveway. Her glass empty, Lulu took a swig of wine from the bottle.

He came to the back door, kicked his boots off, and walked out to her. She was calmed by his loving smile. Her abuela's voice rang in her ears. *This is why we named you 'Little Wolf'. Your instincts will always guide you, like the stars.*

'Hey, beautiful,' Aiden said, settling beside her.

She kissed him and poured him some wine in her empty glass.

'What a day,' he sighed, as he took a sip. 'How was Alice when she left?'

Lulu watched the glowing fairy lights outside Alice's house. She shook her head.

'Are you okay?' he asked.

She took the glass off him, drank more wine. 'I will be,' she said, looking up at the stars.

Aiden held her hand and rubbed warm circles into her palm with his thumb. Lulu filled with love and gratefulness. Once she found the courage to tell him the poisonous story about Dylan that she'd kept hidden from him for so long, she knew he'd do whatever it took to support her. She had no doubt he'd agree to move on from desert life. She'd already started looking for jobs in Tasmania; Aiden was always talking about how much he'd love to live there.

Lulu waited until her voice was strong before she spoke.

'I've got a meeting with Sarah in the morning. I need to tell her something, but first, I need to tell you.'

He looked at her, waiting.

In the distance Alice's fairy lights trembled, each one a tiny, fluttering fire, burning into the night sky.

By the time Alice arrived in Agnes Bluff the sky was scattered with stars. She swung into the vet clinic and left the engine running when she got out. Stood at the door. Traced her fingertip over his name on the glass. Slipped her letter through the mail slot and watched it fall to the floor inside, the back of the envelope facing up, her forwarding address scrawled in her handwriting.

As she drove away she thought about the flowers she'd sketched for him. Billy buttons. She'd drawn one after the other, bright balls of yellow on skinny stems, over and over again, covering the paper, except for the far right corner where she'd written their meaning.

My gratitude.

Beloved, thou hast brought me many
    flowers ...
... take them, as I used to do
Thy flowers, and keep them where they
    shall not pine.
Instruct thine eyes to keep their
    colours true,
And tell thy soul, their roots are left
    in mine.

Elizabeth Barrett Browning

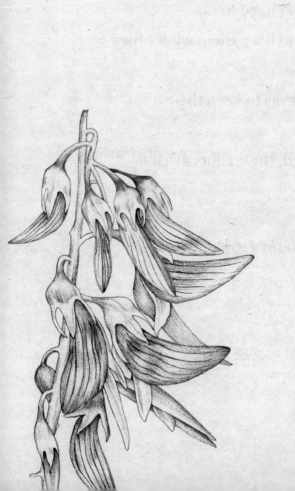

28

Green birdflower

Meaning: My heart flees
Crotalaria cunninghamii | Mid to western states

*Widespread on sandy soils in mulga communities and on
sand dunes, this shrub bears soft hairs on thick and pithy
branches. The flower resembles a bird attached by its beak to the
central stalk of the flower head; yellow-green, streaked with fine
purple lines. Blooms in winter and spring. Pollinated by large
bees, and birds.*

Three long days of driving later, the dusty and barren landscape
became verdant and lush. At the end of her fourth day travelling,
Alice turned off the highway and followed a thin road along the
coast until she reached the small town she'd left when she was a
child. She stood at the main intersection watching farmers' trucks
rumble by. New shops dotted Main Street: a tattoo parlour, a
mobile phone store, a vintage clothing shop and a surfboard
outlet.

Behind her the sugar cane stalks were as vividly green as she
remembered. The cane seemed shorter, but the air was still sweet
and humid. She envisaged herself at seven years old, running
through the stalks to emerge into this new and exciting world
beyond the boundaries of her home. She wrapped her arms around
herself. As if to reassure her, Pip licked Alice's leg.

'Are you okay? Are you lost?' a friendly voice asked. Alice
turned to see a young woman carrying a toddler on her hip.

'I'm fine. Thanks,' Alice replied.

The woman smiled, while the toddler cooed at Pip. At the traffic lights she set the toddler down to push the pedestrian button.

'Sorry,' Alice called her, compelled by nerves to ask for an answer she already knew. 'Is that still the library across the road?'

'Yep, sure is.' The woman and toddler waved as the light turned green.

Over the years, Sally Morgan had pictured so many ways it might happen, when the day came that she'd see Alice Hart again. She never expected it would happen so simply, on an ordinary Tuesday afternoon.

School was finished, the library was full and Sally was crouched by the children's shelves, putting books away. Seemingly for no reason, goosebumps prickled her spine.

She stood slowly. Remembered shabby little sandals poking out from under a tatty nightgown; tousled head bent poring over the library books; the dimple in her cheek; her fiery green eyes; her dark hair falling over the edge of the hospital bed; the click and whirr of the ventilator rising and falling as it helped her lungs to breathe; her cheekbones so sharp in her young, gaunt face; the tiny violet veins in her pale eyelids.

Sally moved cautiously between the shelves. There was nothing unusual that she could see. Nothing out of place. She was just tired, she reasoned with herself. When she was tired she was always more vulnerable to the past. Nevertheless, she couldn't stop herself searching the library.

People browsing bookshelves. Parents with their children. High schoolers huddled together, giggling over their books.

There was nothing out of the ordinary. Nothing that wasn't like any other day. Her pulse began to slow.

Chiding herself for her foolish hopes, Sally walked through the shelves towards her desk, gathering stray books. Her cheeks were hot with disappointment.

Late afternoon light poured through the stained-glass windows. As Sally headed for her desk, a flare of aquamarine light from the Little Mermaid's tail fell straight into her eyes. She stepped sideways, shielding her face from the glare. And, when she looked up again, she saw the little girl she'd loved in the face of a bedraggled woman standing in front of her. The books Sally was carrying fell to the floor.

For twenty years Sally had yearned for the moment when Alice Hart might fall like a star back into her life.

Here she was.

Alice drove through town, following Sally's hatchback, reeling from the scene that unfolded in the library. When Sally had spotted her, her eyes had lost focus, almost as if she was looking straight through her, but then she swiftly enveloped Alice in a fierce hug, rocking to and fro, repeating her name. Alice stood unmoving, overwhelmed by the memory of Sally's rose-scented perfume, unsure of how to react.

'Let me have a look at you,' Sally cried, sniffling, wiping her cheeks. 'What a beautiful woman you are.'

Alice's face flushed with unexpected pleasure.

'How about we have that cup of tea, hey? All these years later?' Sally asked, her eyes shining.

Alice nodded shyly.

'Everyone, library's closing early today, I'm afraid,' Sally announced. She swept the library clean of people, and ushered Alice out into the car park. 'Follow me, Alice, honey.'

Alice pulled up beside Sally's car at the front of a cottage on a cliff overlooking the ocean. It had wraparound timber decking, covered by a fragrant frangipani vine. From the roof hung wind chimes made of shells, sea glass and drift wood. Flamingo grevillea bloomed in the garden. Chickens pecked at the grass beneath a silver wattle tree.

'Wow,' Alice murmured.

'Come in,' Sally called, waving. 'Let's get that little dog of yours something to drink.'

Inside, Alice sat at the kitchen table with Pip at her feet. Sally made tea and conjured a fruit cake from the cupboard, which she cut and slathered in butter. Outside the ocean roared. Sally drew a chair and sat, sliding a laden plate and a steaming cup of tea in Alice's direction.

'Eat something,' she urged.

Alice was taken aback by the sense of comfort she felt with Sally. They'd met twenty years earlier just for an afternoon, and yet here she was, welcomed into Sally's home as if she were long-lost family.

She took a bite of the fruit slice. Sally did the same, and sipped her tea, watching Alice carefully. They sat together in companionable silence. The ocean sounded so close, as if it were rolling through the house. Memories pulled at Alice like a riptide. Prickles encroached on her vision. She gripped the table to steady herself as she grew increasingly dizzy.

'Alice?' Sally asked, alarmed.

She tried to speak but could only groan. Sally put her arms around Alice and rubbed her back.

'Oh, sweet girl. Steady, now. Deep breaths.'

Alice watched the ocean, breathing deeply, following a silver line of waves crashing blue-green on shore. *The desert is an old dream of the sea.* His voice ran through her. *Ngayuku pinta-pinta.* She danced barefoot around their winter fire, his eyes on her body, watching her twirl through the flames, drinking her in. *Ngayuku pinta-pinta. My butterfly.*

'Deep breaths, Alice. Focus on my voice. Just stay with my voice.' As Sally held her, memories stirred. *Stay with my voice.* The ocean of fire. *Sleeping Beauty.* Feathers aflame. *Flap, flap, swoop. Up, up, away.*

Alice clung to Sally, clutching fistfuls of her shirt, suddenly fearful that if she didn't tether herself, she would fall apart, off the cliff, over the edge of the world.

Dusk. Sally made leek and potato soup while Alice lay on the couch, watching as the sun finished painting the clouds and passed its brush to the stars.

They ate without talking, the silence between them filled with the clink of cutlery against china, the music of the wind chimes, the rolling sea, the warbling of the chickens, and Pip's occasional yawns.

'You'll be needing a place to up stumps,' Sally said, wiping her hands on her serviette.

Alice tore a piece of bread in half and mopped up the last of her soup. She nodded as she chewed.

'I've got more space here than I need,' Sally offered. 'The spare room is all yours. It gets full morning light, and has a view of the garden and the sea.' She fidgeted with her soup spoon. 'Bed's made up.'

'I couldn't –'

Sally reached forward and put her hand over Alice's. Warmth spread up Alice's arm.

'Thank you, Sally.'

Sally raised her glass with a nod. 'Cheers to you,' she said, her eyes full.

Alice copied the gesture.

'And you,' she replied.

When dinner was cleared away Sally showed Alice to her room. She gave her fluffy towels and extra-plump pillows.

'Do you two have everything you need?' Sally rubbed Pip's ears. Alice nodded.

'I'll see you in the morning then,' she said, hugging Alice.

'See you in the morning.'

Alice turned off the light and left the curtains open. Moonlight poured through the windows. The view of the sea was wide and full. She lay on the bed and pulled Pip into the curve of her body, holding her tightly through the ebb and flow of tears.

The next morning Alice found her way around the kitchen, made a cup of coffee, and took it into the garden before Sally was up. She was grateful for the solitude. The sky was cloudless and powder blue. The sea sparkled, serene. Pip chased her tail. Bees hovered by a blooming lilly-pilly. Alice smiled. She yawned and rubbed her eyes. Her sleep had been fractured; the ocean and her memories were too loud. She wandered around Sally's garden, sipping coffee, stopping to admire the grevillea and talk to the chickens. As the warmth of the sun unknotted the tension in her spine, Alice noticed a lush alley of potted tropical plants alongside the house: monstera, bird of paradise, agave, staghorns and ferns.

Alice was filled with a sense of wonder; it was a garden within a garden, so meticulous and well-tended in contrast to the wild beauty surrounding it. The sumptuous blends of greens. The varying, glossy foliage. But as she walked on, Alice's wonderment began to fade. She gripped the handle of her coffee cup. Cracked and discoloured plastic toys stuck out of the dirt in some of the pots: a waving mermaid, a seashell, a smiling dolphin, a starfish. Alice's steps faltered.

In the centre of the garden was a life-sized wooden statue. A young girl, offering up a flower. A statue Alice had seen before.

'Alice.'

She spun around, her heart racing. Sally stood at the end of the alley, her face lined from sleep and heavy with sadness.

'What the fuck is that doing here?' Alice asked, her voice too high, her hand shaking hard as she pointed to the wooden statue. 'Why do you have one of my father's carvings?'

Sally took a step back. 'Come inside.'

Alice didn't respond.

'Come in, Alice. I'll make more coffee. We'll sit and talk.'

Inside, Sally set a fresh coffee pot on the table by the couch. When she gestured for Alice to sit, Alice obliged.

'God.' Sally laughed awkwardly. 'I've been praying for the chance to have this conversation with you for years, and now I'm tongue-tied.' She fidgeted with her hands. 'The truth is I don't know where to start. How about you ask me questions, Alice, anything you want to know, and we'll go from there.'

Alice leaned forward, struggling to control her voice. 'Start with why you have one of my father's statues of me in your garden,' she said. 'Or start with why my mother left guardianship of me and my brother to you in her will.' The question she'd been carrying ever since she'd opened Twig's thick envelope came out in a rush.

Sally's face paled. 'Wow,' she said. 'Okay.'

Alice jiggled one knee as the words of her mother's will flared in her mind. *Should June Hart not be fit to raise my children, I, Agnes Hart, hereby leave guardianship to Sally Morgan.*

'Did you know her? My mum?' Alice demanded.

'No,' she said. 'No, Alice. I didn't. Not really. No more than occasionally passing each other in town.'

Alice shook her head. 'That doesn't make sense. Why would she leave us to you?'

'I didn't know her, but your mother knew me, Alice,' Sally said. 'She knew me.'

'I don't know what that means,' Alice said. Her heart felt constricted, as if her ribcage was too small to contain it.

'When I was young,' Sally said slowly, 'I fell in love. With someone who wasn't mine to fall in love with.' She shook her head. 'I was eighteen. Never had a boyfriend. I'd seen your father here and there. He was a new cane farmer in town. Quiet, hardworking, brooding. Kept to himself. There was something about him, I guess.' She paused. 'I watched him from afar for a long time. No one knew much about him. He didn't wear a wedding ring. It was just one night. One. I was at the pub with girlfriends, tipsy on shandy, and got some Dutch courage. Walked straight up to him at the bar and asked him if I could buy him a drink ... Two months later I found out I was pregnant.'

Alice stared at her. 'When was this?'

'The year after you were born, when –'

'No?' Alice interjected. 'That can't be right.'

Sally nodded solemnly. 'I'm afraid it is.'

'No,' Alice said again. Nowhere in her mother's stories was there a sister. Her mother couldn't have known about Sally.

Sally waited, her face open, her eyes heavy.

Alice's head spun. 'You have a child with my father?'

'Had,' Sally murmured. 'I had a child.' She looked down at her hands. 'Gillian died when she was five. Leukaemia.'

Alice couldn't bring herself to speak.

'I told Clem about Gilly when she was born, just so he knew about her, but I made it clear I didn't want anything from him. Still, the love of a child changes you. I couldn't stop myself from hoping he'd acknowledge her. The night she died, as morbid as it may sound, I sent him a clipping of her hair, tied in one of her favourite ribbons. Although Clem wouldn't have anything to do with her while she was alive, I wanted him to have something of her. The truth is, I was a mess. Angry. I wanted to hurt him, to punish him, to remind him of how he'd ignored her life, in her death.'

The smell of kerosene filled Alice's nose as she remembered opening the drawer of her father's workbench to find the photograph of Thornfield, and a curl of hair, tied in a pale ribbon. Gillian's hair. Her sister's hair.

'The carving of Gilly was at my front door when I got home from her funeral,' Sally said.

In Alice's memory, the lamplight flickered over his carvings of June, and a young girl. Who Alice had wrongly presumed was herself.

'Your mother came to the funeral.'

Alice looked sharply at Sally.

'I saw her,' Sally said, 'at the back of the congregation. I couldn't find her after the service. She left a pot plant at the grave with a card to Gilly, signed in your name.'

Alice whimpered, covering her face with her hands, imagining what it must have taken for her mother to get herself into town, to the funeral and back home, without her father finding out. What it must have taken to discover such a betrayal yet still find compassion for Sally. The pain she must have carried, knowing Alice would never meet her half-sister. The trust her mother must have had in Sally's decency; the point of desperation she must have reached to leave guardianship of her children to Sally. The point of fear her mother must have reached to have had the need for a will.

'What plant?'

'Sorry?'

'What plant did Mum leave, at the grave?'

Sally went to the open window and reached through to pick a peach-coloured flower from a blooming bush. She offered it to Alice.

'Beach hibiscus,' Alice cried softly, remembering the flower crown her mother made when she was a child. Remembering its meaning in the Thornfield Dictionary. *Love binds us in eternity.*

'A year later you walked into the library,' Sally went on. 'I recognised you straight away. I knew you were Clem and Agnes's daughter. My Gilly's big sister. After the fire, I made it my business to look after you.'

'Look after me?'

'I was there. In hospital.' Sally's voice was nearly inaudible. 'I sat with you while you were in a coma. I read you stories.'

Stay with my voice, Alice, I'm right here.

'I sent you a box of books ...' Sally trailed off.

Her childhood books, which she was told were a gift from June.

'I stayed with you until I found out June was coming. After you'd left with her, your nurse rang and told me your brother survived, but June didn't take him. Then a solicitor contacted me about Agnes's will ... I made my John find out where you were, though. I needed to know you were safe. Once I knew you were at Thornfield, I forced myself to accept June's wishes and make peace with things.'

Alice looked at her blankly. 'What wishes?' she asked.

Sally studied her face. 'Oh, Alice,' she said after a moment.

'What wishes, Sally?'

'June made it clear she didn't want you to have any contact with me, or your brother.'

'Made it clear, how?'

Sally blanched. 'I sent letters, Alice. For years. Letters and photographs about your brother, as he grew up. I always wanted contact with you, but never got a reply. With June being your legal guardian, I couldn't impose upon her. I had no power. All I could do was make sure I didn't cause any additional pain. Especially not for you, or your brother.'

Alice cried out in frustration. Desperate for fresh air she got up and went to the window. Pressed her forehead against the cool glass.

After a while Sally cleared her throat. 'Your brother grew up knowing he was adopted. I wouldn't have raised him any other way,' she said quietly. 'He's always known about you.'

Alice turned.

'He'll be twenty soon. Such a gentle soul. Just moved in with his girlfriend and works as a landscaper. Never as happy as when he's in a garden.'

Alice sank back to the couch. 'What's his name?' she whispered.

'I named him Charlie,' Sally said, smiling for the first time that morning.

29

Foxtails

Meaning: **Blood of my blood**
Ptilotus | Inland Australia

*Tjulpun-tjulpunpa (Pit.) are small shrubs that form spikes of
purple flowers covered in dense white hairs. Leaves are covered in
closely packed star-shaped hairs that slow the rate of water loss.
Traditionally, women used the soft furry flowers to line wooden
bowls in which babies could be carried.*

Alice pedalled uphill, as hard as she could bear. Her locket swung
back and forth, hitting her chest as she puffed along. She wanted
to kick herself for not driving into town; her backpack was cutting
into her shoulders, filled to the zipper with ingredients for dinner
that night. But the exercise was helping. She'd needed to work her
nerves through her body ever since Sally had arranged the dinner
date. This morning, she'd pulled the cobwebs off a bike in Sally's
garage and decided to ride. As she cycled into town, the sea had
glittered turquoise. Alice took it as a good sign.

Riding home, Alice thought through the menu one more
time. Barramundi tacos with salsa and homemade guacamole, and
Anzac biscuits, crunchy on the outside, chewy in the middle. Sally
had taken care of everything else. She seemed determined to bring
Alice and Charlie together gently.

In the weeks following Alice's arrival, Sally had made room
in her house for Alice to feel at home. She helped Alice to unpack
her books, and hang the Frida Kahlo print Lulu had given her.
She sat with Alice while she cried. Sally had explained that June
paid for Agnes and Clem to have full funeral services; Sally had

gone to both. She took Alice to the site of the house Alice grew up in, which was no longer a secluded pocket between the sugar cane and the sea. It was now a beachfront bar and youth hostel, full of tanned travellers. Her mother's garden was gone. Alice couldn't bring herself to get out of the car. Back at Sally's house, Alice ran down to the shore, took a deep breath, and screamed at the sea. Sally listened while Alice told stories from the flower farm and the desert. She introduced Alice to a grief counsellor she'd used when Gilly died. Alice saw her every week, twice a week after Dylan started sending emails. They were waiting in her inbox when she checked her account for the first time, a month after leaving Kililpitjara. There were a dozen or more; thousands and thousands of words. He started sorrowfully, apologetically. But the longer he went unanswered, the angrier he became. *Don't read them*, Sally implored her. *They'll only do you harm.* They both knew she read every word. Over and over again. Sally could always tell when a new email arrived. She gave Alice a wide berth. Baked fruit slice. Always had time for a walk by the sea, but never pressed Alice to talk if she didn't want to. The depth of Sally's kindness, her astute intuition; it was as if she'd been preparing for Alice to come back to her for years.

After she was done at the supermarket, Alice had stopped by the post office to send her reply to Lulu's latest letter. *It's a rainy, lush and misty dream here,* Lulu had written. *We've acquired a pot-bellied wood stove, a goat, donkey (you'll love knowing Aiden named her Frida), two dairy cows and six chickens. Please come and visit us soon. We can hike the Bay of Fires together.* As Alice stuck the stamp on her envelope she smiled at the thought of the words she was sending back to Lulu. *I'd love to visit you guys sometime.*

On her way home, Alice had gone to the library. Walking through the foyer still felt like walking through time, back to when she was a girl and Sally first shone a light into her world.

'There's mail here for you,' Sally said, beaming when Alice walked in.

The envelope was addressed to Alice in handwriting she didn't recognise. The postmark was from Agnes Bluff. For a moment Alice struggled to breathe. Had Dylan found her? But no. He couldn't. He had no idea where she was, he only had her email address. She slid her finger under the seal and tore the envelope open. Inside was a card.

> *I hope you're well, Alice.*
>> *Here's to courage. And to heart, right?*
>> *How about, here's also to the future, and everything it holds.*
>> *Moss.*

Alice shook the envelope; a packet of desert pea seeds fell into her palm.

'That looks like some kind of magic,' Sally said.

Alice gave her a small smile. 'It is.' She closed her hand around the packet of seeds, feeling their individual shapes and thinking of the colour they would grow. *To the future.*

'You okay? Keeping nerves about dinner in check?'

Alice swallowed. 'I'm okay. Nervous. Kind of sick, actually.' She sighed. 'But, it's all I've thought about since I left Kililpitjara, meeting him. So …'

'It's going to be wonderful.' Sally got up to give Alice a hug. 'You off home now?'

'One more stop,' Alice had said.

She stood on her pedals, heaving to get up the last hill before home, her lungs burning. The image of her parents' gravestones played on her. She gritted her teeth and kept riding until she reached the crest.

Stopped to let the breeze cool her sweaty skin, and to look out at the sky and the sea. How vast they were. She followed the black ribbon of road with her eyes, seeing where it unspooled through cane fields and climbed the cliff before turning off to Sally's house. Seeing the very route her little brother would soon drive.

Alice sat on the bike seat. After another lingering glance at the sea she lifted her feet, and began to coast downhill, into the tranquillity that lay ahead.

After she finished work, Sally took a last-minute detour. She parked by her favourite white scribbly gum. Bellbirds rang in the branches. She crossed the empty street and walked through the ornate cemetery gates. Down the avenue of gums, past the carved angel with her wings outstretched, and left at the walkway covered in flowering bougainvillea. Straight ahead to the shady knoll by a paperbark tree, where she always let her shoulders fall.

Sally sat with John and Gilly, her back straight, her hair swept off her face by the sea air. She ran her fingertips over the letters of John's name. Kissed the cold marble bearing Gilly's. She stayed for a while, listening to the birds sing and the trees rustle. The shooting water of a sprinkler. Somewhere, a mower. When the light started to dim she checked her watch.

On her way back to her car, something caused her to stop and consider the northern lawn of the cemetery. It'd been years. She felt herself turn and wander through the rows of graves, checking the names on the headstones.

At the sight of Clem and Agnes's graves, Sally was taken aback. Someone had been there. Strewn across Clem's grave were used stickers. As she got closer, Sally recognised the butterflies, streaked with turquoise paint. Alice must have torn them off her truck doors. Remorse swelled in Sally's chest. She turned to face the wind, letting it blow the years away until she was eighteen again, wide-eyed, crazy-in-love with Clem Hart.

She was wearing plastic daisy earrings the night they'd met. *Where I come from they mean 'I attach myself to you'*, was the first thing he said to her. When he took her hand, she held tight and kept close by his side. They fucked against the brick wall of the pub. She'd almost not wanted the grazes on her back to heal, each one proof that he hadn't been a dream. But the next time they saw each other, Clem looked through her as if she was no more than vapour.

Not long afterwards, Sally's father brought John Morgan, a young policeman relocated from the city, home for dinner. When she shook his warm hand, saw the kindness in his eyes, Sally knew he was her answer. After a whirlwind courtship, they were married, and there wasn't one scandalous whisper when Sally started to show. People were overjoyed for them. Sally got so swept up in her own lie she heard herself say that she hoped the baby would have John's eyes or calm disposition. Although Sally didn't hide from John the story that she'd once fancied one of the farmers in town, when Gilly died and she saw John's spirit break, she knew Clem Hart was a secret she would never tell him.

Sally opened her eyes and turned to Agnes's grave. Her headstone was covered in bindweed, lemon myrtle and a palm of kangaroo paw, lovingly arranged. She imagined Alice sitting there, building a shrine of flowers for her mother.

A moment passed. Sally cleared her throat. 'Agnes,' she said. 'She's home. She's come home, and she's beautiful.' Sally reached for a fallen gum leaf and broke it into pieces. 'She's safe. They're both safe. And wonderful. Oh god, Agnes, they're so wonderful.'

Somewhere above, hidden among the crowns of the gum trees, a magpie sang.

'I'm looking after them.' Sally's voice grew stronger. 'I promise you.'

The shrill ringing of her mobile phone interrupted her. She rummaged through her handbag, flustered, until she found it.

'Hi, Charlie,' she said.

Sally stood and pressed a hand to Agnes's headstone, taking a moment before she turned and walked away, listening to the sweet sound of her son's voice.

He walked up the front steps of the house he grew up in, taking shaky breaths.

It's going to be amazing, Cassie said as she kissed him goodbye. *This is what you've always wanted. This is your family, Charlie. Don't be afraid.*

He tightened his grip on the bouquet. After his mum rang and they'd agreed to dinner, he'd Googled her. Again. *Alice Hart, Floriographer. Thornfield Farm, where wildflowers bloom.* He'd bought her a bunch of waratahs after reading that at Thornfield they meant *Return of happiness.*

Standing on the deck he listened to the familiar sounds of the sea, wind chimes, chickens clucking, bees hovering drowsily, and his mum's voice coming from the kitchen. Collectively they were the backing track of his life. Then, a new addition, a dog barking.

'Pip!' A voice filled with laughter, a voice he didn't know, came towards him.

He gulped. Readjusted the flowers in his sweaty hands.

Her shadow reached down the hall ahead of her. He opened the screen door. Relaxed his shoulders. Tears prickled at the corners of his eyes.

His big sister. She was here.

30

Wheel of fire

Meaning: The colour of my fate

Stenocarpus sinuatus | Queensland and New South Wales

*Profuse bright red and orange flowers create a spectacular display
from summer to autumn. Shaped like the spokes of a wheel before
they open, these symmetrical blossoms get their name from their
resemblance to a spinning fire.*

It was late afternoon when Alice got home with a bunch of fresh
fire flowers.

She greeted Pip and went into her room to get the other things
she needed: a bundle of books and papers. She roped the ininti
necklace Ruby had given her around her throat, inhaling the
smoky scent of its seeds. Tucked a pen, box of matches and ball of
string into her pocket. Carried everything through the house and
out onto the verandah. Pip stayed close to her heels as she went
down the steps, into the garden. They sat together in the spot
where she'd spent the last week building a bonfire. Pip licked her
arm as she set down her things.

Alice basked in the stillness. The early autumn sun warmed
her skin; the sea shimmered molten, aquamarine. She looked at
the corner where her desert peas had flourished through their
first season. *They're notoriously fickle to grow,* she'd written to Moss
in a recent email, *but yours haven't given me any trouble.* In his
reply, Moss had mentioned he was coming to the coast for a
conference towards the end of the year. *Are you too far away for a
visit?* When she'd typed her answer, Alice couldn't stop herself
from smiling.

A northeasterly blew in, ringing the wind chimes. She checked her watch. Sally would soon be on her way home, and Charlie and Cassie were coming to stay for the weekend, before Alice's flight out on Monday. They were having one last celebration before she left to take up a three-month writing residency she'd won in Copenhagen, the city to which Alice had traced Agnes's ancestry. When the acceptance email had arrived, Charlie was the first person Alice told. *You'll get to see the real Little Mermaid*, he'd said proudly. *Tell her g'day from me too.*

Since Alice had met her brother, she could no longer imagine life without Charlie in it. The night of their first dinner at Sally's, they'd sat across the table and studied each other's faces, bursting into awkward laughter and, occasionally, tears. From then on, they'd hung out twice a week, and met with the counsellor once a fortnight as they tried to make sense of a new life together. Alice took Charlie to the backpacker hostel to show him the place where she'd grown up with their parents. They walked on her old beach and lay on the sand, watching the clouds change as Alice told him their mother's stories. When she described how much their mother loved her garden, Charlie suggested he take Alice to visit some of the local plant nurseries and flower markets he worked with. Seeing the wonder in his face when he was among plants and flowers, an idea came to Alice; as soon as Charlie dropped her home, she set things in motion.

A couple of weeks later, Twig and Candy were waiting on the verandah when Alice and Charlie drove up the Thornfield driveway, his truck loaded with supplies to help finish the long process of rebuilding after the floods. Twig was strong and angular but gentle as ever. Candy still wore her hair long and bluer than a flower. Alice reunited with Myf, Robin and a few of the other Flowers who'd stayed on, and met the new women Candy and Twig had taken in. Charlie was quiet, watching and listening, as he absorbed the landscape and stories he and Alice came from.

They spent nights around the dinner table together, eating Candy's feasts and sharing memories. The women taught Charlie about Thornfield and its language of flowers; Alice had taken the dictionary with her, waiting until she was with Twig and Candy to show him. They fussed over him like maternal hens, especially Twig. There was a joy in her face Alice couldn't recall ever seeing before.

Charlie stayed in June's bedroom, and Alice climbed the spiral staircase to her old bell room. She slept with the windows thrown open and the moonlight pouring in.

A few days before they were due to drive back to the coast, Charlie asked Alice if she'd show him the river.

'It's all through Thornfield's story. Will you take me there before we go?'

Alice caught Twig and Candy glancing at each other. 'I saw that.' She wagged her finger at them. 'What is it?'

Twig nodded at Candy, who left the room and came back with an urn.

'It didn't feel right to do it without you …' Candy trailed off.

The day they held the ceremony was bright and vivid. Sun filtered through the eucalyptus canopy, green and gold. Twig and Candy each said a few words, and when the time came, Alice scattered June's ashes. Watching the ash flow down river, Alice wiped her face of tears and exhaled deeply, as if letting go of a breath she'd long been holding. She hugged Twig and Candy tightly. Years of memories swayed around them. When everyone else headed back to the house, Alice tugged on Charlie's sleeve, signalling for him to hang back with her.

'I want to show you something,' she said.

Alice led him to the giant gum.

'This is where our parents found each other, for better or worse.' Her voice shook. 'This place is why we have each other. It's as much your story as it is mine.'

Charlie studied the engraved tree trunk. Held his hand to the scar beside their father's name. Though his chin wobbled, he grinned at Alice; when he reached into his back pocket for his knife, eyebrow raised in question, she nodded, grinning. They walked home from the river arm in arm, smelling of tree bark and sap, his and their mother's names freshly carved into the gum.

On the morning they left Thornfield, Alice brought some papers with her to the breakfast table. She slid them across to Charlie. He looked at her, puzzled. Twig and Candy, who Alice had spoken to about her intentions, watched on, smiling. For the rest of her life, one of Alice's most treasured memories would be Charlie's face the moment he unfolded the statutory declaration she'd signed, giving her third of Thornfield to him.

Alice put the fire flowers aside, and took the first book from the top of the pile. Her eyes ran over her grandmother's handwriting in the Thornfield Dictionary. She thumbed through the stories she'd read dozens of times already, of Ruth Stone, Wattle Hart and June herself. Of Clem and Agnes. Of Candy and Twig. Alice twirled the stem of a fire flower between her fingers, considering their meaning. *The colour of my fate.* Steeling herself, she put the dictionary a safe distance away on a garden chair.

Next, she went through the folder of papers; printed copies of every email Dylan had sent her since she'd left the desert, daily, weekly, and still, monthly. Her eyes snagged on lines she knew by heart, from one of the first.

You've left, yet you're still here, appearing and disappearing from me. The last coffee cup you used. Your dresses amongst my clothes.

Your toothbrush by mine. It rained yesterday. I haven't been able to go outside today; I don't want to see your footprints gone from the red dirt.

Alice scrunched the page in her fist, breathing through the pain behind her ribs. Held her face to the sea breeze, letting it cool her skin. She glanced sidelong at the Thornfield Dictionary. *Pay attention now, Alice,* she heard June's voice, speaking her written words. *These are the ways we've survived.* She smoothed the page out, placed it back in the folder, and put it aside.

Finally, she turned to her notebooks, full of the story she'd been writing in flowers since Agnes Bluff, during her months in the desert, and over the last year at Sally's; the story that had become her application for the writing residency. *You've written a book*, Charlie had stated in awe when Alice showed him and Sally the first printout of her manuscript. When she read the title, Sally had shaken her head. *You've spun seeds into gold*, she'd said softly, grinning through tears.

Alice took a notebook from the pile and ran her hands over its cover. When she lifted it, a wisp of red sand trickled from the pages onto her lap, glinting in the light, otherworldly. Alice balanced the notebook between her palms and let it fall open. Ran her fingertips over the red granules caught in the stitching of its exposed centre. Life and other people's stories had always told her she was blue. Her father's eyes. The sea. *Alice Blue*. The colour of orchids. Of her boots. Of fairytale queens. Of loss. But Alice's centre was red. It always was. The colour of fire. Of earth. Of heart, and courage.

She pored over the books. Paused to name every sketched and pressed flower aloud, and speak its meaning; an incantation to end the burden of carrying an untold story inside her.

Black fire orchid	Desire to possess
Flannel flower	What is lost is found
Sticky everlasting	My love will not leave you
Blue pincushion	I mourn your absence
Painted feather flower	Tears
Striped mintbush	Love forsaken
Yellow bells	Welcome to a stranger
Vanilla Lily	Ambassador of love
Violet nightshade	Fascination, witchcraft
Thorn box	Girlhood
River Lily	Love concealed
Cootamundra wattle	I wound to heal
Copper-cups	My surrender
River red gum	Enchantment
Blue lady Orchid	Consumed by love
Gorse bitter pea	Ill-natured beauty
Showy banksia	I am your captive

Orange Immortelle	Written in the stars
Pearl saltbush	My hidden worth
Honey grevillea	Foresight
Sturt's desert pea	Have courage, take heart
Spinifex	Dangerous pleasures
Desert heath-myrtle	Flame, I burn
Broad-leaved parakeelya	By your love, I live and die
Desert oak	Resurrection
Lantern bush	Hope may blind me
Bat's wing coral tree	Cure for heartache
Green birdflower	My heart flees
Foxtails	Blood of my blood
Wheel of fire	The colour of my fate

When she was ready, Alice uncapped her pen and scrawled the title of her manuscript across the cover of every notebook, amid her flower illustrations. She piled them in her lap and bound them with string. Gathered them together with the folder of emails and put the bundle on the bonfire. As she reached for the fire flowers and then, the matches in her pocket, Alice faltered. Took a moment to collect herself. *Breathe.* She slid a match from its box, steadied her hand, and struck it against the flint. A quick intake of oxygen, the smell of sulphur, and a quiet hiss and crackle; the bonfire came to life.

The blaze rose against the backdrop of the ocean. Alice watched the flowers catch alight and burn; the corners of Dylan's emails blacken and char; all her notebooks turn incandescent. She watched the words she'd written on the covers until they were no longer legible.

The Lost Flowers of Alice Hart

After a while she went to the garden chair and sat, cradling the Thornfield Dictionary in her arms. Pip lolled against her legs. Alice took a deep breath full of salt, smoke and flowers, gazing at the flames. Their changing colours. Their transformations. Her beautiful mother, forever in her garden. Alice pressed a hand over her desert pea locket and ininti seed necklace. *Trust your story. All you can do is tell it true.*

The memory came clear and unfettered: in the weatherboard house at the end of the lane, she sat at her desk by the window, dreaming of ways to set her father on fire.

Her heart beat slow.

I'm—here.

I'm—here.

I'm—here.

AUTHOR'S NOTE

There are stories and characters from varying cultures in this novel. I'd like to acknowledge the generous friends, experiences, and resources I consulted, drew from and used to write them.

In the opening chapter the line, *life is lived forward but only understood backward*, was inspired by the work of Danish philosopher, Søren Kierkegaard.

Candy's favourite fairytale, about a queen who waits for so long for her lover to return to her that she turns into the orchid on her gown, was inspired by the Filipino fairytale, *The Legend of Waling-Waling*.

The Indian stories of Sita and Draupadi that one of the Flowers shares with Alice were shared with me by Tanmay Barhale.

The story of the king's daughter who always wore the same shade of blue was inspired by Alice Roosevelt Longworth, daughter of Theodore Roosevelt, who always wore the same pale tint of azure, and was known for never abiding by the rules of her society.

The Bulgarian fairytale Oggi refers to in his letter to Alice, about the wolf and fox, was inspired by a version of the Bulgarian folktale, *The Sick and the Healthy*, which was translated and shared with me by Iva Boneva.

Lulu's stories of monarch butterflies, fire warriors and daughters of the sun were inspired by Mexican tales shared with me by Viridiana Alfonso-Lara.

It was important to me that I fictionalised the central Australian settings Alice visits, lives and works in because to set those parts of this novel in existing places would be telling stories that aren't mine to tell. I consulted Ali Cobby Eckermann, Yankunytjatjara woman and internationally acclaimed poet, about creating such settings. She agreed that it was a wise thing to do.

Kililpitjara, or Earnshaw Crater, and everything to do with it – its name, its story, its landscape – is fictional. The place name Kililpitjara is fictional in the sense that I made it up, but the Pitjantjatjara I used to create it, and that is used throughout the novel, is the language spoken by Anangu. *Kililpi* (noun), means star. *Tjara* (noun), means some or part of a larger group or thing. Basic translation of the combination in English is *belonging to stars*. The main reference text I used was the IAD Press Pitjantjatjara/Yankunytjatjara to English Dictionary.

To create a sense of Kililpitjara's geological structure I was inspired by images of Kandimalal (Wolfe Creek Crater) and Tnorala (Gosse Bluff) but its enormity, energy, and presence has been informed by my experience living in the central desert.

In 2016 I met with Dr John Goldsmith in Perth, who talked me through his first-hand experiences of Kandimalal and photographing western desert stars. Dr Goldsmith was also a great help in enlightening me to the concentric circles of stars and craters, and the very likelihood of a patch of desert peas growing in the formation I have described.

Kililpitjara's creation story was inspired by the public Arrernte creation story of Tnorala, the crater where a baby fell from its wooden carrier in the stars to the earth, and its parents in the sky who search for it eternally.

The returned sorry flowers and accompanying letters from tourists that Ruby shows Alice are inspired by the 'sorry rocks' received by park staff every day at Uluru, sent by guilty tourists around the world.

Ruby's poem, *Seeds*, is written by Ali Cobby Eckermann, who gave me full permission to use it in this context. While I lived in the desert I had the pleasure of meeting and knowing many women like Ruby. They shared their stories and their spirits with me, which taught me lessons I hadn't learned anywhere else. Australia has a black history. It always was and always will be Aboriginal land.

IN GRATITUDE

As a reader, I love reading the acknowledgements section of novels. It's always felt a little like being able to slip into an after party while it's in full swing and see the people in the wings of an author's story step into light. It is an immeasurable thrill to be able to now write my own for my first novel.

My respect and gratitude to Yugambeh people on whose land many drafts of this novel were crafted; to Bundjalung people on whose saltwater country I grew up; to Butchulla people on whose land my grandmother lives, where the sugar cane fields grow that have long enchanted my mind. My respect and gratitude to Arrernte people, and Anangu on whose Ngaanyatjarra Pitjantjatjara Yankunytjatjara (NPY) Lands I worked and travelled through during the time I lived in the Northern Territory. I would especially like to acknowledge with gratitude the NPY women who shared culture and stories from their ancestors with me.

To my extraordinary team at HarperCollins Publishers Australia, thank you for completely exceeding my wildest childhood dreams. Alice 'Whizzy' Wood and Sarah Barrett, thank you for your tireless energy, hard work, and our out-of-hours chats and giggles. Hazel Lam, thank you for creating one of the most beautiful book covers I have ever seen for Alice Hart's story. Mark Campbell, Tom Wilson, Karen-Maree Griffiths, Erin Dunk, Essie Orchard and Andrea Johnson, thank you for your passion and belief in this novel, and me. Nicola Robinson, thank you for your deft and intuitive edits, knowing where I could be and do better, and seeing me through. Catherine Milne, story sister, you have made me and Alice the best we can be. Thank you for imploring and teaching me to trust in the novel I had written, to trust in myself. I am indebted to you.

To Zeitgeist Agency: Benython Oldfield, Sharon Galant, and Thomasin Chinnery, my agents, thank you for believing in me, and Alice, and being the dream team of near-mythical wonders you are. There is no one else I would rather be in a war room with than you three.

Thank you Stéphanie Abou of Massie & McQuilkin Literary Agents for your hard word and tireless dedication.

To my incredible team of international publishers and translators for bringing Alice to readers around the world, deepest thanks to you for making dreams I didn't even know I had come true.

My love, respect and heartfelt thanks to Ali Cobby Eckermann, desert-and-sea-bracelet-twin and tjanpi-T-shirt-giving ininti-sister. Thank you for appearing in my life when you did, and for your permission to include *Seeds* as Ruby's own poem. Thank you for sharing your powerful words and big heart with me, malpa.

Alice Hoffman, thank you for replying to my first letter in 2009, and for your generosity of spirit sharing letters with me ever since. Thank you for your unwavering encouragement, magic, and the permission to quote from one of your letters in this novel. Thank you for writing the books that I have carried with me around the world, they have shown me the way to be brave and to believe.

To Anne Carson, thank you for honouring me with permission to quote your translation of Sappho's poetry. Thank you Gracie Dietshe and Nicole Aragi of Aragi agency for your wonderful assistance in facilitating my request.

To Julianne Schultz, John Tague, Jane Hunterland and the team at *Griffith Review* in 2015, thank you for all you do and have done for Australian readers and writers. Thank you for being home to my first paid publication, and for giving the first chapter of this novel your annual writer award. Your investment in me changed the course of my life.

Thank you to Varuna the Writers' House, for the perfect amount of eeriness, beauty, and solitude I didn't know I needed so much to begin editing this book. To the women I wrote through the dark with on my residency: Biff Ward, Jackie Yowell, Helen Loughlin, and Bec Butterworth, you are always in my heart, around a banquet table of Sheila's cooking. With wine.

To David Jayet-Laraffe of Frog Flowers, Giulia Zonza of On Love & Photography, and Nancy Spencer of Nancy Spencer Makeup, thank you for your alchemy, conjuring a tropical garden fairytale within a Manchester winter snow globe and placing me in the centre. Thank you for creating a once-in-a-lifetime author photo, and a joyous love-filled experience I will never forget.

To Edith Rewa, flower queen and enchanting botanical artist, thank you for flower illustrations that cast such powerful spells they don't let go.

To the booksellers who supported Alice Hart, and me, in the lead up to publication: thank you for all the book magic you bring into the world, and for sharing some of that with me and this novel. To the booksellers who will read this novel, give it a place on a bookstore shelf, and share it with readers, thank you for being a light in every city and town, and making my childhood dream as a booklover and aspiring writer come true.

Thank you to Kate Forsyth and Carol Crennan for offering me a sponsored place on the History Mystery and Magic writing retreat in Oxford, 2015, an experience that had a profound effect on my writing and me as a writer. To my fellow retreat writers Sarah Guise, Kellie Watson, and Bec Smedley, thank you for sharing your hearts and stories with me. Thank you, Kate, for your friendship and for reminding me Alice was an ember that fear and anxiety could not extinguish.

To those who lit the way for me while I was in the dark woods writing this novel, thank you for your steadfast friendship, love, empowerment and encouragement: Favel Parrett, Courtney

Collins, Nicole Hayes, Alys Conran, Meredith Whitfield, Anni Sartorio, Nick Benson and the Benson family, Simone Gingras-Fox and the Gerlinger family, Dimi Venkov, Ashley Hay, Khela Hutchinson, Gregoreen and PD, Eva de Vries, Olga Van Der Kooi (and Rogier and Louise), Helen Weston and JP, Sarah Rakich, Vanessa Radnidge, Lilia Krasteva, Jesse Blackadder, Andi Davey, Philippa Moore, Jenn Ashworth, Jane Bradley, Chris and Debbie Macintosh (and Beth and Lil), Cerys Jones, Helen Fulcher, Fraser How, Derek Henderson, Vicki Henderson, Stephen Ashworth, Lorena Fernandez Sanchez, Alex D'Netto, Linda Teo, Ian Henderson, Jenn Ashworth, Rachael Clegg (and Roberto, Joe, Francis, and Ruben), Susan Fernley and Brian Fox, Kate Gray, Cheryl Hollatz-Wisely, Jackie Bailey (Yen Yang and Ellie Belly), Jeremy Lachlan, Josie and James McSkimming, Sani Van der Spek, Dervla McTiernan, and Andy Stevenson (and Lou, Sam and Gina).

Particular heartfelt thanks to Kate Forsyth, Brooke Davis, Favel Parrett, Ashley Hay, Jenn Ashworth, Myf Jones, and Ali Cobby Eckermann for reading early proofs and endorsing this novel with such warmth, love, and generosity of spirit.

Thank you to Dr John Goldsmith for taking the time to meet with me, answer my relentless questions and share stories of stars and craters.

To the women I met at Singing Over the Bones training with Dr Clarissa Pinkola Estés in 2015, thank you for sharing your love and stories with me. Thank you for howling me along the way ever since.

To the men and women I studied and practised alongside at Mindfulness Self Compassion training with Christopher Germer and Kristin Neff in 2017. The timeliness of your work, empathy, support, and friendship carried me over the line, for which I am deeply grateful.

I had a public school education and some of my teachers throughout primary and high school remain standing examples of the power encouragement can have on shaping a life. Mrs Smart, Ms Pearce, Mr Chandler, Mrs Reynolds, and Mr Ham, thank you for seeing something in me I couldn't see in myself and for teaching me how to believe in what might be possible with hard work and courage.

To the International Society, an independent charity that has been promoting diversity and providing a haven for international students, refugees, asylum seekers and locals in Greater Manchester for the last fifty years, thank you for being a place of warmth and welcome, safety and imagination, for so many thousands of us. Thank you to my International 16s around the world, I wouldn't be the storyteller I am without you and the stories you shared with me.

Samantha Smith, incredibly talented tattooist, artist and storyteller, thank you for bringing Alice to life in and on my skin. I'm so grateful to have found you and to know you.

Melissa Acton, you are a woman who can turn a sensory deprivation chamber into a wonderland. Thank you for being one of my first readers and giving Alice a home in your book-loving heart.

Tanmay Barhale, Batman might have the notoriety, but you're my favourite superhero. Thank you for telling me stories, some of which I hope to have honoured in this novel.

Viridiana Alonso-Lara, fire warrior, thank you for sharing your heart with me through your Mexican stories, right from the first night we met. Thank you for sharing your family and guacamole with me. Thank you for your love. Lulu wouldn't be who she is without you.

Thank you Ammna Winchester for your friendship, and for doing me the honour of sharing your experiences with me. I couldn't have written Alice's time in hospital the way I have without your generous support and inspiration.

Boryana Pashova, beloved Banana, thank you for help with Bulgarian translations, for believing in me as a writer, and for showing me how to yell at a dish in the oven to make it bake faster.

Iva Boneva, Money Honey, woman extraordinaire, thank you for sharing Bulgarian fairytales with me. Thank you for all the belly-aching laughter we have had between Manchester and Sofia as we live fairytales of our own together.

Matt Warren and Nick Walsh, thank you for reminding me that laughter and love are medicine, and for teaching me never to be afraid or ashamed of being a honker.

Brooke Davis, there is not an In Gratitude section long enough for me to name everything I love and am grateful for about you. Nor are there enough daisies. Thank you for seeing me, for loving me, for letting me love you in my Doug apron whether you're up or down your tree. Thank you for absolutely everything you have done to enable and empower Alice Hart, and me. I am bettered by the mere thought of you.

Myf Jones, incomparable friend, captain of our floating worlds, teacher of wind-leaning and sister through it all, there is no one I would rather eat my congratulations with than you. Thank you for being the very first to wholly bring Alice to life.

Sophs Stephenson, thank you for making my first year of writing in Manchester magnificent, and proving Elizabeth Bennet is alive and well. Jonny, thank you for putting Mr Darcy to shame. And HazelPop, Violet Crawley doesn't hold a candle to you, my dear girl.

Sarah de Vries, my love-at-first-sight sister soul, there are not enough 1 pm starts to a day, naked trees, road trips, dogs in flower crowns, trinkets, house pants, king prawns, nutritional yeast, fabreezay, dark horses, fairytale collections or choreographed GoT arm dances in existence to measure the love and joy you bring to my life. Thank you for picking me up and dusting me off through all weather. Here's to our future of purple rinses and butterfly hoarding.

Libby Morgan, when I was a kid and wished for a Golden Book best friend, I never thought she actually existed outside of the pages in my books. Thank you for surpassing my wishes and for fifteen years of true and extraordinary love. Thank you for talking every knot in this novel through with me and being a tireless and always loving voice of reason. Thank you for every hour of the countless hours we've spent talking over land and sea. Andy, Jess, Nath, Raff, Mick, Jordy, Lani, Rainy, and Razor: thank you for loving me like your own.

To my extended Harris family, Merilyn, Matt, Gabe, Leo, Arley, Buggy, Chris, Vicky, Sue, and Annie, thank you for believing in me and cheering me on, with love.

Lee Steindl, thank you for screaming with me every step of this way. Thank you for teaching me the power of a broom, how to stare down crows, and making me belly laugh all my life. And for Moët. Always, for Moët.

Matty Hutchinson, Lulu and I will love you forever. Thank you for championing Alice into being, for naming your sunflower girl after her, and for bringing me her cupcake.

Joan Mary Corfield, thank you for growing an incomparable fairy garden that we all roamed wild in, and for the deep love of stories and writing in my blood.

Dadgee, Toby, Goose, Teapot, and Coco, there is nothing that compares to coming home to you. Thank you for giving me love and the safest place I could ever hope for to write my way through the dark into bloom.

To Hendrix, the littlest Thor, and Kira Navi, Queen of the Wild Frontier, thank you for reminding me how powerful and essential imagination and stories are.

To my mother, Colleen Ringland. You taught me how to be brave. You taught me how to read by the time I was three. Thank you for my life, Mamaleen. Thank you for showing me what it means to never give up.

To the rest of my family and friends, thank you for your love and support.

Saving the best to nearly last, Sam Harris, you are the best thing that's ever happened to me. Thank you for teaching me that peace is a fire. Your love is the truest magic I know.

My final thanks are to you, dear reader. A writer's words are brought to life by being read: Alice Hart would not fully live without you. My gratitude is yours.